PENGUIN

A New Era for H

Maggie Campbell grew up on a rough estate in north Manchester. Exchanging the spires of nearby Strangeways prison for those of Cambridge University, she gained a Masters in German and Dutch. Maggie has now returned to Manchester, where she writes full time and enjoys a heart-warming, uplifting ending.

Also by Maggie Campbell

Nurse Kitty's Secret War
Nurse Kitty's Unforgettable Journey
Nurse Kitty: After the War

The Housekeeper of Holcombe Hall

A New Era for Holcombe Hall

MAGGIE CAMPBELL

PENGUIN BOOKS

PENGUIN BOOKS

UK | USA | Canada | Ireland | Australia
India | New Zealand | South Africa

Penguin Books is part of the Penguin Random House group of companies whose addresses can be found at global.penguinrandomhouse.com

Penguin Random House UK,
One Embassy Gardens, 8 Viaduct Gardens, London SW11 7BW

penguin.co.uk

First published 2026

001

Copyright © Maggie Campbell, 2026

The moral right of the author has been asserted

Penguin Random House values and supports copyright. Copyright fuels creativity, encourages diverse voices, promotes freedom of expression and supports a vibrant culture. Thank you for purchasing an authorized edition of this book and for respecting intellectual property laws by not reproducing, scanning or distributing any part of it by any means without permission. You are supporting authors and enabling Penguin Random House to continue to publish books for everyone. No part of this book may be used or reproduced in any manner for the purpose of training artificial intelligence technologies or systems. In accordance with Article 4(3) of the DSM Directive 2019/790, Penguin Random House expressly reserves this work from the text and data mining exception

Set in 12.5/14.75pt Garamond MT Std
Typeset by Six Red Marbles UK, Thetford, Norfolk
Printed and bound in Great Britain by Clays Ltd, Elcograf S.p.A.

The authorized representative in the EEA is Penguin Random House Ireland, Morrison Chambers, 32 Nassau Street, Dublin D02 YH68

A CIP catalogue record for this book is available from the British Library

ISBN: 978–1–405–96640–5

Penguin Random House is committed to a sustainable future for our business, our readers and our planet. This book is made from Forest Stewardship Council® certified paper

For the real Dr Haslam. Holcombe's loss is Hale's gain.

A New Era for Holcombe Hall

1931.

I

The muscles in Florrie's forearms complained as she pushed the heavy old pram along the gravelled path that skirted the grand frontage of Holcombe Hall. She'd been walking only twenty minutes, and the starched blouse of her housekeeper's uniform was already clinging to her skin from the effort. Yet Florrie relished being away from the stifling warren of rooms and corridors below stairs, feeling the sun on her skin.

'Look at all this, eh?' she said to the chubby baby sitting in the pram. She stopped to take in the deep flower beds to her left, where bright blue delphiniums swayed in the warm breeze, and clambering pink roses and honeysuckle snaked their way up and around the tall drawing room windows. To her right, the groomed turf of the lawns was already starting to yellow ever so slightly in the June heat, but the glossy leaves of the magnolia sapling that the staff had planted in memory of her predecessor were still a lush green. 'One day, Sir William, all this will be yours. Imagine that! The house. The gardens. The farmland beyond. Even Bertha's tree. And I tell you what, chuck, it doesn't get much better than Holcombe Hall on a sunny Sunday morning.'

The baby squinted up at her, nonplussed. He sneezed in the strong sunlight.

'Bless you!'

Florrie paused momentarily to wipe the baby's nose on a lace-trimmed handkerchief, then she continued on her way. When the old Victorian wheels sank into a particularly deep patch of gravel, the pram ground to a halt.

'Oh, fiddlesticks! I wish your mother had forked out for a better pram than this old bucket from the year dot,' Florrie said. 'I'll have to get Thom to see if he can do something about the paths . . . or the wheels, or both.'

The baby sneezed a second time, this time losing his balance and falling backwards on to the soft pillow at his back. He let out a cry of complaint.

Florrie leaned over and sat the baby up. 'There, there, Sir William! Oh, what a fuss!'

A bumblebee flew over and started to lazily buzz around the baby's face, just as Florrie was trying to adjust the brim of his sunhat to shield his eyes. William let out a horrified shriek.

'It's only a bee, young man. Just a buzzy bumble. Keep still and it won't harm you.' Florrie waved the insect away, but the baby was still fretful. She regarded his screwed-up little face – the image of his grandfather, the old Lord Harding-Bourne. 'Ooh, I do wish that nanny of yours would take you out in the fresh air more often.' She straightened the Peter Pan collar of his little outfit and stroked his cheek. 'You need a distraction, other children.' She sighed. 'I wish our Nelly, Alice and George could have come out with us for a walk today. It's supposed to be my day off, after all, and they're my nieces and nephew – flesh and blood. Me and my mam are all they've got left.'

A bitter memory of her sister's untimely demise presented itself: gasping for her last breath on a Manchester

Royal Infirmary ward, leaving three children under the age of five behind. If only Irene hadn't been living in slum conditions. If only she'd had the money to see a doctor before the pneumonia had really got a grip . . . Florrie batted the mental image away and looked down at her infant charge.

'But here am I, babysitting you . . .' She spoke in a sing-song voice and softly tickled him under the chin so that he started to giggle. 'Just so Miss Talbot can sit in chapel for half the day. And you're not even allowed to mix with my lot, are you? No! "Hoi-polloi", Lady Charlotte calls them.' She tutted.

In the distance, Florrie could hear the thrum of a biplane's engine. Shielding her eyes from the bright sunshine, she looked up into the azure skies.

'There she is,' Florrie said, pointing to the dot in the distance, growing ever larger as it flew towards them. 'There's your mother. Fancies herself as Amelia Earhart, does our Lady Charlotte.' Florrie shook her head. 'And your Aunty Daphne's her willing sidekick. What a pair!'

Frowning momentarily, Florrie bit her tongue, though her only audience was a tiny babbling babe. She advanced towards the library windows and peered in, spotting Lady Elizabeth sitting in an armchair, reading in the strong sunlight that streamed in.

'Oh, good. Your grandmother's up and about,' she said to the baby. 'First time in a while and all. Very glad to see her out of her sickbed. It's a right shame her gout took a turn for the worse, just as you arrived. She's definitely not herself, these days . . . unsurprisingly, I suppose.'

A moving shape within the shadows of the library stacks caught Florrie's eye – a tall, slender man, instantly recognizable as Sir Richard. He emerged from the gloom and took his place by Lady Elizabeth's side, placing his hand on his mother's shoulder, a smile in his eyes as he spoke to her. Though he was dressed simply in light slacks and a short-sleeved polo shirt, buttoned down at the neck, he was ever the elegant nobleman Florrie had privately worshipped since she'd arrived at Holcombe Hall at the tender age of fifteen.

'And there's your father!'

When Sir Richard looked up and through the window, he locked eyes with Florrie.

Florrie smiled and waved tentatively, aware that her cheeks had flushed and her pulse had quickened. Even though she'd been courted by handsome, dependable Thom for the last eleven months, there was still a secret place in Florrie's heart for her employer. Had Sir Richard not gone out of his way to give Mam and Irene's destitute children the chance of a new life, enjoying comfort and security beneath the lovingly repaired roof of the old gamekeeper's cottage? Had he not been true to his word, raising money to fill the new Harding-Bourne Trust's coffers, so that laid-off mill workers, coal miners and ship builders might avoid penury?

'He's a grand feller, your father,' she told the baby. 'You're a very, very lucky boy to have a daddy like that. I hope you'll realize that when you grow up.'

Sir Richard waved back, pointed to them both, and said something to his mother. Lady Elizabeth looked up and peered through the window. She smiled weakly, raising a handkerchief at Florrie and the baby by way of greeting. Yet even with distance and a window between them,

Florrie could see uncertainty in the old lady's eyes. Lady Elizabeth knew that affection for her middle son was not the only secret that Florrie guarded.

'Families, eh?' Florrie said. She held Sir William's chubby little hand and waved it at his doting father and grandmother. Turning away from the window, she resumed their walk along the path. 'Doesn't matter how rich you are, families are always complicated.'

She was just reflecting that she and Sir Richard had both lost siblings too young when she became aware that the distant buzz of the biplane was no longer quite so distant. Florrie looked up to see the aircraft nearing Holcombe Hall.

'Ooh. Looks like your mother is coming into land at last. She might actually pay you some attention before . . .'

Florrie's words drifted away on the light summer breeze as she tried to make sense of the sight of the biplane approaching in entirely the wrong direction for the makeshift airstrip in a neighbouring field. 'Hang on a minute . . .' It was also flying altogether too low, and the engines were now making a sputtering noise. 'What's going on here? Oh, blimey!'

The biplane buffeted, skimming the treetops of Holcombe's woods with its wheels. Lady Charlotte was clearly visible in the cockpit. Though her head was clad in her close-fitting leather helmet and she was wearing goggles, it was clear she was grinning. But why?

The propeller slowed and the engine cut out.

'They're going to crash!' Florrie yelled. 'Good Lord, no!'

Closer and closer the biplane glided, heading straight for the Hall, with Florrie and the baby directly in its path.

Florrie snatched Sir William out of his pram and clutched him to her chest, then ran away from the sandstone walls of Holcombe Hall and on to the lawn. Her foot caught in her long skirt and she stumbled.

At that moment, Sir Richard sprinted out of the library's French doors towards them. The biplane was seconds from impact, with Lady Charlotte and Daphne waving absurdly at them, as if they hadn't a care in the world; as if they weren't about to coast to a fiery death.

Just as Sir Richard reached Florrie and the baby, pulling them to the ground and sheltering them with his body, Florrie heard the engine of the aircraft cut back in. She craned her neck to see the propeller start to spin again, and then the biplane shot up, up, up and over the steep rooftops of the stately home.

The sound of Lady Charlotte and Daphne's hoots of laughter trilled on the air.

'What in God's name . . . ?' Sir Richard sat up, freeing Florrie and the baby from the protective cage of his arms and torso. He looked up, scowling at the aircraft. 'Wanton recklessness! I shall have to have stern words with my wife when she returns.'

Florrie gently shushed the fretting baby. 'There, there, Sir William. What a to-do! What a to-do! All over now, eh? All safe and sound.' She eyed the biplane as it banked steeply, this time heading for the landing strip that had been mown into the neighbouring field. Much as she would love to tell Sir Richard exactly what she also thought of Lady Charlotte and Daphne, she kept her opinions to herself. 'And the main thing is, nobody was hurt.'

'But we could have been,' Sir Richard said, getting to

his feet. He helped Florrie up and then held his hands out to take his son. 'Here. Give him to me.' Supporting the little boy on his hip, he kissed his cheek and wiped the tears from his eyes. 'There, there, William. Papa's here.' Sir Richard turned to Florrie wearing an inscrutable expression. 'Thank goodness Charlotte pulled the nose of that blasted toy of hers up in time. I could have lost everything I hold dear to me in a split second of poor judgement.'

Florrie watched his Adam's apple rise and fall in his throat. She glanced rapidly down at the bulky seat of the baby's trousers before Sir Richard could catch her eye. 'Well, there's not a scratch on the house, and your son and heir's fine, too,' she said with a forced chuckle. She took the baby back from him and sniffed his bottom with a grimace. 'Though I think this one could probably do with being changed. Let me take his little lordship back to the nursery. My mam's had a load of his nappy squares drying on the line all yesterday.' She cooed at the baby. 'Kitten soft and white as the driven snow, they are. Yes!'

She turned to leave Sir Richard – scratching his head and peering at the distant hedgerow, beyond which his wife's biplane was just landing.

Florrie retrieved the pram, settling the baby back inside. She wondered how much of the fiasco Dame Elizabeth had witnessed through the library windows. As she pushed the cumbersome pram towards the grand stone staircase of the main entrance, Sir Richard's younger brother, Sir Hugh, came skipping down the steps, taking them two at a time. He was wearing tennis whites, and his button-down collar was unfastened, his brilliantined hair dishevelled, as usual. He carried a tennis racket over his shoulder.

'What ho, Florrie! Was that my daredevil sister-in-law I just saw, almost crashing into the house, with my reckless wife in the passenger seat?' He laughed, as though Lady Charlotte's stunt had been a terrific wheeze.

Florrie had no time for Sir Hugh's nonsense. 'Sir Hugh, would you mind terribly helping me up the stairs with the pram, please?'

Behind her, she heard laughter in the distance, coming from the direction of the makeshift airstrip. She turned around to see Lady Charlotte, walking side by side with Sir Hugh's wife, Daphne. Both women were swinging their flying hats and goggles, elbowing each other and erupting into fits of giggles.

Sir Hugh ignored Florrie's plea entirely. He jogged towards the women, leaving Florrie to carry the baby and heave the pram up the stairs on her own. Grumbling beneath her breath, Florrie paused in her ascent when she saw Sir Richard, marching across the lawn from the direction of the library to meet his wife and sister-in-law. The summer breeze carried his voice towards Florrie.

'Charlotte Harding-Bourne, I wish to have a word with you! In fact, I wish to have several.'

Lady Charlotte merely pushed her hat into her husband's chest. 'Oh, don't be such an interminable bore, Dickie. Didn't you see our terrific, death-defying stunt?' She flashed a mischievous grin at Daphne.

'*Such* fun!' Daphne said. 'I swear, Dickie, she's every bit as good as Earhart!'

'But, need I remind you, Charlotte, you're *not* Amelia Earhart. You are not even a skilled pilot.'

'I beg to differ!' Lady Charlotte blinked defiantly at him. 'A mere hobbyist could never have pulled off a manoeuvre like that.'

'You are a wife and mother, Charlotte. A member of the nobility, who should be behaving in a seemly manner, befitting her social standing.'

'Oh, do stop being such a stick-in-the-mud. You know I love flying,' Lady Charlotte said. 'Hans was an absolute darling for teaching me. I think my aerobatic skills this morning were sublime.'

'*Sublime?* Surely you jest? You could have crashed and died, taking half the house with you!' Sir Richard's face flushed an uncharacteristic shade of red. He balled his fists so tightly that even from a distance, Florrie could see his knuckles stood proud like white marbles. 'More to the point, you could have killed *our son*!'

'Nonsense. I can see William over there on the steps with Florrie.' Lady Charlotte waved to Florrie absently. 'He's in perfectly capable hands, and is one not allowed a break from the travails of motherhood on a delightful Sunday morning?'

Florrie was so engrossed in eavesdropping on the conversation that she jolted with surprise when the pram seemed to move of its own accord.

'May I?' A familiar man's voice, at her side.

She turned to find Arkwright, the butler, yanking the pram from her. 'Come inside, Florence,' he said. 'It will do no good to bear witness to the antics of our employers.'

'No. I suppose you're right.'

'Sir Richard sails to India tomorrow.' With his back to the house, Arkwright started to pull the cumbersome pram up one step after another. 'And the maids you've tasked with packing are at each other's throats over which of his suits to put in the trunk.' He glowered at her pointedly. 'Best you concern yourself with the ructions below stairs, rather than the tomfoolery of our betters above, eh?'

2

'I see you've picked out heavy gabardine slacks for India, Clary,' Florrie said to the new junior maid who had been tasked with packing for Sir Richard. 'Do you think that's wise? I mean, he's going to Bombay, not Penrith! It's going to be boiling hot one minute and tipping with monsoon rain the next.'

Clutching the offending trousers, Clary stared at Florrie, wide-eyed and unmoving. It was as if fear had frozen her to the spot. Then her lower lip started to tremble.

'Don't cry! I wasn't rebuking you. I was asking you a question. In a job like this, you have to show some initiative.'

Rummaging in Sir Richard's wardrobe, Florrie's friend and one-time contemporary, Sally, glanced back at her, wearing an exasperated expression. 'I told her, and she wouldn't listen. If I say black, she says white. Take no notice of this "little girl lost" routine. This one's got plenty to say for herself when you're not in earshot.'

Adjusting a fidgeting Sir William on her hip, Florrie looked enquiringly at Clary.

'That's not true!' Clary said, shaking her head vehemently. 'I'm trying my best.'

Before her, Florrie saw a girl of fifteen, whose second-hand maid's uniform was sack-like on her diminutive frame. She wondered if she had appeared equally vulnerable when she'd arrived at Holcombe Hall twelve years earlier as a fifteen-year-old domestic trainee – little more than a child.

'Put the trousers back, Clary,' she said gently. 'And listen to Sally, please, because she's more experienced than you. I know you think you're being told off, but Sal's only got your best interests at heart. If you pick up sloppy habits now, you'll struggle down the line. Running this house like clockwork depends on us all knowing our place, trusting those above us, and doing our jobs to the very best of our abilities.' She watched Clary fumble with the trousers and hanger. 'Neatly, mind!' She turned to Sally. 'Sir Richard needs white tie, black tie; he's got an ivory dinner jacket somewhere.'

'Got it!' Sally pulled the jacket out of the wardrobe with a flourish.

'Aye, he'll want that.' Florrie nodded. She addressed both of them. 'His smoking jacket, too. Linen suits only for formal daytime, please, girls. Short-sleeved shirts and polo shirts; as many pairs of Bermuda shorts as he's got for sightseeing and suchlike. Cricket whites, tennis whites, golf attire.'

'He's doing all that in the heat?' Sally took out a dust bag and hung it on a door of the triple wardrobe. 'What's that new Noël Coward song? "Mad Dogs and Englishmen"?' She lifted the cotton bag to reveal a burgundy velvet smoking jacket, which sported a black satin quilted collar and a fringed belt.

Florrie strode over to the jacket. Between the finger and thumb of her free hand she tweezed a stray piece of white cotton from the collar and smoothed down the velvet. 'Ours is not to question why, Sal. If Sir Richard wants to go "out in the midday sun", I'm sure there's some thinking behind it. It's a business trip, isn't it?' She turned the jacket over to check for moth holes but was satisfied there were none. Before little Sir William could grab the fringes on the belt, she moved back towards the dressing table. 'The new Viceroy Lord Willingdon's a bit long in the tooth for cricket and tennis, I shouldn't wonder, but Sir Richard's after securing HB Steel's stake in the Raj's rail network. Apparently a lot of deals get done on the golf course and the cricket pitch.'

She turned back to Clary, who was still fumbling with the hanger and the gabardine trousers.

'I can't do it, Miss Bickerstaff,' the girl said. 'I can't get them to stay on. They're right fiddly.'

Sir William grabbed at the tight bun in Florrie's hair and tugged hard, squealing with delight.

'Well, Sally will have to teach you, because I've been left holding the baby, quite literally.' She prised her bun free and looked at her charge with affection.

'I've already showed her twice,' Sally said.

'No, you didn't,' Clary insisted.

'I most certainly did, so you couldn't have been paying attention.' Sally turned to Florrie, a look of exasperation on her face. 'I *did* show her.'

Florrie sighed. 'Clary, you must pay attention to Sally and do as she says.'

'Yes, Miss Bickerstaff. But what if I disagree with her?'

'Sally has packed more trunks for Sir Richard than you've had hot dinners. Do what you're told and do it well, please. Is that clear?'

Clary bobbed a curtsey, little blotches of red appearing

on her wan cheeks. 'Yes, Miss Bickerstaff. Sorry, Miss Bickerstaff.' The trousers slid on to the floor.

'Get on with your work, ladies. Sir Richard departs at six o'clock tomorrow morning, and his trunks and cases must all be locked, labelled and ready for Thom to load into the luggage car at half past five, sharp.'

'There. That's much more comfortable, isn't it, Sir William?' Florrie said to the baby, once she'd cleaned him up and wrapped a fresh nappy around him.

Happily lying on a quilted pad on top of a Louis XIV dresser that had been repurposed to suit his nappy changing needs, the baby gurgled at her and kicked out his chubby legs. He looked up at the playful cherubs Lady Charlotte had insisted be painted on to the walls of the spacious nursery and blew a raspberry.

'Now, let's get this nappy fastened, and maybe I can hand you over to your mother, seeing as your nanny's absconded to spend a leisurely morning with Holcombe's Methodists.' Florrie struggled to get the stiff, oversized safety pin open and pricked the pad of her thumb. 'Ow!' She wiped a bead of blood on to the corner of the muslin she'd used to wash her temporary charge's bottom. 'Darn it! Where on earth *is* that nanny of yours? She should have been back for midday, but Miss Talbot thinks her religious fervour means the rules don't apply to her, doesn't she? Yes!' She tutted. 'My own day off, and here I am, wiping your noble little bottom when I'm supposed to be taking our Nelly, Alice and George for a walk up Holcombe Hill.'

Once she'd put Sir William's trousers back on, Florrie picked him up and descended the servants' staircase, emerging by the drawing room. From the hallway, she could hear the chatter and laughter of Sir Hugh, Daphne and Lady Charlotte, accompanied by the crackling, tinny sound of jazz music coming from the gramophone.

'Here we go . . .' Florrie kissed the silken wisps on Sir William's head and knocked on the door to the drawing room. She pushed the door open to find the two women still in their flying garb – jodhpurs, knee-length leather boots, fine-knit jumpers with scarves tied jauntily at their necks – foxtrotting to the music. Sir Hugh was pouring gin into tall crystal glasses which had clearly already held at least one drink already. There was no sign of Arkwright or any of his valets.

'Ah, Florrie!' Sir Hugh said. He held the bottle of gin towards her. 'Do pour us each another Tom Collins, there's a good girl.'

A good girl? Florrie thought, her face already starting to ache from the accommodating smile she was willing herself to maintain. *I'm the housekeeper. I thank God every day for the opportunity that prematurely came my way because of poor Bertha dying, but I am the most senior female member of staff now. Yet to this lot, I will never be anything more than 'good girl'. And I'm still holding the baby.* 'Of course.' She turned to Lady Charlotte. 'Ma'am, would you like to take your darling son so I can pour the drinks?'

Lady Charlotte's smile was fleeting. 'Hand him here.' She took Sir William from Florrie, holding him at arm's length, as if she were his distant relative with no real experience of children. Then she lowered herself into an armchair, stiffly perching the baby on her knee. 'There, there, William. Mama's here.'

Little Sir William started to struggle against her grip. Grunting and wriggling in complaint, he accidentally hit his mother in the face.

Lady Charlotte looked down at him, aghast. 'William! You perfectly horrid little boy. I'm your mother!' Getting to her feet, she thrust the baby back at Florrie.

'He's teething,' Florrie said, swapping the gin bottle for the distraught baby. 'It makes babies short-tempered, is all. And I really don't think he meant to hit—'

'Where is Miss Talbot?' Lady Charlotte snapped.

'She's at chapel,' Florrie said. She patted Sir William's back gently as he started to sob. 'She'll be back any minute now, I'm sure. In fact, she should have been back an hour and a half ago.'

'Very well. I suppose *I'll* fix these drinks, then, shall I?' Lady Charlotte turned away from Florrie and started to pour gin into the glasses. She glanced back at Florrie and her son, wearing a look of exasperation ... or was it disgust? 'Thank you, Florrie. That will be all.'

Florrie curtseyed. Much as she ideally needed to leave Sir William with his mother – to bond if for no other reason – she knew a room full of stinking cigarette smoke and gin fumes was not the place to entertain a baby. Furthermore, she wouldn't have felt comfortable leaving Lady Charlotte in charge of him.

'Come on, flowerpot,' she told the drooling, fractious boy. 'Let's take you down to the kitchens and see if Cook's got something tasty for you to teethe on.' She peered into his mouth and spied florid gums. 'Bit of ice-cream might numb that pain.'

*

As soon as Florrie arrived at the foot of the stairs leading down to the kitchen, it was as if she'd entered the steam room of one of the Turkish baths Sir Hugh regularly eulogized about.

'Hey up! Here she is,' Cook said, rolling out pastry with gusto, her sleeves folded up to reveal the giant forearms of a woman who spent her life either kneading dough or else beating sugar and butter together with a spoon. 'The Pied Piper of Holcombe Hall.'

Florrie groaned. 'I don't think carrying one babe-in-arms makes me a Pied Piper. I haven't seen our George, Nelly and Alice for days, because Miss Talbot insists Sir William be kept well away from them.'

Cook set down her rolling pin and approached Florrie and Sir William with floury hands held out. She rubbed Sir William's florid cheeks. 'Has our little lordship come to visit Cookie? Yes, he has! Does Sir William want a biccy to chomp on?'

'Oh, I don't think a biscuit would do him much good,' Florrie said, swinging her charge out of Cook's floury reach. 'And you told me you don't even like babies!'

'Rubbish! Come here!' Cook beckoned to Florrie as she marched across the kitchen, past the huge staff dining table. 'Babies love chomping on something hard when they're teething. It helps the tooth come through. Even *I* know that. And I've got some rock-hard macaroons that overcooked because a *certain* housekeeper has got my apprentice packing for Sir Richard's trip to India.'

Florrie followed in her wake, savouring the buttery, almondy smell of baking that she trailed behind her. 'It's an economizing exercise, Cook. Sir Richard's orders. We must save money where we can, so all the girls have to double up on their duties now. Sally's no different. She might be your apprentice, but she still has to pitch in above stairs when we're stretched. I can't give you preferential treatment.'

Cook looked back at her, rolling her eyes and waving her hand dismissively. 'Don't act like you're doing me no favours, Florrie Bickerstaff. I'm not daft. Sally's only training under me because she were terrible at everything else!' She came to a halt by her oversized sideboard, on top of which she'd left her baked wares to cool on racks. 'Anyhow, never mind all that.' She picked up a deep brown, thick biscuit and held it out to Sir William. 'I was saving these burnt offerings for the staff to dunk in their tea later . . .'

Sir William took the biscuit and chomped down on it. He grimaced and threw it on to the terracotta tiles of the floor.

Cook guffawed with laughter. 'Charming! Be like that, then!' She grunted as she crouched to pick up the broken pieces of macaroon.

'I say, is my son causing a stir?' A man's voice emanated from the far side of the kitchen.

Florrie looked around to find Sir Richard standing at the foot of the stairs. She immediately bobbed a curtsey and smiled. 'No, sir. I just thought I'd bring Sir William down to see if Cook had any ice-cream for his sore gums.'

'Something cold? Why didn't you say in the first place? I've just the thing.' Cook reached into the Frigidaire that Sir Richard had recently had shipped over from America, and brought out a tub of something icy-looking. 'Sorbet for tonight's dinner do him?'

Sir Richard took his wriggling, fractious son from Florrie and accepted a spoonful of sorbet from Cook. The baby chomped down on the spoon and started to make grateful noises. 'Ah, I do believe Cook has discovered the cure for all ills on a sultry June afternoon!' His brow furrowed and he locked eyes with Florrie. 'But why are you playing nursemaid to my son, Florrie? You told me you'd planned to spend your free day with your family. Where's Miss Talbot?'

In Florrie's peripheral vision, she could see the kitchen maid emerge from the labyrinth of corridors that extended below stairs. As soon as the girl spied Sir Richard, she retreated, carrying her mop and pail of sloshing water back towards Arkwright's office. 'Miss Talbot should have been back from chapel a while ago. But she's not.' She shrugged.

Sir Richard frowned. 'And my wife?'

'Lady Charlotte was . . .' Florrie chose her words carefully. '. . . fatigued after her flight.'

Her employer tutted. 'This really won't do. Miss Talbot should return promptly to her nannying duties as soon as her chapel's Sunday service has concluded. If her timekeeping is poor while I'm here, what on earth is going to happen while I'm in India? I can hardly postpone my trip to keep tabs on the nanny. It's ludicrous.'

'No, Sir Richard. Absolutely not.'

Sir Richard studied his son's face intently, as if he was mulling something over. 'Europe's economy is in tatters since German and Austrian banking collapsed. I *have* to go to Delhi. If Harding-Bourne Steel goes under because I failed to drum up Indian locomotive orders, this young man will have nothing to inherit at all, and the future of Holcombe Hall will suddenly be in question.' He turned to Florrie. 'We're all cogs in a complex machine that keeps this estate running.'

Florrie nodded. 'I know, sir. I know.'

'The businesses, the staff, my family and I ... *Miss Talbot*. If one part fails, the whole house of cards collapses, forgive my mixed metaphors.' He smiled fleetingly. 'I know my wife's technically responsible for the nanny, but can *you* see to it that Miss Talbot improves her timekeeping? This tardiness can't continue.'

Florrie knew better than to challenge Sir Richard on his assumption that she could make the slightest bit of difference to Miss Talbot's behaviour. Nevertheless, she knew that fretting over his son's nanny was the last thing her employer needed, just as he was about to set sail for a six-week-long odyssey. 'Of course not.'

Cook caught her eye and nodded almost imperceptibly towards the window, set high into the wall. The kitchen was partially subterranean, so not only was the window the sole source of natural light and fresh air, but it also gave a limited view of the utilitarian courtyard next to the servants' and tradesman's entrance. Through the window, Florrie spotted a familiar pair of spindly legs, clad in thick black Lisle stockings, with feet wedged into highly polished but extremely old-fashioned, low-heeled shoes. Miss Talbot had returned, and Florrie determined to challenge her.

'Leave it with me,' she told Sir Richard, taking Sir William back from him. 'I'll have a word.'

3

'Get out of the way, girl! You're obstructing the corridor.'

The sound of Miss Talbot's sharp voice made Florrie turn around. From the direction of Arkwright's office, the shy young kitchen maid had suddenly reappeared, carrying her mop and bucket. Behind her was Miss Talbot, who unceremoniously pushed the girl aside.

'Ah, at last,' Florrie said.

The kitchen maid pointed at herself. 'What? Me?'

'No, Ginny, love. Not you. Sir Richard's gone back upstairs now, so you can get on with your duties, please.' Florrie fixed her gaze on Miss Talbot and then pointedly looked up at the large clock on the kitchen wall. 'You took your time.'

Miss Talbot removed the black felt hat she'd been wearing and smoothed her grey hair, which had been tied tightly in a bun at the nape of her thin neck. 'Is that any way to speak to a senior member of the household, Miss Bickerstaff?'

Florrie readjusted Sir William on her hip, her arm and leg muscles now aching after having carried or pushed him around for much of the day. 'Need I remind you, Miss Talbot, that I am the housekeeper of this great home? Younger than you I might be, but junior to you I am not.'

'I don't answer to you, girl. I answer to the *lady* of the house. And I *must* go to church on a Sunday morning. As a practising Christian, that is my right.' She clutched her hard-framed handbag in front of her. 'Now, when I've had a cup of tea, which Cook here is going to make me, I will *then* take over responsibility of Sir William.'

Cook wedged her fists on to her hips. 'Hey! I'm not your lady's maid. Don't get me involved in all this. I've got three big game pies to make for dinner – for that lot above stairs *and* for us lot down here. You'll be the first to grumble if your stomach's rumbling at tea time and there's nowt to eat.' She pointed to the large pine Welsh dresser, where an array of crockery was neatly displayed on its shelves. Wedged in among the stacked plates was an urn. 'You want a brew? There's boiled water in the urn. Make it yourself!'

Florrie took the sorbet spoon from Sir William's mouth and set it down on the dining table, taking a deep breath before she said something she regretted. It wouldn't do to have Miss Talbot running with tales about her to Lady Charlotte or Dame Elizabeth. 'Very well. Make yourself a cup of tea. But remember this, Miss Talbot: it's my day off, and you're reliant on my goodwill to attend chapel, because if you're not looking after Sir William, someone else has to – either me or one of my girls. I've missed much of my day off thanks to you being back two hours late.'

Cook pointed to Miss Talbot with her rolling pin. 'Taking advantage of Miss Bickerstaff's good nature, you are. That's not on.'

Miss Talbot glared at her with a sour-looking down-turned mouth. 'I thought you didn't want to get involved, Cook.' She marched over to the urn, ignoring Sir William's outstretched hands, and spooned some tea into a small earthenware pot. 'I'd take your own advice, if I were you, and keep your opinions to yourself. I know my job. My references are impeccable. I'm not frightened by your schoolyard bullying, and if you two continue, I'll not hesitate to report you both to Lady Charlotte.' She rammed her hat back on her head emphatically. In awkward silence, she poured water from the urn into the pot, decanted some milk into a small jug, assembled a cup and saucer for herself and started to carry the lot on a tray up the back steps. 'Kindly deliver Sir William to me in twenty minutes, Miss Bickerstaff. I'll be in the nursery.'

Florrie felt suddenly cold and light-headed. She looked at Cook.

'Well,' said Cook. 'She's a piece of work.'

'What am I going to do?' Florrie bit her lip. 'I can't have her taking liberties like that every Sunday.'

Cook shook her head and started to roll her pastry out again with noticeably more aggression than before. 'She's a troublemaker, that one.' She looked up and fixed Florrie with narrowed eyes. 'Watch your back, love. That's all I'm saying. We're all expendable, and don't kid yourself otherwise.'

Florrie thought about how her mam and her nephew and nieces – George, Nelly and Alice – depended on her to supplement her mam's insufficient income as the estate's laundress. She nodded. 'Aye. Point taken. Thanks.'

With Sir William delivered to his nursery and the care of a stony-faced Miss Talbot, Florrie finally found she could return to her stiflingly hot room to change out of her housekeeper's plain black dress with its restrictive white collar into a comfortable outfit of her own. Since becoming the housekeeper some eighteen months earlier, she had not only moved into a larger room (though it was still at the top of the house, under the eaves, along with all the other servants' quarters) but she had also expanded her wardrobe for days off to include three new outfits – a striped, sleeveless summer dress that Mam had made for her, a green winter two-piece with a pleated skirt that Daphne had put out for the church jumble sale, and a pair of sky-blue wide trousers to be paired with an ivory fine-knit, short-sleeved top. Mam had made the trousers by repurposing and dying a fine linen tablecloth that Dame Elizabeth had insisted had reached the end of its useful life. The top was a hand-me-down from Lady Charlotte, but the silken fabric felt luxurious and was still in perfect condition but for one small ladder.

Now, Florrie stood in her scratchy, utilitarian undergarments, staring into the wardrobe. She unpinned her hair, pulled out the wide-legged trousers and ivory top, put them on and headed outside into the afternoon sunshine. As she walked across the lawn towards the gamekeeper's cottage, she sensed eyes on her. She looked back at the hall, but couldn't spy anyone watching her from the windows, either on the ground floor or upstairs.

'You're being paranoid, Florrie Bickerstaff,' she told herself, folding her arms over her chest. 'Don't let Lady Charlotte and Miss Talbot's antics ruin the rest of your day off.'

'Mam? Mam, it's me!' When Florrie knocked on the door of the gamekeeper's cottage, nobody answered. She stepped on to the sun-baked earth of the deep border that Thom had planted for her mother before moving-in day. Pushing aside the bushy hydrangea which hadn't yet bloomed anew, since it had been cut back hard to reveal the old leaded windows, she peered through the glass. There was nobody in the parlour, and no sound coming from inside. Had her mother given up the ghost and gone out alone with the children?

Tracing her steps back to the front door, she looked up at the bedroom windows of the house. Always a handsome place, even when it had been abandoned to the elements, after undergoing the expensive refurbishment that Sir Richard had ordered, the cottage was now chocolate-box perfection. The afternoon sun highlighted the blush-pink lime mortar that sat between the lovingly restored upper storey timbers. The flint that the ground floor had been built in seemed to gleam today. The place was a welcoming sight. Yet nobody appeared to be at home.

Florrie heard a high-pitched shriek, carried on the breeze. She walked around the side of the house, pushing past a lilac-blooming potato vine to reach the back garden with its large vegetable patch, mature rhododendron bushes and clumps of perennial flowers spilling on to a lush lawn. Mam was pegging out brilliant white washing. In the middle of the lawn were the children.

'It's Auntie Florrie!' George squealed, pointing. He was seated on the swings Thom had fashioned for the children with spare rope and timber.

Nelly and Alice were bouncing up and down on the homemade seesaw – also a gift from Thom. 'Auntie Florrie! Yippee!' they yelled in unison.

The children all dismounted and ran across to her.

Florrie felt Alice's little arms wrap around her knees, while Nelly's encircled her hips. George hugged her middle. 'Hello, my darlings. Sorry I'm late.'

Mam picked up the empty laundry basket and walked over to them. She kissed Florrie on the cheek. 'Hey up, love. I thought you were never coming. What took you so long?'

Florrie revelled in the familiar scent of her mother: clean washing and carbolic soap. 'Miss Talbot.'

Mam raised an eyebrow. 'Say no more. She reckons she's a cut above us all, that one. Will you tell Sir Richard she's taking liberties?'

Kneeling down to kiss the children, Florrie shook her head. 'He's seen it with his own eyes. He even commented on it earlier. But he's off to India in the morning for six weeks, so he's got more important things on his plate. He's got no jurisdiction over the nanny, anyhow. That's Lady Charlotte's domain.'

Scoffing and tutting, Mam walked to the back door of the cottage. 'The liberties we have to put up with, just because we need the wages coming in! Never changes.' Mam looked up at the cloudless sky. 'Still, at least the washing will dry, and her ladyship isn't flying around like a drunken wasp.'

Given there was too little time left in the afternoon to allow for a walk, Florrie prepared a picnic and took the children into the walled rose garden, where the rose bushes were at the peak of their first flush and smelled like heaven.

'When I grow up, can I go and live in the big house with you?' Nelly asked, chewing thoughtfully on a ham sandwich.

'Don't speak with your mouth full, young lady,' Florrie said. She turned her attention to Alice, who was taking her sandwich apart, layer by layer. She picked up the toddler's mess and put it back on to her plate. 'And don't play with your food, Alice!'

'But can I?' Nelly cocked her head to the side.

Florrie gazed through the archway that led to the formal flower gardens beyond. She could see her darling Thom and his apprentice, hoeing the beds. Would Thom propose to her soon, she wondered? Her gut tightened as she considered the terrible choice she'd be forced to make if he did. There was no having her cake and eating it. She could get married and start her own family, but she would have to give up not just her job and income, but also her home for the last decade. Or she could continue to work, live in one of the country's most beautiful stately homes and support Mam and Irene's children, who were now all but orphaned, given their mother was dead and their father had absconded without so much as a forwarding address. Securing their future would be at the expense of her ever marrying. She sighed deeply. 'The only way you could ever live in Holcombe Hall itself, Nell, would be to go into service like I did at fifteen.'

The little girl's eyes widened. 'Ooh, can I? Can I please?'

George studied his chicken drumstick. 'I like the horses, me. If I get a job as a stable lad, can I live in the big house, too?'

Florrie shook her head. 'No, love. You'd have to live above the stable block or in the coaching house with the other lads.' She took a sip from the bottle of homemade lemonade that her mam had included in the picnic basket. 'But, if I'm honest, I think you'd do better to work as hard as you can in school and get normal jobs.' She reached out and rubbed Nelly's arm. 'Wouldn't you like to work in a shop? The post office, maybe? You could even be a nurse!' She turned to George. 'And you could be anything. A mechanic, maybe? Graham the chauffeur could teach you to fix cars, and then one day, you might even own your own garage – be your own boss.'

'Could I be a pilot, like Lady Charlotte and that German feller she's pally with?' George got to his feet, spreading his arms wide, and started to run around the rose garden. 'I could fly to the Americas and seek my fortune.'

Florrie chuckled. 'Who knows? But just apply yourself in school. Being in service has a lot to recommend it – we'll never go hungry or want for a roof over our heads – but only as long as me and Nana keep our jobs. And there's lots we can't do.'

Alice got to her feet and flung her arms around Florrie. 'Don't be sad, Auntie Florrie. Love you.'

Drinking in the pungent smell of the Derbac soap her mam had used to wash Alice's hair, to ward off the headlice that were so easily passed on from George and Nelly's school friends, Florrie held her niece tight. She pushed away imaginings of how her own children might look and feel and smell. *Just be happy with what you've got, Florrie Bickerstaff*, she reminded herself. *It's not perfect, but you've come a long way from the slums of Manchester. That's worth something.* 'Love you too, chuck.'

4

That evening, when dinner had been served to the Harding-Bournes upstairs, she and Thom dined with the other staff at the oversized kitchen table.

'By heck, that were a cracking pie,' Thom told Cook. He slapped his stomach and rocked back on his chair, lacing his hands together behind his head. 'Smashing spuds, too. Just what the doctor ordered after a day's weeding.' He reached into the breast pocket of his shirt and took out a pack of playing cards. 'Who's up for a game of poker?'

Cook pulled her chair in noisily and grinned at him, a mischievous glint in her eye. 'Naturally, I'll be defending my title.' Leaning back, she rummaged in the drawer of the dresser and pulled out a packet of matches. 'Stakes are high, Thomas.' When she rattled the packet, it sounded full. 'Question is, are we evenly *matched* in skill?' She threw her head back and laughed heartily at her own pun.

Florrie watched, amused, as Sally rolled her eyes at her mentor.

Thom reached into his pocket and threw a packet of matches on to the table. 'Sparks are going to be flying tonight, Cookie.'

Sally and Danny, the valet, both groaned.

'Go on, then,' Graham the chauffeur said. 'I'm game.'

Miss Talbot, who had been sitting primly in the corner pushing the same forkful of pie around her plate for the last twenty minutes, eyed Thom over the top of her round, wire spectacles. 'Should we really be gambling on the Lord's rest day, Thomas?' she asked in a voice that seemed to chill the warm kitchen by several degrees.

Florrie watched Thom for his reaction. Would he be able to brush off her killjoy comments with good-natured humour? The tendon in Thom's jaw flinched. He inhaled, poised to answer.

At the far end of the table, Arkwright set down his newspaper and cleared his throat. 'I'm not sure playing cards for matches constitutes gambling, Miss Talbot. And we're all adults here, relaxing after a hard day's work.' He smoothed his gleaming, brilliantined hair with a perfectly manicured hand. 'And most of us have not had the benefit of spending an idle half-day in church.'

Pressing her lips together to stop herself from laughing out loud, Florrie caught Thom's eye and winked. She was sure he was thinking the same thing: that the sudden death from a heart attack of former housekeeper and object of his unrequited love, Bertha, and his more recent blossoming closeness with Mam had all changed Arkwright for the better. He was still a formidable butler, but he seemed now to err on the side of being the staff's champion, rather than their eternal tormentor. She squeezed Thom's hand beneath the table, grateful for the food in her belly and the bond that held the staff of Holcombe Hall together.

Arkwright's scathing comment left most people around the staff dining table smirking or nudging one another.

Miss Talbot, however, got to her feet, gripping her napkin like a weapon and wearing a thunderous expression. 'I don't like your tone, Mr Arkwright.'

'I was merely—'

'And I don't like what you're insinuating.' The loose skin around her jaw seemed to tremble with outrage. 'Making me out to be a shirker, when I'm merely observing the Sabbath like a good Christian.' She pointed to Florrie. 'Has *she* been dripping poison in your ear?'

Florrie gasped. 'I beg your pardon!'

Thom leaned forward. 'Hey. Hang on just a minute, Miss Talbot! Who are you to speak to our Miss Bickerstaff like she's some scullery maid? She's our housekeeper. She deserves a bit of respect.'

Laying her hand on Thom's forearm, Florrie could feel her cheeks reddening. 'Thanks, Thom, but there's no need to—'

'She's not *my* boss!' Miss Talbot threw her napkin down on to the table. 'And respect is earned, where I come from.' She glared at Arkwright. 'A couple of hours late, I was. Unavoidable. I was doing the Lord's work at chapel. I consider that rather more important than Miss Bickerstaff's planned gallivant with her snot-nosed nieces and nephew.'

Before Florrie could respond to the insult, Miss Talbot scraped her chair backwards and marched out of the kitchen and up the back stairs.

Tossing and turning into the small hours of the following morning, Florrie replayed the confrontation in her mind's eye, like a flickering film reel on a loop. Miss Talbot accusing her of dripping poison into Arkwright's ear. Thom speaking up for her. Her crippling embarrassment at being argued over at the table as if she wasn't even present.

By half past four in the morning, the sunlight was streaming into Florrie's room. She threw back her sheet and thin blanket and exhaled ruefully.

'I was only trying to do her a favour while she went to chapel,' Florrie told the dust motes on the air. 'Now, suddenly, *I'm* in the frame as some sort of godless monster. Flipping Nora. What have I done to deserve this?'

Scrambling out of bed, Florrie threw her curtains wide and flung open her window. Outside, the dawn chorus was already in full song, and the air was blissfully warm. Yet today was the day Sir Richard set sail for India. Arkwright was increasingly supportive of her, but how would she fare with her true champion gone for six weeks?

'Stand in a line,' Florrie told the maids and Cook, just before six o'clock. 'Straighten those mob caps and no slouching!'

The female domestic staff under her jurisdiction stood a little straighter, though some still stifled yawns. Notably, Miss Talbot stood apart from them with her hands laced in front of her. She was looking back at the house – towards Dame Elizabeth's quarters on the ground floor.

Florrie cleared her throat and spoke with as much authority as she could muster. 'Turn to face front, please.'

Miss Talbot either didn't hear her instruction or else was deliberately ignoring her.

On the other side of the grand stone staircase, Arkwright's valets, stable lads and the gardeners were already standing to attention. Arkwright prowled from one end of the line to the other, inspecting everyone's uniform and the cleanliness of their footwear.

Just beyond the foot of the stairs, Graham was already standing by the Rolls-Royce, dressed smartly in his grey chauffeur's livery. Behind him, Florrie could see Thom in the luggage car, awaiting the last of the baggage.

'Easy, easy. I'll go in front.'

Florrie turned around to spy the owner of the voice. It was Danny, the valet, emerging from the hallway, carrying one end of the final trunk to be loaded into Thom's luggage car.

Carrying the other end was Matthew, the former stable lad who had recently been promoted to household duties. The men climbed down the stairs slowly and with some ceremony, as if they were pallbearers at a funeral.

Finally, Sir Richard appeared, looking crisp in a pale linen, double-breasted suit. He donned his Panama hat and descended the stairs.

'I say, you lot,' he said. 'It's jolly good of you to wave me off, but really, there's no need at this ungodly hour.'

Arkwright bowed stiffly. 'On the contrary, Sir Richard, we are always awake and busy about our business at this hour in any case.'

'It's only right we wave you off,' Florrie said, curtseying. 'You'll be missed, Sir Richard. But have a safe and successful trip.'

Sir Richard raised his hat to her. 'My dear, you are so kind. I know my house is in the very best hands while I'm away. Please do keep an eye on my daredevil wife and my reckless hedonist of a brother, won't you?' He rocked back on the heels of his brogues and chuckled. Then he turned to Arkwright. 'Lock the wine cellar if you must, Arkwright. There's a good chap!'

He waved to the rest of the staff and, thanking Graham for holding the rear passenger door open for him, he climbed into the back of the Rolls-Royce.

When both cars pulled away, Florrie felt her heart sink. Thom would be back by the afternoon, since the Liverpool docks were only a couple of hours' drive away. Sir Richard, however . . . There was always the possibility her beloved employer might never return, given how treacherous such a long journey could be and given the civil unrest the papers were currently reporting in India.

Florrie said a silent prayer that Sir Richard would return to them safe and sound, but when she turned to address her staff, she caught sight of Miss Talbot staring straight at her, wearing an expression that made the hairs on Florrie's arms stand to attention. At that moment, Florrie wondered if the next six weeks wouldn't be more arduous for Holcombe Hall's residents than for their intrepid voyaging employer.

5

'I say, Florrie! Do send Arkwright up with the newspapers,' Sir Hugh said, as he bashed the top of his boiled egg with a teaspoon. He looked over at his wife, Daphne, who was seated on the opposite side of the long rosewood dining table. 'I'm desperate to see if Oswald is in *The Times* and the *Telegraph*. He said something about giving an interview regarding the New Party.'

Daphne, who had been staring dolefully at the tomato juice-based hangover concoction Cook had prepared for her, suddenly perked up and smiled. 'Walter's so excited about being chosen as a parliamentary candidate, darling.' She absently ran her finger around the rim of the glass, a look of longing in her eye. 'I rather think we should hold a luncheon to help him raise money for his campaign.'

While Florrie raised the lid to check that the steel chafing dish was keeping the sausages and bacon warm, she cast her mind back to when else she had seen that longing look in Daphne's eyes. Hadn't she seen it at Sir Hugh and Daphne's own wedding, when the blushing bride had turned around, quite obviously to seek out Walter Knight-Downey? It was a look Florrie had also witnessed on the many occasions since, whenever Walter visited Holcombe Hall – usually accompanied by a flutter of eyelashes.

Sir Hugh was clearly oblivious to his wife's continuing affections for his best friend. He clicked his fingers.

'That's an excellent idea, darling. Though Walter hasn't actually been selected yet, of course, but if we can throw a fundraising luncheon for the New Party more generally and get Mosley here as our guest speaker, that will reflect very well on Walter. Make it clear he's got a wealthy, powerful patron behind him.' He flung one arm over the back of the empty seat next to him, drained his tea and held his cup out for a top-up without even looking to see where Annie, the recently promoted maid, was.

Florrie raised her eyebrows at Annie. 'Go on, then,' she whispered. 'Quickly.'

Annie darted forward with the teapot. 'Here you go, Sir Hugh.' Her hands shook as she poured, however, and some tea spilled on to Sir Hugh's fingers.

Yelping and snatching his hand away, Sir Hugh let the half-full cup drop on to the Persian rug. He glowered at the maid. 'I say, girl, are you trying to scald me to death?' He sucked at his fingers. 'Damn it! I shall be lucky if the skin doesn't blister.'

Florrie rushed over to pick the cup up. She gently manoeuvred Annie backwards, away from the table. 'Oh, dear. Would you like me to get you some ice for that, Sir Hugh?'

'Yes, I would,' he said, grimacing. 'It stings like stink. What a way to start the day!'

'I'm so, so sorry, Sir Hugh,' Annie said, still clutching the teapot.

Florrie clapped her hands at the maid, who seemed to be rooted to the spot. 'Go and get ice wrapped in a cloth from Cook. And get towels and a soapy rag to clean the rug before the tannins stain the wool permanently. *Immediately*, please.' She spoke calmly. The last thing she needed was an inexperienced young maid bursting into tears in front of family members at breakfast. It was only Annie's second day of serving in the dining room, after all.

Pale-faced, with the lid rattling in the teapot held between her visibly shaking hands, Annie nodded and fled the dining room.

'Florrie, you really must get rid of her,' Sir Hugh said. 'She's cack-handed in the extreme.'

'And terribly plain,' Daphne added. 'She has a ghastly complexion.' She touched her own cheek. 'It's rather off-putting to look at when one's trying to eat.'

Kneeling to lay down napkins that would absorb some of the tea, lest it stain the precious rug – which (according to Dame Elizabeth) had been shipped all the way from Persia by Sir Richard's grandfather, when the plaster on Holcombe Hall's brand-new walls had barely dried – Florrie chose her words carefully. 'Annie's only just been promoted from chamber maid. She's young and terrified of making mistakes, bless her.' She pressed on the snowy-white napkins until they turned orangey brown. 'But fret not! I'll make sure she has a little more training before she serves in here again. And I'm dreadfully sorry this happened.' Collecting the damp napkins up, she got to her feet.

'Honestly, Florrie, we shouldn't have dumpy incompetents on our domestic staff.' Sir Hugh clutched at his throat. 'This morning's bacon has left me terribly thirsty, and she didn't even leave the teapot, the dunce.'

Florrie forced a smile on to her lips. 'While we're waiting for fresh tea to arrive, why don't I pour you a glass of orange juice?'

Whipping the soggy napkins into the used linen bin beneath the service table, Florrie poured a glass of juice for Sir Hugh and set it down before him.

'I don't want that,' he snapped. 'It'll bring on indigestion after all that bacon.' He pushed the glass away and craned his neck to see beyond the threshold into the hallway. 'Where is that dratted girl with my tea?'

Realizing that Sir Hugh was getting himself worked up, and that a tantrum might ensue, Florrie tried to distract him. 'Annie will be along presently. How about I pour you a glass of water, and you tell me what you'd like in terms of a fundraising lunch for Mr Knight-Downey?' she asked.

He smiled. 'Ah, well . . .'

Clearly just about to regale Florrie with his grand ideas, Sir Hugh was interrupted by Lady Charlotte entering the dining room, clutching her head.

'Charlotte!' Daphne said. 'Darling, you made it up before noon. Well done!'

As she poured water into a fresh glass, out of the corner of her eye, Florrie observed Lady Charlotte slump into the seat at the head of the table. There were dark circles beneath her eyes, her hair was lank and her colour wan. She wondered if Lady Charlotte had seen her baby son at all in the last twenty-four hours.

'I feel simply ghastly,' she said, yawning. 'Why on earth did you keep me up until three in the morning?'

Sir Hugh took the water from Florrie without a thanks. 'Oh, come now, Lottie! Dickie's been gone for a week, now. There's nobody to tell you to go to bed before midnight, like a good girl.'

'Why shouldn't we dance and have fun into the small

hours?' Daphne asked. She flung her slender arms into the air triumphantly. 'We're the haut monde. We can all sleep when we're dead.'

'I'm a mother,' Lady Charlotte said. 'Aren't I supposed to be responsible and boring?'

'Nonsense,' Sir Hugh said. 'You have a nanny for all that. Get some sausages down you. Maybe hair of the dog. I'm sure Florrie wouldn't mind fixing you—'

'Stop!' Lady Charlotte raised her hand. 'Stop, Hugh. You are perfectly disgusting. I couldn't possibly drink alcohol until after lunch, at least.' She turned to Florrie and held out her hand. 'Darling Florrie.' She opened and closed her hand, clearly expecting Florrie to come to her side.

Florrie obliged and found herself being claimed by Lady Charlotte. Her hand felt cold and clammy.

'Hey up, chuck,' she said, mimicking the flat Lancashire vowels of the local Rawtenstall accent. 'Can tha get me a sausage barm, love?' She turned to Daphne. 'You know, I really should have trodden the boards myself! If only I hadn't been related to the King.' Throwing back her head with laughter at her own joke, she immediately winced and yanked her hand free of Florrie's to press her fingers to her temples. 'Ow. Just bring me some food as quickly as you can, please. There's a dear.'

Florrie curtseyed. 'Of course, ma'am.' Over the years, she'd learned to bite her tongue and simply smile whenever Lady Charlotte tried to humiliate her – and she regularly did. Florrie knew that bringing in a wage to support her family would always be more important than defending herself against ridicule. At least now she had Mam and Thom to confide her hopes, fears and irritations to.

While she buttered a barm cake and sliced up two sausages, Sir Hugh planned his grand political luncheon.

'So, the plan is to have Oswald Mosley as our guest speaker. I rather think we can get ... what ... two, three hundred guests to take tables of ten?'

'Are you going to *charge* them?' Lady Charlotte asked, wrinkling her nose. 'Isn't that a bit *nouveau riche*?'

Florrie served the barm cake on a plate and set it in front of Lady Charlotte.

Sir Hugh took out a cigarette and lit it, puffing plumes of blue smoke into the air. 'Of course not. How vulgar. No, I shall invite Dickie's wealthy businessmen friends and urge them to make donations.' He turned to Florrie. 'You can ask Cook to come up with a stellar menu, can't you? Five courses, perhaps. Good wines. Get them all tipsy and loosen their wallets.'

Opening her mouth to respond, Florrie found Daphne talking over her.

'But Richard has got such a bee in his bonnet about fascism and authoritarianism. So has your mother. Neither of them can see the attraction at all. Imagine the fuss he'll make if you use his business address book to recruit people for an expensive lunch in honour of British politics' up-and-coming fascist leader!'

Lady Charlotte looked thoughtfully at her barm cake and started to pick the sausages out, setting them on the side of the plate. 'Hans says Dickie and my mother-in-law are both naïve idealists! Everyone who has their wits about them knows the whole of Europe is going to be fascist within the next few years. Italy's already there.' She leaned over to Daphne. 'I hear Mussolini gives very *rousing* speeches.' She snorted with mirth and sliced off a sliver of sausage, slipping it into her mouth but then spitting it into her napkin. She pushed the plate away and caught Florrie's eye. 'Perhaps I will try a Tom Collins. Just a weak one.'

Sir Hugh got to his feet and wandered over to the window. He faced the rolling lawn. 'Mosley's an outstanding orator. I believe he's the future of Britain.' He turned back to his wife and sister-in-law. 'Dickie's an idiot, and he's not my father. And actually, if we hold the lunch in the next few weeks while he's in India rubbing shoulders with the Viceroy, Dickie needn't even know.'

6

'Shut the door!' Arkwright ordered. He was sitting behind his desk in his office, where the family silver was kept in locked wall cabinets and where he also slept, guarding the silver with his very life. He got up from his chair and closed the window that faced on to the courtyard next to the staff and tradesmen's entrance. He turned back to Florrie, lowering his voice. 'I don't want the others privy to our conversation. You understand?'

'Of course.' Florrie sat in the visitor's chair, lacing her hands in her lap.

Arkwright returned to his seat. 'Right, now tell me again. Slowly this time. What has Sir Hugh asked you to do?'

Florrie told the butler of Sir Hugh's plans to host a fundraising luncheon for Mosley's New Party.

Arkwright inhaled sharply. 'Sir Richard is going to have an apoplexy when he finds out,' he said.

'Exactly my point.' Florrie nodded. 'Sir Hugh might think he can hold the lunch without Sir Richard finding out, but in a house with such a large staff we can't hope to keep it under wraps forever.'

Steepling his fingers beneath his chin, Arkwright looked suddenly weary. 'Like chalk and cheese, those two.' He shook his head and sighed. 'But my loyalties as butler are to Sir Richard, as are yours. He's the head of Holcombe Hall, the head of the family.'

Florrie thought of the terrible secret that she was guarding: that Sir Richard wasn't the true heir to the Harding-Bourne fortune and Holcombe Estate at all; that he had allegedly been conceived following Dame Elizabeth's indiscretion with an old college friend of the late Lord Harding-Bourne. She bit her lip. 'Yes, but in his absence we're rudderless and answerable to Sir Hugh.'

Arkwright peered thoughtfully at the framed photograph of himself in conversation with the Prince of Wales, when the heir to the throne had visited Holcombe Hall during the late Lord Harding-Bourne's final years. 'Dame Elizabeth,' he said. He locked eyes with Florrie. 'You're closest to her out of all the staff. Tell Dame Elizabeth, and see if she can't put a stop to her son entertaining fascists at the house.'

'I can't promise anything,' Florrie said. 'It's not my place to tell any of the family members what to do. You of all people know that.'

'Try,' Arkwright said simply. He got to his feet and opened the window again, signalling that their summit was at an end. 'Please.'

'Get the windows in the sitting room cleaned today, please,' Florrie told Gracie, one of the maids, as she made her way through the reception rooms downstairs, assessing which cleaning tasks were pressing. 'And tackle the ones in the dining room when you're finished with those. They're all getting terribly yellow and cloudy from nicotine.'

'There's pollen on the outside and all,' Gracie said, blushing.

Florrie scribbled 'windows outside' in her notebook.

'I'll get Thom to have one of his lads clean the outsides. We shouldn't try to negotiate those flower beds. That Miss Wilmott's Ghost sea holly might look lovely, but it doesn't half slice through skirt fabric and stockings like razor blades.' She turned to another maid. 'And Elsie, I'd like you to work with Agnes to take the rugs from Sir Richard's study and give them a good beating while he's away.' She leafed through the notes she'd written that morning. 'And it's time the nursery was given a good do. I notice little Sir William's been sneezing a lot.'

Gracie grimaced. 'Miss Talbot told us to leave the nursery and her room be.'

Florrie looked up, puzzled. 'What reason did she give for that?'

Gracie shrugged. 'She reckons a bit of dirt's good for his health, and she also says us maids should keep away from him, in case he starts getting attached to us.'

Not for the first time, Florrie acknowledged the ice in her gut that told her something was amiss with Miss Talbot's nannying techniques. 'Nonsense. I'm the housekeeper. If she doesn't want her room cleaned, that's one thing, but the nursery's another matter entirely, and I say it needs a good bottoming. That baby has hay fever. Don't need to be a doctor to work that one out. The dust won't be doing him any favours.'

With her orders given, she turned her attention to visiting Dame Elizabeth. The old lady's rooms were situated on the ground floor, beyond Sir Richard's study and the library. Of late, the grand doyenne of the family had taken to staying in her rooms, blaming a flare-up of her gout. Florrie wondered if she hadn't also fallen into something of a malaise as a result of being blackmailed by Miles T. Brooke – the man who Dame Elizabeth herself had reluctantly confided to Florrie was Sir Richard's true father. Could the burden of guarding such a grave family secret be exacerbating the old lady's frailty? Was Brooke still extorting money from her?

'Dame Elizabeth?' She knocked lightly on the door to the suite.

There was no response from within.

'Dame Elizabeth? It's Florrie.'

Momentarily, Florrie could hear Dame Elizabeth's voice. Was she being asked to come in or go away? The old lady sounded progressively weaker as each month passed.

'I'm coming in, Dame Elizabeth.'

Pushing the door open, Florrie slipped inside. The suite of rooms had been recently rearranged and redecorated, so that one first entered a reception room that faced on to the grounds at the rear of the house. In here, it was warm and stuffy, as if the window hadn't been open for days. Lifting the window open, Florrie sensed that nobody other than family had been to visit Dame Elizabeth for some time. The cushions on the seating were all perfectly plumped and the side tables gleamed, yet the place felt like a stage set in an abandoned theatre. She moved through to the study, in which (she'd discovered more than a year ago) Dame Elizabeth had been writing correspondence to Brooke. Finally, Florrie passed through Dame Elizabeth's dressing room, where her widow's weeds adorned a mannequin, and then ventured into the reconfigured bedroom, which overlooked the gardens at the front of the house. The curtains were partially drawn. A solitary shaft of strong sunlight sliced through the gloom, illuminating dust motes that drifted like slivers of gold on to the parquet floor.

'Ma'am, are you well?' Florrie asked, curtseying.

The old lady was lying in her old four-poster bed, still in her nightgown. 'I was just resting, dear.'

Advancing to the curtains, Florrie gripped the edges and started to tug at them. 'May I?'

'If you must.'

Florrie yanked the heavy brocade curtains open, letting bright light flood into every nook and cranny of the room. 'Fresh air. That's what you need, Dame Elizabeth. You've been missing out on a glorious day.' She lifted up the heavy window. In the distance, Thom was pushing a wheelbarrow across the lawn, towards the greenhouse.

'Have I indeed?' Dame Elizabeth's voice was little more than a croak, as though she hadn't spoken in too long. 'Here! Help me to sit up.'

Florrie moved swiftly to the head of the large bed and helped prop her against her pillows. 'Have you eaten today, ma'am?' She poured a glass of water from a heavy jug and offered it to the old lady.

'Yes, yes.' Dame Elizabeth sipped at the water and then pushed the glass away. 'Dilys brought me some porridge for breakfast, but I've no appetite.' She patted the counterpane. 'Sit, sit, dear girl.'

Florrie took the glass from her, set it back on the nightstand and sat gingerly on the edge of the bed. She allowed Dame Elizabeth to take her hand, noticing that the old lady's arms were too thin. Of late, the puckered skin hung loose from the bones, as if her very body were a garment that had been washed poorly, becoming overly large and ill-fitting. 'I'm worried about you, ma'am. We rarely see you in the dining room any more. It's not right, you being holed up here on your own, when little Sir William needs his grandma.'

Dame Elizabeth patted her hand. 'How right you are, Florrie. It's the dratted gout. I've had the terrible misfortune of it flaring up, just as my darling grandson arrived, and I fear I am not long for this world.'

'Surely not!'

'My energy seems to desert me daily in increments, and soon there will be nothing left but an empty husk.'

Florrie looked into Dame Elizabeth's eyes, cloudy with the start of cataracts. She sensed the unbearably heavy weight of sadness in the old woman. 'The household needs your steady hand on the rudder, with Sir Richard away. We need to get you back to full strength. I shall call the doctor!'

Dame Elizabeth shook her head. 'No, no. It is not merely the gout that ails me, nor age, nor even ennui.'

'Then what is it?' Florrie smoothed a renegade lock of Dame Elizabeth's white hair from her brow. She pressed her lips together, wondering if she dare broach the topic of the clandestine visitor. 'Are you still receiving ... unwanted letters? Because you're entirely within your right to call the police if that's—'

'Don't breathe a word of that out loud, girl. Not even in here.' Dame Elizabeth gripped her hand tightly; surprising strength in those bony fingers. She looked around the room, as if spies might lurk behind every stick of furniture, then lowered her voice to little more than a whisper. 'Nobody must *ever* know that Sir Richard is not the true heir to the Harding-Bourne fortune.'

'I swear on my life that your secret will die with me,' Florrie said, willing the old woman to see how deep her loyalty ran. 'You have my word.'

Tears pooled in the old woman's eyes. 'Miles was the most foolish mistake I ever made. He presents himself as a gentleman, but he's little more than a well-spoken scoundrel who took advantage of me when I was at a low ebb. And even now, even after I threatened to expose his blackmail and sent him packing . . . The barefaced cheek! Is it any wonder I have fallen into melancholia?'

Florrie frowned. *So he is still extorting money from her*, she reflected. She opted not to press Dame Elizabeth further, however. It wouldn't do to aggravate an already distressed woman. 'Don't give Mr Brooke a second thought,' she said blithely. 'He's nowt but mud on your shoe.'

'It takes more than a misspent night to be a true father to a son.' Dame Elizabeth drew her close, her milky eyes searching Florrie's. 'Please, Florence. Promise me again that you'll never breathe a word that Richard . . .'

'My lips are sealed. I know exactly what's at stake.' Florrie thought about Sir Hugh, and the consequences of him taking over the ownership of the Holcombe Estate and the considerable Harding-Bourne industrialist fortune. She shuddered. 'But I do need you to nurture your strength of spirit, ma'am, because we have a problem.'

She conveyed the news that Dame Elizabeth's reckless younger son wanted to use the house to entertain the new enfant terrible of the British political fringe.

'Damn that boy!' Dame Elizabeth said, sitting up straight. She threw back the counterpane and swung her swollen legs out of bed. 'I will not have this! Besmirching our family's good name, just as we've recovered from the indignity of being associated with Clarence Hatry. Of all the reprobates my son could have gone into business with, he chose the very cad who practically brought Wall Street crashing down, with his fraudulent steel merger. I sincerely hope Hatry's now rotting in his prison cell,' she said with disgust. 'No. We've suffered enough, and I will not have it!' Her voice rose to a shout and she clutched at her chest, wheezing.

'Oh, blimey!' Florrie said. 'Don't be doing a Bertha Douglas on me, ma'am, please! Don't exert yourself if you can't catch your breath. I shouldn't have said anything.'

'Nonsense, dear girl. Nonsense.' Dame Elizabeth allowed herself to be tucked back into bed. 'I'm afraid I am not myself.'

'Would you like me to convey a message to Sir Hugh? A note, perhaps? Or shall I send him in to see you?'

Dame Elizabeth gestured to her study. 'There's paper and a pen on my writing desk. Do bring it in. I don't want to see that buffoon of a son of mine, however, until you tell me he's cancelled this tomfoolery.'

Florrie brought her the writing materials, concerned at the shaky hand in which the grand doyenne of Holcombe Hall wrote. She chided herself inwardly for having bothered her with the matter. Dame Elizabeth's health was clearly more precarious than Florrie had realized.

'Here. Give this to him and make sure he reads it.' Dame Elizabeth folded the note into a tight square with shaking hands. 'I expect an answer and an apology. Hugh knows this family does not tolerate fascist nonsense. He's like a rebellious child!'

Florrie slid the note into her pocket and curtseyed. 'I'll send Dilys in with a light lunch, and she can freshen you up.'

Dame Elizabeth shook her head. 'I couldn't eat a thing. I don't wish to be fussed over.'

'Please, ma'am. Let her take care of you. That's what a lady's maid is for. At least let her bring in some of Cook's lemonade. She can give you a bed bath, change your sheets and help you into a fresh nightgown.'

Dame Elizabeth nodded then. 'Very well.'

'And shall I send Miss Talbot in with Sir William?'

At first, Dame Elizabeth looked up at her with a hopeful smile. Then the smile faltered. 'Miss Talbot doesn't think it fitting to have Sir William at my bedside while I am sick.'

Florrie could feel irritation prickle on the end of her tongue. 'Not meaning to be disrespectful, like, ma'am, but wouldn't spending time with your grandson help with your . . . melancholia? And wouldn't it be good for the baby to have a close and loving connection with his grandmother?'

Dame Elizabeth sighed. 'Miss Talbot's reputation precedes her, according to my daughter-in-law. She's an expert in infant rearing, apparently.'

Florrie cocked her head to the side. 'Oh? I thought she had some historical tie to the family.'

'No, no, no. My boys' nanny is long passed away, sadly. No, Lady Charlotte received the recommendation – from a trusted source, she said. I expect it's one of the other women in her social circle, or maybe from someone at the palace.' Perhaps Dame Elizabeth could see the uncertainty in Florrie's expression, because she went on to elaborate. 'She showed me Miss Talbot's references, and I have to say, they were entirely commendable.'

Florrie nodded, careful to smile. 'Good.' It would not do to share her misgivings over Miss Talbot's character and nannying techniques. It wasn't her place to interfere with family matters and the old lady was already rattled enough by talk of her blackmailer and by the news of Sir Hugh's luncheon. 'Very well. I'll pass your note to Sir Hugh, and Dilys will be along shortly.'

When she showed the note to Sir Hugh at the dining table, he crumpled it into a ball and threw it squarely into a jardiniere that contained a lush palm. He turned to Florrie. 'Have Cook send up suggested menus for my luncheon. And next time I make plans to host a meal in my own home, Florrie, please desist from running with tales to my dear mama.' He looked her up and down, naked disdain etched into the lines around his mouth. 'I am no schoolboy to be reported on, and you are nothing but a glorified maid.' He looked to his wife and sister-in-law for approval and sat taller in his seat, clearly enjoying the spectacle. 'Do I make myself clear?'

Florrie felt tears threaten. A prickly response to the humiliation was trying to fight its way out, but she dug her nails into her palms and willed both the tears and the words to disappear. 'Of course, Sir Hugh.'

7

'Now, let's go over the table settings,' Florrie said to the maids and valets tasked with serving at the grand fundraising luncheon. 'There's ten to a table. I want to see cutlery for hors d'oeuvres, a fish course, sorbet, main; dessert will be some kind of fool served in sundae dishes, Cook says, so long sundae spoons, butter knives... oh, and there's a cheese course and petits fours to be brought out with the port.'

'What wines does Mr Arkwright want?' Danny asked. He seemed to be chewing something.

'Mr Arkwright's on his way. Are you chewing gum, Danny?' Florrie asked.

He shrugged.

'Go and dispose of it, please. I will not have staff indulging in dirty habits while they're on shift.' She pointed to the door.

Danny rolled his eyes at her and smirked at one of the other valets.

'Out!' Florrie said.

As Danny slouched out of the ballroom, where the lunch was to take place, Arkwright strode in, deftly carrying several different bottles of wine. He glared at Danny as they passed one another. 'Have you been sent out with a flea in your ear *again*?' He tutted loudly and shook his head at the insolent looking valet. 'Come and see me in my office before dinner, young man.'

Turning to focus on Florrie and her charges, Arkwright shouted, 'Wines! Pay attention, now. Anybody caught serving the wrong wine with the wrong course or spilling any will have their pay docked.'

Arkwright delivered a swift masterclass on the wines he'd selected for the lunch, testing each member of serving staff afterwards to ensure they could trot out a satisfactory description of the wine's origin and bouquet, should a guest ask them. He demonstrated to even the old hands how to pour perfectly without spilling a drop.

Florrie watched the young staff hanging on the butler's every word, and she smiled at the memory of herself and Sally being lectured in identical fashion, when she had still been a maid. How much had changed in such a short space of time!

'Right,' she said, clapping her hands together when Arkwright had finished. 'Before you set the tables, I want to see everyone's hands.' She watched the younger staff look at each other, clearly puzzled. 'There must not be a single fingerprint on any of the cutlery, crockery or crystal.'

The maids and valets lined up with their hands held out for inspection. Florrie walked along the row, grabbing each server's hands and checking to see if they passed muster.

'Elsie, your hands are filthy, girl.' She looked at Elsie's hair, which was tied in a greasy-looking bun. 'Dirty fingernails and greasy locks? Not on my watch. Tonight, make sure you wash your hair and give yourself a good scrub.' She spoke sternly to her charges. 'I don't want to see any of you looking less than immaculate tomorrow. Do I make myself clear?'

'Yes, Miss Bickerstaff,' they mumbled in unison.

She sent Elsie and a young valet packing to wash their hands, and then supervised the laying of the tables. Mam had laundered and laid the snowy-white tablecloths on the round tables earlier in the day. But where were the trolleys loaded with crockery and the centrepieces?

'Carry on, ladies and gentlemen. I'll be back presently.'

Making her way down to the kitchen, Florrie reflected on her misgivings about the political luncheon being hosted at Holcombe Hall. Even so, she had to admit that, she always enjoyed the military-style preparation required for such events, taking pride in presiding over the fine detail that was expected at a high-society lunch or dinner.

'Come on, Sal!' she said, entering the kitchen to find the china was still being loaded on to the trolley. 'We'll still be setting up at dinner time if you don't get a move on.'

'Pots were streaky,' Cook said. She stared at Ginny the kitchen maid with eyebrows raised. '*Somebody* hadn't washed and dried them properly last time Sir Richard held a business dinner, so *somebody* had to wash the bloody lot again!'

Drying a coffee cup, Ginny looked contrite. 'Sorry, Cook.'

Florrie folded her arms. 'Not good enough, young lady. If I'd done that when Mrs Douglas was housekeeper, she would have had my guts for garters. Think yourself lucky I'm giving you a second chance.'

'Thanks, Miss Bickerstaff. Sorry, Miss Bickerstaff.' The girl looked down at her damp tea towel and the cup, utterly forlorn. Tears stood in her eyes.

'No time for that nonsense, eh? Stiffen your spine and crack on, please.'

Though Florrie hated seeing the younger staff burst into tears when she gave them a ticking off, she knew that she had to be firm if the Holcombe Hall domestic staff were to operate like a well-oiled machine. She tried to be as kind as she could, careful to praise the girls whenever they did something well, but she was always mindful of how Bertha Douglas, her beloved predecessor, had successfully tempered motherly warmth with strict discipline, inspiring respect.

She patted Ginny on the shoulder. 'There, there. Practice makes perfect. You'll know for next time.'

The girl managed a weak smile and dabbed at her eyes with her apron. 'Yes, Miss Bickerstaff.'

Returning to the dining room, Florrie oversaw the rest of the preparation. With the dazzling rainbow light of the crystal chandeliers bouncing off the pristine wine glasses and silverware, the ballroom had a magical feel to it. Florrie pictured Thom taking her for a spin around the parquet dancefloor – covered in tables tonight – on those few occasions when they had danced in silence together, barefoot in the darkness, while the rest of the household slept. Dear Thom.

'That'll do for tonight, ladies and gentlemen,' she said. 'Go and get your dinner. I'll supervise the flowers in the morning, and you must all attend to your usual duties first thing. But I want you all back in the ballroom tomorrow morning at ten o'clock sharp, shipshape and ready to extend a legendary Holcombe Hall welcome to Sir Hugh's guests. Champagne and canapés will be served from the gazebo on the back lawn.' She clapped her hands together and the staff were dismissed, leaving Florrie alone to put out the name cards, painstakingly penned in Arkwright's scrolling calligraphy.

'I don't know whether to be terrified or excited, Miss Bickerstaff.'

Florrie recognized Thom's deep, gravelly voice immediately. She turned around to find him leaning against the door frame, arms folded and smiling at her so that the dimples in his cheeks deepened.

Giggling, Florrie made her way over to him, noting his clean slacks and collarless linen shirt. On his feet were his leather indoor shoes, rather than his gardener's muddy boots. His golden hair was darker with damp and combed back off his tanned forehead. Only one errant lock had escaped and now hung loose over his bright blue left eye. 'My, my, you're looking very handsome this evening, Thomas Stanley.'

'Freshly scrubbed up to take you to dinner, milady.' He bowed and winked.

Checking that nobody was loitering in the hallway, she allowed his muscular arms to enfold her in an embrace and craned her neck upwards to kiss him. He tasted of Parma Violets and smelled of soap and sunshine.

Thom stroked her face gently, though the hardened skin of his gardener's fingers was rough from manual toil. 'You're a sight for sore eyes, Florrie Bickerstaff. You've been that busy this last week, I've barely seen you except from a distance.' He kissed her full on the mouth again. 'I missed you.'

Florrie could sense his ardour. She pushed him away playfully. 'Now, now, Thom. You know I've been up to my eyes in it, what with this lunch and pandering to that lot's every whim.'

He grabbed her around the waist and pulled her close to him. 'Never mind their whims. What about ours? When are we going to get some time to ourselves? When am I going to visit you in your room again, eh, Miss Bickerstaff?' He nibbled at her ear and kissed her neck.

Hearing the chatter of two of the ladies' maids in the hallway, growing louder as they approached, Florrie disentangled herself from Thom's embrace. 'You're incorrigible,' she said. 'Let's go to dinner.'

'I'm a red-blooded man.' With his index finger, he traced the line of her collar bone beneath her blouse. 'And you're the most beautiful girl I ever laid eyes on.'

'Dinner!' she said, removing his hand.

'I'm hungry for *you*. Can I come to your room tonight? Go on!'

Florrie giggled, flushing hot at the idea the maids might overhear them. 'Pack it in, for heaven's sake, and let's get going! Cook's doing a practice run for tomorrow's lunch. Something fancy with chicken. Come on, before it gets cold.'

Knowing that the maids weren't far behind them, Florrie refused to link Thom in the hallway. It wouldn't do to parade their romance in front of the other staff.

'I don't know why you're getting all bashful. Everyone knows we're courting,' he said.

'It's nowt to do with being bashful,' Florrie said. They had reached the sitting room. The door was only slightly ajar, but she could hear Sir Hugh, Daphne and Lady Charlotte within, singing along to the tinny music coming from the gramophone. 'I'm the housekeeper, the most senior female member of staff, and that means I have to set an example.'

'You're on your own time now, though.'

She sighed and looked up at Thom. 'But I'm never truly off shift, am I?'

They walked quickly along the hallway, but just as Florrie was about to bear right at the grand staircase to head for the servants' stairs down to the kitchen, Thom steered her left, towards the main entrance.

'Where are we going?' she asked.

He placed his hand on the small of her back and gestured towards the front door. 'You'll see.'

They passed beneath the giant dome that covered the marble-floored vestibule, where the late Lord Harding-Bourne gazed down on them from his portrait, softly lit in the glow of the angled picture light that hung above the frame.

Thom clasped Florrie to him, as though they were waltzing. He swept her off her feet, swinging her around and setting her back down.

'Hey up, Fred Astaire. What you up to?' Florrie asked, bemused.

'A surprise.'

'Oh?'

Pushing the door open, Thom took Florrie by the hand. 'Nobody to see us here, my love. No spies where I'm taking you.'

The hairs on Florrie's arms stood proud. Was it gooseflesh as she moved from the stuffy house into the cooler night air, or was it the thrill of anticipation that Thom had some romantic subterfuge planned?

'You're a right rum beggar, you are. Are you out to take advantage of me in the woods, Thomas Stanley?'

'You'll see!'

He led her over the moonlit lawn, where the long shadows from a cedar of Lebanon stretched away over the grass, like some secretive nocturnal picnic blanket. Wordlessly, they entered the corner of the woods closest to the house.

'I'd like to go back now,' Florrie said, wrenching her hand free and slowing to a standstill, irritated that Thom was pressing her into a clandestine meeting when her stomach was rumbling and she was bone-tired from being on her feet since dawn. 'Those stable lads are like a plague of locusts. They'll have eaten everything and left cob all for us.'

'Flipping Nora, Florrie. Will you just trust me for five minutes?' Thom took her hand again. 'I've got something to show you. You'll want to see this.'

Reluctantly, Florrie followed him deeper in until she saw lights a way ahead.

'What's all this, then?'

They emerged from the dense tangle of trees into a grass clearing that was strung about with lights – the sort Florrie had seen at fairgrounds, where glowing white bulbs hung from thick cable. She gasped with delight. In the middle of the clearing was a table set for two, complete with a pristine tablecloth, a red rose in a slender rose vase and a candle, flickering inside a glass shade.

'What on earth is this?'

'Dinner à deux,' Thom said, pulling out a chair for her.

Florrie found she was grinning so hard, her back teeth ached. 'All this for me?'

'Am I not allowed to take my sweetheart on a date?'

Thom pushed her chair in as she sat down. He took his own seat and unfolded his napkin with a flourish.

Before each of them was a dinner plate, covered by a steel cloche. Florrie could smell Cook's signature chicken dish on the air. She lifted the cloche and peered beneath at the beautifully presented plate.

'Blimey,' she said. 'This is a far cry from servants' rations, dumped on a plate with a big spoon. Look at all these fancy garnishes! It's just like what gets served to the family and their guests at one of their posh dinners.'

'You are the best so you deserve the best, milady!' Thom took a bottle of white wine out of an ice bucket that had been hidden from view until now. He picked up a corkscrew that had been left on the table and removed the cork with a triumphant squeak and a pop. 'Would madam like to try the wine first?'

Florrie roared with laughter. 'Ooh, you are a wit! Just pour it, will you, and let's get stuck in. My stomach's growling like an angry tiger.'

They dined in style beneath the golden glow of the lights, talking and laughing, revelling in their blissful solitude, where only the owls eavesdropped. Every mouthful of Cook's chicken dish tasted heavenly to Florrie, as she gazed into the azure eyes of her Thom. Yet at the end of the meal, when the wine bottle was empty and the harsh edges of the world of servitude had been blunted to a warm, soft fuzz, Florrie felt her gut tighten, when Thom stood and reached into his pocket, as if it already knew something her brain hadn't yet considered.

'What you doing, Thom?' she asked. 'Thom?'

'I, er . . . there's something I've been meaning to . . .' He took out a small square case and sank on to one knee.

Florrie inhaled sharply and clasped her hands to her chest.

'Er . . . I've got something important I want to ask you,' Thom said, grinning.

8

'Marry me, Florrie,' Thom said, opening the box to reveal a slim gold band with a tiny glinting stone set into it.

Marry me, Florrie. More a command than a question, Florrie thought as she stared down at the ring, then Thom, gazing up at her hopefully. When his smile started to falter, she realized she was likely wearing a look of puzzlement rather than delight, since the scenario in which she said yes to his proposal was already playing out in her mind's eye. They would have a glorious wedding, held in Holcombe Hall's chapel, and then catered by Cook, with her family and colleagues – people who had become true friends over the years – seated around the kitchen table. So far, so good. Perhaps she and Thom would even go to Blackpool or the Lake District on a honeymoon, if Sir Richard would agree to them taking an entire week off. But she could already see the disappointment in Sir Richard's grey eyes, as she handed her notice in. Her career would end abruptly, her delightful, sunny room at the top of the house being given over to another, while she and Thom would have to secure costly, cramped accommodation in the village befitting a married couple, or else move into the gamekeeper's cottage with Mam and the children. Their income would wither overnight to that of a solitary Head Gardener, meaning there would be little spare to give to Mam and the children. No more easy camaraderie with a large coterie of domestic staff. No more sense of being woven into the rich tapestry of the Harding-Bourne dynasty, and of being as much a part of the glorious Holcombe Hall – her home for the last twelve years – as the foundation stones and the roofs and the sandstone bricks. No more sense of purpose or pride that she mattered to the likes of Sir Richard. *Stop! Stop it, Florrie Bickerstaff! What are you thinking? Isn't it every girl's dream to be asked by a handsome and honourable man to be his wife? Nothing short of a miracle at your age!*

'What do you say?' Thom asked, looking up at her, clearly disconcerted.

Florrie sank to her knees and took his hands and the ring in its box between hers. 'I'm so flattered, Thom. It's a grand ring.'

'It were my mother's, left to her by my grandmother. She'd have wanted you to have it. She'd have loved you. *I* love you, Florrie. Be my wife.'

'Oh, Thom. I want to . . . but—'

'But what?'

'Mam and the kids. Giving up a job I love in a household I love, where I've worked darn hard to move up the ranks.'

He looked at her quizzically. 'Them lot – below stairs and especially above stairs – none of them will look after you in your dotage. Our jobs are a means to an end, not an end in themselves. Think of how lovely it would be to have a family of our own.'

'Aye. You're not wrong.' She sat on her heels, thinking wistfully of the laughter of small children and the warm, comforting weight of a baby in her arms. Yet Thom was not the one being asked to give up everything he'd known since the age of fifteen. 'But this proposal ... getting married ... It's all a bit sudden.'

'*Sudden?*' He pulled away from her grasp and looked down at the modest ring, his eyebrows gathered together over eyes that had lost their sparkle. 'We've been courting a year.'

Grabbing his face between her hands, she pulled him close and kissed him passionately. 'I do love you, Thom. But getting married will mean a huge change – not just for me, but for Mam and the kids, too. Do you understand?' She forced him to meet her gaze. Did the hardness in his eyes soften, or was she imagining it?

'I just thought ...' He snapped the ring box shut. His Adam's apple rose and fell.

What could she say to give herself a little breathing room, yet avoid breaking his heart? 'I just need a little time to think on it; how we can all manage without my wages, where we'd live ... that sort of thing. Can you give me some time, love? Let me get my head round it? Doesn't mean we can't still be lovebirds.'

At last, a smile, albeit unconvincing, reappeared on Thom's lips. 'Don't keep me waiting forever, will you?'

Preferring not to return to the house straight away, Florrie made her excuses and slipped through the woodland to the gamekeeper's cottage. It was late. Would Mam still be awake?

Not wishing to disturb the children, Florrie tapped gently on the window of the parlour. The curtains were shut and there was no light coming from within. Next, she walked around to the back of the cottage and peered inside the kitchen window. The room was in darkness and there was no sign of life in there, either.

Casting around on the ground, she found a small stone. She stood on the back lawn, looking up at the window of her mother's bedroom. Though the curtains were drawn, she was sure she could make out the glow of a paraffin lamp inside the room. Perhaps her mother was reading in bed. She threw the stone at the glass, praying it wouldn't crack a pane.

Presently, the curtains were wrenched open and her mother appeared. She opened the window and leaned out.

'Whatever's the matter, Florrie?' Mam spoke in little more than a hissed whisper. The moon had gone behind a small patch of cloud, and there was annoyance evident in what Florrie could see of her face.

'Sorry, Mam,' Florrie said. 'I needed to talk to you about something.'

'Don't you know what time it is? Shouldn't you be turning in for the night?'

'Please.'

'Wait there.'

Within a few minutes, her mother opened the back door and admitted her to the small kitchen, which was chillier than usual.

'I'll get a fire going in the stove,' Mam said, opening the fire box and filling it with some kindling. She struck a long match, and soon flames were dancing merrily. She filled a kettle from the cold water tap over the butler's sink and set it on top of the stove. 'You smell like a brewery.'

'I've just had dinner with Thom. We shared a bottle of wine.'

'Oh, aye? Special occasion, was it? Well, judging by the smell of you, young lady, I'd say you could do with sobering up. Tea do you?'

'Aye. Ta, Mam.'

Her mother draped a cardigan around her shoulders and spooned some tea leaves into an earthenware pot. She set out two cups and decanted some milk from the cool larder into a small jug. Then she turned back to Florrie. 'Come on then. Out with it. I'm guessing summat untoward's gone on for you to be paying me a visit after bedtime.'

Feeling tears threaten, Florrie exhaled hard and looked at her outstretched fingers. 'Oh, Mam. I reckon I've stuffed everything up good and proper.'

'Oh, love!' Her mother pulled her chair next to Florrie's and put her arms around her. 'It can't be that bad. Tell your mam. A trouble shared is a trouble halved.'

Florrie started to relate all that had come to pass in the woods between her and Thom.

'Oh, that's *marvellous*, love,' Mam said, clasping her to her chest at the juncture where Thom had got down on one knee and asked for her hand in marriage. She was beaming and nodding. 'If I'm honest, I knew it was on the cards.'

'How do you mean?'

'Well, he did come to me the other day and asked me permission for your hand, given you've no dad and all. Obviously, I said yes. I mean, he's such a good lad, he really is.' She kissed Florrie on her forehead. 'Congratulations, lovey! You've not stuffed up owt in the slightest. This is the *best* news!'

Florrie shook her head and pulled away. 'But it's not, is it? How can I marry him when we stand to lose so much? My job, the money I bring in for you and the little'uns. How will you survive on the tuppence ha'penny you earn as a laundress? You didn't think of that when you were conspiring to give me away like some chattel, did you?'

Her mother sat up straight, her eyes narrowing. 'Hey! Now, hang on a minute, young lady. There's no need for *that*!' Her delight had been quickly supplanted by alarm. 'I was thinking of your best interests. I've already got one daughter dead and buried. I don't want my only surviving child turning out a spinster on my account!' On the stove, the kettle began to whistle.

'Mam!'

Her mother got to her feet and made the tea, then sat down again at the small kitchen table. She closed her eyes and groaned. 'I can't believe you turned down a good man like that. I mean, are you *barmy*?'

'Oh, behave, Mam. I didn't turn him down. I just told him I needed time.'

'And what did he say?' Mam looked at her hopefully, worrying at the collar of her cardigan with arthritic fingers.

'He said he'd wait . . . for now, at least.' Florrie rubbed her face. 'What should I do, Mam?'

Her mother poured the tea, took some biscuits from a tin on the side and set them on a plate in the middle of the table. She took one, snapping it in two emphatically, then pointed a half at Florrie. 'My advice is to stop shilly-shallying around and get wed. Don't worry about me and the kids.'

'How can I not? How can you make your money stretch to keep three growing children clothed and fed?'

'We've got a roof over our heads, and I'm in work. We'll manage.' She bit into her biscuit and chewed, frowning. 'But you're on the wrong side of twenty-five, Florrie Bickerstaff, and you can't expect Sir Richard and his clan to be there for you in sickness and in health, 'til death do you part. You'll be on the scrap heap by sixty, alone and skint.'

'Charming!'

'It's true, Florence. If you lose this opportunity for a normal family life ... if you lose Thomas, at your age, you're likely going to end up on the shelf. Don't be a mug.'

9

'Are those centrepieces ready?' Florrie asked Daisy the following morning, rubbing the gooseflesh on her arms.

Though it was only just nine, the sun had been up for a good five hours, and below stairs the air was already stiflingly warm, humid and full of delicious smells from Cook's luncheon preparations. Florrie had found Daisy – the maid who showed the greatest flair for arranging flowers – sitting at a small table in the old slate-lined cold larder, where perishables had been kept before Sir Richard had bought Cook the Frigidaire. It was the only place in the house that escaped the heat of the summer, and where the flowers wouldn't wilt prematurely.

'Not yet, Miss Bickerstaff,' Daisy said, pushing a long-stemmed carnation into the supportive ball of chicken wire that was wedged in a shallow, uranium glass bowl full of water. The bowl already held a number of flower stems and foliage. Scattered on the table and in the buckets behind it was a dazzling array of flowers, freshly harvested from the Holcombe Estate gardens and smelling heavenly. 'I've done eight, as best I can . . .' She pointed to the arrangements sitting on the deep shelving that ran along one wall of the store. 'I've got a few more to do, and then I'm waiting on Thom for the roses.'

Thom. Florrie saw him in her mind's eye. Had he slept as fitfully as she had, wondering what would become of them, after Florrie had all but turned down his proposal? 'Have you seen him today?'

Daisy nodded, trimming the stem on a bright blue delphinium. 'Aye.'

'How was he? In himself, I mean.'

The maid shrugged. 'Usual, I suppose. Can't say I really noticed.'

'Right.' Florrie nodded, relieved to hear that he wasn't obviously inconsolable, at least. 'Very well. Make sure all the flowers are finished and awaiting my inspection by eleven o'clock, please. The guests will be arriving at twelve for drinks and canapés. You always, always get a few what turn up too early. I want everything ready for half past.'

By the time the Mosleys arrived, pulling up in the Rolls-Royce which Graham had driven to the station to collect them in, one hundred and fifty guests dressed in lounge suits and day dresses thronged the lawn at the back of the house. In the ballroom, the tables had all been perfectly set, complete with exquisite flower arrangements, gleaming cutlery and glinting crystal. Yet Florrie knew she must still keep a watchful eye on every detail: outside, where maids milled around, offering canapés to the guests; inside, where the valets were pouring champagne to be loaded on to trays (though Arkwright bore the bulk of the responsibility for his lads); below stairs, where spent glasses and platters were being carried to be quickly washed up and dried by Ginny for reuse, and where Cook and Sally were already assembling delicate cold plates for starters.

'Cook, are you on top of your timings?' she asked, checking the clock on the kitchen wall.

Cook looked up from the lobster concoction she was corralling into a shell. She fixed Florrie with a ruddy-faced stare. 'Is the Pope a Catholic, Florence?'

Florrie grinned. 'That's a yes, then.'

Cook suddenly stepped away from the kitchen table and took Florrie by the elbow. 'Need to have a word with you about . . . chicken.'

Bemused, Florrie allowed herself to be led into the overspill kitchen, where Cook kept her spare ovens for catering large functions. The room was stiflingly hot, but they could not be overheard in there.

'What's going on?' Florrie asked. 'Is there a problem with the grub?'

Cook eyed her suspiciously. 'Thom looked like he'd been ten rounds with Knuckles O'Rourke at the pub on a Saturday night when he came in for breakfast.'

'How do you mean?' Florrie tensed.

'Red, puffy eyes. And I noticed you both came in at different times. Everything all right with you two?' She looked down at Florrie's wedding finger and raised an eyebrow. 'Oh. No ring? Say no more.'

Florrie shoved her left hand into her pocket. 'Jesus Christ! Did everyone know about that proposal before me?'

'There's nowt goes on under this roof that Cookie doesn't know about.' She folded her arms and blew a stray lock of hair from her forehead. 'Especially since I'm the one what prepares *special* dinners!' She winked and tapped the side of her nose.

'I don't want to talk about it,' Florrie said, her insides

churning. 'There's work to do, and none of it concerns either me or Thom's personal business. Right? Please get on with your tasks at hand, Cook.'

Feeling like the walls were closing in on her, Florrie undid the top button of her blouse and hastened back up the service stairs. *Damn this household!* she thought. *Is there nothing I can do without everyone knowing my business?* She marched into the ballroom and hurried across it to the open doors for some air.

Outside, the guests were all gathering around Sir Hugh, who was tapping a fork on the side of his crystal goblet.

'Gather, ye! O gather, ye, mighty political minds of His Majesty's Great British Isles. I say!' Sir Hugh turned to Arkwright, who had been standing close to the doors, clutching a bottle of champagne. 'I say, dear chap.' He held his glass out to Arkwright. 'Top me up for the toast, will you? There's a good fellow.'

Arkwright poured more champagne into Sir Hugh's goblet and then moved back to stand next to Florrie.

'Are you ready for the circus to begin?' he whispered in Florrie's ear.

Florrie had been so engrossed in thoughts of Thom that she initially looked at him askance before she realized he was referring to the crowd that had gathered around Sir Hugh. To Sir Hugh's left stood Daphne in a silk floral sundress. Next to her was Walter Knight-Downey, whose fingers seemed to be surreptitiously touching Daphne's. To Sir Hugh's right was a dapper man with a thin moustache and beady eyes whom Florrie recognized as Oswald Mosley, and to his right was a woman who must have been his wife, chatting with Lady Charlotte.

'What's the collective noun for fascists?' Florrie whispered to Arkwright. 'A clutch? A fist?'

'A degeneracy,' Arkwright said quietly. 'Whatever bilge they vomit up this afternoon, we must continue to serve them to the best of our ability and remember that Sir Richard is our employer. He'll throw a hissy fit when he hears of this.'

Florrie nodded and turned her attention back to Sir Hugh.

'Erm, before we take our seats for a splendid luncheon, my lords, ladies and gentlemen, I propose a toast to our guests of honour, the founder and leader of the glorious New Party, the Right Honourable Sir Oswald Mosley, and his wife Lady Mosley. To Sir Oswald and his New Party! May they restore Britain to her former glory!'

Everybody raised their glasses and toasted the Mosleys. Some young men wolf-whistled and cheered.

Florrie heard Sir Hugh ask Oswald Mosley if he'd like to address the other guests.

'Pray silence please, for the great Sir Oswald Mosley,' Walter shouted.

Daphne patted him on the arm encouragingly, all fluttering lashes and smiles.

Dame Elizabeth could surely see what was unfolding from her reception room, and she would not like it one iota, Florrie thought. Fanning herself with a table menu, anticipating Sir Richard's reaction when he eventually, inevitably found out about this political gathering, she watched the guest of honour clamber on to an occasional table so that he towered over the rest of the guests. He waited until everybody had fallen entirely silent. All eyes were on him.

'On behalf of the New Party, I would like to thank our host, Sir Hugh Harding-Bourne, for his generosity today in hosting this luncheon in aid of our great political undertaking.' He looked around at the applauding guests, waiting for them to fall silent again before continuing. He grabbed the lapels of his jacket and spoke slowly, over-enunciating in an almost comical fashion. 'As our friend, Mr Adolf Hitler, and his trailblazing National Socialist Party make significant gains in Germany, promising to raze the rotten, dead wood of the Weimar Republic to the ground so that a powerful new Germany can rise from the ashes, so too will my New Party sweep aside all that is holding Britain back from glory.'

Florrie's gaze travelled over Mosley's wife to where Lady Charlotte was standing wide-eyed with her mouth ajar, clearly hanging on every one of the politician's words.

'... But the New Party is so much more than a political movement, my lords, ladies and gentlemen,' Mosley continued. 'We will take our fight from the front benches of the Commons and into the streets. Just as Hitler has shocked and awed the German public with his brave, marching brownshirts, my own newly formed militia – my "Biff Boys" – will overcome the Communists and Jews that threaten to weaken this magnificent Anglo-Saxon nation of ours with their degenerate ideas and their impure blood. My New Party will beat them in parliament with our vision of a reinvigorated Britain for the British, and the Biff Boys will beat them in the gutters and slums with their fists.' Mosley's eyes seemed alight with the fanatical zeal coming from within.

'I can't abide this,' Arkwright said. 'Mrs Douglas will be turning in her grave. I'm going below stairs.'

Florrie nodded. 'I don't blame you one bit. I hope Dame Elizabeth can't hear what's being said. It'd be the end of her.' She wondered briefly if she might ask Lady Charlotte to cut Mosley's speech short somehow, perhaps blaming the need for precision timing with Cook's entrée. Yet she was well aware that the word of a housekeeper counted for nothing, and she couldn't risk her position for the sake of Dame Elizabeth's sensibilities.

Just as Arkwright retreated to his below-stairs domain, Florrie caught sight of something that made her wonder if sleep deprivation hadn't caused her to imagine things.

'Miss Talbot?'

She saw the unmistakable, austere figure of the nanny moving through the throng, carrying Sir William. Miss Talbot came to a halt alongside Lady Charlotte and passed the wriggling baby to her. To Florrie's horror, when Mosley finished his speech to rapturous applause, Lady Charlotte offered the baby boy to him to kiss.

Mosley stroked the baby's cheek. 'What a fine specimen!'

'Do you think so? Oh good.'

'We'll make a good fascist of him when he's grown, don't you worry.'

Lady Charlotte giggled. 'Oh, my Dickie would be perfectly horrified at the thought.' She batted her eyelashes coquettishly at the politician. 'Though I personally think that's a sterling idea. You know, my very good friend, Prince Hans von Grunwald – a Prussian Prince who's a fervent supporter of Herr Hitler – he would have admired your speech greatly.' She handed the baby back to Miss Talbot. 'Nap time for baby, yes?'

Miss Talbot curtseyed.

Immediately turning back to Mosley, Lady Charlotte said, 'I hear you're planning a trip to Italy to gain inspiration from Mussolini. You know, I'm something of a pilot myself. I could fly you there, personally.'

'Are you really, my dear?' Mosley asked, staring at her intently with those beady eyes. 'What a charming idea. I might take you up on your offer. I am indeed due to spend several months with him.'

Florrie had heard as much as she could stomach. She returned to the ballroom and clapped her hands. 'Let's get those starters on the tables, girls. The sooner this lunch is over, the better.'

10

'I'm absolutely shattered,' Cook said, rubbing her eyes. She yawned and looked around the kitchen table at the other staff who had gathered to eat dinner. 'I don't know if it's my age or what, but those big meals are getting harder and harder to cater.'

Florrie yawned too. She shook her head, trying to dispel the sleepiness that the warmth of the kitchen seemed to encourage. 'I think it's because we get less practice since Sir Richard insisted on tightening the household belt. We haven't really had a big lunch or dinner since Sir Hugh's wedding. Not big like today's fiasco.' She glanced surreptitiously at the place immediately to her right, where Thom normally sat, but where today, Sally was sitting. Where was Thom?

'Fiasco?' Matthew, the newly promoted valet, helped himself to some more of Cook's potato salad and banged the large serving spoon on the side of the dish emphatically. 'I wouldn't call that lunch a fiasco at all.'

Arkwright looked up from slicing his quiche and fixed his subordinate with a steely glare. 'Oh? And what would you call a gathering of fascists in the Holcombe Hall ballroom?'

Matthew shovelled potato into his mouth and pointed his fork at Arkwright. 'I know you're not right keen on fascists, Mr Arkwright,' he said, speaking with his mouth full, 'but there wasn't a single thing that Mosley feller said what I didn't agree with.' He looked at the others sitting around the table, presumably looking for nods of approval. 'I mean, Britain for the British? What's wrong with that? Coming down hard on Commies and Jews?'

'Hey! What's wrong with Communism?' Danny the valet asked. 'Workers' rights? Sharing wealth? Taking from the rich and giving to the poor?'

'Since when were you a Communist sympathizer?' Matthew asked. 'Them lot are as bad as the Jews. In fact, a lot of Jews *are* Bolsheviks. Upsetting the apple cart. It's not proper British.'

Arkwright slapped the tabletop. 'Enough. I don't want to hear any more of your prejudiced nonsense at this table. Do you hear me? Our Mrs Douglas might still be here if she hadn't overheard that lot upstairs coming out with their appalling, ignorant claptrap about the Jews.'

'I thought it were an argument yous two were having what brought on her heart attack,' Danny said.

Florrie set down her cutlery, astounded at Danny's daring. 'Are you seriously challenging the butler – *your boss* – in front of the rest of us? It weren't just Mr Arkwright in that dining room with Mrs Douglas the night she died. I was there too.' She thumbed herself in the chest. 'And yes, it was von Grunwald, Sir Hugh and that idiot Walter's despicable chit-chat that upset Mrs Douglas so in the first place. Imagine a Jewish lady having to listen to such ignorant talk! There was no need for it then, and there's no need for it now.'

'I think there's every need,' Matthew said. 'Country's in a mess. Foreigners are taking our jobs.'

'The Depression is taking jobs, son,' Florrie said. 'And that came about for more complicated reasons than the likes of Mosley and Hitler and that Mussolini would have you believe. It's all lies, packaged up as a political excuse for a fight. You heard him today, going on about his "Biff Boys". "Biff Boys", I ask you! Common thugs, and nowt more. You should know better.'

Matthew sneered at her. 'It's a free country. I can make my own mind up about Mosley and his lads. And it sounds about right to me.'

'You're as impressionable as Sir Hugh, daft little ha'porth.'

'Should you be having opinions on the toffs upstairs' political leanings, Florrie?' Danny joined in, raising an eyebrow, clearly enjoying an excuse to belittle her, even though he'd been defending Communism a moment ago.

There was the sound of someone clearing their throat dramatically.

Looking down the table, Florrie realized the throat-clearing was coming from Miss Talbot, who until now had been sitting primly in the far corner, pushing a piece of lettuce around her plate. Dressed all in black and clutching her fork in a sinewy hand, she put Florrie in mind of a malevolent crow.

'Spit it out, Miss Talbot,' Cook said. 'Or are you choking on my delicious, melt-in-the-mouth quiche? How would you like me to come and give you a thump on the back?' She sought out Florrie, mischief sparkling in her eyes.

Miss Talbot shifted in her seat, then spoke in a small voice. 'I happen to agree with Daniel.'

All eyes were suddenly on the nanny. Sally kicked Florrie beneath the table.

'Oh, aye?' Florrie asked. 'What, are you a Communist sympathiser and all?'

When Miss Talbot turned to Florrie, her gaze was so dead-eyed that Florrie felt the need to look away.

'My views are between the good Lord, the ballot box and my own conscience,' she said. 'I am talking about the inappropriateness of commenting on the Harding-Bournes' political affiliations. They are our employers and our betters. Is it our place to pass judgement on their political allegiances?'

'Mr Arkwright used to say that, didn't you, Mr Arkwright?' Cook said, nodding towards the butler. 'Not any more though.'

Arkwright looked down at his manicured hands. 'I'm afraid the loss of our old housekeeper rather cast things in a different light.' He looked up to address the nanny directly. 'I realize now that none should be above scrutiny, comment or well-meaning advice, when it comes to such controversial matters. Especially not the Harding-Bournes, who find themselves in the sharp glare of the public eye. They should set an example, and in my view, they ought to behave like the educated nobility they are.'

'But your view is unsolicited, Mr Arkwright,' Miss Talbot said. She turned to Florrie. 'And younger staff need to learn to know their place.'

Florrie balked.

Before she could respond, however, Arkwright cut in. 'Had I been frank with Sir Richard about how intolerable some members of staff might find the unsavoury views on Jews expressed by his brother, his wife and their friends at the dining table . . .' His eyes glazed momentarily, as if he could visualize the past. Then he turned back to Miss Talbot. 'I missed my opportunity to speak up for what I believe is right, and a good woman paid for that cowardice with her own life. I believe Sir Richard regrets what happened even now.'

'I wholly disagree with your sentiments. I've heard all about the Mrs Douglas incident, and I'd say you're exploiting the untimely demise of an already ailing woman to justify your position.' Miss Talbot had raised her voice, seemingly unaware of the knowing looks that the other staff members were giving each other. 'That's manipulative. The fact remains that it is *not* our place to judge, Mr Arkwright.'

There were a few audible gasps and nervous sniggers from the younger members of staff. Beneath the table, Sally squeezed Florrie's hand. Florrie was glad of her show of support, but it was Thom's that she truly missed. How she wished he had been present to witness this extraordinary battle of wills. Would Arkwright be able to resist Miss Talbot's challenge? It seemed not.

Arkwright put his cutlery together neatly on his empty plate and stood up. 'Need I remind you that *you* are *not* my keeper, Miss Talbot?' His demeanour was stiff and unyielding. 'It wouldn't do to bother Sir Richard with a telegram while he's thousands of miles away in India. But on his return, I *shall* be speaking to him about today's luncheon and his brother's political aspirations as a fascist kingmaker. I think he would want to know what goes on under his roof when he's not around.'

He marched over to the kitchen sink and set his plate on top of the stack of dirty dishes. Without a backwards glance, he headed for the warren of corridors that led back towards his office and was gone.

Florrie couldn't help but steal glances at Miss Talbot during the uncomfortable silence that lasted throughout the remainder of the dinner.

The nanny seemed entirely unconcerned by any upset she might have caused Arkwright. She finished her food, dabbed primly at her mouth with her napkin and rose to leave. 'I'll leave my dishes for the kitchen maid to clear away, shall I?' She smiled without mirth. 'I wouldn't like to do her out of a job.'

She wafted out of the kitchen like a swooping crow.

'Charming!' Cook said. 'Who the hell does she think she is, that one?'

Florrie shook her head. 'I'd better check on Mr Arkwright before I turn in for the night. Poor beggar! He seemed quite shaken by such a set-to. At the dinner table and all!'

'Shocking,' Cook said, pulling off her mob cap to reveal greying hair, braided and pinned close to her head, apart from the stray locks that had sprung free in the course of the day. 'I've not seen Arkwright that rattled in many a year.'

Florrie watched the valets, stable boys and gardeners all put their plates and cutlery on the side and leave for their quarters. She then clapped her hands at the maids who were loitering at the table to exchange gossip. 'Girls! Off to bed, now, please. I want you all up with the larks, bright-eyed and bushy-tailed. That ballroom floor won't polish itself after today's shenanigans.'

Most of the young maids bade Florrie and Cook

farewell. Only Sally and the kitchen maid, Ginny, remained seated at the table.

'You two and all,' Cook told them. 'Go on. Off to your beds. I'll see to that lot.' She gestured at the pile of washing-up on the side by the sink. Clearly, she realized that Florrie wanted to talk in confidence. 'Consider it a treat for you both working so hard today.'

'Ooh, ta, Cook,' Ginny said, grinning.

'Are you sure?' Sally asked, looking uncertainly at Cook and Florrie.

'Off you pop, Sal,' Florrie said, nodding.

Once they were alone, Florrie turned back to Cook, lowering her voice. 'She's not right, that one. Miss Talbot, I mean. Am I being paranoid?'

Cook shrugged and folded her arms. 'I think she's just . . . contrary. And let's face it, Arkwright was just as much a contrarian not two year ago. I suppose, for the first time since Bertha died, he's come up against a challenger.'

'What? Am I no match for Arkwright?'

'No, you daft beggar! I mean, yes. Course you are! But you and him don't clash so much any more. He's right calm around you, nowadays. You've got him eating out of your hand. But Miss Talbot . . . There were sparks flying tonight round this table. She threw down the gauntlet, and he went for it.'

'I think there's more to it than that, but I can't put my finger on it.' Florrie pressed the tip of her index finger down on to the tabletop emphatically. 'She gives me the heebie-jeebies.'

Cook raised an eyebrow quizzically, scratching beneath her braid. 'Supposed to have glowing references, isn't she?'

Florrie recalled what Dame Elizabeth had told her. 'Apparently she came highly recommended to Lady Charlotte.' She was tempted to comment that Lady Charlotte was hardly the most discerning of women, but Florrie considered her own position of authority and Cook's propensity to gossip and thought better of it. 'I suppose as long as Lady Charlotte's satisfied that Miss Talbot is kind and nurturing towards that baby, she's doing her job.' The knot in her stomach tightened.

Cook got up from the table and opened the oven door to check on the contents, and Florrie noticed that there was a portion of dinner sitting in a Pyrex glass dish on the middle shelf. Miss Talbot had not been the only topic she'd wanted to discreetly broach with Cook.

'Who you keeping that warm for?' she asked, though she already knew the answer, since only one member of staff (apart from Mam, who always ate at the gamekeeper's cottage with the children) hadn't turned up to dinner.

Cook slammed the door closed, not looking Florrie in the eye. 'Keeping what warm?'

'The man-sized meal in that dish. Come on, Cook! I'm not daft. That's for Thom, isn't it? He's avoiding me, isn't he?'

'I think he was busy servicing some garden equipment or summat,' Cook said airily. She took the kettle from the stove and walked over to the sink, her back to Florrie while she filled it.

'And pigs might fly.' Florrie sighed heavily. 'I honestly didn't think he'd take it like this. All I said was, I didn't want to rush into anything.' She waited until Cook had turned back to face her. 'I was right not to throw my job and financial independence away willy-nilly, wasn't I?'

'Is accepting a serious proposal of marriage throwing owt away "willy-nilly", though?' Cook set the kettle on the stove to boil. 'I'm guessing, after courting you for a good twelve month, Thom'd given it plenty of thought. He'd certainly been planning that romantic dinner in the woods for a good while.' She took a clean ceramic teapot for two from the Welsh dresser and spooned tea leaves into it. 'He's head over heels in love with you, is that lad. Marriage is a big commitment for men and all, and it's *you* he wants to settle down and raise a family with.'

'I can't . . .' Florrie tried to find the words to explain her conundrum: that she did eventually want a family of her own but that she was first and foremost duty-bound to the one her sister had left behind. 'I can't—'

'You can,' Cook said, taking the whistling kettle from the stove and pouring the water into the pot. 'But maybe you just don't want to. And that's fine. Take me, for example. *I* like my independence, me. I don't need no man to put food on *my* table or a roof over my head. I do that for myself. I've got some money put by for my dotage too. If I'm honest, I'll be happy if I snuff it here, in my kitchen. I know my place and I *like* my place.'

'Queen of all you survey,' Florrie remarked.

'Happy as a pig in muck, I am.' Cook's grin faded. 'But if *you'd* rather keep your independence . . . if you're made of the same stuff as me, our Florrie, make sure you let Thom down quickly and gently. Don't string the poor lamb along.'

Florrie held her hands aloft. 'I'm not! I do love him. It's not an easy decision to make.' What she could never admit to Cook was that, while she loved Thom, there was a corner of her heart still foolishly devoted to the unattainable Sir Richard, whom she'd been smitten by from the moment they'd met, twelve years earlier. She couldn't shake the feeling that accepting Thom's proposal would be a dishonest act.

Cook carried the teapot to the table and set it down. 'Look, I understand your situation, what with your mam and your sister's kiddies and all. But your mam's got a damn good roof over her and the kids' heads. Sir Richard'll let her do the washing till the cows come home with whites like that. She's only in her early fifties, right?'

Florrie nodded. 'She's fifty.'

'Right, well, there'll be no pressure for her to retire for donkeys' years, if ever. Certainly not until she wants or needs to. And kids aren't kids forever. They might be tots now, but by the time your mam loses her regular wage, those little'uns will be all grown up.' She took clean cups and saucers from the dresser cupboard and handed one to Florrie. 'He's a cracking lad, is Thom. Handsome like a film star, honourable, a grafter. And you're twenty-*seven*, love. Women can't shilly-shally like men when it comes to starting a family. Maybe if a feller like Thom had got down on one knee for me . . .' Her eyes glazed momentarily and her cheeks flushed. She grinned. 'Well, if you reckon you're the kind to settle down and start a family, I'd grab his hand. But only if you want to, of course.'

Through the open window came the sound of crunching gravel. Cook, who was sitting closer to the window than Florrie, craned her neck to get a glimpse of who was walking towards the servants' entrance.

'Speak of the devil,' she said.

Florrie got to her feet. 'I can't face seeing him right now. Especially not if he's got the hump after last night. I need some kip and a clear head, so I'm going to turn in.' She leaned over and squeezed Cook's hand. 'I'll give what you said some thought, but don't say nowt, will you?'

'Course not, you silly beggar.'

'Thanks. I appreciate talking woman to woman like this.'

'You can always come to Cookie with your problems, chuck.'

Before Thom could put in an appearance in the kitchen, Florrie hastened to the back stairs and climbed quickly away from a confrontation of her own that she wasn't ready to have.

11

'I can't believe our Nelly's such a big girl,' Mam said, grabbing Nelly by the cheeks and smothering her in kisses. 'Four! You're going to be *four*!'

'I *am* a big girl, Nana,' Nelly said in her squeaky voice. 'I'm having a party with all my friends.'

'Yes, you are, my darling.' Mam held Nelly's hands, staring at her adoringly. 'And a cake.'

Nelly burst into a fit of delighted giggles and jumped up and down. 'Birthday cake, birthday cake! All the cake for Nelly!'

At her side, Alice copied her older sister by jumping up and down and giggling, though Florrie was fairly sure the two-year-old wasn't entirely sure what she was celebrating.

'Will I get a doll's house?' Nelly asked, putting her hands together as if in prayer. 'Will I? Please, *please* let me have a doll's house for my dollies.' She picked up the collection of tiny wooden peg dolls Thom had carefully whittled for her, with clothing made by Mam from offcuts of old clothes.

'You'll have to be a *very* good girl and see.'

'Can I bring some of my friends too?' George asked.

Mam's eyes narrowed. 'You can if you get off the arm of that settee, young man. You're not John Wayne, riding a horse.'

George slid off his makeshift steed. 'But I'm bored,

Nan.' He peered through the leaded panes of the parlour windows at the heavy rain that was falling for the first time in weeks and wrinkled his nose. 'There's nowt to do.'

Florrie watched her nephew fold his arms and sigh melodramatically at her mother, who had turned her attention back to the mustard boiled-wool tank top she was knitting for him. George was growing rapidly. He was one of the tallest boys in his class, she knew, and had colour in his cheeks and a healthy sheen to his hair. She smiled, wondering if Irene could somehow see how her children were all flourishing in the rural idyll of the Holcombe Estate, under the protection of the Harding-Bournes.

'Why don't you get some paper and coloured pencils?' Florrie suggested. 'You could do our Nelly a birthday card. It's only a week till her big day, after all.'

'But I want to play cricket in the back garden. Thom said he'd teach me how to bowl overarm properly.' He mimed bowling, windmilling his arms.

Mam looked up from her knitting. 'Well, you can't go in the garden today. It's like a monsoon out there. So, unless you want to spend the afternoon learning your times tables or ironing pillowcases for me—'

'No ta.' George looked horrified at the suggestion.

'Well then. The devil finds work for idle hands, so use your imagination and entertain yourself. Read a book.'

Florrie relished sitting in her mam's parlour, drinking tea during a quiet spell at the main house. Sir Richard was still in India, and Lady Charlotte, Sir Hugh and Daphne had all gone away for the week to Coco Chanel and the Duke of Westminster's not-so-secret Scottish retreat, Rosehall

House. She put her feet up on the footstool and let out a long, contented sigh.

'By heck. It's so lovely to see my family and switch off from the goings-on at the big house,' she said. 'Last week or so has been . . .' She shook her head.

Alice jumped on to her lap and curled up with her thumb in her mouth. 'Cuddles, Auntie Florrie?'

'I've always got time to snuggle you, sweetheart.'

Stroking Alice's hair, Florrie briefly imagined how it might feel to stroke the hair of her own daughter. Hers and Thom's. She batted the thought aside because she couldn't envisage a place where that might happen – likely tiny two-roomed digs in the village. That would be bringing a family into the same cramped living conditions that she had helped Mam and her sister's children to escape from. She felt a clammy cloud of sorrow descend on her, absorbing any warmth and light in the parlour.

'Hey! Are you crying, love?' Mam asked, looking up from her knitting. Her brow furrowed.

Florrie wiped the unexpected tears from her eyes. 'Must be an eyelash or something. It's nowt. Hay fever, maybe.'

'Don't cry, Auntie Florrie,' Nelly shouted, looking up from her spinning top.

'I'm not.' Shaking off her doldrums, Florrie was keen to divert attention away from herself. 'Now, about this birthday party. I'm going to have one last try at getting Miss Talbot to bring Sir William over, if that's all right, Mam. Or if it's a Sunday morning, and she's at church, I can bring him anyway. She'll be none the wiser, and I think it will do him good to be around other little'uns.'

Mam looked at her uncertainly. 'I completely agree it's

unhealthy to keep that baby cooped up on his own. They learn everything faster when they're around other children. But if Lady Charlotte has swallowed this codswallop about the boy needing to be kept separate from ordinary folk, should you be flouting her wishes?'

'Will she know? Will she even care?'

'Miss Talbot will find out, and she's a troublemaker, that one, from what you've told me. You go behind her back and . . .' Mam pressed her lips together and cocked her head to one side. 'You don't want to lose your position because you went behind her back.'

'I'll just have to ask her then.'

When the rain abated, Florrie set off on the walk back to the house. The path from the old gamekeeper's cottage was winding and led through a patch of long grass that was bent double under the weight of fat rain droplets still clinging to the tips. A sudden gust of wind shook the grass, wetting Florrie's feet.

'Ugh! Bugger.'

She looked down at her sodden shoes and tights. Feeling like her wet feet were somehow a bad omen, Florrie held her breath when she heard the squeak of a wheelbarrow coming her way. Through a sparse copse of birch trees, she spotted Thom. He was whistling to himself, blithely pushing the wheelbarrow towards her, no doubt on his way to the arboretum, which was out past Mam's cottage. It was the first time she'd seen him since his proposal.

Peering around, Florrie realized that, even if she'd wanted to avoid talking to Thom, there was no place to hide.

Thom rounded the corner and pulled up short. 'Florrie.' His smile was uncertain.

Feeling her gut tighten at the sight of her sweetheart, Florrie bit her lip and looked down at her wet shoes. 'Thom.' She laced her hands together over her stomach and stood to the side to let him pass. The questions inside her fizzed and bubbled uncomfortably. *Why have you been avoiding me? Why have you acted so childishly over me asking for time to think? Don't you still love me? Can't what we have be enough? Are you breaking up with me?* She looked up to find he had set the wheelbarrow down and was staring straight at her.

'I didn't expect to bump into you,' he said.

'I was coming back from Mam's. We were planning our Nelly's birthday party.' Florrie felt like she was talking to a long-lost acquaintance, rather than the man she loved.

'Oh, aye. I'm looking forward to that. Not often I get to go to a birthday party.' He chuckled and then fell awkwardly silent. 'Your mam invited me, like. I've made Nelly a doll's house.'

Florrie felt some of the tension in her shoulders dissipate. 'She'll love that. She was talking about it just now. She adores those peg dolls you made her.' Finally she smiled. 'You're so good with the kids. We're so grateful – me and Mam, like ... we're dead thankful they've got a man like you in their lives. Someone for George to look up to. Someone who cares enough to bring presents.'

'Aye, well ... They deserve better than the bumpy beginnings they've had. They're lovely kids.' His expression softened, then he peered down at Florrie's shoes and grinned. 'With a *really* lovely auntie, who's got *really* wet feet.'

Pressing her feet into the path, Florrie saw how her shoes squelched. She grimaced. 'I'm going to get trench foot at this rate, aren't I?'

'Come to the shed? I've got some spare socks and wellingtons you can put on. Clean socks, mind. Or would mademoiselle like me to wheel her back to the house in style?' He gestured at the wheelbarrow.

Noticing the mound of compost in the tray, Florrie wrinkled her nose. 'I think I'll go for the wellingtons, ta.' Her heart lifted at the thought they would finally get an opportunity to talk about the distance that had unexpectedly opened up between them. 'As long as the socks are genuinely clean.'

Thom held the crook of his arm out to her. 'I guarantee it. May I?'

Sighing with a mixture of relief and resignation, Florrie took his arm. 'Are we still pals, then?' She locked eyes with him.

He swung her into an embrace and kissed her squarely on the lips. 'I'm not just some "pal", Florrie Bickerstaff. I'm your lover. I could be your betrothed ... if you'll eventually have me. Come here and give us another kiss.'

'Ooh, get away, you rum pig! You are forward.' Florrie pretended to push him away playfully but then reciprocated his kiss. His arms felt good around her. 'Are you trying to take advantage of me, Thomas Stanley?'

'Come to the shed and find out.'

'And there was me, thinking you just wanted to share your spare boots with me.' Florrie giggled. The low-hanging cloud from her mother's parlour was lifting, but the knot in her gut hadn't completely loosened. There was still the issue of him acknowledging all she'd have to give up if they were to marry. She broke away from him in earnest. 'Seriously, though, I feel like you've been avoiding me. You have, haven't you?'

Thom picked up the handles of the wheelbarrow, turned it around and started to push it back towards the large shed.

Florrie walked alongside him. 'Well?'

'I'm sorry,' he said. 'I wasn't deliberately giving you the cold shoulder or owt. I just needed a day or two to calm down. I had it in my head that the proposal were going to go one way, but then it went the other. And I had to take a step back and get my head straight. That's all.'

'A day or two? It's been longer than that!'

He shrugged sheepishly. 'I got busy making Nelly's doll's house, and I reckoned you probably didn't want to speak to me, after the way I acted. I were embarrassed, I suppose. It seemed easier for Cook to keep a plate warm for me and for me to keep my distance for a bit. And you said you needed time. I don't know what I were thinking, to be honest, but I *am* sorry, and I hope we can go back to where we were.'

Florrie reached out to put her arm around him. He felt so solid and dependable and familiar. 'We're already there, Thom.'

He came to a standstill. 'I really love you, Florrie Bickerstaff.'

She gazed into his azure eyes and found truth and honesty there. She grabbed his hand. 'And I love you. But you realize I can't leave my sister's three children in the lurch to ride off into the sunset with you? Not yet, anyway. Not while the girls are still such tots, and our George needs to get through his schooling before he can bring home any bacon.' Telling him felt like a valve had been turned deep inside her and the pressure had been released.

He nodded. 'I'll wait for you. When you're ready, I'll still be here.'

'You're here now.' Florrie drew him close to her. She revelled in the reassuring solidity of his body and the warmth of his skin. He smelled of toil in the outdoors and carbolic soap. 'Kiss me.'

They rekindled their romance with a passionate kiss, and her world, which had felt as though it was spinning on the wrong axis for over a week, was set back in its proper place.

Florrie accompanied Thom to the shed, donned the spare rubber boots and made her way back to the house, swinging her wet shoes in her hand.

12

'Oh, Sal. Have you seen Miss Talbot?' she asked, walking across the kitchen's terracotta tiled floor in her socked feet.

Sally, who was busy basting a joint of meat, peered over her shoulder. She balked at the sight of Florrie's footwear. 'Aye, aye. What happened there? Did your mam confiscate your shoes?'

'Long story. Miss Talbot? You seen her this afternoon?'

Sally nodded at the clock on the wall which showed that it was a little before three. 'Sir William's nap time, isn't it? So your guess is as good as mine.' She turned back to her basting.

At that moment, Dame Elizabeth's lady's maid Dilys reached the bottom of the stairs to the kitchen and made straight for Florrie, wearing a hopeful expression.

'Ooh, Miss Bickerstaff, just the woman I was hoping to bump into.' She glanced down at Florrie's feet and frowned momentarily. 'I've took Dame Elizabeth's luncheon up to her and made sure she's comfortable.' She removed her mob cap. 'Do you think I could slip away for a couple of hours, please? It's just my sister's finally given birth.'

'Congratulations,' Florrie said. 'Boy or girl?'

Dilys grinned. 'A boy. A reet big'un and all, apparently. She were a fortnight overdue, so I want to see with my own eyes that mother and baby are both doing well. She's only in Rawtenstall, so I wouldn't be long.'

Florrie considered Dilys' priorities and her own housekeeper's duty of care to the family. 'Did you check her ladyship ate something?'

'I tried, but she insisted I leave her to it. She promised she'd pick at her sandwich when the mood took her.' She shrugged. 'What could I do? I can hardly force-feed her. But she seemed happy enough and I made sure she had a cup of tea.'

Florrie nodded. 'I'll drop in on her ladyship later.' She smiled. 'You get yourself off, *Aunty* Dilys!'

'Is that Florrie?' Cook called from the direction of the large larder, where Florrie knew she was doing her weekly stocktake. 'Florrie Bickerstaff, I want a word with you about this substandard flour the wholesaler sent.'

Florrie dropped her voice to a whisper. 'Tell her I'll be back when I've sorted my feet out.'

Making a swift exit before Cook could take her to task on her most recent economies, Florrie ascended the stairs to the ground floor of the house. If Miss Talbot had put Sir William down for a nap, might she be in the library? She had often found her there of an evening, reading some dour book of war poetry or else the bible, when she should have either been below stairs or in her own room, adjacent to the nursery. Yet no matter how many times Arkwright had told the nanny what the etiquette was regarding using the family's living accommodation upstairs, Miss Talbot seemed not to give a fig for rules, and apparently Lady Charlotte didn't try to remind her of where the boundaries lay between those below and those above stairs.

Florrie walked past the empty dining room, then the

living room, which was deathly still but for the tick tock of the clock on the mantel. No jazz music. No blue haze of cigarette or cigar smoke hanging in the air. No smells of expensive perfume and cologne. No erudite or even inane chatter or raucous laughter. Realizing that the heart of the house beat only feebly without the family present, Florrie felt quite dejected as she passed the silent music room to push open the door to the library.

She stepped inside. 'Miss Talbot? Miss Talbot! Are you in here?' She walked through the stacks of books but spied nobody – not even Dame Elizabeth on a rare foray beyond the bounds of her personal suite of rooms.

Florrie looked up at the mezzanine, beyond the bounds of the ornate balustrade, where she'd once found Dame Elizabeth arguing in secret with the man who had turned out to be Sir Richard's true father. There was nobody up there.

Might the nanny have gone for a turn around the gardens? Florrie gazed out through the windows to the manicured grounds in front of the house. There was nobody to see on the path except for one of Thom's apprentices, digging out dandelions from the lawn.

'Dear Lord and Father of mankind, forgive our foolish ways . . .'

Suddenly, Florrie caught some tuneless singing on the air, accompanied by the piano. Miss Talbot was in the music room after all!

Turning to retrace her steps, she made her way back along the hall to the music room.

'. . . reclothe us in our rightful mind; in purer lives thy service find . . .'

Selecting her words before she entered, Florrie opted not to knock. She opened the door, took several steps inside, and happened upon a scene she had not been expecting. Miss Talbot was indeed seated at the grand piano, plonking away as if she were entertaining a room full of adoring, musical recital enthusiasts. Her voice put Florrie in mind of a distressed, honking duck, or perhaps a squawking crow, given her attire. Yet what was most alarming was the sight of baby William, shuffling apace on his bottom towards the cello that had belonged to Sir Richard and Sir Hugh's elder brother, the late Sir James. Florrie knew the cello was a prized family memento of the elder brother's life, cut short in the Great War, and it took pride of place in the middle of the room, perched rather precariously on the stand. Now the baby boy was pawing at the instrument, which towered ominously above him.

Miss Talbot had clearly not noticed that Florrie had entered the room.

'Get off that, you stupid boy!' she shouted at the baby. 'Idiot!'

Despite Sir William being on the brink of pulling the heavy cello on to himself, Miss Talbot turned a page on her sheet music and drew breath.

Florrie had heard enough. 'Miss Talbot! Stop at once!' She ran over to where the baby was trying to pull himself up on the body of the cello. He started to fret and complain as he'd ensnared his fingers between the bridge and the strings. The cello was falling, falling . . .

In her peripheral vision, Florrie could see the look of alarm on Miss Talbot's face.

Florrie's only concern was the baby. 'There, there, Sir William. That's not a plaything for you.' Holding the cello steady, she disentangled the baby's fingers from the strings and deftly hoisted him off the floor and on to her hip.

Miss Talbot was out of her seat, holding out her hands. 'Give him to me.'

Florrie held her free hand up. 'Now, just wait a minute, Miss Talbot—'

'I said, give him to me.' The nanny's expression was pure fire and brimstone.

Instinctively, Florrie swung around, keeping the baby out of reach. 'I'm sorry, Miss Talbot, but what have I just happened upon? Sir William, almost pulling a large instrument on to himself – which could have done him grave injury, by the way – while you bash out some hymn on the family's Steinway . . . an instrument worth a small fortune, I might add.'

'I beg your pardon. Are you calling my religious instruction of the boy, "bashing out some hymn"?'

Florrie blinked hard. 'Hang on, are you trying to turn this into *me* insulting your religious ardour, when the issue is *you* dangerously leaving a baby to his own devices, while you entertain yourself? And what's really scandalous is the way you just spoke to that baby, like he was dirt on your shoe.'

Miss Talbot inhaled sharply, glaring at Florrie. 'Whatever do you mean? I did no such thing. I resent what you're implying, young lady.'

'"Stupid boy"? "Idiot"? Is that any way to speak to your charge?'

'I said nothing of the sort.' Miss Talbot reached out

again to take the baby. 'You are a fanciful girl . . . or hard of hearing, perhaps?'

Again, Florrie kept him out of arm's reach, taking a step backwards. 'There's nothing wrong with my hearing. You said what you said. And incidentally, you'll address me as Miss Bickerstaff, not "girl" or "young lady". I am the housekeeper, not some junior dishrag that you can abuse at will. And to think I'd come here, trying to persuade you to bring Sir William to my niece's birthday party! Ha. How deluded I was. There's nothing wholesome about your nannying methods, and there's nothing genuinely nurturing about you. This child is just a pay packet and a way for you to wield power – nothing more. Am I right?'

'Hand me my charge *at once*!' Miss Talbot's voice now had an edge of steel. 'Or Lady Charlotte shall hear of this.'

'Fine,' Florrie said. 'We can tell her together, when she returns from her travels, and see who she believes then. Me, a longstanding member of staff in a position of authority, or you, a nanny who's been here five minutes?' With no real idea who Lady Charlotte might side with, Florrie was bluffing, but the nanny wasn't to know that.

'Give me that baby right now, you insolent hussy.'

'What did you just call me?'

Miss Talbot's eyes narrowed to mean slits. 'Carrying on with the gardener out of wedlock? What would you call that, if not the actions of a harlot?'

Florrie gasped. She felt her pulse race and her cheeks flush hot. 'You are a bad-minded women, Miss Talbot. Me and Thomas are courting. There is nothing immoral about our relationship whatsoever, and need I remind you that it is also none of your business? What *is* your business, however, is the proper care of this baby.'

'Pass him to me, right this minute!'

Florrie stroked Sir William's fluffy hair and kissed the top of his head.

'Bah-bah,' he said, pointing to a photograph of Sir Richard on top of the sideboard that contained reams of sheet music. 'Bah-bah.'

'Papa! Yes, that's right!' Florrie said brightly to Sir William. 'Your very first word! Well done, you clever boy!' She turned back to Miss Talbot, the thunder returning to her voice. 'I'll give him to you on one condition.' Her heart was pounding against her ribs in earnest now. 'Don't let me *ever* see you neglect him like that again, and don't let me *ever* hear you speak to him unkindly like that again. Not ever.' Finally, she handed the wriggling boy back to the nanny. 'You would do well to remember that I have eyes and ears all over this house, Miss Talbot.' She pointed to her own eyes. 'I'll be watching you.'

Leaving an open-mouthed Miss Talbot clutching a disgruntled Sir William, Florrie strode out of the music room, swallowing down the icy dread that stuck in her throat. She was certain that Miss Talbot was utterly untrustworthy and a menace. With everyone in the family apart from Dame Elizabeth away for at least a week, however, what should she do with such sensitive information?

13

'Dame Elizabeth?' Florrie knocked quietly at the door to Dame Elizabeth's suite.

Feeling that Miss Talbot's neglect of the baby couldn't go unchallenged and unchecked by a member of the Harding-Bourne family, and given nobody else would be in the house for a week, Florrie had resolved to broach the topic with the old lady. She felt as though she might burst if she kept the details of what she'd observed in the music room to herself.

She knocked again, listening for sounds of life within. 'Dame Elizabeth?' Yet nobody answered and there was no sound of movement either. Might the old lady be at the far end of the suite, where she might not hear?

Pushing the door open, Florrie shouted, 'Only me!'

The reception room was empty. Venturing further into the suite, Florrie could see no sunlight coming from the bedroom at the far end, though the door was ajar. Perhaps the old lady was sleeping. She often took a nap at this hour.

At that point, Florrie had a decision to make. Should she return at a time when Dame Elizabeth was clearly up and about, or could the maltreatment of her beloved and only grandson not wait? As she hesitated on the threshold of Dame Elizabeth's study, she heard a soft moan come from the bedroom.

'Dame Elizabeth? Is that you? Are you all right?'

Instinctively, she felt that this was not merely a case of the old lady being in the grip of some troubling dream. Advancing through the study and dressing area and into the bedroom, Florrie could see little in the dark. The moaning continued. Hastening to Dame Elizabeth's bedside, she switched on the small electric lamp on her nightstand. The lamp shed light on to a ghoulish scene: Dame Elizabeth was hanging half out of bed, her head dangling only inches above the rug and her arm outstretched at an untenable angle. Several objects were on the floor – a book, a glass, with its contents staining the rug in a dark patch, the bell which Dame Elizabeth rang to call for assistance, since the suite had not yet been connected to the system of servants' bells that were rigged up in the main reception rooms. The worst thing about the scene Florrie beheld was the old lady's face. She stared blankly into nothingness, her eyes glazed; her mouth hung open.

'Oh, good Lord. What on earth has gone on here?' Florrie said, feeling herself succumb to panic's vice-like grip. 'Did you reach out to get something from your bedside table and fall out of bed?' She tried to keep her tone bright but could hear a waver in every word. Her throat was suddenly dry.

Moaning was the only response she could elicit from Dame Elizabeth – louder, this time.

Had the old lady hit her head somehow?

'Let's get you back into bed, shall we?'

Grabbing her beneath the shoulders, Florrie tried to manoeuvre her back on to the bed, but Dame Elizabeth was a dead weight.

'I'm going to get help,' Florrie said, striving to sound calm and authoritative in spite of her mounting fear that Dame Elizabeth had suffered some sort of funny turn.

First, she made the old lady as comfortable as possible by wedging a pillow behind her head. Then she ran back into the hall, hoping to call on a passing member of staff.

'Help! Somebody fetch Mr Arkwright. Help!'

Miss Talbot would surely come to her aid. Hadn't she just been in the music room with Sir William? Florrie ran there, but the room was now standing empty. She pressed the servants' bell once, twice, three times in quick succession, knowing that that would signal an emergency to Arkwright.

It took only a minute or two for Arkwright to appear in the hallway.

'Come quickly, Mr Arkwright!' Florrie shouted, beckoning him. 'Dame Elizabeth's bedroom.'

Arkwright started to run down the hall.

By the time Florrie had returned to Dame Elizabeth's side, Arkwright had caught up with her. He was short of breath when he spoke. 'Whatever's the matter, Miss—? Oh dear.'

'Help me get her on to the bed, will you? And then telephone the doctor immediately. Tell him it's an emergency. I think she's had some kind of apoplexy.'

Together, they managed to get Dame Elizabeth back on to her bed. Florrie made her as comfortable as she could, propping her lolling head between an inverted V made from cushions. She held her hand, stroking the mottled skin that hung loose over a cat's cradle of prominent blue and purple veins.

'There, there, Dame Elizabeth. Florrie's here. Mr Arkwright's gone to telephone the doctor. He'll be with you in a jiffy, and I'll take good care of you till he comes.'

The old lady's intermittent moans were no indication that she understood a word of what Florrie was saying, and Florrie was certain that the left side of her face had slackened.

It didn't take long before Arkwright returned. 'I've rung the doctor. Any change?' he asked.

Florrie shook her head. 'She's not been right for a while, you know. Fretful, listless, not really eating or sleeping.' A tear rolled down her cheek and she wiped it away hastily. 'We should have seen this coming.'

'Did her lady's maid not say anything about her physical or mental decline?'

'If you see someone every day, you don't necessarily notice they're deteriorating, do you?'

'I suppose not.' Arkwright sounded unconvinced. 'Where is Dilys, by the way?'

'She tended to Dame Elizabeth only this lunchtime.' Florrie gestured at a tray on the chaise longue at the foot of the bed that contained the remnants of a barely nibbled sandwich. 'She never made any mention of her ladyship being taken badly.'

'Yes, but where is she *now*? Why was nobody else looking after Dame Elizabeth? And why did *you* find her in this predicament?'

Florrie tutted and huffed at Arkwright. She had known the butler long enough to understand that he was casting around for someone to blame. 'Right now, Dilys is in Rawtenstall, visiting her sister, who's just given birth.'

'Leaving an infirm woman to fend for herself?'

'Dame Elizabeth wasn't infirm at lunchtime. You can see she's eaten something from the tray, can't you?' Florrie stared pointedly at the tray, then crossed her arms and turned back to Arkwright. 'I didn't think for a moment Dilys would be needed for the next couple of hours, given it was Dame Elizabeth's nap time anyway. There's nobody else experienced enough who could have stood in to be on call while Dilys is out. Dame Elizabeth's gout is a challenge. I wouldn't have trusted one of the new girls to do anything more than bring her a drink.'

'*You* came. Eventually.'

The comment seemed pointed. 'I needed to speak to Dame Elizabeth about a delicate matter, and it's lucky I came when I did. But what's important now is not finding someone to blame, but making sure she gets the right medical attention.'

Arkwright inhaled sharply, as if to deliver a retort, but he was interrupted by Dame Elizabeth letting out an ungodly sounding moan. He got up from the bed and muttered that he would do better to wait for the doctor by the front entrance.

'How do you do? I'm Doctor Haslam.'

'Oh, thank heavens you're here, doctor,' Florrie said. 'I'll take you to the patient. Follow me.'

She had been waiting nervously at the threshold to Dame Elizabeth's suite for almost forty minutes, praying that medical help would come swiftly. The maids and valets had all heard through the grapevine (which was almost certainly Cook) that the old lady had fallen gravely ill. In ones and twos, they'd all approached Dame Elizabeth's quarters, seeking any further nuggets of news. Florrie had had to scold them all for being sensationalists and had sent them back to their duties. It wouldn't do to have young maids and valets gawping at a gravely ill elderly woman on what was potentially her deathbed, but nor did she relish being left alone to guard a woman who might slip away at any moment.

Holding back tears of relief, grief and ragged panic, she led Dr Haslam through from Dame Elizabeth's reception room to her bedroom. 'I do hope you can help her ladyship, doctor. She's in a terrible way. She's not able to communicate at all, though she does seem to be suffering. I can't bear it. I don't know if she's hit her head or had an apoplexy or what.'

'Let's see, shall we?' The doctor set his fat leather Gladstone bag on top of Dame Elizabeth's dressing table and opened it up. He rummaged inside and brought out various contraptions, including his stethoscope and a blood pressure monitoring device. 'I came as soon as I could, given I was in the middle of delivering a baby when Mr Arkwright's message finally reached me!'

Arkwright was leaning against the wall by the window, studying the doctor. 'You're *new*, aren't you?' He was clearly judging this doctor's more casual attire of slacks and a shirt with the sleeves rolled up, open at the neck, compared to the tweed three-piece suit and bow tie that the old doctor had always worn.

Dr Haslam smiled brightly and plugged his stethoscope into his ears. He sat on the edge of Dame Elizabeth's bed. 'Yes. I've taken over Dr Fleming's practice in the village, now that he's retired. I assure you, there's no need to balk at my lack of tie. I'll be happy to tell you all about my medical pedigree, but only once I've treated this patient.' He looked pointedly at Arkwright. 'And I've taken the liberty of telephoning an ambulance from Moorlands Infirmary in Rawtenstall. So keep a watch out for that while I examine her ladyship? There's a good chap.'

Arkwright frowned. 'You see to it she gets the very best care, or—'

'Thank you, Mr Arkwright. I'll come and find you when I've finished.'

With Arkwright gone, the doctor turned his attention to Dame Elizabeth. 'Now, what have we here?'

Florrie watched as he listened to her heartbeat and lungs, took her blood pressure, lifted her eyelids to examine her pupils in bright light, checked her bodily reaction to various other stimuli and checked her head for signs of injury.

He sighed and then nodded. 'I was right to call the ambulance. I'm fairly certain she's had an apoplexy.' He pointed to where the left side of her face sagged. 'See this? It's paralysis. Classic symptom of a haemorrhage somewhere in the brain affecting movement and speech.'

Florrie clasped her hand to her mouth. 'Good Lord. Will she live?'

Dr Haslam started to pack away his things. 'She'll be in good hands at the infirmary. The doctors there will be able to monitor her and do what they can, though it's often the case that in the event of a major haemorrhage . . . Well, let's see how she fares.' There was sympathy behind his fleeting and uncertain smile.

'Dear God. Poor woman. What could have caused it? The gout? Melancholia? She's been rather distressed for a while, I reckon.'

The doctor shook his head. 'Distress wouldn't have helped, assuming it was severe. It pushes the blood pressure up. But the causes of an apoplexy are rather more involved than that.'

He looked thoughtfully at Dame Elizabeth, who was taking shallow breaths and still moaning softly, then turned his focus back to Florrie. 'If you're in touch with her next of kin . . .'

'Sir Richard, her eldest – he's head of the household. On business in India at the moment.'

Dr Haslam closed his case and checked his wristwatch. 'Well, I'd send him a telegram immediately and advise him to return home as fast as he can. Anyone else you can tell?'

'Yes. There's Dame Elizabeth's youngest son, Sir Hugh. He's also away, but I'll inform him too.'

'I'm sorry I don't have better news.'

Florrie nodded. 'Oh, poor Sir Richard. They're very close, him and Dame Elizabeth.' She pressed her lips together, willing the tears that pricked the backs of her eyes to dissipate. 'Perhaps he can fly home with Imperial Airways. I've heard it can be done in just under a week, now, if he can get a ticket at such short notice.' She swallowed hard.

'Good. In the meantime, I'll sit here with her ladyship until the ambulance drivers arrive, and then I'll follow her in my car to the hospital.'

By the time Dame Elizabeth was stretchered away to the ambulance and packed off to the Moorlands Infirmary,

Florrie had all but forgotten her argument with Miss Talbot and the original reason for wanting to speak to the old lady in private. She got Thom to drive her to the post office in Holcombe village where she composed a telegram to Sir Richard first, and then Sir Hugh. They were the hardest words she'd ever had to write.

```
Dame Elizabeth had apoplexy STOP Taken to
infirmary in bad way STOP Come home immediately
STOP Florrie Bickerstaff
```

14

On her return from sending the telegrams, Florrie had called an emergency meeting of all the domestic staff members who were under her jurisdiction, instructing them to muster in the empty drawing room. The girls who hadn't already been privy to Cook's grapevine reports had appeared distressed when she'd informed them of what had come to pass with Dame Elizabeth. Dilys had burst into tears. The others had dispersed to carry out their duties. Now, only three of the chambermaids remained.

'Right, I want you girls to give the family's bedrooms a good bottoming before Sir Hugh, Daphne and Lady Charlotte get home,' Florrie said. 'Everything should be shipshape and ready for my inspection by . . .' She looked at the time on the grandfather clock in the corner. 'Ten o'clock tonight.'

Gracie, the most recent addition to the team of young girls whose responsibility it was to keep the house sparkling clean, scratched at her hair beneath her mob cap. 'What's the big rush? Why do we have to work tonight? We always put our feet up after dinner so we're fresh for the morning.' She was slouching with an air of insolence about her, looking to Elsie and Agnes for support. 'It's not like we get paid any extra for working out of hours.'

'Straighten up, Gracie, please, and use your loaf.' Florrie

tapped her temple. 'I've already told you about Dame Elizabeth's condition. It's critical, apparently. Sir Hugh, Daphne and Lady Charlotte are setting off from Scotland *tonight*. I sent a telegram but managed to telephone them as well. They'll be with us in the early hours so they can visit the hospital, first thing. And need I remind you, you aren't paid by the hour, young lady? Though if you'd like to try your chances at one of the local mills that haven't already shut down, working some dangerous loom instead of dusting and polishing here, where your bed and board are guaranteed, as well as your pay packet, then be my guest.' She gestured towards the open door. 'No?'

Gracie rolled her eyes, then stood up with drooping shoulders.

'Less eye-rolling, please. And stop slouching.'

'Sorry, Miss Bickerstaff.' She straightened up.

Florrie nodded and then addressed the three as a group once more. 'Right. Where were we? Yes. Fresh bedding. Beat the rugs. Above and beyond the usual dusting and wiping down. Treat it like an extra spring clean. And put some nice-smelling flowers in a vase to lift the ladies' spirits. I'll inspect at ten sharp.'

'What about Sir Richard?' one of the other chambermaids asked.

'He's been informed, like I said during my briefing to all of yous. Mr Arkwright's waiting on his reply, confirming his travel arrangements.' Florrie wondered if she should confess her private concerns that soon they would be preparing the house for a large funeral and wake. No, she would keep those misgivings to herself for now, to keep morale high. She clapped her hands together. 'Right, take pride in your work, ladies, and crack on!'

'Wake up! They're here. Florrie! Florrie, wake up!'

In the middle of her strange dream about Sir William being trapped inside a cello, Florrie felt someone shaking her urgently. She opened her eyes to see Arkwright towering above her. It was then that she realized she'd fallen asleep on the camp bed in one of the cubbies below stairs – a makeshift place to get her head down that she sometimes used when she needed to be on call overnight.

Wiping her mouth and blinking hard, she pushed the thin blanket off to reveal she was still fully dressed. She swung her legs over the edge of the camp bed. 'Yes, yes. I'm awake.' Shivering, she realised that the heat of a midsummer's evening had long since been replaced by the chill of early morning. She pulled her cardigan back on. 'I'm coming. Let me put the kettle on. Tell them I'll bring a camomile infusion to their rooms.'

With Cook still asleep at Florrie's insistence, she started to prepare tea for the three weary travellers. The kitchen clock said it was just after three – a good hour or so before Cook would be up to bake the day's bread. Florrie's thoughts were sluggish, but she slowly worked through all that had come to pass with Miss Talbot, and then, the terrible drama of discovering Dame Elizabeth's apoplexy. *I mustn't let Miss Talbot's unseemly behaviour get lost in all of this*, she thought. *That baby's safety is at stake.* She resolved to discuss the matter with Arkwright as soon as she had the chance.

When the tea was ready, Florrie put two china teapots – one large, one small – and three cups and saucers on to a tray. Yawning, she climbed the back stairs, repairing first to Sir Hugh's room.

He and Daphne were inside, still dressed in their travelling clothes.

'Oh, Florrie, good girl,' Sir Hugh said. He was sitting on the end of his bed, hands on his knees. There was a waxy pallor to his skin with dark patches beneath his eyes. His hair was dishevelled. He looked up at her. 'Tell me, was my mother compos mentis when the ambulance drivers took her?' There was a whiff of stale spirits and cigars on his breath as he spoke.

Florrie set the tray down on an occasional table next to the tallboy. Sir Hugh had never set any obvious store by considering the feelings of others. Should she consider his? Should she give him the unvarnished truth or soften the true course of events a little?

'She was confused, but she was in good hands. Dr Haslam, the new doctor, attended her, and he was very thorough. And I've heard good things about Moorlands Infirmary.'

Daphne, who was seated at her dressing table, taking out her earrings, turned to Florrie. 'She's not on a *ward*, is she?'

Sir Hugh's features crumpled into a look of disgust. 'Oh, don't say that. Mama would be simply mortified to be on an open ward with the great unwashed.'

Florrie poured the tea in silence and set the cups on embroidered doilies. *Don't rise to it. You know what they're like, so just smile sympathetically and keep your gob shut, Florrie Bickerstaff.* 'I'm sure all will be revealed when you visit the hospital in the morning. And I'm certain they've made her as comfortable as possible.' She took up the tray again. 'Will that be all, sir?'

Sir Hugh had already turned away from her to speak to his wife.

Moving on to Lady Charlotte's bedroom, Florrie entered to find her employer's wife struggling to pull off her riding boots.

'Camomile tea, Lady Charlotte? I'm sure you're exhausted after such a long journey.'

Lady Charlotte looked up from her boots. Her eyes seemed unfocussed. 'It was hellish.' She slurred when she spoke. Was she drunk? 'We almost crashed into a blasted sheep on some godforsaken country lane, and Gareth drove like a Chelsea Pensioner all the way home.'

'Gareth, milady?'

'The chauffeur!'

'Oh, you mean Graham.' Florrie wondered how her mistress *still* didn't remember the name of the chauffeur, though she'd lived at Holcombe Hall for five or more years.

'Yes, that's the chap. I swear, I could have got back in half the time if I'd driven us all in the Bugatti.' She grunted as she tugged ineffectually at her boot. 'Here, give me a hand with these. They're welded to my legs after half a lifetime spent sitting in the car.'

Florrie set the tray down and took a hold of Lady Charlotte's leg. With her back to her employer, she yanked the boot forwards and off.

'At last.' Lady Charlotte wiggled her toes on the freed foot.

Florrie pulled off the other boot. 'Better, ma'am?' She took the box for the boots from the triple wardrobe that contained all of Lady Charlotte's footwear – years of being her lady's maid had taught her where everything was kept – and put them carefully away.

'Oh, what a dratted inconvenience it is to have been dragged back from Rosehall House,' Lady Charlotte said, thumping the bed dramatically. 'We were having such a lovely time with Coco and Bendor. Your telegram came just as the party they were throwing in our honour was really getting going. There was a band, Florrie. You know how I love to dance to a big band. And they'd arranged a grouse shoot for tomorrow . . . well, *today*, I suppose.' She harrumphed. 'Just our luck my mother-in-law should choose to fall ill, right in the middle of a well-needed Scottish sojourn.' She stifled a yawn. 'New motherhood is *incredibly* tiring, you know.'

Florrie stood perfectly still, staring down at Lady Charlotte; studying how she slurred when she spoke and how her eyes were glazed. They were the same age, born a day apart under very different circumstances, yet Florrie realized Lady Charlotte had started to appear years her senior, and busy new motherhood was certainly not the culprit for such rapid ageing. What could she say to this spoiled, self-regarding hedonist – a good-time Charlotte, rather than a 'good-time Charlie' – that wouldn't result in her instant dismissal?

'Would you like to know how Sir William has been while you were away, milady?' she asked.

Lady Charlotte looked up at her and yawned again. 'Oh, my darling son! Yes. Of course. Is he well?'

'I believe he may have said his first word while you were away.'

Smiling, Lady Charlotte touched the tight waves in her platinum hair. 'Was it, Mama?'

'Papa, actually. Though it sounded more like bah-bah!'

The smile faltered. 'My husband will be thrilled. Ask Miss Talbot to bring Sir William to see me . . . perhaps tomorrow afternoon, after lunch?'

Florrie curtseyed. 'Of course. Will that be all?'

'Yes. Thank you, Florrie.'

Climbing the stairs to her room to get a meagre two hours' sleep before she'd have to be up again, Florrie wondered that she prized her position at Holcombe Hall, serving vain and silly members of the nobility, who were anything but noble in their behaviour and motivations.

In her room, she cracked open the window to let the fresh early morning air in. Outside, it was still black as night and quiet but for a solitary owl, with the dawn chorus an hour away.

A cat cares more for its kittens than that lot above stairs care for each other, she thought, changing into her nightdress. *All these years I've given them. My best years. If it wasn't for our George, Nelly and Alice needing me . . . I could have my own family with Thom, a normal life.*

As she drifted off into a fitful sleep, she entertained the idea of seeking out Thom in the morning to accept his proposal. When she rose again at five, however, two things caught her by surprise.

Florrie tiptoed down to the first floor, deciding to check on Sir William. She found the tiny boy awake in his cot, happily grabbing at his own feet and gurgling at the sunlight that already streamed on to the ceiling through gaps in the curtains. As soon as he recognized Florrie, he cackled and beamed at her, reaching out to touch her face as she leaned in over the side of the cot.

'Bah-bah. Bah-bah.'

Florrie took his chubby little hand and kissed it. 'Not your Papa, darling. It's Florrie.'

'Ba-ba-bah.'

She was pleased to see he was in good spirits after the previous day's conflict between her and Miss Talbot. He did, however, smell strongly as though he needed his nappy changing. Florrie saw that the clean terry-towelling nappies her own mother had washed and other changing accoutrements had already been laid out, ready for use on the special counter top that one of the handymen had nailed to an antique chest of drawers to facilitate nappy changing. When she uncovered the boy's bottom and started to clean him up, however, he shrieked. He had an angry, florid rash that had all but taken his delicate skin clean off.

Florrie reeled at this horrifying sight. 'Dear God. Is that harridan not even changing your nappies regularly?' she whispered.

Shushing the baby, she patted his bottom dry carefully and then liberally applied the zinc and castor oil cream she had seen Mam use on Alice before she'd been potty trained. She fastened the baby into a clean nappy, and his fretful whingeing soon subsided.

She held him close and kissed his head before putting him back into the cot. 'Don't worry, Sir William. I'll keep an eye on you, son. Daddy will be home soon, and I'll tell him everything. We'll get you a new nanny that cares.'

Slipping out, Florrie descended to the ground floor and emerged by Dame Elizabeth's suite, which had been cleaned but which now stood empty. At first, it wasn't the strange noise coming from within that alerted Florrie to something being amiss. It was the fact that the door stood open, where she had shut it herself last night, after the ten o'clock inspection.

'Odd,' she said beneath her breath.

As she stepped into the reception room, she realized that somebody was either crying or laughing further inside – it was hard to tell which. She knew it was a man, however. Creeping further in, Florrie got as far as the dressing room. She concealed herself behind Dame Elizabeth's voluminous widow's weeds, which adorned a tailor's dummy. Who on earth was in the old lady's bedroom?

The curtains had been left open and the early morning sun – shining on the other side of the house at that time of day, but still risen enough to brighten the place – illuminated the forlorn figure sitting on the end of the bed. Though the figure faced the window, so that Florrie could only see it from the back, she could see he was a man, dressed in purple cotton pyjamas, his hair in disarray. He was sobbing like a desolate child who had lost everything. Who was this strange man? Surely one of Arkwright's lads hadn't snuck into Dame Elizabeth's suite for a private sob over being snubbed by some girl or perhaps bitterly regretting a prank that had gone badly amiss?

When the man turned a few degrees to his right, Florrie could see that he was clutching some kind of cloth to his cheek that glistened with his tears.

At first, Florrie couldn't make any sense of what she was seeing, but then she realized all at once that the cloth was the black cashmere knitted shawl that Dame Elizabeth wore around her shoulders on a cold night. Her second surprise of the morning was that the man sitting on the end of the bed, wracked by grief, was Sir Hugh.

15

'What do you think, then?' Thom asked. He was standing in the woodshed with his arms folded, studying the doll's house he had just put the finishing touches to. 'I painted the roof that red colour last night and glued in the last of the curtains.'

Florrie put her arm around him and squeezed him affectionately. 'It's a work of art, Thom.' She pointed to the furniture he'd painstakingly fashioned from wood, perfectly scaled down to fit the miniature peg dolls he'd already made. There was a table and chairs, a settee, a bed, a tiny lamp. He'd even covered the wooden walls with intricately patterned wallpaper. 'Look at all these tiny details! You're so clever.'

He slid a muscular arm around Florrie's waist. 'Do you think Nelly'll like it?'

'She'll love it.'

'I wish I was making a doll's house for our own daughter,' Thom said quietly. He looked down at Florrie expectantly.

Sighing and putting her head on his shoulder, Florrie wondered how she could tell Thom that she'd strengthened her resolve to keep serving the Harding-Bournes, just at the point where she'd been ready to throw in the towel and marry. She thought about the dawn revelations of a few days earlier – Sir Hugh, sobbing like a small boy on his gravely ill mother's bed, and the evident neglect that was being visited on Sir William by his manipulative nanny. It was not just her nieces and nephew who needed her. The Harding-Bourne family needed her too. Hadn't Sir Hugh begged her to accompany him to the infirmary only the previous afternoon, to arrange for Dame Elizabeth to be brought home – either to eke out the rest of her life in her current stable but uncommunicative, paralysed state, or else to die? She'd found it gratifying to have been the one person he'd turned to in the Harding-Bournes' hour of need. However much Thom wanted desperately for them to start their own family, she simply wasn't ready.

Wracked with guilt, she patted Thom on the back. 'You never know what the future might bring.' She turned to focus on the doll's house. 'It's all part of life's great adventure. But for now, I've got to settle Dame Elizabeth back in.'

'Why's she coming home? I thought she were at death's door.'

'There's nowt they can do for her, is there? They can't keep her in an infirmary indefinitely if she's not ... "acutely ill", the doctor called it. So I've got to help the family recruit a live-in nurse, and I've got to—'

Thom spun her around and kissed her squarely on the mouth. 'Never mind what you've got to do. Let's get away somewhere. Just me and you.' His eyes shone with glee. 'I've been saving up and I've got enough to take us to Blackpool for the weekend. How do you fancy? Fish and chips by the sea. A nice little bed and breakfast.' He winked.

'And how would that work? I'm *Miss* Bickerstaff, remember.'

'Who's going to ask questions if we book as Mr and Mrs?'

Florrie felt her cheeks flush hot. 'Oh, you are a one! Are you trying to take advantage of me?'

'Maybe.' He kissed her again, this time more languorously. His rough stubble stung against the delicate skin of her lips. Breaking away, Florrie placed her hand on his chest. 'That's quite enough of that. You knocking me up on some squeaking old bed in a Blackpool boarding house would rather take the romance out of that lovely woodland proposal.'

'How could it? We're in love, aren't we?'

Irritated, she realized that he *still* didn't understand her predicament. 'I don't want a shotgun wedding, Thomas. I've already made it clear I'm not yet ready to tie the knot, so please . . . just give it a rest.'

'But I'm not pushing the marriage thing. I know you're worried about supporting your mam and Irene's kids. I understand all that.' Now he looked positively crestfallen. 'But we are still courting. And it's not like we're pure as the driven snow. We both have . . . urges.'

'If you can't be good, be careful, my mam always says. But booking a dirty weekend away isn't exactly being careful, is it?'

'How is it any different than being here?' he asked. 'Except we wouldn't have to sneak around.'

Florrie shook her head. 'Having to snatch intimate moments under the spying eyes of the other servants reminds us not to take silly risks.'

Thom was frowning, clearly nonplussed.

She sighed. 'Look, I know there's no upside for you in waiting or limiting what we get up to behind closed doors, but if we go away for a dirty weekend, and I let my hair down in earnest . . . ? If I slip up and get pregnant before I'm ready for motherhood, it's life-changing . . . for *me*.' She thumbed herself in her chest. '*Me!*'

'It's not just you, though, is it? We're a couple. I'll do right by you.'

Withdrawing from his embrace, she slid her hands into the pockets of her skirt. 'I'm not having this conversation again and again, Thom. I love you, but if you want to rush into living the life of a married man, I suggest you court one of the girls in the village instead.'

'Florrie, I'm sorry!'

'I'll see you at our Nelly's party.' She waved dismissively and left the shed without looking back.

Nelly's party went off without a hitch on the following Saturday morning. The sun had shone over the gamekeeper's cottage, warming the blush-pink of the lime mortar and casting light into the shadiest corners of the lush garden that Thom and Mam had cultivated over the last year. Florrie had revelled in seeing her nieces and nephew mixing so well with the children from the village. With rosy cheeks and a love of rough and tumble in the garden, it was now as if they'd never struggled on the margins in Manchester's slums. She'd chatted amiably with the local parents who had accompanied their small children to the Holcombe Estate. Thom had brought over the doll's house, wrapped in brown paper.

'I think it's time the birthday girl opened her biggest present,' Mam had said.

The children had all immediately paused in their play, keen to know what magical offering might be concealed by the paper.

'Oooh, what's this? Is it for me?' Nelly had asked, looking up at Thom, wide-eyed.

'Aye. It is that, chuck.' Thom had set the gift down on the grass and was then surrounded by an audience of young party guests, all craning their necks to see what he'd brought.

'What is it?' Nelly had asked. 'Is it a doll's house?' She'd sunk to her knees and clasped her hands in prayer. 'Please, *please* let it be a doll's house.'

'Why don't you open it and see?' Florrie had said, chuckling at her melodramatic little niece.

Nelly had squealed and jumped up and down with delight when she'd torn away the brown paper concealing her gift. 'A doll's house! I knew it! Thanks, Uncle Thom. Thank you, thank you, thank you.' She'd grabbed his legs in a tight hug of gratitude and then immediately started to stage the peg dolls in the various rooms, her tongue protruding from the corner of her mouth and her little brow furrowed in concentration.

Yet again, Florrie had found herself holding hands with Thom – all hard feelings forgotten . . . for now, at least. Together, they'd delighted in the wholesome scene, and it had struck Florrie that, while the Harding-Bournes were suffering so much upheaval and turmoil, here at the gamekeeper's cottage, all was truly well in the garden.

The warm feelings that Nelly's birthday inspired in Florrie soon cooled abruptly on the Monday morning when the ambulance returned to Holcombe Hall bearing Dame Elizabeth. The staff assembled on the steps of the grand entrance to greet her, their uniforms slowly darkening in the drizzle.

Sir Hugh, who had been waiting alone at the top of the steps, holding an umbrella, descended past the phalanx of staff as soon as the vehicle came to a standstill and the drivers emerged from their cab. Grim-faced, he made his way over to the ambulance. From where Florrie was standing, she couldn't hear what was being said, but she observed how Sir Hugh seemed to have aged some ten years in the space of a week. The erect bearing of an arrogant man was gone, leaving a hunched, haunted-looking stranger in their midst.

'Good God,' Cook said, crossing herself when the old lady was stretchered from the back doors of the vehicle. 'I've seen sides of beef with more life in them. Handled more carefully, and all.'

'Shush!' Florrie gave her an admonishing look. 'Show some respect.'

Arkwright clicked his fingers and two valets immediately made their way over to the stretcher, opening umbrellas to protect Dame Elizabeth from the rain.

In Florrie's peripheral vision, she saw Arkwright checking his fob watch, no doubt wondering where Dr Haslam was.

As if he'd been magically summoned by the butler, there was the rumble of an engine and Dr Haslam's old Ford appeared at the end of the gravel driveway. When he parked up, he got out of his car and shook hands with Sir Hugh, then sought Florrie out.

Florrie abandoned the ranks of her staff to greet the doctor.

'Morning, Dr Haslam. I've got Dame Elizabeth's room all set up for her, just as you requested. The study's now a little bedroom-cum-office for the nurses, and I've had our handyman knock together some rails that he's fixed to the sides of her ladyship's bed.'

'Good, good,' the doctor said. 'We don't want her rolling out and injuring herself.' He walked over to Dame Elizabeth, took her hand and spoke loudly to her. 'You'll be much more comfortable in your own bed, your ladyship. I've arranged some nursing for you. Margaret, your day nurse, will be here after lunch. She'll do a twelve-hour shift, and then you get Dorothy overnight. Both lovely, caring ladies and very experienced. I'll check in on you regularly.'

Dame Elizabeth stared up at him blankly, groaning softly in response.

The grand matriarch, whom everyone had always revered and feared, had been reduced to a shell of a woman. How frail she looked. And those haunted eyes . . . Florrie exhaled hard, willing herself not to show either horror or grief at Dame Elizabeth's deteriorated state. She said a silent prayer that Sir Richard would make it back to Holcombe Hall in time to say goodbye, for Dame Elizabeth's end was surely imminent.

'His nappy's just been changed, he had a bottle an hour ago, and I fed him some rusk and some milk,' Miss Talbot said the following Sunday when she came down to the kitchen to find Florrie. She carried a struggling, wriggling, complaining Sir William, holding him at arm's length as if he were made from toxic stuff, presumably to conserve the cleanliness of her prim, Sunday-best dress. 'Now I must be on my way to chapel.' She looked up at the clock and tutted. 'I'm going to be late, and latecomers are always frowned upon.'

Without waiting for a response, she hefted the boy into Florrie's arms.

'I thought Dilys had offered to take him while you're at church,' Florrie said.

'Chapel. I'm going to *chapel*. And Dilys was nowhere to be found when I went looking for her. No doubt she's taking a Sunday morning tumble in the hay with one of the stable—'

'Miss Talbot! Whatever are you implying about one of my girls?'

Miss Talbot shook her head. 'I don't have time to start combing through haystacks for hussies.' She patted the tight bun of hair tied at the nape of her neck. 'I'll be back as soon as the good Lord permits.'

Before Florrie could complain that she'd been left holding the baby yet again, Miss Talbot marched off towards the servants' entrance.

Florrie looked down at the now-smiling baby and then turned to Cook. 'Well, how do you like, eh? She's done her usual trick.'

Cook, who was already preparing soup for Sunday lunch, pointed her wooden spoon at Florrie. 'She knows you're a soft touch, that one. She's not daft. She bends the rules to suit herself and ends up skiving a half-day a week. "Lord permit" indeed! Maybe I'll go all holy-holy and apply for a bloody "Lord permit".'

Florrie covered the baby's ears. 'Language, Cook! Not in front of the baby.'

Scoffing, Cook returned to stirring her soup with gusto. She looked through the high window at the shining wet cobbles in the rear courtyard. 'What you going to do with him this morning? It's bucketing down outside.'

Sir William reached out and grabbed a stray lock of Florrie's hair in his fist, then yanked it hard.

'Ow. Less of that, young man.'

Florrie prised her hair free, licked her thumb and wiped away the ghost of milk and rusk from around his mouth. 'I know exactly what I'm going to do. His mam's in bed, sleeping off another heavy night of hedonism. It's too wet to take him over to see Alice and Nelly, even if Miss Lord Permit allowed it. I'll take him to see his grandmother.'

'Ooh, are you sure that's a good idea, Florrie? I mean, the old lady's on her last legs. It's not right for a babba to be around death and decay.'

Getting to her feet, Florrie pushed her chair out noisily. 'She's not dead yet! Doctor Haslam said she could go at any time, or she could be like this for years. There's no way of knowing. Are you going to stop Sir William from ever seeing his grandmother? And what if the baby's babbling rouses her? The specialists at the hospital didn't rule that out.' She looked down at the baby, who straddled her hip. 'No, this child needs to see more of his flesh and blood, and less of that old crow of a nanny.'

Cook threw back her head and laughed. 'Old crow. I'll tell her you called her that.'

'Just you dare!'

En route to Dame Elizabeth's suite of rooms, Florrie stopped by the nursery to pick up some picture books.

'How about I read to you, eh?' she asked Sir William.

The baby lunged for a brightly coloured book about a farmyard, grabbing it with both hands.

Kissing his soft baby hair, Florrie carried him downstairs. She knocked on the outer door.

'Nurse Margaret? It's only me,' she said. 'Miss Bickerstaff.'

'Oh, hello, dear! Come in!' the nurse's voice sounded cheery.

Florrie entered the suite to find Dame Elizabeth partly propped in her bed. The old lady's eyes tracked sluggishly from Nurse Margaret, who was sitting on the edge of the bed, clutching a bowl and spoon, to the baby, and Florrie was sure she could detect one corner of Dame Elizabeth's mouth twitching upwards slightly.

'Is she smiling?' Florrie asked, sitting in the armchair that had been put out for visitors. She placed Sir William on her lap.

The nurse studied her charge's face. She shook her head. 'I don't think so, love. She's not very responsive at all, and she's not eating, neither. I'm just trying to wet her whistle with a bit of jelly. See how cracked her lips are? Terribly dehydrated.' Her sympathetic expression brightened suddenly. 'But tell me, who is this lovely bonnie baby?'

'This is Dame Elizabeth's grandson, Sir William,' Florrie said. She took one of the boy's hands and waggled it at his grandmother. 'Wave hello to Grandma!'

'Oh, what a grand idea to bring him in,' Nurse Margaret said. She turned back to her task of spooning jelly from the dish. 'Nobody but her son has been to visit her ladyship since she was brought in.' She shook her head and tried to tempt the old lady by rubbing her lips with the ruby red jelly. 'Sir Henry? Or was it Harold?'

'Hugh. Sir Hugh. He's Dame Elizabeth's youngest. We're expecting her eldest son, Sir Richard, home from India any day now,' Florrie said, keeping her criticism of Lady Charlotte and Daphne to herself. It hardly surprised her that the women were too selfish to visit their mother-in-law, even when she was likely at death's door.

Margaret sighed and set the spoon back in the bowl with a clank. 'I'm not getting anywhere here, am I? Listen, I'm going to go to the kitchens to ask the cook to make something cold and creamy. Her ladyship's comfortable for now. She's not in any pain. So am I all right to leave you and the baby to it for a bit?'

Florrie smiled. 'Absolutely.' She looked down at Sir William. 'We're going to read a book, aren't we, sweetheart?'

The baby burbled at her and blew a raspberry.

With the nurse gone, Florrie read to the baby and intermittently spoke encouraging words to Dame Elizabeth. She had just turned to the final page and was explaining to Sir William what all the various farmyard animals were, when she heard rapid footsteps behind her and caught a whiff of cigars and sandalwood that could only belong to one man.

She craned her neck to confirm by sight what all her other senses were telling her. 'Sir Richard! You're back!'

16

'I got here as soon as I could, dear Florrie,' he said, never taking his eyes from his now sleeping mother. 'Dear God! She looks . . . Oh, how dreadful. How positively terrible.'

'I thought Sir Hugh had been in touch with news of her condition,' Florrie said.

'Yes. He sent me a telegram when I stopped over in Baghdad. He did tell me she was in a bad way, and I sent him a communiqué in response, saying I'd be arriving today.'

'He never said a word.'

'Well, here I am. Better late than never. But . . . good Lord.'

He approached the head of his mother's bed and leaned over the rail that Margaret had put back up. He stroked the old lady's lopsided face. 'Darling Mama. This is perfectly dreadful, and I'm so, so sorry that I haven't been here to oversee your care.'

Florrie was taken aback when Sir Richard started to sob. 'Oh dear. Would you like us to leave?'

He shook his head and sat on the end of his mother's bed, sobbing so hard that he started to hiccup. He reached out to take Sir William, and as Florrie transferred the baby from her hands to his, she found herself entangled in a clumsy, desperate embrace. Sir Richard kissed his son's head and leaned into Florrie, his body quaking with sorrow.

Suddenly, Florrie found tears pooling in her own eyes, as though his abject misery was contagious. 'There, there.' She put her arm around him gingerly, torn between wanting to comfort him and not wanting anybody to see either him or her compromised, should someone walk in at that very moment. Though surely, any feeling person would immediately grasp the perfectly innocent chain of events that had come to pass. 'Shall I get you a hanky?'

First, he shook his head. Then he nodded. He did not shift his position, however, and Florrie found herself embracing him tightly, rocking him softly, as though he too were a small boy. As he wept, so did she. She felt all of her frustrations and worries from the past few weeks coalesce into a hot, messy ball of sorrow, its only means of escape through tears.

It was Sir William who put an end to the impromptu entanglement. Clearly agitated at being constrained by the adults, he drummed his little fists against them and shrieked.

They broke apart.

'Oh, I say. I'm terribly sorry, Florrie.' Sir Richard wiped his eyes on his shirtsleeve and then sat his son on his knee. 'I didn't mean to . . . I hope you don't think I . . .'

'It's fine, sir.' Florrie dabbed at her own eyes. 'Fully understandable. It must have been very hard to be in a far-flung destination while your mother was taken badly. But rest assured, the doctor says she's comfortable, and we're doing all we can to care for her.'

'Poor Mama.' He looked forlornly at his mother, who was now so soundly asleep that her only movement came from her eyeballs moving to and fro beneath the loose, lined skin of her eyelids. 'She has been so fretful this last year. I have no idea why her mood deteriorated so abruptly. One minute, she was positively giddy at the prospect of being a grandmother; the next . . .' He gasped and looked up at the ornate plasterwork of the ceiling, his eyes still glassy with tears. 'She reverted to how she'd been when my father first passed away. Fell into a kind of malaise. She wouldn't come out of her room, her health seemed to deteriorate, she was morose – paranoid, even – and easy to upset.' He locked eyes with Florrie. 'Have you any idea what might have changed in my mother's life to bring about such a pronounced shift in mood and temperament? And could such a shift have been a prelude to this apoplexy?'

Florrie bit down on her tongue and dug her fingernails into her palms. She was desperate to tell Sir Richard that his mother had been blackmailed over an extended period of time by Lord Harding-Bourne's college chum and her former lover, Miles T. Brooke. But a vow of silence was a vow of silence. Surely there was nothing to be gained by telling Sir Richard that his profligate brother was the true heir to the Harding-Bourne fortune; that the man he'd looked up to and loved all his life wasn't, in fact, his biological father. With a shake of her head, she pushed the truth away. 'Not that I'm aware of. Sorry.' Should she confide in him her misgivings about Miss Talbot? No. Now was not the time.

Clearing her throat, Florrie got to her feet. 'Would you like me to take Sir William so you can be alone with your mother?'

Sir Richard rubbed noses with his son. 'No. Thank you,

Florrie. William will be fine here, until Miss Talbot returns from chapel.'

'Are you sure? He's due a bottle soon.'

'Then have one of the maids bring it to me here. I've been away for far too long, and the world has crumbled around us in my absence. The least I can do is spend a little time with my son at my mother's bedside.' He picked up the boy's picture book. 'We'll read a lovely story, won't we?'

'Very well.' Florrie curtsied. 'It's so good to have you back.'

At lunch, Florrie oversaw service in the dining room, while Arkwright poured the wine. With Sir Richard back, it was the first time in weeks that the place had felt full. Cook had prepared roast pheasant. Though the smell of the food was mouth-watering, and the sun streamed merrily in through the stained glass of the oriel windows, the mood was sombre.

Florrie busied herself at the serving table, helping the maid to stack the spent plates and cutlery from the starter, but she could not help eavesdropping on the family's conversation. She turned around surreptitiously to see what was going on.

'It's been perfectly horrid,' Sir Hugh said, slumped in his seat. 'I hate seeing her like that.'

'Did the doctor say there's even the slightest chance she'll recover?' Sir Richard asked. When Arkwright offered him wine, he put his hand over the glass.

'They don't have a clue, old bean. The specialist at the infirmary seemed only too happy to shove her back in the ambulance and send her on her way back home. He said it was a "wait and see situation". Wait and see, indeed!'

'What does this new doctor say? Haslam? Is he any good?'

Lady Charlotte held her glass up to Arkwright. 'I think Dr Haslam's rather fun, actually.' Florrie observed her exchanging a glance with Daphne. 'You'd like him, Dickie. He's not stuffy at all.'

Sir Richard raised an eyebrow. 'A doctor isn't trained to be fun, dear. He's trained to heal and care for the sick.' He turned to engage his brother. 'Well?'

'I do think Haslam knows his onions,' Sir Hugh said. 'He came the other day and said there are signs that Mama's vital organs are struggling to function. She's terribly jaundiced, for a start. And while she isn't able to eat or drink, the prognosis isn't at all good.'

Florrie regarded Sir Hugh. The usual blank smile had been replaced by a furrowed brow.

'Can she not be force-fed until she's regained her strength?' Lady Charlotte asked, slurring slightly. She drained her glass, then held it out to Arkwright for a top-up.

Florrie noted how Sir Richard wore a frown as he studied his wife's behaviour. 'Darling. It's only lunchtime. Wouldn't you do better to switch to lemonade?'

Lady Charlotte turned from her brother-in-law to blink slowly at her husband. 'I asked Hugh a perfectly valid question. And no, I don't want to switch to lemonade.' She shook her empty glass at Arkwright but turned back to Hugh, wearing an expectant half-smile. 'Well? Don't they normally feed people in Elizabeth's condition through a tube?'

Sir Hugh shook his head glumly. 'The specialist said we must let nature take its course. Dr Haslam feels our main priority is to keep Mama comfortable.'

Sir Richard rose from the table and sought Florrie out. The colour in his cheeks from having spent time in the Indian sunshine seemed already to have drained away. 'Florrie, could you have my main course brought to my study, please? I feel I ought to deal with the daunting pile of correspondence that's accrued on my desk in my absence. And there's the not insignificant issue of an accident at one of the collieries to deal with.'

Without looking back at his wife, brother and sister-in-law, Sir Richard marched out of the dining room.

'Honestly, Dickie is *such* a bore,' Lady Charlotte said, shaking her head while Arkwright poured her a fourth glass of wine. She looked around the table at her fellow diners. 'We haven't seen him in weeks, have we? And the moment he returns to Holcombe, he's banging on about the business and scolding me like a schoolgirl for having a thimble of wine with my Sunday lunch.' She tutted. 'And then there's all this beastly business with your mother, Hugh. Just when we were having such a lovely time in Scotland. It hardly seems fair.'

Daphne threw down her napkin. 'I know. Let's take the Bugatti out for a spin. Blow away the cobwebs. That will cheer us up no end.'

Lady Charlotte smiled and got to her feet. 'Smashing idea. I'll drive!'

'Nonsense,' Daphne said. 'You've had too much wine already. I've only had three glasses. I'll drive. Let's go and get changed.'

The two women left Sir Hugh alone in the dining room. 'Emancipated women, eh?' he said to Arkwright. 'Those suffragettes have much to answer for.'

Arkwright bowed stiffly. 'Will sir be requiring anything else?'

Sir Hugh scratched behind his ear and sighed. 'I'll eat in my mother's rooms. Leave me what's left in the bottle, there's a good chap.'

Before the main course had even been sent up from the kitchen, Florrie and the other serving staff found themselves alone, with the family dispersed to the four corners of the house.

Three days passed with monotonous uniformity. Dr Haslam attended Dame Elizabeth in the morning, checking her for signs of improvement and shaking his head apologetically when he spotted none. Sir Richard would take his breakfast by his mother's bedside, evidently preferring to read the news to her than to spend time with the rest of his family.

'I do wonder if she isn't a little more responsive this morning,' he'd said to Florrie each day, when she'd brought him his tray.

Florrie had noticed no such change, however. She'd observed the old lady waking with only slightly more regularity, still staring wildly into the middle distance and breathing more rapidly, as if she was now in pain. On the third day, Dr Haslam decided to medicate her, instructing the nurse to administer some strong painkiller by injection, which he said would allow her to rest without discomfort.

After the check-up, Florrie pulled the doctor to one

side in the hallway. She lowered her voice. 'She's dying, isn't she?'

Dr Haslam smiled sadly. 'I'm afraid I can only discuss her ladyship's condition with her next of kin.'

'Is it worth arranging for Dame Elizabeth's little grandson to visit her?'

The doctor merely patted Florrie's arm. 'The family is very lucky to have such supportive staff, really they are. Look, if it gives Sir Richard some measure of comfort, by all means he should bring the baby to see his grandmother – perhaps soon and briefly would be best. But in terms of it helping her ladyship ... I'm not sure how *aware* she is at this point.'

Florrie realized then that there was truly no hope left for the grand doyenne of Holcombe Hall.

Later that evening, she carried in a tray containing a plateful of dinner, kept warm beneath a silver cloche.

Sir Richard was sitting in the armchair by his mother's bed. The remains of the summer's evening sunlight still streamed through the closed window, warming the bedroom and giving the place a hot, sickly smell. 'Oh, Florrie. You really needn't have brought me anything. I don't feel I could eat a single mouthful.'

Florrie set the tray down on the table at the side of the chair. 'Now, now, Sir Richard. You must keep up your strength if you will insist on carrying the weight of the world on your shoulders.'

'You are such a good egg, Florrie.' He lifted the dome to reveal braised beef cooked in stout, mashed potatoes and carrots. 'I suppose I could have a bit. Cook will be terribly cross with me if I let her delicious stew go to waste.'

He pointed to the additional visitor's chair beyond the table that held the tray. 'Keep me company?'

Soon, her own dinner would be served, but Florrie could tell that her employer needed to unburden himself. 'Of course.' She looked over at Dame Elizabeth, who lay on her back, breathing noisily and shallowly. 'Keeping vigil like this must be very emotionally taxing.'

Sir Richard forked some stew into his mouth, peering thoughtfully at his mother. 'I've accepted whatever fate lies ahead for Mama, now. But still ... It really is heartbreaking to see such a vibrant woman reduced to a pale imitation of her former self.'

'She seems peaceful, at least. And I'm sure she knows you're here, and that's got to be a comfort to her. I know she loves you deeply.'

Looking at her quizzically, Sir Richard cocked his head to the side. 'How do you know?'

Florrie realized then that she'd rendered herself vulnerable to being cross-examined, and she was not content to reveal Dame Elizabeth's guilty secret when the woman was on her deathbed. 'Oh, just the way she's always spoken about you with such evident pride.' *Idiot! Keep your gob shut, Florrie Bickerstaff!* she thought. *Change the subject.* 'Anyway, are you happy with Sir William's progress? He's such a bonny baby.'

Sir Richard glanced over at the old lady. 'I'm truly blessed, and I'm so glad my mother got to see her grandson properly before her illness.' He set his fork down and turned to Florrie. He lowered his voice, 'But I'm relieved she doesn't know that seventeen men were killed in a mining accident that took place at one of our collieries.'

'*Seventeen?*' Florrie echoed.

He nodded. 'The day before I returned home. I haven't even been able to visit the families of the dead miners yet, let alone the injured men. I feel dreadfully guilty about it.'

'I'm sure they understand. You've only been home five minutes. Family first and all that.'

'But it's never that simple when you're an industrialist with the fate of thousands of families in your hands. You're responsible for each and every one of them. I feel that burden acutely at the moment.' He peered over at his mother again. 'I'm relieved she can't now know the extent to which our businesses are struggling with this blasted Depression.' He closed his eyes solemnly. 'Even after my trip to curry favour with the Viceroy of India to get him to place an order for locomotives built with Harding-Bourne raw materials, we're still having to lay off workers left, right and centre. I fear we may end up having to parcel off bits of the business to sell to the highest bidder at this rate.'

Florrie chewed the inside of her cheek, planning her next words carefully. 'Could you not trim the staff here even more? Miss Talbot, for example ... Maybe Lady Charlotte could take on more mothering duties?' She knew she was treading a fine line between helpfulness and inappropriate familiarity. Had she said too much?

Sir Richard's eyes darkened. 'Nice idea, but there's the small matter of my wife drinking far more than is good for her. At the moment, she's neither keen enough nor in a fit state to take on parenting full-time. At least Miss Talbot is teetotal.'

'But do you think she's ... ?' Florrie wondered how to

phrase her misgivings without seeming to overtly criticize Lady Charlotte's judgement. 'I mean, Sir William's inside a lot – an *awful* lot – and doesn't ever mix with other children. And Miss Talbot is quite ... severe. So I just thought—'

Florrie was interrupted by a terrible rattling, gurgling sound coming from Dame Elizabeth.

Sir Richard set the tray aside and leaped to his feet. 'Mama!'

Florrie had heard that noise before, however, at the end of her own sister's life. She stood, looking down at the old lady's wizened face. The gurgling continued for a full half-minute and then stopped abruptly.

'Mama?' Sir Richard took his mother's hand into his. He glanced back at Florrie, panic in his face, tears in his eyes. Then he looked back at his mother. 'Mama?'

Florrie could just about hear a long breath being exhaled. Then, there was nothing.

She approached the dressing table, picked up a long-handled mirror and held it over Dame Elizabeth's open mouth to see if the glass steamed. When it didn't, she set the mirror down on the end of the bed, turned to Sir Richard and curtseyed low, bowing her head. She wiped away a tear. 'I'm very sorry for your loss, sir.'

17

'How long are they keeping her in the chapel for?' Cook asked, twiddling her pen between her fingers.

Florrie sighed and looked up at her. She tapped her notepad with her index finger. 'Er, do you think we can just get back to these plans for the wake?'

'Have you seen her?' Sally asked her, wide-eyed. 'Have you been in? Is it an open coffin? Does she look like Bela Lugosi in *Dracula*?'

At Florrie's side, Thom started laughing, rocking back on his chair as he did so. 'Aye. You go paying your respects after dark, you'd better go with a wooden stake and a bulb of garlic!'

'You're all very disrespectful,' Florrie said. She glared at Thom. '*You*, I can't do much about. You're a law unto yourself.' Then she turned to Cook and Sally, pointing accusingly. 'But you two are under my jurisdiction, so stop messing around and show some respect for the dead, or I'll be docking your wages.' She flicked back through her notebook and read what she'd written there, when she and Arkwright had met with Sir Richard earlier that morning. 'Funeral service is in three weeks at Manchester Cathedral.'

'Manchester?' Sally asked. 'Why the heck is she getting buried there?'

'She's not getting buried there. They're holding a service for her in the cathedral, so the great and the good of the north's industrialists can come and pay their respects. Not just northerners, neither. Sir Richard had to consult over a date with the King himself *and* the Prince of Wales. Ramsay MacDonald and all. Couldn't commit to a date until he'd made sure they could all make it.'

'And then they're bringing her back to Holcombe for the actual burial?' Cook asked.

Florrie nodded. 'Exactly. And all the dignitaries will be coming to Holcombe Hall for the wake on the same specially commissioned train what leaves from Victoria Station.'

Cook whistled low. 'Crikey. When I die, I'll be lucky if any of you lot turn up to weep for me over a bag of chips and a pint of ale. And then, you'll likely chuck me in a pauper's grave.'

'If you're planning on dying, Cookie,' Thom said, pulling a dried seed pod from the tangle of his hair, 'make sure you plan ahead, so you can at least bake us all a good meat pie before you pop your clogs. Sal here still can't stew beef to save her life. It's like boot leather.'

Sally screwed her notepaper into a ball and threw it at Thom's head, while Cook guffawed with laughter.

'Enough!' Florrie shouted. 'Right, that's a shilling out of your pay packet, Sally. I did warn you.' She turned to Thom. 'And I'm not going to speak to you for a week if you carry on like that. Come on now. Show some decorum. The great lady of Holcombe Hall has passed, and we've got to arrange a funeral reception to remember. The King, the heir to the throne and the Prime Minister are coming *here*. All the big newspapers will be reporting on it.'

Thom leaned over to where Arkwright had been sitting

during lunch and pulled across that day's edition of *The Times*. 'Dame Elizabeth's obituary's in here. Have you read it?'

'When have I had time to read the flipping paper?' Florrie asked. 'It's been mayhem. The telephone's been ringing non-stop. We've had Uncle Tom Cobley and all turning up to pay their respects.'

'And they always want feeding,' Cook added. 'I must have baked a thousand scones in the last few days.'

'Aye, and I've been run off my feet.' Florrie cast her mind back to the hours following Dame Elizabeth's last breath. The house had immediately fallen into emotional turmoil, but as soon as the undertaker had taken the body away to be prepared for burial, Florrie had locked herself into the old lady's suite and searched the place from top to bottom. She'd been looking for correspondence with Sir Richard's true father, Miles T. Brooke, hoping to destroy it to protect the family from scandal, but her search had proven fruitless. Yet Dame Elizabeth had allowed herself to be blackmailed for years. Wouldn't bank statements, now fully available to Sir Richard as executor of Dame Elizabeth's will, at least reveal regular payments to the man, prompting Sir Richard to investigate further? There might be no hard evidence that Brooke was his true father, but the statements might at least point to longstanding extortion. Or had Dame Elizabeth parted with cash to ensure no damning trail could be traced back to Brooke? She shivered at the thought and looked at the newspaper. 'What does it say?'

Thom started to thumb his way to the obituary, but he paused midway, frowning at an article on another page. 'Hang on a minute. I didn't notice this earlier.'

'What?' Cook asked.

He folded the oversized paper to read it more easily. 'Article here about Sir Richard in the business section.'

He turned the paper around to show them a photo of two men, one of them Sir Richard, standing outside a colliery.

'Is that where they had that cave-in and all them fellers got killed?' Sally asked.

'Aye. Says under the picture.'

In the photo, Florrie saw Sir Richard was standing next to Edward, the Prince of Wales himself – both men looking grim-faced as they examined some machinery.

Thom turned the paper back. His lips moved as he read silently. Then he read aloud. 'Says here, "Even those too pragmatic to harbour superstition might be persuaded that Harding-Bourne Enterprises are cursed, given that the disaster at their Lancashire colliery, where seventeen miners were killed in a mineshaft collapse, was immediately followed by the death of the family's matriarch, Dame Elizabeth, widow of the late, great Lord Harding-Bourne of Holcombe. Harding-Bourne Steel was one of the steel companies that invested in Clarence Hatry's failed merger, which is now believed to have triggered the Wall Street Crash of 1929, leading not just to a series of tragedies befalling the Harding-Bournes, but the Depression itself. Can Sir Richard Harding-Bourne, current Chairman and majority shareholder of the Harding-Bourne industrial empire, shake off the dreaded Curse of Clarence Hatry?"'

'Bloody hell.' Thom pressed his lips together and shook his head. 'I'm almost sorry for them.'

Florrie looked askance at him. 'How do you mean, "almost"?'

He flung the paper down. 'Well, let's face it, they've never really wanted for owt, have they? All this cobblers about a curse? They're multimillionaires! Dame Elizabeth died warm in her Louis XIV bed, after a long life of luxury, knowing that her most sensible son had inherited the family fortune and married the King's cousin or summat, who pushed out a male heir. I mean, come on! Talk about having a silver spoon in your gob.'

'You're not wrong, Thomas,' Cook said, folding her arms. 'But at the end of the day, that lot put a roof over our heads and food on the table for us all. So our fate is bound up with theirs.'

'And they're still real people with real feelings,' Florrie added, alarmed that Thom should be so callous about Dame Elizabeth's death.

Thom chuckled. 'You really reckon Sir Hugh and that lot are real and have feelings like you and me? Pull the other one. It's got bells on.'

'I saw Sir Hugh weeping like a little boy when her ladyship got taken to the infirmary.'

'And one show of humanity in the twelve years you've been here makes him just like us? Come on, Florrie! Even Sir Richard, the supposedly sensible one, is nowt like us. Married to that alcoholic clothes horse he calls a wife, just so the family moves up in the pecking order? They hate each other! How is that normal?'

'Plenty of women marry out of expedience, Thom,' Florrie said, folding her arms tightly. 'Not everyone has the luxury of being financially self-sufficient. Seems to me the likes of us are just as motivated by money and social standing when it comes to making a marriage as the nobility.'

'That's not true though, is it?' He took her hand. 'We marry for love.'

Florrie shook herself free of his grip. 'Well, maybe we should be more savvy! If my sister had given some thought to marrying better, she likely wouldn't have been left in a slum by a drunkard whoremonger to struggle alone with three kids under the age of five, until she died young, six months later.' She placed her hands emphatically on the kitchen table, spread her fingers and took a deep breath. 'But none of that is relevant to our planning, and we shouldn't be casting aspersions on the moral fibre of our employers, especially not while they're freshly bereaved. Now, let's turn our thoughts back to this wake.' Returning to the most recently written page in her notebook, she read out a list of people who would be attending the funeral reception only, and those who would also be staying overnight. 'So, Cook, you have to come up with a menu for the day. Canapés, sit-down lunch. Nothing too lavish or heavy. And Thom, I'd like the gardeners to provide as many of the flowers and foliage for the funeral decoration as possible to keep costs down. Keep it to whites and the odd splash of blue or purple. Lilies, if they're still in flower.'

'Lilies will be mostly done by early August.'

'Can we pick them in bud and refrigerate them somehow?'

Cook gasped. 'Hey, you're not putting blinking flowers in my Frigidaire! They can go in the cold store.'

'Look, leave the flowers to me,' Thom said. 'We've always got plenty knocking about that would suit funeral arrangements. I'll make sure you get them in time and in good condition for arranging, and I'll let you know in advance what you might want to order in extra from a florist.'

The lead-up to Dame Elizabeth's funeral passed in a dizzying blur of preparation. Florrie found herself liaising regularly with Sir Richard's personal assistant at Harding-Bourne Enterprises' head office in Manchester, the secretary to the head of the charitable foundation that Dame Elizabeth had established at Florrie's suggestion, the undertaker, the Anglican priest who led the services at Holcombe's own chapel . . . even the local railway authority, which was organizing the specially commissioned train. As she performed her duties, alongside the usual management of the Hall, she wondered if her predecessor, Bertha, hadn't succumbed to heart disease in part thanks to the additional pressures of organizing Lord Harding-Bourne and Sir James's funerals.

The day before the funeral, Florrie and Arkwright were in the butler's office, going through some last-minute changes to the schedule, when there was a knock at the door.

'Enter!' Arkwright looked up from his paperwork expectantly.

'Ah, glad to have caught you both.'

Florrie turned around to see her employer standing in the doorway. Sir Richard's complexion seemed tinged with grey. The shadows beneath his reddened eyes spoke to sleepless, sorrowful nights. His demeanour, however, was as dignified as ever. He smiled and closed the door behind him.

Arkwright was on his feet now. 'Is anything the matter, sir?'

Sir Richard held his hand up. 'Not at all. No.'

Florrie stood and bobbed a curtsey. 'We're just putting the finishing touches to the funeral reception, Sir Richard. Dame Elizabeth is getting a send-off to be proud of. But if there's any more changes you want to make . . .'

'Not at all. No. The reason I sought you both out is that I wanted to ask if you would both come to Manchester Cathedral for the funeral service.'

Arkwright looked momentarily puzzled. 'To assist the family, sir?'

Sir Richard shook his head. 'No. As guests. My mother thought very highly of both of you . . . as do I, of course . . . and I think it only fitting that the household's two most senior members of staff attend the cathedral service. Assuming you'd like to, of course.'

Florrie and Arkwright looked at one another, exchanging silent surprise.

'I wouldn't miss it for the world,' Florrie said. 'Thank you, sir.'

Arkwright bowed. 'I'm deeply honoured.'

Later that evening, Florrie made her way over to the gamekeeper's cottage to visit her mother, though by the time she'd ended her working day at ten o'clock at night, she knew seeing the children would have to wait for another occasion. Revelling in the evening scent of the nicotiana in the flower beds, she walked around to the back of the cottage and knocked on the door.

Mam answered quickly. 'What took you so long?' she asked, pulling Florrie into the kitchen. 'I were expecting you a while ago. First pot of tea I made went cold.' She squinted at Florrie's face in the light of the wall-mounted gas lamp. 'And you're looking peaky, young lady. Are you sickening for summat?'

Florrie kissed her mother on the cheek. 'I'm fine,' she said. 'It's just bad light in here.' She yanked her shoes off her throbbing feet and padded through from the kitchen to the front parlour, where she all but collapsed on to the old settee.

Mam followed her, carrying a tray that contained a fresh pot of tea, a jug of milk, two cups and two cheese sandwiches. 'We've barely seen you for weeks, and I'm telling you, I can see a difference. You look washed out, our Florrie. They're working you too hard.' She set the sandwich down on the coffee table, in front of Florrie. 'Eat. You look thin.'

Florrie's stomach growled audibly. 'I'm barely getting a chance to get down a proper square meal because I'm so rushed off my feet.' She took a hefty bite out of the sandwich and swallowed before she'd even chewed the food properly. 'But this is my job, and it helps put food on this table.' She pointed to the ceiling, indicating the bedrooms upstairs where the children slept. 'It puts clothes on their backs.'

Mam poured the tea, her expression souring like curdled milk. 'Our Irene . . . we could barely afford a proper send-off for my girl, and now here's you, run ragged for flimpence a week, all so a bunch of dignitaries can pay their respects to a woman who never did a day's graft in her life.'

'Mam! You sound just like Thom.'

'And Thom's not wrong.'

Florrie set her sandwich down and picked up her teacup. 'Need I remind you that the Harding-Bournes took our family out of squalor and saved George, Nelly and Alice from the same sort of short and brutish life our Irene had? I thought you loved it here – your job, this house, the fresh air and greenery?'

Mam's eyebrows shot up. 'I do! It's just . . . It's complicated. I don't like seeing you exploited, is all. I want to see you walk up the aisle with Thom and have a family of your own. And it's frustrating, because that lot have got us all over a barrel, and you're letting your best years slip away in service to a bunch of toffs that wouldn't notice or care if you died tomorrow.'

Florrie winced inwardly at her mother's barbed appraisal. 'First of all, I'm delaying marrying Thom so I can keep giving you wages to help with the costs of raising George, Nelly and Alice. And secondly, it's not true that the Harding-Bournes don't care if I live or die. Sir Richard values me. If he didn't, I wouldn't be going to the cathedral service tomorrow as a guest.'

Florrie thought about the impending trip to Manchester and the strange blurring of boundaries between her and the family. If she was a guest, wouldn't she stand out as an impoverished domestic servant in her uniform skirt and a borrowed top (seeing as her Sunday best wasn't black), surrounded by socialites and nobility, dressed in

Paris fashions? And though she was honoured to attend the funeral as some sort of family friend rather than as the paid help, how awkward she would feel once she returned to Holcombe Hall and transformed back into the housekeeper, waiting on the very people she'd just been rubbing shoulders with!

That night, as she struggled to fall asleep, Florrie wondered if Sir Richard hadn't inadvertently set her and Arkwright up for an awkward day of making fools of themselves.

18

The train chugged into Manchester's Victoria Station an hour ahead of the funeral. Florrie hadn't been back to the city since she'd attended the grand opening of the HB Charitable Foundation – her very own brainchild which had been set up to alleviate the suffering of those employees who had found themselves suddenly jobless, thanks to the Depression biting in earnest. Back then, her visit had been a happy occasion in a smart bit of town, but spending time in her old birthplace more than a decade after she'd had to leave it in order to enter service, had still felt like passing a vagabond in the street and realizing he was a long-lost relative. On the day of Dame Elizabeth's funeral, Florrie still experienced that feeling of dislocation, with even the bright August sunshine unable to cast the grime of the city in a more flattering light.

'It feels like it should be raining on such a sad day,' Arkwright said, peering out of the window.

'At least Lady Charlotte and Daphne's hand-lasted shoes won't get wet,' Florrie said. 'But I should imagine the sunshine feels like a joke told in bad taste if you're out of work and starving.' She thought of her aunt, who was eking out a half-life in a run-down lodging house in Lower Broughton, to the north of the city centre. Suddenly, Thom's and her mam's bitter words seemed to resonate with her in a way that they hadn't back in Holcombe. 'Never mind. Come on. Let's get to the cathedral.'

The immediate family had gone on ahead in the Rolls-Royce and would almost certainly be already installed at the cathedral to receive mourners. So, when Florrie and Arkwright disembarked, the undertakers were the only other people on the platform, preparing to unload the coffin.

'I feel like we've been on babysitting duty,' Florrie said.

'Perhaps we have.' Arkwright put on his bowler hat and offered Florrie his arm. 'Shall we?'

With a thudding heart, Florrie looked up at the cathedral clock tower. The intricately carved gargoyles leered down at her, reminding her that she was out of place there. She had not been raised in a particularly religious household. Attending midnight mass in Holcombe on Christmas Eve because the other maids were going was about as close to being an observant Christian as Florrie got. More daunting than never having been inside the cathedral before and having to sit through an Anglican funeral service, was the prospect of possibly sitting next to some member of the nobility.

'I'm used to serving these people, not rubbing shoulders with them,' she said to Arkwright. 'They'll sniff me out as an interloper within a minute.'

Arkwright let go of her arm, straightened up and smoothed down his suit. 'Just remember why we're here, Florence. We're here to pay our respects to a woman we knew far better than most of those who are here today. We're invited guests of Sir Richard himself. Try to leave your insecurities at the door. Act like you belong. Acting. It's what they all do.'

Florrie heard a car horn toot. She turned around to see the crowd of onlookers that had gathered across the road from the main entrance – men wearing flat caps and shirt-sleeves, women in old-fashioned summer dresses, boys in short trousers and little girls, dressed in their Sunday best. Most were waving Union Jack flags. The crowd was pushing forward into the road, blocking the approach of a Rolls-Royce. The horn tooted again, and the crowd parted, allowing Florrie to see that, attached to the radiator grille, was a coat of arms.

'Hang on,' Arkwright said. He pulled Florrie back. 'Is that . . . ?' A smile spread across his face. 'It's the Royal car! I don't believe it. The King and Queen and the Prince of Wales. It must be!'

'Should we go inside or wait for them to go in first?' Florrie asked.

'Let's slip inside now, sit at the back, and we can watch them come in.' The excitement was audible in Arkwright's voice.

The cathedral was lit not just by candles, but also by the sun streaming in through the stained-glass windows, casting a kaleidoscope of colourful light on to the black-clad guests, as if God himself wished to defy the sombre mood. The scent of lilies hung heavily in the air, almost but not quite disguising the underlying tang of damp and Victorian-era dust. No sooner had Florrie stepped into the central aisle than she all but forgot about the Royal party arriving outside. Her gaze was drawn straight to the front, to the plinth where Dame Elizabeth's coffin would be set down. With a lump in her throat, she cast her mind back to Irene's simple funeral, when she and Mam had had so little money between them that they had all ridden to the cemetery in the vicar's car. The memory had not been so bitter or so sharp for many months.

'Florrie! Over here!' Arkwright said. He was beckoning her to a pew, three rows from the back, where there was enough space for two to squeeze in.

Florrie swallowed her grief and took her place. She craned her neck to glance again at the front and finally caught sight of Sir Richard. He was shaking hands with a moustachioed elderly man she recognized as Ramsay MacDonald, the beleaguered Labour Prime Minister. Both men appeared to exchange solemn words, and Florrie felt she was observing her employer's professional life through a new window that had hitherto always been obscured. Next to Sir Richard was Sir Hugh, who merely stared dolefully at the plinth. Lady Charlotte and Daphne were out of sight, hidden by mourners in the packed pews behind, though thanks to the acoustics of the vaulted roof, Florrie was certain she could hear the high-pitched trill of Lady Charlotte tittering inappropriately at something a guest might have said.

Suddenly, the congregation started to turn around, and an excited murmur rippled around the cathedral's interior, echoing off the vaulted ceiling. Everybody seemed to stand a little straighter as the King and Queen proceeded in stately fashion to the front, followed by the Princes Edward and Albert, who were unaccompanied.

'Blimey,' Florrie whispered. 'I wish my mam could see this.'

Arkwright shushed her. Then his stern face softened. 'I'm not entirely sure she'd be impressed,' he whispered. 'I think Matilda Bickerstaff is something of a republican on the quiet.' A corner of his mouth lifted in a smirk.

Florrie looked askance at Arkwright, realizing that the butler was on more familiar terms with her mother than merely having the odd turn around the gardens together or occasionally sharing a Sunday lunch at the cottage. 'Don't be coming out with things like that in here. You'll get us hung for treason!'

It didn't take long for the coffin to arrive. Sir Richard, Sir Hugh and their male relatives went out to meet it.

Dame Elizabeth's coffin was carried on the shoulders of the Harding-Bourne menfolk, with Sir Richard and Sir Hugh standing shoulder to shoulder at the front. The sight of Sir Richard's anguished expression as he bore his share of the coffin's weight brought tears to Florrie's eyes. It was almost as if she could taste the bitterness of his grief on the stale air.

The funeral service passed by in a blur of kneeling and standing, of sermon and prayer and recitation. The choir led the congregation in the singing of solemn hymns, and soon it was all over.

'By heck, it's crammed to the gills in this carriage,' Florrie said, once they had boarded the special train back to Holcombe.

The Royals had now departed, but the remaining dignitaries being ferried to the wake glanced at Arkwright and shifted awkwardly in their seats. It was as if they could smell the servitude on him, Florrie mused, and knew instantly that he was no business associate, friend or relative. They seemed not to notice her at all, but she was glad about that.

Arkwright looked distinctly uncomfortable, clutching his hat against his belly and smiling uncertainly at people Florrie remembered visiting the house at one time or another. They all turned away from him.

'Let's walk through to the next,' she said.

She led the way past women dressed in elegant black day dresses and black straw hats adorned with feathers. Their faces were perfectly made up, with no signs of having shed tears at any point during the service. The men wore expensively tailored black suits and puffed on cigarettes and cigars, chatting away about commercial matters, while the women shared society gossip and commentary over who had been wearing what at the funeral.

In the next carriage, Florrie found them empty seats at a table, facing two elderly women – dowager queens, she privately wagered. They fleetingly looked her up and down and then turned back to their conversation. It wasn't until the train pulled out, however, that Florrie realized who was sitting at the table to their side.

Arkwright's pained smile alerted her to their august travel companion. He pointed surreptitiously and mouthed, 'Prime Minister' at her.

Stifling a nervous giggle, Florrie listened to the conversation between Ramsay MacDonald and his companions.

'Well, we'll keep going as long as we can, of course,' the Prime Minister said in his inimitable clipped voice, with its almost imperceptible hint of a Scottish accent. 'The voting public entrusted a Labour government to bring them out of the doldrums, and I still intend to do that.' He shook his fist determinedly.

'How can you possibly when there's been a run on the pound?' one of the other men asked. 'We're ruined!'

A third man spoke. Florrie was certain she had seen him at one of Sir Richard's business luncheons at the house. 'Nothing but a change of government can save us from economic disaster. You must call an election, surely?'

MacDonald touched his moustache thoughtfully. 'We shall see what the next fortnight brings, gentlemen. The German banking system may have collapsed, but I'm not Heinrich Brüning and I don't frighten easily. We are British. We're made of sterner stuff. If I can avoid calling a general election, I shall.'

'But if it is what the nation requires? If a coalition government is the only way out of this economic quagmire?'

'We shall see . . .'

Florrie caught Arkwright's eye. She whispered behind her hand, 'Can you get over this? We're earwigging the Prime Minister, nattering about elections and that!'

Arkwright merely pressed his index finger to his lips, cocked his head to the side and continued to eavesdrop.

It didn't take long for Florrie to lose concentration as the Prime Minister continued to debate a remedy for the parlous state of the country's finances. Her focus wandered around the carriage, as the cramped urban architecture gave way to undulating farmland with small hamlets and villages dotted here and there. She had started to think about the long list of tasks she had to oversee on her return to the house, when her idle gaze came to rest on one man at the far end of the carriage, dressed in a black suit with a cravat. She recognized him as the smartly dressed man from a professional class that she had once caught sight of in the library at Holcombe Hall – Dame Elizabeth's clandestine visitor, her blackmailer, and Sir Richard's alleged father. Miles T. Brooke Esquire had had the temerity to attend his ex-lover's funeral.

Florrie gasped and clasped her hand to her mouth. Her heartbeat sped up to a thunderous pace, and she felt a bead of cold sweat roll down her back.

'Are you quite all right?' Arkwright asked.

She nodded, realizing Brooke couldn't possibly know that she was aware of his dastardly secret. 'Just remembered something I need to tell Cook when we get back. That's all.'

Brooke locked eyes with her fleetingly and Florrie was careful to look away, but as she stared out of the window, she worried if Brooke would attempt to blackmail the calf, now that his milch cow was gone. Could anyone be brazen enough to exploit a grieving man at his mother's funeral? The air in the carriage was suddenly stifling. Knowing there wasn't a single thing she could do to warn Sir Richard without exposing him to the full sordid extent of his mother's indiscretion and Brooke's subsequent extortion, Florrie couldn't wait to disembark and escape to the simple hustle and bustle of Holcombe's below stairs.

Once she was back, Florrie changed into her most comfortable shoes and stashed the hat she had borrowed from Cook in her bedroom. She resumed her duties as the housekeeper, and it was as if she'd dreamed the last few hours. The funeral reception passed without a hitch. Oddly, she did not spot Brooke again among the throng. Had she been so fatigued that she'd imagined it was him on the train? Perhaps. *You're overwrought, Florrie Bickerstaff,* she counselled herself. *Once today is over, you've got to allow yourself to rest and recover. You can't keep going at this ridiculous pace. Think of how things ended for poor Bertha.*

It was only once the majority of the guests had left that the private burial took place. Dame Elizabeth's coffin was interred in the imposing family crypt that stood in the graveyard of the Hall's chapel – laid to rest alongside her husband, Lord Harding-Bourne, and her eldest son, Sir James, who had perished in the Great War. The servants were not invited to attend the short additional service – it was a family only affair – but at the end of the long, long day, Florrie was summoned to Sir Richard's study.

'It was a wonderful send-off, Sir Richard,' she said. 'And thanks for inviting Mr Arkwright and myself. We were honoured.'

'Thank *you*, Florrie,' Sir Richard smiled sadly. He swirled the whisky in his glass. 'Please thank the staff for their superlative efforts. They did my mother proud. *You* did my mother proud. She was very fond of you.' His eyes were glassy, but he didn't shed a single tear. 'We all are.'

Florrie's fingers twitched at her sides. She had an overwhelming urge to embrace him but blinked the absurd idea away. 'Your mother was a formidable woman. I admired her very much. It's a sad day, but we all have wonderful memories of her.' She laced her fingers together resolutely. 'But you asked to see me, sir.'

'Indeed.' Sir Richard cleared his throat and reached into

the drawer at the side of his desk. He retrieved a fat package wrapped in brown paper. It was addressed to Florrie, written in Dame Elizabeth's shaky hand. 'My mother wished you to have this. I have no idea what it is, but that's none of my business. Here.' He held the package out to Florrie. 'I hope it's a kind memento that befits your considerate service.'

Florrie took the package with slightly trembling hands, wondering what on earth could be held within the anonymous-looking brown wrapping. 'Thank you.'

At the end of her shift, Florrie took the package upstairs, and in the privacy of her room, she unwrapped it. Letter after letter, written on the same pale blue paper in the same neat hand, fell out on to her bed.

'Flaming Nora,' Florrie said beneath her breath.

It appeared to be the entire correspondence from Miles T. Brooke. Along with the letters was a note from Dame Elizabeth herself.

Dear Florence,

I am trusting you to keep my darkest secret, because I no longer trust myself, especially now that my end is near. Do with these letters as you see fit. I know you have the very best interests of my son at heart.

Yours,
Elizabeth

Florrie read and re-read the note. Then she realized that she had a decision to make. Should she burn the correspondence? Or should she hang on to it as damning evidence? She thought again about the man on the train. Had she imagined him? Or had she witnessed Miles T. Brooke's first effort to reinsert himself into the Harding-Bournes' lives, now that Dame Elizabeth was no longer there to keep him at bay and mollified with money?

19

Early October 1931

'Oh, do come here. *I'll* show you how it's done properly.' Daphne pulled Walter Knight-Downey towards her by his jacket lapels. She had her back to Sir Hugh, and Florrie noted how she was gazing coquettishly up at her husband's best friend, licking her lips lasciviously and grinning. She plucked the New Party rosette from Walter's hands and pinned it to his jacket. 'There.' She spun him around to face Sir Hugh and Lady Charlotte. 'What do you think?' She pulled him close and pressed the rosette flat. 'Do you think he looks like a member of parliament in waiting?'

Sir Hugh applauded. 'Rather! Arise, the Right Honourable Walter Knight-Downey, MP for ... where are you standing again?'

'Do you know, I can't remember!' Walter burst into a fit of laughter.

Lady Charlotte laughed along, slapping her knees with mirth. 'Wherever it is, even if it's somewhere ungodly like Bury or Ramsbottom ...' She said the local town names in an exaggerated rendition of the Lancashire accent. '*Tha'll be reet, chuck*.' She clapped her hands and burst into a fresh fit of giggles.

Florrie looked up from preparing gin and tonics in the drawing room. With Arkwright taking a day off thanks to a stomach bug, she had happily taken on post-dinner drinks duty. The theoretical scenario of Ramsay MacDonald having to call an emergency general election which Florrie had overheard being discussed by the Prime Minister on the funeral train back to Holcombe Hall had become a reality in light of Labour's struggle to keep the economy on an even keel. With a general election now looming at the end of October, she was privy to the preparations for Walter's hastily put-together political campaign.

Outside it had already gone dark. As Florrie had not yet drawn the curtains, the windows served as mirrors to the antics in the drawing room.

'Has Mosley printed leaflets for you, old boy?' Sir Hugh asked.

Walter stood in front of the glass, admiring his reflection. 'Yes, yes. New Party headquarters is a well-oiled machine.' He waved his hand dismissively. 'And obviously, thanks to you, my beloved patrons, my campaign is sure to be a storming success.' He turned to the room and took a bow. 'How can I fail to succeed in our elections, when the political mood is changing all over Europe? Spain's chucked out its royal family. You've got Mussolini in Italy. And Hitler has managed to unite his National Socialist Party, the German National People's Party *and* the *Stahlhelm* as a united *Harzburger* front! One hundred thousand proud nationalists, standing for what's right.'

'Is that actually what's happened in Germany?' Lady Charlotte asked. 'Hans said Hitler's having to play second fiddle to some other chap.'

Again, Walter waved away the detail. 'Look, if the Germans are desperate for a strongman on the right . . . and

I'm told Hitler's the favourite to become Chancellor in the not-too-distant future . . .' He straightened his tie. 'Then I can guarantee you the British will follow suit. I'm going to win my seat by a landslide.'

'I think I favour the odds of Al Capone finally being convicted over the odds of boring old Ramsay MacDonald and Neville Chamberlain winning,' Daphne said. 'They have no charisma whatsoever. Fusty old men, peddling fusty old ideas!'

'Exactly.' Walter clicked his fingers. 'You'll see. This poor excuse for a coalition government will be swept aside, and the New Party will reign with Mosley at the helm.'

'Bravo, sir. Good speech.' Sir Hugh stuck his fingers into his mouth and whistled, while the women clapped.

Florrie stifled the desire to shake her head. Sir Richard had increasingly withdrawn from the antics of his wife, brother and sister-in-law since Dame Elizabeth's death in August, and without his calming influence, the three revellers had seemed to burrow deeper and deeper down the rabbit hole of heavy drinking and planning Walter's entry into politics. Lady Charlotte had already held five fundraising luncheons, and ordinarily Sir Richard would have objected to these on cost-saving grounds, but he was distracted by worries about Harding-Bourne Enterprises. The Gold Standard had been abandoned and the value of the pound had plummeted, but conversely, the demand for cheaper British exports had started to increase rapidly (or so he'd explained to Florrie), and he'd spent much of the last two months in his study or in Manchester, at Harding-Bourne Enterprises' head office. When Florrie had broached the subject of the costly luncheons with him, he'd merely sighed deeply and thanked her for keeping him informed.

What she had been pleased to see, however, was that Sir Richard had started to spend more time with his infant son – holding his hands as he learned to walk; reading to him; opting to feed him at mealtimes, whenever Sir Richard was home and could find the time in his busy work schedule. *This lot don't deserve you,* Florrie thought. *And they don't appreciate a single thing you do for them. Thom's right. They're nowt but parasites.*

She handed out the drinks with a smile.

'What will you be voting, Florrie, dear?' Lady Charlotte asked.

Florrie hesitated, 'I haven't decided yet, milady.' She bobbed a curtsey. 'Will that be all?'

Sir Hugh weighed in. 'See, it's people like Florrie you have to win over, Walter. Not everyone's an erudite scholar of Oxford, with a thorough understanding of the various political schools of thought or economic models.'

'Walter certainly isn't!' Daphne giggled.

'Steady on, Daphne!' Walter said. 'Hugh and I were at Oxford together.'

She batted her lashes at him. 'Didn't you say you spent the entire time rowing?'

Walter stood tall and pushed his chest out. 'Most certainly, I did. I'm an Oxford Blue. Coxed pairs. Up at the crack of dawn, built for speed, and with a prodigious drinking ability.' He raised his glass to Sir Hugh. 'Never let it be said that Oxford isn't a preparation for life.'

Realizing that nobody was taking the blithest bit of

notice of her, Florrie slipped out of the drawing room and headed back down to the kitchen, where she found the other staff still sitting around the big table, finishing their puddings and chatting. Even Miss Talbot had deigned to join them, though she sat at the far corner of the table, crocheting and grim-faced.

'By heck, love,' Cook said when she looked up at her. 'Sit yourself down before you fall down. You look fit to drop. What's the matter? Tell Cookie!'

Florrie took her seat next to Thom. She exhaled the breath she now realized she'd been holding. 'It's nowt. Just listening to Sir Hugh and Walter's plans to take over the world, come election day.'

With a raised eyebrow, Arkwright harrumphed and turned the page of that morning's edition of the *Daily Telegraph*. Florrie was certain she heard him say, 'A fool and his money are soon parted' beneath his breath.

At her side, Thom was shuffling cards. 'New Party? That Mosley berk?' He started to dole out cards to Sally, Cook, Danny and two junior gardeners. 'The way things are going in this country with everybody being skint and out of collar, it wouldn't surprise me if they won a few seats.' He offered Florrie a card, which she declined with a shake of her head. 'I mean, people are gullible, aren't they? They'll listen to snake oil salesmen promising them the earth, if they're on their uppers, like. But I hope to Christ—'

'Is it necessary to blaspheme, Thomas?' Miss Talbot snapped.

Thom treated her to a disdainful glance. 'I hope to *high heaven* that British voters have got more sense than to think the likes of Walter Knight-Downey are the answer to their prayers.'

'I reckon that Neville Chamberlain's a right handsome feller,' Cook said, winking. 'He gets my vote.'

Arkwright lowered his paper. 'He's the Chancellor,' he said. 'A weak politician, if you ask me. The Prime Minister, assuming the coalition wins, will be MacDonald again.'

Cook looked miffed. She gathered up the cards Thom had dealt her. 'All right, spoil-sport,' she mumbled.

Arkwright glared at Cook. 'What was that you just said?'

Cook grinned. 'Nowt.' She waved her cards at Thom. 'I've got a good hand here. Better hold on to your hat, sunbeam.'

'Either way,' Thom said, setting his own cards face down and catching Arkwright's eye. 'Mosley and his pals are nowt but posh berks. I wouldn't trust them as far as I could throw them, and having that daft ha'porth Hugh Harding-Bourne getting involved only makes it more obvious to me that the New Party's a bunch of wrong'uns.'

A small, steely voice cut through the warmth of the kitchen chat. 'Perhaps I plan to vote for the New Party,' Miss Talbot said. 'Would that make me a "wrong'un"?'

Clearly irritated, Arkwright folded his newspaper into precise quarters and slapped it on to the table. He locked eyes with the nanny. 'You think Mosley's big ideas about protectionism and imposing high *tariffs* are any way to get us out of the financial mire, do you?' He all but spat the word *tariff*.

'You seem to know a lot about economic matters for a mere *butler*,' Miss Talbot said. She turned back to her crocheting, wearing the suggestion of a smile on her thin lips.

'A mere butler I may be, Miss Talbot, but a financial and political illiterate I am not.' He flicked the copy of the *Daily Telegraph*. 'One doesn't have to be a lord's son, misspending three years at Oxford pickling one's liver in hock, to be able to read and understand the newspaper.'

'Indeed not, Mr Arkwright,' Miss Talbot said. 'But to dismiss those who have had enough of the current government as "daft" or "wrong'uns" . . .' she shot Thom a venomous look, '. . . is to mistake independent thought for stupidity. I'd advise you not to underestimate your fellow common man.'

In the weeks that followed, Florrie watched Lady Charlotte, Sir Hugh and Daphne leave the house daily to help Walter with his political campaign, always setting off in the Ford (at Daphne's suggestion) to make them appear 'normal' to voters. The discussion about who would win the election and what was the best way to drag the country out of the doldrums continued below stairs as soon as dinner was done, though Florrie noticed that the atmosphere was a good deal lighter when Miss Talbot opted to take her meal in her room.

The day of the general election arrived on the 27th October, and Florrie took an hour out of her working day to walk into the village with Mam and the children to cast her vote.

'Who you going to vote for?' Mam asked, as they approached the polling station.

Florrie shrugged. 'I'm torn. I would vote Labour, but they've done a rotten job. I can't vote Conservative because they might look after the Harding-Bournes of this world, but I don't see what they'd do for the likes of us. I suppose it's this coalition, with MacDonald leaving Labour to share power with the Conservatives and Liberals, or nothing.' She shrugged. 'Me and Thom can't afford to get married, whoever gets in. That's the truth of it.'

That evening, the domestic staff sat in the kitchen, listening to Cook's wireless as the results came in. Labour lost seat after seat. The National Government, as they were calling the cross-party coalition, looked set to win. By the time Florrie repaired to her bed, Mosley's New Party had still not won a single seat.

The next morning, she opted to accompany Arkwright to the dining room to oversee breakfast.

'Did you hear them come in last night?' Florrie whispered in the hallway.

Arkwright nodded, giving her a knowing look. 'Steaming drunk, all four of them. There's a dent in the side of the Ford to prove it.'

'So, Walter didn't win?'

'What do you think?'

Suppressing a smirk, Florrie entered the dining room, ready to take egg orders for Cook with a flourish of her notepad, but there was nobody at the table besides Sir Richard. She curtseyed.

'Good morning, sir. I trust you slept well.'

Sir Richard looked brighter than he had done for months. 'Morning, Florrie. Yes, I slept reasonably, thank you. Until my wife returned home with some apparently disappointing political news, that is.' He grinned. 'It seems Mr Knight-Downey was denied his seat in parliament. *Such* a shame.' His mischievous sarcasm was audible. 'But on the bright side, the country won't be sliding into fascism *or* communism any time soon. I, for one, am rather glad about that. And I think I'll celebrate with two boiled eggs, please.'

At that moment, Sir Hugh staggered into the dining room, still wearing his dressing gown. Florrie could smell the stale alcohol emanating from him, even several feet away.

'What a bloody shambles,' he said. He clicked his fingers at Arkwright. 'Get me one of those hangover concoctions that Cook specializes in, will you? I feel like I'm going to die.'

Arkwright bowed. 'Do I take it Sir did not have a successful evening?'

'No. Sir bloody well didn't.'

'Hugh!' Sir Richard admonished his younger brother, but Florrie could see he was grinning behind his cup of coffee. 'Take it easy on poor Arkwright. He's not responsible for the election result.'

Sir Hugh glared at Sir Richard, his face a picture of insolence. 'Isn't he? It's the Lumpenproletariat, casting their vote for that rotter MacDonald, that kept the New Party from victory. So maybe Arkwright *is* responsible.'

'Take no notice of him, Arkwright,' Sir Richard said. 'My brother is looking for a scapegoat to take his frustrations out on.'

Sir Hugh slumped into a dining chair. 'I don't know why I ever thought it a good idea to back that idiot, Walter. I should have stood for election myself, instead of spending the entire summer raising a war chest for a buffoon.' He turned to Florrie. 'Put the wireless on, will you? Maybe some late counts have come in and we won seats that were too close to call last night or something.' He groaned. 'Oh, and get me some toast before I expire.'

Florrie switched on the wireless. By the time she returned with Sir Richard's eggs, the BBC newsreader was updating the nation with the final election results. It was confirmed. The National Government was in power.

'We didn't get a single seat, damn it. What a waste of money, time and effort.' Sir Hugh held his head in his hands.

As Florrie pushed a rack of toast in front of the defeated Sir Hugh, she caught Sir Richard's eye. He winked at her and with a conspiratorial smile, Florrie found herself winking back.

20

'Hutch up, love,' the woman standing next to Florrie said. She pushed a small girl forward. 'My daughter wants to see her father marching.'

'Sorry.' Florrie moved to her right, squeezing up against a stranger with a red nose, whose breath steamed on the cold November air. 'Is that better, darling?' she asked the little girl.

Shivering in an overly short, faded pink coat that looked like a hand-me-down she'd long since outgrown, and wearing a burgundy hand-knit beret, the girl couldn't have been more than ten. She beamed up at Florrie. 'My daddy's a war hero.' Her teeth chattered.

'Is he, love?' Florrie asked, smiling down at her. 'You must be very proud of him. I'm here to see my boyfriend and my boss marching. It's my first time watching the Armistice Day parade. It's very exciting, isn't it?'

The girl waved her Union Jack flag gleefully. 'I'll say! But I hope they start soon because I'm freezing.'

Her mother opened her coat and wrapped the girl inside. 'I'll keep you warm, cocker. It won't be long now.'

In truth, Florrie's toes had already gone numb with the cold. She realized, however, that she had been lucky to get a space at the front of the enormous crowd that had gathered in Manchester's St Peter's Square, especially given how the Rolls-Royce had been stuck in traffic, making the small and unlikely Holcombe Hall Armistice Day contingent – Sir Richard, Thom and her, awkwardly sandwiched between the men – late. In truth, she would have much preferred to travel into Manchester with Thom by train. Given that Lady Charlotte and Sir Hugh had used their recent election disappointment as a reason for spending the day playing golf instead, however, Sir Richard had magnanimously insisted the three of them all travel in the family's car. By the time Graham the chauffeur had driven them to their destination, parking up near Kendal Milne on Deansgate, she'd been only too happy to spend some time on her own. She'd pushed through the throng of thousands of men, wearing their best suits and hats, that had gathered in front of the Town Hall in Albert Square to watch the procession of war veterans. Florrie had wanted to get a spot close to the cenotaph, however, where the wreaths would be laid to commemorate the dead who had fought in the Great War. She had kept pushing and darting into any free space she could find and had eventually worked her way to a plum spot behind the Town Hall, closer to the imposing round building of Central Library and the tall stone cenotaph. Would she be able to spot Sir Richard and Thom?

The march began. She could hear the crowd over in Albert Square cheer as the city's dignitaries and ex-servicemen passed by to the beat of military drums. Before long, the procession snaked its way through to St Peter's Square, and Florrie caught sight of the marching servicemen and veterans. At the front, where the Lord Mayor of Manchester and various aldermen led, she spied Sir Richard approaching on the side closest to her. Her heart pounded a little faster at the sight of the man she'd idolized ever since joining the household, carrying the huge wreath of poppies on behalf of his fallen brother's regiment. Though the crowd would likely not know or care who he was, Florrie knew that sombre, dignified man bore the weight of his family's world on his shoulders. Grief had visibly aged him since his return from India, yet this most dapper man remained heart-stoppingly handsome. Watching him march forward, set the wreath down at the cenotaph and bow, she felt tears prick at the backs of her eyes. Was it empathy she was overwhelmed by, or feelings somewhat stronger than affection for her kind-hearted employer?

Stop it this instant, Florrie Bickerstaff, she chided herself. *You put those misplaced feelings right back in your Pandora's box where they belong, and close the lid tightly.* Florrie looked up to the grey Mancunian skies and blinked her tears away. By the time she turned her focus back to the cenotaph, Sir Richard and the other dignitaries had melted away into the crowds, perhaps to return to the stage in front of the Town Hall, where she had glimpsed Pathé cameras filming for the news.

Groups of ex-servicemen passed – some missing limbs, pushed along in wheelchairs by their able-bodied compatriots. Florrie mused that the procession told a story of the common man's valour in war; the pride, stoicism and selflessness of the British nation; the terrible sacrifice and human tragedy that was the inevitable result of defending one's homeland, values and way of life. Aware that the economic hardship everyone was suffering provided the perfect conditions for unrest and global uncertainty, she said a silent prayer that the menfolk she loved – Thom, her nephew, George, and Sir Richard – would know only peacetime in the future.

'There's Daddy!' the little girl at her side cried. 'Look, Mammy! There's Daddy!' She started to jump up and down.

Florrie was snapped out of her reverie and watched the approaching battalion. She spotted Thom among them instantly by his height and his shock of blond hair, untamed by either Brilliantine or Brylcreem, the new unguent that barbers were using. He too was carrying a wreath, albeit more modest in size than the one Sir Richard had laid.

She waved. 'Thom! Thomas Stanley!' Would he hear her? She could see he was looking around to see who was calling his name. 'Thom! Over here!'

Finally, Thom spotted her in the crowd and blew her a kiss. Florrie flushed with happiness, though not a little guilt, too, that moments earlier she had swooned inappropriately and shed lovelorn tears over her employer. *You're an inconstant fool, Florrie Bickerstaff,* came a bitter, accusatory voice from within her. *You don't deserve a man like Thom. You're toying with him, dangling the carrot and snatching it away. He can do better. If you don't love him enough to marry him, let him go.* Florrie gasped at the vitriol of her inner critic.

'I *do* love him enough,' she said beneath her breath. 'And I can't imagine life without him. What the hell am I doing, dicing with a happy future like this? For what? A stuffy room in somebody else's attic, with a squeaky single bed and a thin mattress?' *Are you forgetting the boon of a pay packet that keeps your nephew and nieces in clothes and shoes?* her inner critic reminded her.

'Did you say something, love?' the girl's mother asked Florrie.

Florrie shook her head. 'No.' She was torn, but she suddenly realized how she might balance her love of and need for her job at Holcombe Hall with her love for Thom.

Buoyed by her epiphany, Florrie pushed forward, closer to the cenotaph. When Thom had laid his wreath, she broke ranks and ran to him.

'Thom!'

He turned around, wearing a bemused smile.

'Let's get engaged,' she said.

'Do you mean it?' he asked, his smile broadening.

She nodded. 'You're the man for me. I'm not saying I want to leave my job and tie the knot right this minute, because I've made a commitment to support our Irene's little'uns. But there's nowt but my daftness stopping us from getting engaged, at least. So if you're willing to wait a while – at least until you get a rise that can cover the money I give Mam, or our George is old enough to earn a few bob. If you'll still have me . . .'

Thom picked her up and swung her around. 'I'll wait for you, Florrie Bickerstaff.' He kissed her passionately. 'The pleasure is all mine.' He looked at his watch. 'Tell you what, let's spend the day in town. We'll have a nice walk round and go to the flicks. Make our own way back to Holcombe on the train. How does that sound?'

'Well, it's Sunday, so everywhere's shut.'

'No, the Deansgate Picture House will be open. Special licence, in't it?'

'Are you sure?'

'Aye.' Thom nodded.

Florrie thought about the prospect of hanging around Victoria Station on a Sunday afternoon, praying for a train that might never come. They certainly had no money for a hotel for the night. 'Because even if the Picture House is open, there's the issue of getting back on a Sunday.'

'Stop worrying, will you?' Thom's brow furrowed. He sighed. 'I know you're in a position of authority at the house and a bit of a blue stocking at heart, but can't you just trust me to take charge and do something nice for you without questioning it?'

Florrie bit her lip. The spontaneous and romantic gesture of accepting Thom's proposal on Armistice Day was not going quite as smoothly as planned, and yet again, she found herself embroiled in a petty battle of wills with Thom. He was clearly keen to fulfil his chivalrous, manly duty as her suitor. Shouldn't she be flattered? Did she have any option but to relent, despite her feeling certain they'd be on a fool's errand, with no transport home? 'Go on, then. Lovely. Let's do it.'

They walked hand-in-hand through the crowds down to Deansgate and found Graham still sitting in the Rolls-Royce by Kendal Milne, waiting for Sir Richard's return. Thom knocked on the window.

Graham wound it down. 'Finished already? Sir Richard's not back yet.'

'We're not coming back with you,' Thom said. 'We'll get the train. I'm taking Florrie here on the town, because guess what . . .'

'You won on the pools?'

'Better than that. Florrie has finally agreed to marry me.'

He put his arm around Florrie and squeezed her tightly, planting a kiss on her cheek. 'What a lucky man I am.'

Graham pushed his hat back and chuckled. 'Blimey. I suppose congrats are in order.' He stared at her stomach. 'When's it due? He he he.'

'Graham!' Florrie snapped amid the chauffeur's mischievous laughter.

'Hey, don't you be casting aspersions on the morals of my missus-to-be,' Thom said, straightening up and puffing his chest out. 'There's no shotgun wedding needed here.'

'Calm down. I were only kidding.' Graham jerked his thumb towards the back seat. 'Though his nibs isn't going to be best pleased if he's got to find another housekeeper so soon after Bertha popped her clogs.'

Florrie nudged Thom aside and leaned down so Graham would hear her over the noise of tooting horns and bicycle bells on the busy Deansgate. 'He won't have to. We're having a *long* engagement.'

'Oh aye? Very modern.'

'And do us a favour. Don't be blurting our news to Sir Richard the minute he sets foot in the car. It's *our* news to tell, and we'll let him know when we're good and ready.' She could feel Thom staring down at her, likely wondering why she was being so cagey about sharing such momentous news. In fact, Florrie could barely articulate to herself, in the privacy of her own thoughts, why she felt so confused and conflicted about announcing the engagement to Sir Richard, let alone explain her reasoning to Thom. She had made her decision though. She knew Pandora's box must be kept shut and locked. 'I don't want to jeopardize my position,' she added.

Thom seemed satisfied with that and kissed her hand. 'Right, we're off to the flicks.' He turned to Florrie. 'Fancy *Night Nurse* with Barbara Stanwyck? You said you wanted to see that, and I noticed when we drove past that it's still showing at Deansgate Picture House.'

Florrie looked around and saw that the cafés were all shut, along with every shop, as was usual on a Sunday. She had committed, however. 'Smashing.' She stood on her tiptoes and stretched up to kiss him on the cheek. 'We can go Dutch if you haven't brought enough money.'

Thom turned away from the chauffer. 'For God's sake, Florrie! Don't embarrass us in front of Graham.' He turned back so that he was once again within Graham's earshot. 'Club together nowt, my darling. This is *my* treat.'

Heading off into the city, Florrie tried to imagine Mam's face when she told her the happy news. She knew her mother would be both delighted and relieved that Florrie had finally committed to a respectable man who would make an excellent husband and father. As they walked towards the cinema, she tried to imagine her future self: an idealistic fantasy of being happily ensconced in a two-up, two-down terrace in Holcombe village, pinning out washing on a summer's day in the back yard, with the green, heather-covered hills rolling in the distance; three small children just like George, Nelly and Alice playing at her feet. Thom would arrive home after a long day's work on the Holcombe Estate, and she would have a hot meal ready for him. Except she didn't recognize the fatigued woman in her mind's eye.

'Are you all right, Florrie?' Thom asked, slowing and looking down at her.

'Why do you ask?'

He held their entwined hands up. 'Your hand's gone all clammy and you started breathing ragged-like. I thought for a minute you were having a funny turn.'

'I'm fine,' she said. 'Come on. We're nearly there.'

Florrie pulled Thom onwards, but as they approached the cinema, she could see, as she had feared, it was closed.

Thom let go of her hand and slapped his thighs. 'Jesus. It's shut. You were right.' He turned around, surveying the street full of Armistice Day attendees ambling along, peering in through the windows of shops that were shut, just for something to do on a Sunday afternoon. 'Damn it. I were sure it were open.'

'Sorry.' Desperate though she was to say, 'told you so', Florrie kept her counsel and looked down at her shoes.

'It's not your fault. It were a daft idea. I got carried away with myself.' He rubbed his chin. 'Do you fancy going for a walk round?'

Florrie stamped her feet to get the blood flowing again. 'Not really, if I'm honest. It's cold. I can't feel my toes.' She narrowed her eyes and looked down the street towards the cathedral's clock tower. She feared the last train back to Holcombe might already have departed. 'We should go back to the car.'

'Aye. Suppose so. Pity.' Thom offered her his arm, and she linked it. 'It's still the happiest day of my life so far,' he said. 'I love you, Florrie.'

She looked up at his smiling blue eyes and traced her finger gently along the crow's feet and the dimples in his cheeks. 'I love you too. And Barbara Stanwyck'll wait.'

Her heart felt a little lighter at the thought of going back to Holcombe, but when they walked past the impressive Victorian frontage of Kendal Milne's and turned the corner to where Graham had been parked, the car was gone.

'No! We're stranded. And we've got nowhere to sleep and no money for a bed for the night.'

The colour drained from Thom's face. 'Bugger it.' He kicked out at the stone façade of the department store.

'Thom! Kicking a wall is *not* going to help us.' Florrie pressed her fingers to her temples. 'Let's just think a minute.' She returned to the main road and peered down towards the cathedral again. 'They're heading north, so they must have passed us when we were walking down to the flicks.' Was that a bottleneck of traffic she saw in the distance? There was certainly a lot of hooting at the traffic lights. 'If they're stuck at that junction and we run, we might catch them up.'

'I'll go on ahead,' Thom said.

Florrie watched him sprinting off into the distance, covering the ground quickly with his long legs. She ran as fast as she could until her chest felt it might burst. *What an ill-fated fiasco this has turned out to be,* she thought. *What the hell am I doing? Why did I try to fix something that wasn't broken?* She cursed as she turned her ankle halfway down the road.

Miraculously, she saw Thom come to an abrupt stop and tap on a window. He had caught it up with the Rolls-Royce. Thom leaned in to speak to someone – likely Sir Richard – through an open window, and then he opened the rear door, holding it ajar for Florrie.

'Madame,' he said, smiling with obvious relief. 'Your chariot awaits.'

By the time Florrie piled on to the back seat next to Sir Richard, she was flustered and dishevelled – still puffing and panting from the sprint.

She glanced at her employer, feeling her cheeks glow hot from more than exertion. 'Sir Richard, you must think we're a right couple of buffoons. We thought . . . Well, it doesn't matter.'

Sir Richard looked as immaculate and debonair as he had at the start of their Armistice Day odyssey. 'It's quite all right, Florrie. Thom has told me all about your little misadventure.' He leaned forward, reaching past Florrie, and offered his perfectly manicured hand to Thom. 'Congratulations, by the way.' He treated him to a brittle smile that didn't reach his eyes. 'You're a very, very lucky man.'

Thom's calloused gardener's hand looked like a shovel next to Sir Richard's. They shook, as if coming to some sort of private agreement that only men were privy to. 'Thank you, sir. I am that. I couldn't ask for a more beautiful, clever and kind fiancée.'

Florrie stared with disbelief at Thom. In her head, she yelled, *You told him, even though we said we wouldn't say anything yet? Doesn't my will count for anything?* Realizing that she didn't want to embarrass either Thom or Sir Richard, however, she merely chuckled. 'It's been quite a day of surprises. We won't be getting married for a good while, mind. So there's no change just now at Holcombe Hall.' She swallowed hard. This was not going as planned at all.

She turned her head and met Sir Richard's gaze. In those grey eyes, she thought she saw a flicker of raw emotion, though she couldn't be certain what emotion that might be.

Good Lord, she thought as they began the long, excruciating journey home. *What have I done? Why can't my life be straightforward like everybody else's?*

21

Christmas Eve 1931

'Good King Wenceslas looked out on the Feast of Stephen,
When the snow lay round about, deep and crisp and even...'

It was Christmas Eve, and the staff had been invited upstairs by Sir Richard for carol singing and mulled wine in the blue room – the reception room he frequently used for entertaining business associates who stayed over at the house. Even as Florrie sang from her sheet, revelling in the warmth from the roaring fire, the heat of the mulled wine in her belly and the glint and glitter of the Christmas tree baubles as they reflected the glow of the lamplight in shades of gold, green and red, she couldn't help reflecting what an odd year it had been.

She was engaged to Thom and now wore his ring. Weeks had passed since Armistice Day, and having given herself a stern talking-to, she finally felt like she was easing into her engagement, just as she might wear in a pair of uncomfortable new shoes. Looking up at Thom, singing along with gusto in his rumbling baritone and merry on wine, she reasoned that he was happy, her mother was happy and therefore all was good in the garden.

Dame Elizabeth had gone, leaving a female vacuum in the Harding-Bourne family that Lady Charlotte couldn't and wouldn't fill. Though Sir William had passed his first birthday and was now toddling around, Lady Charlotte had seemed to withdraw almost entirely from her motherly duties. When she wasn't flying up to Scotland, she was either drinking and dancing to jazz records in the drawing room (as she currently was), or driving down to London with Sir Hugh and Daphne, to attend political soirées held in a bid to revive the flagging fortunes of the defeated Oswald Mosley. Fascism was gaining a foothold in Europe, and Florrie wondered what the committed Conservative, Dame Elizabeth, would make of those strange developments.

And then there was Sir Richard. Florrie studied her employer as he sang from his carol sheet. The colour had returned to his cheeks somewhat, as his mother's burial had started to recede into the past. He seemed to derive great pleasure from spending time with his infant son, much to Miss Talbot's chagrin. Yet Florrie noted how his eyes seemed to have dulled to a deeper shade of grey, as if something had switched off inside him. Was it grief, continuing turbulence in his business fortunes, or Lady Charlotte's increasing detachment?

Thom put his arm around Florrie, jolting her from her contemplative reverie.

'Am I getting a kiss under the mistletoe tonight?' he asked when the singing had come to an end.

'Maybe a very quick one, if you're lucky,' Florrie said, curling into his comforting bulk and laying her hand on his chest. 'I've got to be up at half four to supervise preparations for Christmas Day. And before I even think about getting to bed—'

'My bed or your bed?' Thom whispered in her ear.

Florrie slapped his chest playfully. 'Before I even think about getting to bed, I've got to make sure that Cook's got the turkey in the oven, that the family and staff presents are all nicely arranged under the various trees, and that I've set the presents by for George, Nelly and Alice, ready to drop over to the cottage first thing tomorrow... all the usual malarkey.' She took a deep breath and laughed. 'No rest for the wicked, eh?'

Thom stroked the small of her back. 'Come and be wicked with me. See what Father Christmas brings you.'

Disentangling herself from her amorous fiancé, Florrie caught sight of Sir Richard casting a troubled glance her way. She felt instantly self-conscious and stepped beyond Thom's reach. 'Enough of that now! I've no interest in finding a bun in the oven on Christmas morning, thank you very much.'

She turned to wish her colleagues a happy Christmas, bursting into laughter when Cook chased her around the settee to subject Florrie to one of her notorious bear hugs, which Arkwright had declared terrifying and unnecessary.

'Come here, you bossy little moo,' Cook shouted after her. 'Give Cookie a proper hug.'

'Someone's been at the mulled wine,' Florrie said.

Cook grinned. 'I'm making a beeline for Arkwright next!'

Florrie took her by her meaty arm. 'No, you're not. You're coming with me to put the turkey in, or we'll all be on sausage butties for Christmas dinner.'

In the kitchen, Florrie opted to peel potatoes with Sally, while Cook dressed the giant turkey.

'What's the final count for Christmas dinner, above stairs?' Florrie asked.

'Fifteen,' Cook said, using her fingers to coat the bird with goose fat she'd procured from one of her preserving jars. 'There's the family, obviously, and then they've got that bloody idiot Walter drip-drawers, the big German pillock, Hans von whatsit, some cousin or other of Lady Charlotte and his missus, the Earl of thingy from Tadcaster—'

'Is there an Earl of Tadcaster?' Sally asked, looking up from her poorly peeled potato. 'I think you're making that up.'

'Well, I don't bloody know, do I? Earl of Hell's Waistcoat, for all I care. They've all got silver spoons in their gobs, but they all want feeding Cookie's good grub. And then there's a couple of Sir Richard's business associates from New York and their fancy wives.'

'Yes, they've been here since last Wednesday,' Florrie said, nodding. She smiled. 'It'll be nice to have a decent number of guests around the table. Since Dame Elizabeth passed away and Sir Hugh's political dreams came to nowt, it's been a bit gloomy above stairs.'

'For all the money they've got, they're still miserable,' Cook said.

'Well, it's never gloomy down here,' Sally said. 'Not even with Miss Talbot to curdle the custard with her "Thou shalt not!" cobblers.'

All three of them laughed, and Florrie mused that she

was lucky Thom was willing to wait for her. Every year that she continued to be in service alongside such good women felt like a gift to someone who had started life with so little.

Florrie's eyes shot open some hours later, when her alarm clock rang. Wearily, she made her way to the freezing, utilitarian bathroom that served all the female staff. At half past four in the morning, she knew she would be the only one up apart from Cook, who always rose extra early to bake the day's bread. Giving herself a good strip wash at the sink – a gruesome task when the room was so icy – she then brushed her teeth with toothpowder and combed her no-nonsense bobbed hair, hooking it behind her ears. She looked in the mirror at the shadows beneath her eyes; ran her finger along the fine furrows that were appearing on her forehead.

'Merry Christmas, you old spinster,' she muttered to her reflection. She frowned. 'Why, Merry Christmas, Mrs Stanley!' she said with an American accent, trying to mimic a Hollywood actress. She touched her chin coquettishly, so that she could see her engagement ring in the mirror. No, that didn't sound right either. 'Merry Christmas, Florrie Bickerstaff,' she said in her ordinary Lancashire accent. She shrugged and went on her way.

Padding along the landing on the third floor, where only domestic staff slept, Florrie peered over the banister to the floor below which housed the family's bedrooms. She reasoned that somebody must be awake, since light was coming from somewhere down there. Could she hear footsteps? Perhaps Sir William was restless, and Miss

Talbot was tending to him. Or maybe Sir Richard had risen early and was leaving extra presents beneath the great tree in the drawing room.

Florrie returned to her room and donned her housekeeper's uniform, slipping into a chunky-knit black cardigan that Mam had made her to keep the cold at bay – essential in winter, since the economic downturn demanded they light fewer fires in the house. She took the present she had bought for Thom – a men's grooming kit, with gleaming tortoiseshell handles on the razor, shaving brush, hairbrush and comb – from beneath her bed. She would set that beneath the staff's Christmas tree, which Cook had relegated to the far corner of the kitchen, complaining that it was getting in her way.

Though Florrie was dreaming of a steaming cup of tea and a slice of fresh-baked bread, still warm from the oven, she couldn't resist nipping into the drawing room to look at the haul of presents beneath the tree.

She switched on the light and immediately spied the empty crystal tumblers and gin bottle that had been left on the occasional tables by Lady Charlotte, Sir Hugh and Daphne. They were accompanied by a stinking full ashtray. No matter. The maids would clear the mess up before sunrise, and all would be back to normal. Happily, when she approached the enormous tree that Thom had felled, the stale stink of revelry was replaced by the fresh scent of pine needles. She admired the baubles that the junior maids had hung on the branches and then turned her attention to the brightly coloured packages scattered around the base. She knelt down and started to read the various gift tags attached to the mystery packages.

'*To Charlotte from Richard. To Charlotte from Hugh and Daphne. To Charlotte love Hans xxx.* Ooh, that sounds affectionate.' Florrie raised an eyebrow and continued to read. '*To William, love Father Christmas.* Aw.' She chuckled at the gift tag and the wrapping paper that featured child-like illustrations of the King's Guards, complete with big black bearskin hats and red uniform jackets. 'Very sweet.' She noticed that Sir Richard seemed to have fewer than everyone else. 'Poor man. He makes all the money and gets the least thanks.'

Rummaging at the back, beyond the guests' gifts, she eventually found what she was looking for – what had been left beneath the tree for her to retrieve discreetly, each Christmas since George, Nelly and Alice had come to live with Mam at the gamekeeper's cottage. There were three medium-sized packages, wrapped in delightfully childish paper. The gift tags made out to each child all came, '*With love from Father Christmas*'. Florrie grinned and collected the presents up. There was one more package that caught her eye, however. It was small, as had been the Christmas present she'd received two years ago – the expensive gift of a fountain pen from Sir Richard that she'd felt compelled to return. 'Surely not?' She read the tag, and it simply said in Sir Richard's distinctive hand, 'For Florrie'.

Florrie sighed and sat cross-legged by the tree, knowing she would not be disturbed at this ungodly hour. She looked up at the angel on the top of the tree and rolled her eyes, as if the angel was privy to her frustrations. 'Again! I told him not to.' Hastily, she unwrapped the gift. It was a small, dark green box, its lid inscribed in gold with a name she recognized from the advertising pages of the *Tatler* and Lady Charlotte's copies of *Vogue*, bearing a warrant that marked the company out as jeweller to the King. A note fell out on to the floor.

Reading the message, Florrie felt a maelstrom of emotions tear at her heart. She pressed her hand to her chest.

Dearest Florrie,

My mother wanted you to have this as a token of her gratitude, and I hope you don't find it inappropriate of me to pass it on. You really are our most precious busy bee.

Ever yours,
Richard

'Damn it!' Wiping a rogue tear away, she opened the hard leather box and gasped. Sitting on a black velvet cushion, she found a small but exquisite gold brooch. It was a bee. In the Victorian style, its body was made from large pearls – one round pearl to represent the thorax and one approximately oval-shaped pearl for the abdomen. The creamy lustre left Florrie in no doubt that these were the genuine article. The golden wings were studded with what appeared to be diamonds, and the bee's eyes were rubies. The delicate detail of the golden legs and antennae was rendered in solid gold. 'Flipping Nora. This must be worth a mint. How am I going to explain this to Thom?'

As she re-read the note, she felt herself blushing and couldn't suppress a smile. She was flattered. 'Actually, this is from Dame Elizabeth, so that's fine.' *Isn't it?*

Sliding the box into the pocket of her skirt, she caught

sight of herself for the second time that morning in the mirror above the ornate fireplace. This time, she was positively glowing, and the dark shadows beneath her eyes had disappeared. 'Merry Christmas, idiot.'

Florrie stashed the gifts for her nieces and nephew in the music room's sideboard, which contained a rarely used dinner service and sheet music that hadn't been touched since Sir James had been alive. She determined to nip over to the gamekeeper's cottage with the packages after she'd checked on Cook and before the children woke.

She checked her wristwatch. It was just past five o'clock, and she could hear the domestic staff begin to go about their day. Walking along the hallway with something of a spring in her step, Florrie was just about to make her way to the service staircase when she heard a bloodcurdling cry.

'No! No, no, no!' Upstairs, a door slammed against a wall as if it had been pushed open in haste, and the voice – unmistakably Miss Talbot's – grew louder and more desperate. 'Help! Somebody! Help me!' The nanny appeared, ashen-faced, bending over the balustrade of the galleried landing, wearing a dark grey dressing gown over her nightclothes. Her hair was in a loose braid, dangling over the stairwell. 'Miss Bickerstaff! Come quickly!'

'What's wrong?' Climbing the main staircase as fast as she could, taking the stairs two at a time, Florrie reached the top in time to see Miss Talbot walking briskly into the nursery.

She followed her inside to find her standing over Sir William's cot, clutching her head with a look of abject horror on her face.

'This can't be happening. This can't,' she said, shaking her head.

'I don't understand. What can't . . . ?' Florrie looked into the cot. It was empty. She stared at Miss Talbot. 'Where's the baby?'

Miss Talbot turned to her, tears rolling down her cheeks. 'He's gone.'

'What do you mean, *gone*? Gone where? How can he have *gone*? Don't talk daft!' Florrie hurried out of the nursery and crossed the landing to Sir Richard and Lady Charlotte's bedroom. She knocked and walked straight in, hoping to find the boy with his parents. Perhaps he'd been poorly in the night and Sir Richard had paced the floors with him, finally allowing the baby into the parental bed, rather than have him scream the house down in the small hours of Christmas morning.

She found Lady Charlotte alone in the bed, snoring softly, wearing a black satin sleep mask, with her hair set in demi-wave pins. There was no trace of Sir William and also no sign that his father had slept in the marital bed. The pillows on his side of the bed were plumped and the bedding entirely undisturbed.

Florrie shook Lady Charlotte. 'Wake up, milady!'

At first, she uttered something unintelligible. Then she hastily sat up and pulled off her mask, the ivory satin strap of her nightgown falling off her shoulder. She looked towards the window and then scowled at Florrie. 'It's still dark outside. What ungodly hour is it, and why are you—'

'Never mind that. Where's Sir Richard?'

Lady Charlotte rubbed her eyes and yawned. 'Why? Has something—'

'Where is he?'

'The oriental bedroom. He finds he sleeps better if . . . Wait, is everything all right?'

Florrie didn't pause to explain. She left the master bedroom and ran along the landing to the first guest room, knocked and went straight in. 'Sir Richard! Sir Richard!'

Her employer's eyelid fluttered open. He smiled lazily. Then his smile faltered. 'Florrie?'

Looking beyond him, Florrie could see there was no sign of the baby in the bed with him. 'It's Sir William. He's missing.'

'*What?*' Scrambling out of bed immediately, Sir Richard sprinted barefoot in his pyjamas to the nursery, pushing past Miss Talbot, who was standing in the doorway, white-faced.

Florrie followed him in. 'Is there anywhere else he could be, sir?'

Sir Richard leaned on the cot, clutching the horizontal bar of the side as though he was about to collapse. 'Search the house,' he told Florrie. 'Get everyone out of bed and looking for him. Everyone.' He turned to Miss Talbot. 'How in God's name did this happen?'

The nanny opened her mouth to speak, but nothing came out. Shaking her head, she sobbed and sank to her knees, clasping her hands together in supplication. 'Forgive me!'

'Get up, woman!' Sir Richard shouted. He marched over to her, took her by her upper arm and pulled her to her feet. 'Pull yourself together this instant! There are more important things at stake than your forgiveness. Namely, the safety and whereabouts of my infant son!'

Miss Talbot wailed uncontrollably and his stern expression softened somewhat. He let go of her arm. 'Now, I want you to tell me *exactly* what time you woke, *why* you were up at such an hour, and if you spotted *anything* untoward. Anything at all.'

'Something woke me. A noise. I-I th-thought I heard a strange n-noise coming from the n-nursery,' Miss Talbot stammered. 'So I w-went to check on the b-baby. He often stirs early. And when I p-put the light on and looked in the c-cot, he wasn't there.' She pressed her hand to her mouth and sobbed so bitterly that tears dropped on to the rug.

Florrie approached the cot and looked inside again. She pulled back the baby-blanket that Lady Charlotte had had Mam crochet for him and yanked back the sheet beneath. It was then that she saw the folded piece of paper.

'There's something in the bed,' she cried. 'A note!'

Sir Richard was by her side instantly, snatching up the folded piece of cream paper. He opened it and read its contents, the colour draining from his face.

'It's a ransom note,' he said. With a shaking hand, he held it towards Florrie.

She took the paper from him and read aloud what was typed there. '"If you want your son back alive, you must pay fifty thousand pounds in cash by midday on New Year's Day, or you will never see him again. Further instructions will be given." Oh, my good Lord!'

Though Miles T. Brooke was the first suspect who sprang to mind, she knew that the cream paper bore no resemblance to the pale blue stationery he'd used to correspond with Dame Elizabeth. In any case, it seemed unlikely that, if Brooke *were* Sir Richard's father, he'd abduct his own grandchild. Studying the lettering, Florrie reasoned it looked like it could have been written on any typewriter in the country. A wealthy industrialist might be a target for all manner of extorters, blackmailers and kidnappers. Sir Richard Harding-Bourne was an obvious target among the millionaire few, at a time of desperation and destitution for many.

'"Further instructions will be given,"' she repeated to herself. 'So that means they'll make contact with you again, which could expose them. And if they're after such a large sum of money, I'm sure Sir William will be safe, as long as there's a prospect of them getting paid.'

'How am I supposed to raise that amount of money *in a week*? And over Christmas, too!' Sir Richard clapped his hands to his cheeks. 'Why is this happening? Why, God, why?' he shouted at the ceiling. He locked eyes with Florrie. 'Where is my baby?'

Florrie opened her mouth to respond, but she had no further words of comfort that wouldn't sound empty.

Her employer reached into the cot and took out his son's small blue teddy bear, holding it to his chest, stroking it – a picture of desolation. 'They've snatched my baby boy and they're likely going to kill him, because I can't begin to imagine how I'll raise that ransom, when the bloody bank's closed.' He pressed a fist between his eyes. 'Dear God!' He turned back to Florrie. 'Tell me what to do, Florrie. Please tell me! How can I save my son?' Now it was his turn to sink to his knees and weep.

Florrie crouched down and put her arm around him. 'Come on now, sir. You need to be strong for the baby. We'll get him back, safe and sound. But first, you must telephone the police straight away!' Irritated that Miss Talbot was standing in the doorway, watching their every move and of no practical use whatsoever, Florrie shuffled round so that her back was to the nanny. She took Sir Richard's face in both hands and forced him to look up. 'Look at me! I need you to telephone the police. All right?'

He nodded.

'And in the meantime,' she said, 'I'll have the house and the grounds searched from top to bottom. If Miss Talbot was woken up by the abductor taking the baby from his cot, that's not long ago, and they can't have got far on a private estate.'

22

'I want every single room of this house searched, because we can't afford to make any assumptions that the kidnapper's left the building. And who knows what a clue might look like?' Florrie told the maids gathered in the drawing room, her breath steaming with the cold. The clock on the mantel above the hearth struck six, but in light of the kidnapping and the hullabaloo of the half-hour that followed, when the police had been telephoned and the house's occupants had all been roused from their beds, lighting the fires had not been a priority. 'Every cupboard. Every wardrobe. Keep your eyes peeled. If you find anything untoward, you tell me *immediately*. Do I make myself clear?'

As she gave her orders to the female domestic staff, who were all still yawning, pale-faced and shivering, she heard Arkwright addressing the men.

'Thom, you'll take the gardeners and cover the gardens, the glasshouses, the sheds, the orchard,' Arkwright said.

Florrie glanced over to Thom. He stood to attention like the ex-military man he was, a solemn figure setting an example for the younger men beneath him. 'Aye, I will that,' he said. 'All our normal jurisdiction, then?'

'Yes. Check every nook and cranny for signs of the baby or clues as to who's snatched him and where he might have been taken.' Arkwright cleared his throat and blinked repeatedly, loosening his collar with his finger. 'Beat the long grass and scour the hedgerows, just in case . . . you know.' He then pointed to the gamekeeper and the stable boys. 'You lot cover the stables, the woods, the paddocks, the pastures. Use the horses to cover the distance as quickly as possible, but leave no stone unturned.' Danny and the valets were next to receive orders. 'You lot do all other outbuildings on the estate.'

'Aw, it's Christmas Day, Mr Arkwright,' Danny said, slouching, his shirt untucked and an unlit cigarette behind his ear. 'I haven't even had my first smoke of the day yet. Can't we leave this searching malarkey to the police? It's their job, after all.'

Arkwright glared at him, his left lower eyelid twitching. 'Do you want a felon to escape the estate with a babe-in-arms – the infant son of the man who pays your wages? Or do you want to be the one who catches a kidnapper?'

Danny shrugged.

Arkwright clicked his heels together and barked his orders. 'Look lively, sunny Jim, or you'll be joining the queue for the labour exchange, come the second of January.'

From the corner of her eye, Florrie saw Danny stand straighter and appear contrite. 'Yes, Mr Arkwright. Sorry, Mr Arkwright.' As soon as Arkwright moved on to Graham the chauffeur, she noticed the lad making a rude hand gesture behind the butler's back.

'You're on garaging and cars,' Arkwright told Graham. 'Check no vehicles have been stolen.'

'My garages are under lock and key,' Graham said, folding his arms. 'Nowt gets past me.'

'Well, criminals happen to be adept at picking and breaking locks, so just check, will you? The police will likely look for a vehicle having been driven in and out of the estate. Look for tyre tracks, signs of the gravel being disturbed on the drive, anything out of place.'

'Merry Christmas to you too,' Florrie heard Graham say beneath his breath.

Sensing that there was as much early morning apathy and disgruntlement as there was genuine shock and outrage that a baby had been snatched from the house under their noses, Florrie clapped her hands. She knew that idling and gossip would be the enemy of a fast and successful resolution. 'Everyone report back to me and Mr Arkwright at . . .' She glanced at the clock. 'Seven o'clock at the latest. You've got an hour to complete your searches. Time is of the essence! Off you go!'

The staff members dispersed to search the house and the land it sat in for signs of Sir William and his abductor. Only Florrie and Arkwright remained in the drawing room. Florrie looked at the Christmas tree with all the presents beneath, still unopened. She remembered then that the presents from Sir Richard to her nephew and nieces still sat in the music room sideboard.

'I'll personally search the gamekeeper's cottage,' she said. 'I can go now. I'll run.'

Arkwright had moved to the window and was now peering out. 'No time. A police car is coming up the driveway right this minute.' He turned to face her. 'Listen, I'll take them through to Sir Richard's study and I'll fetch Sir Richard, if you could bring Miss Talbot. Whoever they've sent will definitely want to question those two first . . . and you, of course. But if you could also get Lady Charlotte to join us . . . She's Sir William's mother, after all.'

Florrie's Christmas delivery to her nephew and nieces would have to wait. This was a priority. She would come up with an excuse later, as to why Father Christmas had delayed his visit to the cottage. She nodded.

'How did she take the news?' Arkwright asked.

'Disbelief,' Florrie said. 'At first, at least. She was cross she was being woken up at the crack of dawn. And then hysteria. No idea if she's calmed down since, and I wouldn't blame her if she hasn't.' She shook her head. 'This is a nightmare. I only wish we could wake up and find that baby boy safe in his cot.'

Leaving Arkwright to answer the door, Florrie took a deep breath and climbed the servants' staircase to the first floor. As soon as she neared the master bedroom, she could hear sobbing. She knocked on the door.

'Lady Charlotte? It's me, Florrie. Can I come in?'

From within, there came a strangled, tormented voice. 'Go away. Leave me alone.'

Florrie listened at the door. She could hear Daphne trying to calm Lady Charlotte with encouraging words, but Lady Charlotte was intermittently screaming and sobbing.

'I want my baby! Where's my baby? Get off me. Don't touch me.'

Knowing that the police would still need to question Lady Charlotte, histrionics notwithstanding, Florrie walked in. She found Lady Charlotte kneeling on the floor, her upper body sprawled over the bed. She was thumping the eiderdown. Daphne knelt at her side, rubbing her bereft sister-in-law's back.

'Look, darling. Here's Florrie. She'll have an update.'

Lady Charlotte paused in her angry, wracking sobs, wiped the back of her hand across her eyes and looked sullenly at Florrie. 'Have they found him?'

Florrie bobbed a curtsey. 'No, ma'am, but the police are here. I thought I'd forewarn you so you can get dressed. They'll need to take statements from everyone, and I imagine you and Sir Richard are key interviewees they'll want to speak to, once they've questioned Miss Talbot.'

'How should I bloody know where my son is?' Her face started to crumple anew. 'He's been kidnapped. My baby boy's being held to ransom.' She shook her head, tears rolling down on to her satin nightgown. 'Who could be so cruel? The police shouldn't waste a single moment asking me useless questions. They must get out there and look for him.'

Did she feel sympathy for this cold, self-centred woman who had barely looked at her own baby from the moment she'd given birth? Yes. Florrie decided that even if the only emotion Lady Charlotte was currently feeling was guilt, she would not want to be in her shoes for a single moment. Her son was gone and might never be returned. *It must be hellish*, she thought. *Perhaps all the more so, because she knows if she'd kept more of an eye on Sir William and less of an eye on the limelight, none of this might be happening.*

'I'm sure they just need to piece together the last few hours before his disappearance,' she said. 'They'll have to examine the ransom note and ask you and Sir Richard if you have any ideas who might be behind this. Who might target you for money? Who might bear a grudge against you? Think of it as a puzzle to be completed under timed conditions, milady. If the clock is ticking, it's essential they get off to a good start, and *you* can help them do that. They need you. Your viewpoint could be the key to unlock this terrible mystery.'

Lady Charlotte looked up at her hopefully. 'Yes. I could look for William in my plane!'

Daphne interjected. 'Darling, I sincerely doubt you're going to see a man running through an adjacent field, carrying Willy in his arms. Don't be silly.' She reached out to place a comforting hand on Lady Charlotte.

'Get off!' Lady Charlotte pushed Daphne away. 'And don't call me silly. I'm not a maid.' She got to her feet and turned to Florrie. 'What shall I wear? I need something serious- and studious-looking, don't I? You'll pick the right outfit for me, won't you?'

Florrie knew she needed to find Miss Talbot, but she also realized that denying Lady Charlotte would cost her time in the long run. She strode over to the wardrobe that contained silk pleated skirts and matching tops. 'Here. This is perfect. Now, I really must find Miss Talbot and attend to the police.' She laid the clothes on the bed and left before anything more could be asked of her.

Predictably, Lady Charlotte had turned a manhunt for her missing baby into an opportunity to put herself at the centre of everyone's attention. *Be charitable-minded, for heaven's sake,* Florrie told herself. *I know it's hard in her case, but have a heart! Maybe she does love the baby but just has a funny way of showing it.*

At the door to the nanny's room, Florrie could hear rummaging from within. 'Miss Talbot?'

The rummaging stopped.

'It's Florrie.' There was only silence now. 'Are you all right?' She grabbed the brass doorknob. 'I'm coming in.' Peeking around the door, Florrie found Miss Talbot sitting on the end of the bed looking flustered. Her normally immaculate bun was in disarray and her face was reddened, as though she'd been exerting herself.

'I was praying,' the nanny said.

Florrie nodded. She cast an appraising eye around the room, but everything seemed to be as expected. The bed was made, the few contents of the shelves and dressing table were perfectly neat to the point of being spartan. The only things out of place were a box on top of the wardrobe, where its lid was askew, and the dressing table stool, which was oddly sited in the middle of the bedside rug.

Her gaze settled back on the nanny, who was smoothing her hair flat. 'Come to Sir Richard's study, please. The police are here.'

In the study, Florrie found two young constables and a bald, middle-aged man in a cheap-looking navy blue suit, whose fat, auburn moustache dominated his weathered face. They were all looking uneasy, sitting in the armchairs by one of the windows, beyond the board table, where Sir Richard normally enjoyed drinking whisky with business associates.

'Florrie. Do come in,' Sir Richard said, sitting on the edge of his chair. He indicated that she should take a seat. 'Florrie is our housekeeper. She was the second person to enter my son's room this morning. At which point she discovered . . . Well, she can tell you herself.'

As Florrie took her seat, she realized that Arkwright was also in the study – he had been standing against the wall and had all but blended into the furniture, as was his usual way.

'Shall I arrange tea, sir?' Arkwright asked, stepping forward.

'Oh yes. What a sterling idea.' Sir Richard treated the butler to a wan smile. 'And do have Cook send up some buns or something for the detective here and his men.'

The suited man with the yard brush moustache took a small pad and pencil from his breast pocket. 'That won't be necessary. We're on duty. But thank you.'

'Oh, of course. How silly of me. Yes, yes. So, let us turn to the business of my son's abduction.' Though there were no tears in Sir Richard's eyes, he was markedly pale and the tendon in his jaw flinched. His hands shook so badly that he laced them together on his knees.

'Your wife and the nanny have been told they also need to be present?' the detective asked.

'We're here,' came a voice from the doorway. Dressed in the silk Chanel two-piece that Florrie had selected for her and with no trace of having been weeping uncontrollably only minutes earlier, Lady Charlotte strutted into the study, smiling. She took a seat opposite her husband.

'This is my wife, Lady Charlotte.' Sir Richard barely glanced her way. He looked up at Miss Talbot. 'And our nanny.'

With all the armchairs taken, Miss Talbot pulled out an uncomfortable looking chair from beneath the boardroom table and perched on the edge of it.

The detective nodded at all of them in turn. 'Good

morning, everyone. I am Detective Sergeant Frank Conway, and these gentlemen are police constables, Jefferson and Kemp. We've been sent from Preston Police Station to investigate this very serious matter.'

'I say! That's a long way away,' Lady Charlotte said.

'We're the biggest station in the region,' Detective Sergeant Conway said. 'Which befits a major crime like kidnap of the infant heir to an industrialist fortune.'

'Oh, of course.' She took a handkerchief from her pocket and screwed it into a ball, dabbing at her eye. 'Kidnap. Oh, that dreadful, dreadful word. I can't believe this has befallen us. Will you bring our son home safely?' She smiled weakly.

'That's why I'm here.' Conway remained unsmiling. 'First, the constables are going to conduct their own search of the house.'

'You don't think William's still under Holcombe's roof, do you?' Lady Charlotte asked. 'I gather our housekeeper has had our staff searching high and low already.'

Conway's moustache twitched. 'My lads will comb the place for clues. Fingerprints, footprints, tyre tracks. That sort of thing. A proper police search might reveal who snatched your son, where they may have taken him. Has anyone within the household facilitated the kidnap, et cetera.'

On his orders, the uniformed policemen got up and left with Arkwright.

Conway turned a page on his pad with flourish. 'Now, I'm going to ask some questions on the days and weeks in the run-up to Sir William's abduction, and then exactly what happened this morning, when it was discovered that he was missing.' He stared at them all in turn again. His penetrating amber eyes made Florrie feel like she was being X-rayed. 'I'm going to be asking some personal and searching questions – some of my enquiries will take the shape of formal interrogations in private. Some will be more general, like now, to establish a timeline of events. But I need you all to answer every question I ask honestly and fully.'

The enormity of the situation suddenly hit Florrie. She found herself close to tears at the thought that this terrible story might well turn out to have an unhappy ending. *Please let the baby be all right, God,* she thought. *He's such a lovely, innocent little soul. He doesn't deserve to be torn from the bosom of his loving father – on Christmas Day, too.* Sir Richard would never get over it if he lost his only child. It would kill him. She reached into her pocket and felt the small velvet case that contained the bee brooch. *Please let them find Sir William, dear God.*

Detective Conway interrogated them one by one. 'So, nobody has witnessed anything untoward over the past few days? No strangers on the estate, no odd telephone calls or telegrams or letters? Nobody behaving oddly?'

Everyone shook their head in turn.

'Nothing.'

'Nobody.'

'Not a sausage.'

Conway pointed to Miss Talbot. 'And you were the last person to see Sir William last night?'

'Yes. That's right.'

Sir Richard interjected. 'Not quite right, actually. I popped my head into the nursery at around midnight, when I went to bed. I wanted to wish my son a merry Christmas.' His voice wavered. 'He was perfectly fine then.'

'But he was gone when I went in at five o'clock,' Miss Talbot said.

'What woke you at that hour?'

She frowned. 'Well, I thought I heard noises coming from the nursery, so I got up and went to investigate, to check the baby was well. But there was no sign of him.'

'I came upstairs as soon as Miss Talbot screamed,' Florrie said. 'Around five, as she says.'

Conway scribbled in his pad, addressing Florrie. 'Did you catch sight of anyone out of place after you rose at half past four? Anyone skulking around? Did you hear any noises?'

Florrie shook her head. 'I did my ablutions, first thing. Then, when I got downstairs, I went straight into the drawing room to check the presents under the tree.' She blushed. 'Just to be nosey, like. I didn't see a soul. Didn't hear anything 'til the scream.'

'And after you realized the baby was missing?'

'I went into the master bedroom. Lady Charlotte was sound asleep with her mask on.' Florrie could feel Lady Charlotte's eyes boring into her. Should she mention the separate sleeping arrangement to a man who wasn't a member of the household or its staff? 'Both her and Sir Richard were fast asleep.' Was withholding detail a lie? Technically not, Florrie decided.

Once the timeline of events was established, Conway's brow furrowed. He tapped his pencil on his discoloured teeth. Then he addressed Sir Richard. 'I need you to think very carefully. Is there anyone who might be seeking revenge or trying to get one over on you or the family or your wife, sir? We'll discuss this privately in more detail later, but for now... anything spring immediately to mind?'

Sir Richard shook his head. 'I don't think so. I mean, I've had to lay a lot of staff off recently, and of course, we've had a recent disaster at one of our collieries, where a number of men tragically lost their lives.' He gasped and his eyebrows bunched sorrowfully above his bloodshot eyes. 'You don't think it could be a bereaved family, do you? An eye for an eye or some such?' He rubbed his face. 'Oh, how perfectly dreadful. Now I come to think about it, it could be anyone. A man like me will always have his enemies. *Anyone* could have my boy, and they might be motivated by grief or vengeance.' He choked back a sob and looked to Lady Charlotte. 'That's worse than it being solely about money. Imagine if all you wanted was to take an eye for an eye!'

Conway cleared his throat. 'At this point, sir, I don't think it's helpful to imagine the worst. Let's try to focus on practicalities. You're an industrialist. Do you ever get any trouble from Communists?'

Sir Richard shook his head. 'A bit. I never give them much thought. They're always just trying to stir discontent among the workforce – the workers' unions, you know? But people have to feed their families, first and foremost, so I find being a fair employer usually wins out over the ideologues' offering. Usually. Except strikes do happen. But we've not had any since this Depression started.'

'And what about your brother's political activities? His backing of the New Party. Might that have attracted unwelcome attention from his opponents?'

'Whatever do you mean?' Lady Charlotte asked, clearly affronted. 'My brother-in-law's political affiliations have nothing to do with the disappearance of my son.'

Conway looked back through the pages of his pad. 'But you say you hadn't really seen your son in four days because you'd been in Scotland. And you often travel, you say.' He smiled wryly. 'Not being funny, but how would you know, if you've been away a lot?'

Florrie shifted in her seat and felt suddenly like she wanted to be anywhere but in that study, watching her employers' fallibility be exposed by the harsh glare of Conway's interrogation.

The detective sergeant was staring impassively at Lady Charlotte now. 'You're friends with those Bright Young Things, aren't you?'

She touched her pearls and smiled. 'I don't see what my friendships have to do—'

'Might this be a prank? By one or more of the Bright Young Things?'

'Ridiculous! Be serious, man!' Lady Charlotte had quickly transformed from the heartbroken mother back into her usual imperious self.

'I am deadly serious,' Conway said. 'The sort of life you lead . . . the sort of wealthy industrialist family this is, with royal connections to boot . . . anyone could have taken your son. You're a magnet for ill will, I'm afraid. Unless we turn up a clue during the search, it's going to be devilishly hard to find your son before the kidnappers get back in touch to arrange payment of the ransom . . . whenever that may be. I'm thinking we should have a press conference and get all the newspapers to cover it – conduct a national manhunt between Christmas and New Year.'

'I want this to be kept out of the news entirely,' Sir Richard said. 'Anything that gets printed could jeopardize William's safety, surely.'

'How?'

Sir Richard scowled, clearly agitated. 'If you broadcast that you're conducting a manhunt in a bid to foil the kidnappers . . . well, they're going to think I'm not going to pay, aren't they? What's their incentive to keep my son safe and well then?'

'If I may . . .' Miss Talbot said. All eyes shifted to her. 'Think of the salacious gossip.' She laced her hands together primly and inclined her head towards Lady Charlotte. 'A wealthy household with no real security? A socialite mother who hadn't seen her infant son for days?' She pressed her hand to her chest. 'Clearly, I'm not implying it myself and I know Sir William was well cared for, and that this is highly unfortunate – scoundrels will be scoundrels, after all. But you can imagine that the public will raise the subject of *neglect*.'

Florrie swallowed hard and watched in dismay as Lady Charlotte gasped, her cheeks flushing deep red. Sir Richard's knuckles stood proud as he gripped the arms of his chair.

'Just find my son,' Sir Richard said to Conway. 'Hang the gossip-mongers. I just want my baby back. If you think you need to go public with this, then do it. Whatever it takes.'

23

'Now, I want you to think hard, Miss Bickerstaff,' Conway said, pencil and pad at the ready. 'The list of potential suspects is going to be long as your arm, seeing as we're dealing with rich industrialists, related to His Majesty, but the culprit could be right under our noses.'

Three hours had passed, with neither the staff's nor the police's search of the house and estate yielding any clues at all as to Sir William's whereabouts. Now, the detective sergeant was sitting at Arkwright's desk in the butler's office, which he had requisitioned for the purposes of questioning staff individually, behind closed doors. The Harding-Bournes and their guests had already been interviewed privately above stairs, of course.

'So, is there *anyone* under this roof ... staff *or* family members — airs and graces and fancy titles don't cut the mustard with me — anyone that you think might be involved in the child's abduction? Acting fishy, maybe, or with an axe to grind?' He exuded an air of absolute authority.

Florrie sat a little straighter, considering her answer. She had nagging suspicions surrounding two people: The first was Miles T. Brooke — a blackmailer who might feasibly be involved in this most cynical of skulduggery, even though Sir William was his grandchild. The second was Miss Talbot — the nanny boasting perfect references, who had appeared seemingly out of nowhere and had managed to bend the entire household to her will. Yet Florrie had no evidence whatsoever that Miss Talbot was anything beyond unpleasant and bad at her job. And sharing the letters between Dame Elizabeth and Brooke, on the off-chance they had a bearing on the kidnapping, would be tantamount to lobbing a grenade into the heart of the Harding-Bourne dynasty. Sir Richard would lose his position as the head of the family and its businesses to the profligate Sir Hugh, to disastrous effect. Thousands of HB Enterprises workers would join the ranks of the jobless, and their families would starve.

Should I speak up now, or do a little digging myself, first? she wondered. *There's a lot at stake.* She thought about her predecessor. *Bertha Douglas would have got to the heart of this mystery in a jiffy. Maybe I can too.*

'Er, let me think . . .' She scratched her chin, feeling a nervous rash itch its way up her neck to her face.

The life of a child hung in the balance, but Florrie reasoned she could allow herself one day to conduct her own investigation. If she solved the riddle of the abduction without having to hand over those letters, she could potentially save the boy, protect the reputation and status quo of the Harding-Bournes, and in doing so, safeguard the livelihoods of their thousands of employees.

She shook her head and bit her lip. 'Sorry. I can't think of owt. If something comes to me, I'll let you know straight away.'

As soon as Miss Talbot was called in to speak to Conway, Florrie marched through the kitchen, excusing herself from Cook, who was drunk, not just on Christmas port, but also on the scurrilous news that Sir William had been snatched from beneath his parents' and nanny's very noses.

'But Florrie! You haven't told me what that detective wanted to know,' Cook was speaking slowly and deliberately, but her intoxication was plainly audible in every slurred consonant. 'I need consoling. I've got a staff Christmas dinner here that's drying up in the oven, and them upstairs . . . the guests all buggered off after breakfast and the family's eaten nowt. I'm in the doldrums, our Florrie. I need you to give me juicy updates.'

'I've just got to nip over to Mam's,' Florrie lied, waving her away. 'I'll be back.'

'Your mam's is the other way.'

Ignoring Cook, Florrie hastened to Miss Talbot's room, next to the nursery, calculating that she'd have a good twenty minutes to herself, since Talbot was a key witness. Checking that nobody was watching her, she slipped inside the large bedroom. It was far grander than the rooms that the other staff slept in – unsurprisingly, since the nanny had to be next door to the nursery in case the baby woke in the night. Where furnishings were concerned, however, it contained the same sort of cast-offs that the rest of them had – a basic oak bedroom suite that had been brought up from the cellar full of disused old furniture, and a cast-iron single bed with a thin mattress. It wasn't the sort of room that held secrets.

Her attention was immediately drawn to the box on top of the wardrobe, whose lid was awry. She took out the stool, which had been shoved back in the kneehole of the dressing table, and carried it over to the wardrobe. Climbing on to the stool, she took the lid off fully, took hold of the box and lifted it down to the floor, disturbing a cloud of dust as she did so. Florrie sneezed twice in a row. She froze, listening to the sounds of the house to check her sneezes hadn't attracted unwanted attention. Satisfied that she would remain undisturbed, she peered inside.

'Is that it?' she whispered beneath her breath.

The box contained only an old bible that was falling apart and some summer clothing – all black or white, and all austere, fashioned from cheap fabrics – which had been folded and stored for the next year. Disappointed, Florrie returned the box to the top of the wardrobe, careful to leave the lid half on.

'Where next?'

She had heard Miss Talbot rummaging before she'd walked in, and the woman had been sitting on the end of the bed. Florrie knelt on the rug, lifted the bedspread and peered beneath the bedstead. Nothing but floorboards thick with dust and a dead spider or two. *Eugh! Dirty. I'll have to have a word with the maid that cleans in here,* she thought. She flipped the rug up. There was nothing beneath. She lifted the bedspread up. It hid no secrets between the layers of bedding.

'Damn it.'

Turning her attention to the tallboy and the dressing table, Florrie rifled through the drawers. When they revealed nothing but utilitarian undergarments, two sweaters, a cardigan, a comb, a hairbrush and a washbag containing only soap and a nailbrush, she checked carefully that nothing had been stuck to the backs of the drawers.

'This doesn't ring true,' she muttered. 'This woman has no personality, no history, nothing.'

The wardrobe revealed nothing apart from two sack-like black pinafore dresses and a black skirt. One spare pair of slip-on shoes and a pair of well-polished button-up boots, that were a good thirty years out of vogue, sat on the bottom.

Checking her wristwatch, Florrie saw she was almost out of time. What was left? Barely anything. She looked behind the curtains and the one picture on the wall – a framed embroidery of a psalm. There was nothing. There was no evidence of anything being affixed to the underside or back of any of the furniture. Miss Talbot's reputation remained untarnished. Either the spartan room was hiding her secrets spectacularly well or else the nanny had nothing to hide but terrible taste in clothes, a complete disinterest in anything but religion and an attitude that could poison the trout in Holcombe's lake.

'This is a waste of time,' Florrie said.

She slipped out of the nanny's bedroom and padded along the first floor, past the family's bedrooms. When she came to the master bedroom, where Lady Charlotte had evidently been sleeping alone for some time, she heard voices beyond the closed door. It was Lady Charlotte and Hans von Grunwald.

'Didn't Richard say it would be kept out of the newspapers at all costs?' von Grunwald said.

'You heard that oaf, Conway. And you heard Richard.' Lady Charlotte sounded distraught and resentful. Gone was the familiar nickname, 'Dickie'. 'They're holding a dratted press conference in the ballroom tomorrow morning. It's all arranged, apparently. Everyone's coming. *The Times,* the *Daily Telegraph,* the *Manchester Guardian,* the *Observer, Pathé News!*'

'That's good, isn't it? The more word gets out, the sooner they will find William. Someone is sure to spot him if they print his photograph.'

Now Lady Charlotte raised her voice. 'I don't want my son on the front page! And *I* don't want to have to sit there, in front of the country's journalists, being framed as the world's worst mother. Hell! Maybe they'll ferret out what we've been up to.'

'But this is not your fault, darling. And it's not about you or me. This is about getting your boy back home, safe and sound in time for New Year.'

There was a growl of frustration from Lady Charlotte. 'Damn it. I need a drink. I'm going downstairs. I'm going to open my bloody presents and get steaming drunk until I can't feel my own face. Later, if Richard and the police aren't breathing down our necks, you can join me in bed and make me forget my horrible existence for twenty minutes. Now, get out of my way!'

Realizing she was about to be caught eavesdropping, Florrie slipped into the adjacent bedroom, which one of the guests had just vacated. Her heart thudded inside her chest. She'd had her suspicions about Lady Charlotte and von Grunwald, but now she was certain they were having an affair, right under Sir Richard's nose. Did her employer realize what was going on? When she felt confident that the coast was clear, she opened the door and walked straight into Miss Talbot.

Florrie yelped. 'Flipping Nora! What the heck are you

doing, standing right outside that door like that? Creeping Jesus!'

Miss Talbot eyed her suspiciously. 'Any particular reason you're prowling the first floor, Florence?'

Florrie swallowed hard. Then she realized Talbot was just searching for a weakness she could exploit. Florrie stuck her chin out defiantly. 'I'm the housekeeper. It's my job to check the bedrooms after guests have departed. But I'm surprised you're not spending Christmas Day in silent prayer for forgiveness, seeing as you didn't do your job properly.'

Miss Talbot's eyes widened and she inhaled sharply. Before the nanny could find a riposte, Florrie hastened back downstairs.

She had only just descended the servants' stairs and was en route to the warmth and relative safety of the kitchen, when she heard a commotion.

'It weren't me! I didn't do owt. Let go! You're hurting me.' Danny's voice resounded throughout the ground floor.

With the blood rushing in her ears, Florrie ran to the entrance hall – the source of the hullabaloo. There, she caught sight of Danny, scuffling uselessly on the slippery marble floor. He was being strong-armed by the two uniformed police constables towards the front door.

'Hey! What's going on here?' Florrie asked.

One of the uniformed constables turned to her. 'We've already explained to the butler. We're taking this young man in for questioning at the station.'

'Why? What's he done?'

Danny kicked out at his captors, turning the air blue with his insults.

The constable gave Danny a good shove. 'That's quite enough of that language now, lad! There's a lady present.'

Shooting Florrie a venomous glance, Danny laughed nastily. 'She in't a lady. Did she say summat about me? Don't listen to her. She's a cow!'

The constable retrieved a set of handcuffs from his person and cuffed the struggling, belligerent valet. He shouted over his shoulder to Florrie. 'This is a police matter, madam. Leave this to us.'

Open-mouthed, Florrie watched as the two policemen bundled a wriggling and protesting Danny out through the door and down the stone steps to the waiting police car.

Arkwright appeared at her side, just as she was watching the policemen pushing Danny into the back of the vehicle.

'It's turning out to be quite a Christmas,' the butler said. He sighed deeply.

'What was all that about?' Florrie asked.

Arkwright closed his eyes, his mouth arcing ruefully downwards. 'I have no idea. Truly. One minute, young Danny was being interviewed by Conway in my office, the next . . .'

'So, you don't even know if he said anything incriminating or not? They're taking him . . . what? On a whim? Or do they think he's somehow involved in the kidnapping?'

Arkwright shook his head. 'I suspect he gave Conway a mouthful. You know what Danny's like. His attitude was always going to get him into trouble at some point. I should have sacked the boy years ago. He hasn't warranted all the chances I've given him.' He clasped his hands behind his back and started to walk back towards the grand staircase. His stooped shoulders were those of a defeated man.

Florrie paused to look up at the portrait of the late Lord Harding-Bourne – an informal painting of the kindly patriarch towards the end of his life, pictured in a relaxed sitting pose, his dog at his feet. She offered a silent prayer of gratitude that he had not lived to see this shocking domestic debacle take place beneath the roof of his beloved Holcombe Hall. The world felt as if it was falling off its axis. How could she, a humble housekeeper, rectify it?

'Wait!' she called to Arkwright, walking after him. 'You can't just let them arrest staff without knowing why. I mean, if Danny *is* involved, and you didn't see it coming, that'll reflect badly on you – on all of us. Ask Conway! Maybe they found damning evidence in his room when they did that search.'

Florrie burned with frustration as Arkwright continued on to the kitchen stairs without showing any sign that he'd even heard her. Why was he being so laissez-faire about the arrest of his valet?

She ran to catch him up and placed a hand on his back. 'What's going on? Are you all right?'

Arkwright shrugged her off. He came to a standstill and finally turned to face her. 'I'm tired, Florence. It's Christmas Day, and instead of enjoying dinner around the kitchen table, pulling crackers and wearing silly paper hats and cracking jokes like the below-stairs family we are, the household is burning down around us.'

'I know, but—'

'An innocent child has been abducted from his bed, sowing discord and suspicion among the staff and family members. That child's mother happens to be a wayward alcoholic, who is cuckolding her husband with a German fascist beneath his very roof. Her brother-in-law is a spendthrift buffoon, who rubs shoulders with the scum of politics. By the time the papers hit the newsstands on the twenty-seventh, the Harding-Bournes will be front-page news for all the wrong reasons.' For the first time since the memorial tree-planting that Sir Richard had held for Mrs Douglas, tears stood in Arkwright's eyes. 'I think maybe it's time for me to retire.'

Florrie absorbed the enormity of what Arkwright had said. The butler who had once ruled below stairs with a rod of iron had given up, just when Sir Richard needed him to be strong. 'Pull yourself together, for heaven's sake!' She was taken aback momentarily by her own outspokenness, but quickly realized she was right. 'We need to present a united front. You said it yourself: we're a family. We've got to pull together to get through this. It's not just them lot who will suffer if this thing goes sideways . . .' She jerked her thumb in the direction of the family's reception rooms. 'It's us lot, too. Bertha used to tell me we had to be like swans. Elegant on top and paddling like billy-oh beneath the surface. *You've always told us that!* Time to take your own advice. So, shake off your self-pity. Let's get to the kitchen and see if Cook has any information, or perhaps Conway will tell us why Danny's been carted off in a Black Maria.'

They headed to the kitchen together – Arkwright sheepishly following Florrie down the servants' stairs – and found Cook arguing with Conway.

'I absolutely was not earwigging at the door!' Cook said, red in the face with arms folded.

'Madam, you were,' Conway said. 'And if you call me a liar again, I'll have *you* arrested for obstructing justice.'

His stern words seemed to flip a switch inside the defeated Arkwright. Suddenly, the butler stood tall and marched into the fray. 'If the domestic staff are complicating your investigation, Detective Sergeant Conway, I'd rather you deferred to Miss Bickerstaff and myself to have a word with them. It sounds rather like Cook, here, was just concerned about your arrest of a younger member of staff and was feeling discombobulated – as are we all.' He held his hands up. 'There's no need for threats of arrest simply for staff members being upset. We're all understandably upset.'

Conway eyed Cook warily, but his expression gradually softened when faced with the resolute-looking Arkwright. Eventually, he nodded. 'Fine. But for your information, my officers found revolutionary propaganda in that valet's room that justifies our questioning him further at the police station.' He smoothed his finger over his moustache.

'Since when has it been a criminal offence to be in possession of political pamphlets?' Cook asked, hands on hips. 'Assuming that's what you've found.'

Conway sighed. 'Communists are a threat to national security. They strongly oppose the monarchy, for a start, and given her ladyship is a minor Royal . . . Think of what the Reds did to the Russian Tsar and his family.' He raised an eyebrow. 'It wouldn't be the first time a Commie had done something unlawful to draw attention to their cause or disrupt the status quo.'

'So there will be no need for a press conference?' Arkwright asked. 'You think you've found your man?'

Conway shook his head, his bald pate gleaming beneath the harsh kitchen light. 'Oh, we're far from having tied up this case, Mr Arkwright. Even if Daniel is involved as an accomplice, the kidnapper himself is still at large, and the little boy is still missing. The clock, meanwhile, is ticking. No. The press conference still goes ahead tomorrow morning.'

24

'Right, you lot,' Florrie said to her team as Boxing Day dawned. They were all gathered in the kitchen to be briefed ahead of the press conference. Florrie could feel the fatigue and stress from the previous day weigh her down, as if her bones had turned to lead. Surveying the sea of exhausted faces before her, it looked like her staff members all felt the same. 'At ten o'clock, we'll have the country's top journalists arriving. I want them all ushered through to the ballroom. None of them are allowed *anywhere* else in the house, so if you spot some feller trying to sneak into the other reception rooms or upstairs, get one of our lads to escort them out.'

Agnes was the first to put up her hand. 'Miss Bickerstaff, if there's kidnappers hanging around, are us lot in danger and all?' Her eyes darted to the others at her side, who were all nodding vehemently. 'I mean, if Danny's been arrested and that . . . might there be accomplices still in the house? Among the lads?'

Florrie could see the girls had all been discussing the drama, and she was hardly surprised that they were all feeling nervous. In truth, she had also been horrified, not just by the kidnapping but also by Danny's arrest. Was it possible that a colleague who, it turned out, was a budding Communist in his free time, could have spent the last year planning to abduct his employer's infant son and hold him to ransom? And if Danny *was* in cahoots with a gang of revolutionary kidnappers, might Brooke's scandalous correspondence with Dame Elizabeth remain a secret after all? Brooke struck Florrie as an opportunist without morals, but she thought it unlikely he was part of some Communist cabal.

She felt the girls' eyes on her. 'Look, I have no idea what lines of enquiry the police are pursuing. Danny's annoying as heck, but none of us have ever suffered anything beyond insults and cheek from him. And *we're* all skint, so I don't think we're targets for any kind of extortion racket or ransom demand or suchlike. Rest easy, girls, and remember, our priority is to get Sir William back, and your job today is to protect the privacy and dignity of the family. Right?'

'Yes, Miss Bickerstaff,' the girls answered in unison.

'What about that prat of a detective?' Cook asked. She was already behind her kitchen table, stuffing sprigs of rosemary into a large joint of lamb for the family's Boxing Day lunch. 'I don't like him. He's a pigging big bully, that one. He'd better keep out my road or else.' She picked up the entire leg of lamb and brandished it in the air, much to the young maids' amusement.

'I thought you were going to knock his block off yesterday, when he copped you earwigging at the door,' Sally said, tittering.

Cook smiled mischievously. 'Aye. Well, there's time yet, if he doesn't watch himself. The bigger they are, the harder they fall. It's not called Boxing Day for nowt.' She flexed her right bicep and guffawed.

Under normal circumstances, Florrie might have laughed

heartily at Cook's show of bravado, but with a baby torn from the bosom of his family at Christmas, she knew it was a time for seriousness. 'Enough of this nonsense, ladies. You've all had your orders. Be courteous and comply with the police, please . . .' She eyed Cook pointedly. 'And keep those snooping journalists out of the family's private business.' She clapped her hands. 'On with the motley!'

The microphone's squeal reverberated around the ballroom, where around fifty of the country's leading journalists had gathered for the press conference. On his arrival at the house earlier that morning, Conway had told her most of them had driven overnight from London to make the gathering. The kidnapping of the heir to an industrialist fortune and a not-too-distant relative of the King was national news.

Now Florrie stood by the door to the ballroom, watching the detective sergeant get to grips with the public address system which had been hired in haste from the singer of a local jazz band in Holcombe village.

'Apparently, every house in the village has turned into bed and breakfast accommodation overnight to make a quick killing off this lot,' Thom said, appearing at Florrie's side. He surreptitiously put his arms around her, beneath her cardigan. 'Did you open your present from me?' He nuzzled her ear.

Florrie broke free of his embrace. 'Sorry, love,' she whispered. 'I haven't had time, what with all that's going on.'

Her fiancé looked crestfallen. 'Oh, that's nice. All that thought I put into getting you the perfect gift, and you can't even be bothered to open it. I thought we could unwrap our presents together. Just me and you on the hearthrug, in front of a roaring fire . . .' There was hurt in his eyes.

Florrie felt guilty for rejecting him. 'Look, I'm sure whatever you've got me is lovely. And I've still got your gift in my room. I'll give it you when the dust settles, I promise. But this really isn't the time for talk of a romantic Christmas present exchange, love.' She discreetly shooed him away, blowing him a kiss by way of recompense for pouring cold water on his misplaced festive advances. 'I'll find you later, all right?'

She turned back to Conway and the press conference.

At the front of the ballroom, Sir Richard and Lady Charlotte were seated behind a table, with microphones set up in front of them. To the side, the Pathé News cameras were rolling, filming every word spoken, every question asked and answered, every telling nuance in the distraught couple's behaviour. Florrie noted that Lady Charlotte had a vacant look about her. She kept glancing over at Hans von Grunwald, who still hadn't returned home to Germany, despite the other guests all leaving on Christmas Day as soon as Conway had spoken to them. *Brazen!* Florrie thought. But she was sure it was the last thing on Sir Richard's mind.

Conway started to speak. 'Gentlemen, early on Christmas Day morning, the infant heir to the HB Enterprises fortune, Sir William Harding-Bourne, was found by his nanny, Miss Fanny Talbot, to be missing from his cot at Holcombe Hall, Lancashire.' He went on to mention the discovery of the ransom note.

Florrie noticed that he didn't mention the arrest of Danny, but he did introduce Sir Richard.

Now, everybody's attention turned to the beleaguered industrialist father of the abducted baby. Judging by the shadows beneath his eyes – dark enough to appear like bruising – Florrie could see he hadn't slept a wink. She felt empathy and affection churn inside her as she watched his Adam's apple rise and fall.

'Good morning. Thank you all for coming.' The microphone whistled, but Sir Richard was undeterred. He leaned in. 'My son, William, is fifteen months old. He has my wife's eyes and my nose, and his favourite colour is red.' His voice started to falter. 'William has brown hair with a slight curl to it. He has recently started to walk on his chubby little legs, and he likes cheese on toast. His favourite farm animals are cows.' He inhaled and looked up at the ornate ceiling, ignoring the hands in the air and the calls for questions from his audience. He leaned back in towards the microphone. 'My darling boy is out there somewhere. He was snatched from his cot by someone who apparently only wants money.' He looked into the Pathé camera. 'Please, if you have William, bring him home safely. He's a lovely little chap with a sunny disposition. If you're desperate and poor ... maybe you're a disgruntled employee or the family of a miner from an HB colliery and maybe your father lost his life in an accident in one of my mines or was laid off at one of my factories or shipbuilding yards.' He swallowed visibly and his lips seemed to tremble. His voice cracked. 'I am so sorry for what this Depression has reduced you to. But I need you to expedite the safe return of my son to the loving bosom of his family. You will be shown leniency.' He turned back to the journalists, who had fallen silent now. 'Alternatively, if you're a member of the public and know anything about my son's abductors or whereabouts, please contact the police immediately and pass that information on. I will personally give a reward of one thousand pounds to anyone who can assist in his safe return before New Year's Day. Thank you. That is all . . . Merry Christmas and a Happy New Year.' He added the festive wishes in a small, thin voice.

A ripple of surprise thrummed around the ballroom. Florrie could hear pencils scratching on reporters' pads.

'Lady Charlotte. Would you like to add anything?' Conway asked.

Florrie watched as Lady Charlotte stared blankly out at the audience. She smiled uncertainly. 'One can't believe this has happened to a family like ours . . . at Christmas too! The fabric of this country is in tatters. Tatters, I tell you!' Was she slurring? She pressed her hand to her chest. 'I am bereft.' She continued to speak, but now she was practically shouting into the microphone, and it squealed back angrily. Florrie could only make out 'my cousin, His Royal Highness, the King' among her apparently drunken babble. She finally fell silent and blinked slowly at the journalists.

Hands immediately started to shoot up. Some men got to their feet.

Conway pointed to a rail-thin older man with a stern face who looked like he only drank coffee and smoked cigars. 'You!'

He announced himself as a senior reporter from *The*

Times. 'Lady Charlotte, is it true that your son was an easy target because you're famously an absent mother?'

Sir Richard grabbed the microphone, frowning. 'My wife will *not* answer that question. This is a press conference to ask the nation to look for my son, to appeal to the kidnappers' better nature to hand him back. It is *not* an excuse for the nation's journalists to have a scurrilous field day at my family's expense.'

Another reporter stood and shouted. 'What about your brother's association with known fascists and your living in the lap of luxury while your miners lose their lives? Could this abduction be politically motivated?'

Florrie clasped her hand to her mouth as the reporters quickly degenerated into a pack of ravening wolves, rounding on and then savaging their prey. Flashbulbs popped everywhere, and Sir Richard and Lady Charlotte blinked in their light, shielding their faces from both the glare of the cameras and the journalistic scrutiny.

At last, Conway stepped in, holding his hand up. 'Er, I'm drawing this press conference to a conclusion, gentlemen.' He cleared his throat and his moustache twitched. 'I'd ask you to focus on the fact that a babe-in-arms is somewhere out there, alone with strangers, terribly afraid and missing his family. You've all been given copies of little Sir William's photo to publish, and details of the telephone number members of the public should call if they have information.' He hooked his fingers around the braces holding up his trousers, raising an eyebrow. 'Now, please remember that libel is *against the law*, and kindly leave the Hall in an orderly fashion.'

As the excitable journalists got to their feet, still clamouring to get an exclusive quote from the Harding-Bournes, Sir Richard locked eyes fleetingly with Florrie. Then he dropped his gaze, his shoulders slumped. He looked like a broken man.

25

The following morning at the start of the working day, Florrie found Arkwright in his office. Daylight was still hours away, but the immaculately groomed butler was already sitting behind his desk, writing in his ledger by lamplight. She could smell the black coffee that still steamed in a cup, carefully set atop a crocheted doily to save the French polished surface of his old mahogany desk.

'Good morning, Florence,' he said, setting his pen down and taking a sip from his drink. 'Did you sleep?'

'Not really,' she admitted. 'I had that press conference on my mind all night. Tossing and turning, I was.' She'd also spent a good half-hour staring at the pearl, ruby and diamond bee brooch that Sir Richard had left for her beneath the tree. Feeling the gift was too lavish to explain to Thom or any of the other staff, for that matter, she'd hidden the small box inside one of her spare shoes. There would be a time to wear it, but that time was not now. 'Did you sleep?'

He shook his head. 'Not a wink.'

'Any news on Sir William overnight?'

He shook his head.

'Have the papers arrived?'

Arkwright screwed the lid on his fountain pen. 'Yes.'

'And?' Florrie's gut tightened as she anticipated what might have been written in the press about the family.

Reaching up to the top of the bookcase behind him,

Arkwright took up three broadsheet newspapers, which were already ironed and placed on reading sticks. 'It's not good, I'm afraid. They've really gone to town on Lady Charlotte, especially.'

Florrie took *The Times* first. The story of the kidnapping was headline news. She sat in the visitor's chair to read what had been written.

'Read it aloud,' Arkwright said. 'I only skimmed it first time around because it was so . . . You'll see.'

Florrie started to read.

'"HARDING-BOURNE HEIR KIDNAPPED: KING'S RANSOM DEMANDED

On Christmas morning, multi-millionaire industrialist Sir Richard Harding-Bourne discovered that his infant son, Sir William, had been snatched from his cot at the family's Lancashire seat, Holcombe Hall. A ransom note demanding payment of £50,000 with a deadline of 1 January 1932 had been left among the bedding.

"The police have begun a nationwide hunt for Sir William and encourage anyone who spots the boy (shown in the photographic portrait taken at his first birthday party) to call the dedicated telephone number given at the end of this article, to report sightings at their local station, or to send a telegram to Preston Police Station for the attention of Detective Sergeant Conway – the man who solved the case of the Thrupenny Bit Murders in 1927."

'Seems all right so far,' she said.

'Go on,' Arkwright said, taking a gulp of his coffee. 'It quickly changes tone.'

Florrie continued.

'"At the press conference, Sir Richard spoke movingly about his son."' She looked up. 'He did, as well. I were almost in tears.'

'Florence, concentrate on the task in hand, for heaven's sake! Read!'

Exhaling sharply, Florrie went on . . .

'"He admitted that as a wealthy industrialist, having to lay off thousands of workers during a global depression, his family was always a likely target for those with criminal proclivities or suffering from destitution, brought about indirectly by his business decisions. The Harding-Bournes invested in Clarence Hatry's fraudulent steel merger back in 1929 – considered by expert economists to be the catalyst for the Wall Street Crash, ushering in the Depression. Hatry was tried and convicted of fraud, and is now serving a fourteen-year prison sentence, though Sir Richard Harding-Bourne and those who paid for Hatry's defence have evaded fraud-related prosecution.

In another disastrous turn of events for the Harding-Bourne business empire, seventeen men recently lost their lives at the company's colliery in Lancashire after the collapse of a mineshaft. It took Sir Richard several days to visit the mine, accompanied by HRH the Prince of Wales, to offer condolences to the dead miners' families."'

She looked up at Arkwright again. 'Oof.'

Arkwright simply nodded sagely. 'Go on.'

Finding her place, Florrie continued to read aloud the report of Dame Elizabeth's death and funeral, which had delayed Sir Richard's visit to the mine. 'Hey, get this! "The reception at Holcombe Hall afterwards was said to have cost, *'a small fortune'*, according to an anonymous staff member."' She frowned in concentration. 'Who do you think revealed that titbit?'

'My money's on Miss Talbot,' Arkwright said.

Florrie looked back down at the dense column inches. 'Ooh, this next bit's . . . It's about her nibs. "At the press conference yesterday, Sir Richard's wife, Lady Charlotte, appeared to be intoxicated."' She snorted with wry laughter.

> '"She had not seen her son for *four days*. Lady Charlotte has regularly appeared in *Tatler* magazine and is part of the more recently pilloried 'Bright Young Things' social scene, rubbing shoulders with the likes of Evelyn Waugh and the singer Daphne le Montford, who last year married younger Harding-Bourne brother, Sir Hugh. Youngest of the three Harding-Bourne sons, Sir Hugh recently raised funds to back Bright Young Thing Walter Knight-Downey as a parliamentary candidate for Oswald Mosley's failed New Party. None of the New Party's fascist-leaning candidates succeeded in winning seats in the recent General Election, where the coalition government, led by Ramsay MacDonald, won by a strong majority.
>
> "Given that Lady Charlotte Harding-Bourne is related to HRH King George V, the stakes are high in the kidnapping. In light of the Harding-Bournes' considerable wealth, status and power, which persists at a time when families are starving in our cities and living in rat-infested slum dwellings, it is perhaps apposite that aspersions have been cast on the hedonistic behaviour, profligacy and political allegiances of Lady Charlotte, Sir Hugh and his wife, Daphne. Questions are also being

asked as to how an intruder managed to snatch a baby from his bed without the alarm being raised."'

Florrie pressed her lips together and sighed. 'Well, quite. I still can't believe someone snuck in and took the baby on Christmas morning. I was awake, for God's sake! Doing my morning ablutions, and I saw nowt. Unless you think it *was* Danny?' She raised an eyebrow at Arkwright.

He shrugged. 'Conway will be the judge of that. If Danny's in the pink, he should be released any day now.'

Florrie shook her head and turned back to the damning report.

> ' "Childrearing expert Mrs Dorothea Tattersall, authoress of the parenting manual, *And Baby Makes Three – a Guide to Perfect Mothering*, commented that, 'the emotional neglect of children by our affluent upper echelons gives rise to a ruling class that has neither the common sense nor sufficient empathy to preside over Great Britain's struggling economy or crumbling civic infrastructure. The Harding-Bournes seem to typify the concept that I call *opulent dysfunction*.' "'

Florrie drew breath sharply. 'That's . . . Blimey. And the *Telegraph* and *Manchester Guardian*?'

Arkwright pulled out the *Guardian* from the pile and pushed it before her. He steepled his fingers. 'They haven't spared them any quarter either. The *Manchester Guardian* journalist was wholly unimpressed by Lady Charlotte's obvious inebriation at eleven in the morning, and I can't say I blame them.'

Florrie tutted. 'She's getting worse, isn't she?'

Arkwright rocked back on his chair and looked up at the yellowing ceiling. He pursed his lips and then met Florrie's gaze. 'You know what she's up to with that German?'

Florrie shrugged, not wanting to get drawn into tittle-tattle.

'Oh, come now, Florence! Occam's razor – the simplest, most obvious explanation is usually the truth! Why else is von Grunwald still hanging around when the other guests are gone? And Lady Charlotte sleeping in a different bedroom to her husband? Two plus two makes four, in my book. I've been butler here for decades, and before that, I was a valet. I've spent my entire adult life in service of this family, and believe me, by now, nothing escapes me.'

Florrie examined her short fingernails, wanting to turn the conversation back to the baby's disappearance. 'I didn't see something like this coming. Did you?'

He shook his head. 'Of course not. Don't be absurd. This has taken us all by surprise. But the von Grunwald thing . . . Ideally, we need to somehow engineer putting a stop to it. It will destabilize the household.'

Florrie thought about Dame Elizabeth's indiscretion with Brooke. Had Arkwright known about that? Should she mention the letters? 'Do you think there's a big family secret that could make Sir Richard and Lady Charlotte vulnerable to these kidnappers?' She watched for his reaction.

He merely shrugged. 'I don't know about a big family secret, but I'd warrant Hans von Grunwald bedding Lady Charlotte under Holcombe Hall's roof, while Sir Richard sleeps down the hall, is surely vulnerability enough. Our employers don't do themselves any favours. They think they're untouchable, and they're not.'

'How are you going to break this news to them?' Florrie asked, tapping the paper.

'Carefully,' Arkwright said. 'Do you think you might join me in the dining room when I put the papers out?' He smiled wryly. 'I might have to run for cover. Shoot the messenger and all that . . .'

It was strangely heartening that Arkwright felt he could reveal his concerns to her. It occurred to Florrie then that she had finally grown up and into her role. The officious butler was treating her as an equal, and he seemed to have learned from Mrs Douglas's untimely demise, where they had left so much unsaid and parted company forever following the harshest of words.

'Don't worry.' She pushed the paper back on to his desk. 'I'll be right by your side.'

In the dining room Sir Richard was sitting at one end of the table, drinking coffee in silence. He still had that defeated look about him. Sitting at the other end of the table were Lady Charlotte, Sir Hugh and Hans von Grunwald.

Florrie turned her attention from assembling a bacon sandwich for Sir Hugh to Arkwright, who had just entered with the newspapers. They exchanged a glance.

Sir Richard looked up, grim-faced. 'Ah, good morning, Arkwright. I'll take the *Daily Telegraph* first, thank you,' he said.

Lady Charlotte, still clad in her dressing gown over her nightclothes, pushed her uneaten boiled egg away. She frowned. 'I say, Arkwright. Pass *The Times* here, will you?'

'I'll take the *Manchester Guardian*,' Sir Hugh said, clicking his fingers.

Arkwright bowed and handed out the newspapers. Florrie watched as the butler stood back, his hands laced together behind him. Ordinarily, he would ask 'Will that be all?' and then depart, but this morning, he was clearly hanging back to gauge the couple's reaction.

Florrie heard Sir Richard sigh heavily. He slapped the *Telegraph* down. 'It's a damned hatchet job.'

Lady Charlotte looked aghast. 'How *dare* they describe me in such unflattering terms! How dare they focus on my perceived inadequacies, when the story is about our missing son?' She looked over at Sir Richard. 'You must sue them!'

'I'll do no such thing.' Sir Richard's voice remained calm. 'The main thing is that we're headline news. William's photograph is on the front page of all these papers, which means people will be looking for him. Conway's already conducting a nationwide hunt for our boy, and these news articles make it more likely he'll be found quickly, spotted by some member of the public. Fortunately, I've also managed to gather the ransom in cash from my business associates, who were all kind enough to empty their safes for me and have their drivers drop the money round without hesitation, and Christmas be damned. Getting Willy back is all that matters. If we find our boy safe and sound – even if it means paying the fifty thousand pounds, once the kidnapper's sent the instructions through – that's all I care about.'

'But our reputation! *My* reputation!' Lady Charlotte looked to Sir Hugh and von Grunwald for support. Both men nodded enthusiastically.

'Harding-Bourne Enterprises' share price will plummet,' Sir Hugh said.

Sir Richard got to his feet. 'I don't remember you taking an interest in the share price at any other time in the past, Hugh. A business mogul you are not, so I suggest you reorient your layman's priorities and start praying that your nephew returns to us in one piece.' He turned to his wife. 'Darling, I don't give a fig about your reputation, and there's not a word I've read printed so far that isn't true.'

Florrie watched as her employer marched out of the dining room, leaving his brother, his wife and her German lover exchanging horrified glances across the dining table.

26

'Jesus!' Florrie yelped, exiting Arkwright's office at the crack of dawn. She'd bumped straight into Danny. 'You're back!' She clutched at her chest.

Danny smirked. 'Aye. Course I'm back. Bad pennies always turn up, right?'

Arkwright's voice boomed from within. 'In here, please, young man!'

Florrie followed the swaggering valet into the butler's office, keen to hear how his three-day-long incarceration at Preston Police Station and ensuing interrogation over the kidnapping had gone.

'I've got to hear this,' she said. 'We all thought you were gone for good.'

Danny stuck his hands in his waistcoat pockets. 'Sorry to disappoint.'

'What on earth happened?'

'Well, I had absolutely nowt to do with the kidnapping, before you ask,' he said. 'I reckon they just wanted to make an example of a Communist. Anyhow, they grilled me for days, and when they couldn't get me to confess . . .' He looked to Arkwright. 'Obviously that Conway was after an easy scapegoat to make it look like he had it all under control from the start. Well, I wasn't confessing to summat I didn't do, so they finally let me go last night. Took me all this while to hitch lifts back to

Holcombe. I walked it from the village. Got back about ten minutes ago.'

'My word,' Arkwright said, leaning back in his chair and putting his hands behind his head so that his waistcoat rode up slightly. 'That's quite an ordeal.'

'You're telling me.'

Studying the valet's face, Florrie thought he'd lost weight in the few days he'd been held in the cells. And was that the suggestion of a bruise she could detect around his eye socket and on the curve of his cheekbone? However loathsome Danny had been in the past, she now felt sorry for him. 'You'd best ask Cook for a bite to eat before you start work for the day. Looks like you could do with it.' Florrie thought about the letters she had in her possession. If Danny had been found innocent of involvement in the kidnapping, perhaps it was time she shared the blackmailing correspondence from Brooke with the detective sergeant.

Danny nodded. 'Grub at the police station was slop.'

Arkwright laced his hands together over his stomach and cleared his voice. 'Listen, young man. It's all very well you being released with no charge brought against you, but there's still the issue of you having been arrested in the first place and bringing disrepute to the household.'

Stiffening, Danny glared. 'Hey! That lot bring themselves into disrepute without any help from me, Mr Arkwright. I'm an innocent man, and there wasn't a damn thing they could stick on me. It's not against the law to be a Communist.'

The butler got to his feet. 'But I can't have you bad-mouthing our employers, Daniel. They pay our wages, and they're our social betters.'

'They're not worth the dirt from under my fingernails,' Danny said defiantly. 'That lot ponce off the hard graft of the likes of us. Betters, my arse!'

Arkwright smoothed his precisely combed hair. 'Look, Daniel, Miss Bickerstaff and I have a large staff to manage and keep on an even keel. You spreading fringe political ideas and sowing discontent among your colleagues does nobody any good. So, once you've had your breakfast, lad, you can clean your room out and sling your hook. If you leave me a forwarding address, I'll send your wages on, paid up to the end of the month.'

Danny's eyes widened. 'Are you having a laugh?'

'I'm deadly serious.'

The valet's thin face drained of all colour. 'But what will I do for a job? We're in the middle of a bloody depression, or hadn't you heard?'

'You should have thought of that before you started shirking and giving everyone lip. You've been trouble from the minute you started here, so just count yourself lucky I didn't give you your marching orders years ago.' He pointed to the door. 'Now, get out.'

Danny hurled abuse at Arkwright, then turned on his heel and stormed out of the office, slamming the door behind him.

Florrie pressed her hand to her mouth. 'Flipping heck, Mr Arkwright. I can't believe what you just did.'

Arkwright shook his head. 'It's bad enough that the baby's still missing, with the eleventh hour almost upon us. The last thing we need is Danny swanning around, telling tales on Conway and his team. He'd only make matters far, far worse, and I think eventually he'd have spoken to the press. We can't have troublemakers like that on the staff.'

'Will that be all, sir?' Arkwright asked, a few days later, once the family had gathered in the drawing room for Conway's update.

With tea and biscuits served, Florrie stood by the door, waiting for them both to be dismissed by Sir Richard. Keen to find out as much as she could about the ongoing investigation, Florrie had opted to take the place of Annie, who might normally have brought up the refreshments. The eleventh hour of New Year's Eve and the ransom deadline itself, the following day, were almost upon them. As far as Florrie knew, however – mainly from reports in the newspaper – the police were still no closer to finding the baby or his kidnappers.

Sir Richard shook his head. 'No, Arkwright. I want you to stay.' He nodded at Florrie. 'You too, Miss Bickerstaff. You and Arkwright are our most senior staff members, so it's vital you also know where we're up to with finding my son.' His left eye twitched as he spoke. His face was drawn and haggard and his hair hung loose.

Florrie felt a sharp pang of empathy for him. 'Of course, sir.' She curtseyed and retreated to the far corner of the room, where she might blend unobtrusively into the wooden panelling.

Arkwright positioned himself by the window, behind the armchair where Lady Charlotte was curled up, nursing a glass full of one of Cook's revolting hangover 'cures' and sporting a doleful expression. Hans von Grunwald was seated by the gramophone, clad in lederhosen and a traditional Bavarian collarless jacket. His sharp blue eyes were fixed on Sir Richard, and the downward turn of his mouth implied loathing for his host and rival for Lady Charlotte's affections. On the settee, Sir Hugh was dressed casually, ruefully examining his half-smoked cigar. Daphne lay next to him with her head on his lap.

Only Sir Richard, sitting on the edge of his father's favoured winged armchair, appeared fully focussed on the task at hand. 'So! Here we are with the deadline for payment almost upon us, the money sitting ready in my safe, and I *still* haven't heard from my son's kidnappers. Conway, do tell us where you're up to with the investigation.'

The detective was standing by the fireplace, chewing on his pipe. He pointed to Sir Richard with the mouthpiece. 'We've spent every waking hour and plenty more besides pursuing every angle. Communists like your valet, who don't have any love for industrialists, republican types who might take exception to your lady wife's royal connections, disgruntled employees . . . and I have to admit, there's a fair few . . . madmen, known conmen operating in the northwest. You name it, we've had 'em all in for questioning.' His moustache twitched. 'That produced a fair few lines of enquiry that me and my lads have exhausted.'

Sir Richard smiled hopefully. 'Yes?'

Conway looked down at his highly polished shoes. 'No leads yet, I'm afraid.'

'What about the news coverage?' Lady Charlotte asked. 'All I've read in the papers every day since the press conference have been stories about Willy's abduction and how dastardly we are as a family. Surely those and Willy's photograph have generated tip-offs from the general public.'

'We're still looking into possible sightings of your son.'

Sir Hugh exhaled a plume of smoke. 'I say, have you been going door-to-door, asking the people in the village if they saw anything untoward on Christmas morning?'

Conway took a pouch of tobacco from the inside pocket of his jacket and pushed some into his pipe. 'It was one of the first things we did. We've searched Holcombe Hall and its grounds *and* the village, *and* the surrounding villages from top to bottom. Nobody reported seeing anything or anyone out of place.'

Sir Richard clapped his hands to his head. 'I can't stand this any longer, God damn it! We're no further forward than we were the morning Willy went missing.'

'I'm so sorry, Sir Richard.' Conway shook his head. 'Every lead we've pursued has been a dead end. At this point, it's as if your son has vanished into thin air.'

'Vanished? I don't believe in magic or jiggery pokery, Conway,' Sir Richard said. 'My son is out there somewhere, and we've got less than twenty-four hours to find him before . . .' He strode to the window and stared out. 'I shudder to think what will happen.' He turned back to Conway. 'Are they likely to hurt him?'

'Darling!' Lady Charlotte cried. 'Don't imagine such a terrible outcome.'

'We have to be pragmatic, Charlotte!' Sir Richard snapped at his wife. 'The kidnappers haven't been in touch. There's no sign of our boy. What else are we to think?'

Conway struck a match and relit his pipe. 'The thing

is not to panic. The kidnappers asked for fifty thousand pounds. They're motivated by money, so my guess is they'll be in touch today. Once they've stipulated how and where they want to take payment, I feel confident we'll know how we can intercept them.'

'How?' Sir Richard demanded. 'Holcombe Hall is now closely guarded by staff and police officers. How are the kidnappers going to get word to me if they can't get into the house? Maybe *that's* why we've heard nothing. Maybe with all this security, we're making things worse.' Tears welled in his eyes. 'And we'll never get my son back.'

Daphne sat up suddenly. 'Don't cry, Dickie. Anybody greedy enough to take a babe-in-arms in return for money is going to prioritize getting the money. They won't hurt Willy. Maybe they'll take out an advertisement in the press.' She looked at Sir Hugh and then at Conway. 'You're scouring the press for hidden messages, aren't you?'

This was the first sensible suggestion to come from Daphne, Florrie thought. She cleared her throat. 'If I may, we have every edition of every national newspaper . . . some of the locals too . . . everything what's been published in the last seven days,' she told Conway. 'Cook likes to keep them in the kitchen. For kindling, like. I don't think she's touched this week's papers yet. I could have my girls re-read through them for coded messages if you like.'

Conway shook his head. 'I've had my men doing all that already. They're professionally trained in these matters, of course. Didn't find a thing, I'm afraid.'

Sir Richard was pacing up and down the drawing room now, with the tense energy of a caged tiger. 'What is the point in having the constabulary involved in this investigation if you've turned up nothing?' He came to a stop in front of his wife. 'We should hire a private detective. I'll find the best money can buy.'

Lady Charlotte got to her feet, pushing him aside. Her bloodshot eyes were filled with tears. 'It's too late for that, you nincompoop! You should have done that when Willy first went missing.' She set her empty glass down on a side table, seeking out Hans. 'I need some air.'

Taking her arm, Sir Richard spun her around so she was forced to look at him. 'You can't give up, Charlotte. We still have one more day and night! It could be just the ticket. Fresh eyes and all that . . .'

She shook herself loose. 'Don't be so naïve, Richard. For heaven's sake, if you commission the services of a detective now, it will take him a day to get here, let alone conduct a nationwide manhunt.'

Florrie noted how Conway appeared to be studying the exchange between the two. Did he see how Lady Charlotte kept glancing over at the German? For a moment, Florrie wondered if Hans von Grunwald could perhaps have coerced his lover into staging a kidnapping, so that Lady Charlotte could ransom her own child to raise sufficient money to flee the country. Was it possible? *You're being ridiculous*, Florrie told herself. *Everyone's grasping at straws, because the prospect of a snatched baby never being returned to the bosom of his family is too grim to bear.* It was time to tell Conway about Brooke and the letters.

'Where are you going?' Sir Richard called after his wife as she marched towards the door.

Lady Charlotte paused momentarily but didn't turn

back. 'Outside. Anywhere but stuck in here with you.' Then she was gone.

Sir Richard turned to Conway. 'What do you propose? What are our next steps? Shall I hire a private detective?'

'I'd rather there wasn't a third party, getting beneath my team's feet.'

'I know the Chief of Police. Need I have a word with him? Get some higher authority involved?' Florrie could see Sir Richard was testing Conway's authority and resolve.

'I've cracked tougher cases than this, sir.' Conway grabbed his lapels and rocked on his heels. 'I feel we'll have our breakthrough when the kidnappers make contact about the ransom payment. They're bound to resurface, and they'll trip up at some point. But you must do as you see fit.'

The two men stood eye to eye: the desperate father, and the detective whose reputation was on the line. Had they reached an impasse? Florrie couldn't bear to watch. She turned her attention to Arkwright, who was looking out at someone. Who was it, walking the grounds? A figure in black. Miss Talbot.

The sight of the nanny brought Arkwright's words back to Florrie. *Occam's razor*. Arkwright had recently used the phrase in the context of Lady Charlotte's suspected affair with von Grunwald, but it now struck Florrie that the concept of the simplest explanation being the likeliest might apply to Sir William's abduction too. Talbot was the most suspicious-acting member of the staff and therefore the most likely culprit.

As soon as Conway had convinced Sir Richard to continue to put his faith in the local police and had taken his leave, Florrie slipped upstairs. She reasoned that she had perhaps quarter of an hour in which to search Miss Talbot's room again before the nanny returned. If she unearthed nothing, she would first tell Sir Richard about Brooke's blackmail, and then, with his permission, pass the correspondence between Brooke and Dame Elizabeth on to Conway.

Checking that she was not being observed, Florrie slipped into the room that was next to the nursery. Before launching into the same systematic search she had conducted before, Florrie thought about how the furniture had been placed last time. A stool had been left on the rug in the middle of the room, whereas it was currently shoved into the kneehole of the small dressing table. Why had it been out of place?

Lifting the rug, Florrie checked the floorboards beneath once more to see that they weren't loose, concealing some hidey-hole between the old oak joists. They were all solid, as before. Irritated, she checked again under the bed. The dust and dead spiders she'd found previously had since been thoroughly cleaned away, yet there was no sign of loose boards. She lay on her back and manoeuvred herself beneath the iron bedframe to check nothing had been hidden on the underside – perhaps wedged in between the springs or fastened to the bottom of the mattress.

Footsteps outside caused Florrie to hold her breath. The door opened. From her vantage point she could see Miss Talbot's stout black schoolmarm shoes. The nanny entered and closed the door behind her.

Flipping heck, she's going to find me under her bed! She'll hear me breathing, and then she'll know I'm spying on her!

The feet approached the bed and stopped mere inches from where Florrie lay concealed. She squeezed her eyes shut and waited for the inevitable.

27

Just as Florrie was certain that the bedspread would be lifted, revealing her subterfuge, Miss Talbot turned to face the door. The mattress and latticework of springs supporting it plunged suddenly downwards, pressing alarmingly close to Florrie's face. Stifling a yelp, Florrie squeezed her eyes shut and prayed the nanny wasn't lying down for a prolonged nap.

Above her, she could hear scratching, as if something was being written on paper with a fountain pen.

Persevere! Don't move an inch. She mustn't find out you're here, Florrie told herself.

Miss Talbot yawned. There was the sound of rustling, then, mercifully, she rose from the bed and walked out of the room. Had she written a note? Had the rustling been the sound of her putting the note into an envelope?

Reassuring herself that she could now safely emerge from her hiding place, Florrie edged her way out from under the bed. Remaining on her back for a moment, she closed her eyes and exhaled with relief that the danger had passed. When she opened her eyes, she gazed up at the ornate plasterwork of the ceiling. It was then that she realized that, directly above the spot where the dressing table stool had been left on her previous search of the nanny's room, there was a square hatch – easy to miss in the square design of the old plasterwork.

Florrie felt her senses sharpen.

'Aye-aye,' she whispered beneath her breath. 'A hidey-hole? How have I never noticed that before?'

The ceilings were so high, Miss Talbot couldn't possibly have reached up to the hatch, even if she'd been standing on a stool. Florrie realized she would have needed a pole or similar to open the hatch and retrieve something hidden between the joists that supported the servants' floor and the roof structure above.

Getting to her feet, Florrie looked around the room. There was nothing.

'A window pole,' she whispered, peering up at the hole in the top rail of the window casement, designed to be pulled down with the hook on the end of a pole. All the bedrooms on the first floor had a window pole, but where was Miss Talbot's?

Florrie leaned over the bed, shoved up against the window, and pushed the left curtain aside. There was nothing there. Then she pushed the right curtain back.

'Aha!' Florrie felt her stomach tighten at the sight of the pole that had been concealed from view by the faded old curtain.

Praying that nobody on the landing would hear her movements, Florrie took up the pole, moved the stool into position beneath the hatch and climbed on top. The stool wobbled beneath her weight. She felt the room spin, but tried to trick her brain into thinking she was merely dusting the tops of the curtains as a young maid once again – a job that had entailed climbing on step ladders infinitely more rickety and high than the stool.

Regaining her balance, Florrie reached up with the

pole and pushed at the hatch. At first, it wouldn't budge. She tapped the pole along the perimeter and suddenly felt it give a little. Pushing harder, she realized the thing was spring-loaded. If she pushed upwards in the right place . . .

The hatch swung abruptly open and a bundle of paper fell out on to the floor, scattering everywhere – correspondence written on light blue paper. Florrie stared down in horror at the mess. Suddenly, she could hear the light footsteps of a woman coming towards the room – the click-clack of Miss Talbot's schoolmarm shoes?

Florrie had perhaps thirty seconds before the nanny entered the bedroom.

She nudged the hatch upwards and pushed until it was back in place. Clambering down off the stool she set it back beneath the dressing table, then flung the pole back behind the curtain and gathered up the letters in shaking hands. The footsteps were closer now. There was no time to slide herself back beneath the bed.

Florrie stood at the side of the door, praying that Miss Talbot wouldn't immediately close the door behind her; praying she could somehow slip out when the nanny's back was turned. *She's going to find me. How the hell do I explain this?*

The footsteps stopped outside the door. Talbot was surely coming in. Florrie grimaced and squeezed her eyes shut, the blood roaring in her ears. But then the door on the far side of the landing opened – the door to the guest bedroom occupied by Hans von Grunwald. There was the rattle of a mop bucket being set down. It was Elsie, arriving to clean the room!

'Thank you, good Lord!' Florrie whispered.

The guest bedroom door closed again. Once silence had descended, Florrie snuck out and headed straight up the back stairs to her own room. Knowing she was unlikely to be disturbed there – if some calamity demanded her urgent attention, her own bedroom would be the last place anyone would go looking for her – Florrie spread the letters on the bed and reordered them by the date of the postmark. She already knew who the correspondence to Miss Talbot was from, because she recognized the light blue stationery and distinctive hand of Miles T. Brooke Esquire. Miss Talbot had been in contact with none other than Dame Elizabeth's old blackmailer and Sir Richard's alleged true father. With a thudding heart, Florrie started to read and confirmed her suspicions . . .

She began with the first letter, dated just before Miss Talbot had arrived at Holcombe Hall. It had been sent to a private post box in Bolton, rather than a home address, and a private post box had been given for return correspondence.

Dearest Fanny,

Congratulations on securing the job as Sir William's nanny. I knew you would, and I was always confident that Lady Charlotte would prove lacking in the motherly dedication required to ask searching questions of you, especially since you had already provided her with your glowing references. The letterheads on which I wrote your letters of recommendation were convincing, not least because I had purloined them from the households of Lady Charlotte's 'closest' chums – people I felt certain she wouldn't have rubbed shoulders with in aeons, and unsuspecting types in social circles I could easily inveigle my way into as one of them. It appears we are off to a good start, my dear.

Now we must play the long game. Embed yourself in the household and in the child's life. Do not attract attention to yourself, but listen and learn the family's secrets, reporting back to me.

Your remuneration for your expenses will be deposited weekly – in cash, beneath a loose turf of grass on the grave of Ermintrude Bishop at the Holcombe Methodist Chapel's graveyard. I advise you to collect the monies each Sunday, before or after the service. Please be discreet. Be sure to burn my correspondence after reading.

Yours admiringly,
Miles T. Brooke Esquire

Florrie gasped and clasped the letter to her chest. So Brooke and Miss Talbot had been in cahoots all along! Were they lovers? Friends? Something else entirely? There was certainly more to their relationship than a confidence trickster contracting the assistance of a co-conspirator. But though the letter implied the two had been up to no good from the start, this did not provide concrete proof of kidnap.

Florrie read on at speed.

Letter after letter from Brooke to Talbot revealed how the nanny had conveyed the sordid family secrets of the Harding-Bournes to him in her own missives: Dame Elizabeth's melancholia, brought about by her being extorted; Sir Richard's struggle to keep the businesses afloat during the Great Depression and his estrangement from his wife; Lady

Charlotte's almost wholesale abandonment of mothering duties in favour of fast parties, fast cars and flying; her descent into alcoholism and affair with von Grunwald; Sir Hugh's profligacy, fascist proclivities and the frightful company he kept.

Florrie skipped over several of the letters and skimmed the more recent correspondence. It didn't take long before she came across Brooke's plan, some three months before the abduction.

My dearest Fanny,

Since your last letter, I have given great thought as to how we might proceed in rendering your position within the household profitable. In short, we must abandon our plans to persuade Sir Richard to part with money in return for our discretion over his family's unseemly secrets. I have an altogether better ruse – namely, we might kidnap Sir William and hold the boy for ransom to the tune of £50,000. I have heard that this is increasingly being done in America, since the hard pinch of the Depression. Industrialists make magnificent targets for those who are prepared to shelve their moral misgivings. One might even consider it doing the Lord's work, redistributing the ill-gotten gains of business moguls to lesser mortals – in this case, you and me. My dear, this will give us the opportunity to begin a new life together . . . perhaps in France or Spain.

I will send instructions anon, once I have paid meticulous attention to the detail of how we might commit this perfect crime.

'Bastard!' Florrie said. 'His own grandchild, too!'
There was a knock at her bedroom door. 'Florrie? Are

you in there?' Sally's voice sounded hollow on the uncarpeted servants' landing.

Should Florrie answer or pretend she wasn't there? If she kept quiet, Sally might come in to check she wasn't collapsed on the floor, and then her spying would be discovered. 'Don't come in, Sal,' she shouted. 'I've got a terrible . . . er . . . women's trouble. Just leave me to it. I'll be down as soon as I can.'

On the other side of the door, Sally sounded discombobulated. 'Oh. Right. Do you want me to get you any rags and hot water or owt?'

Florrie was touched by Sally's thoughtfulness, but the last thing she needed right at that moment was her friend's attentiveness. 'I'm fine, love. I'll be down in a bit.'

'I'll come and check on you after lunch, shall I?'

'No need for that. I'll be down before then.'

Florrie heard Sally's footsteps growing fainter. Alone again, she hastily looked over all the most recent letters until she found one that appeared to outline the logistics of Brooke's dastardly plan.

Darling Fanny,

The wheels are set in motion. On Christmas Day, you are to wake William for a drink of milk around two o'clock in the morning, which you must lace with a good quantity of whisky to ensure the boy sleeps through the transportation. Once he is sound asleep, you are to take him from his bed and bring him to me. By three in the morning, everyone in the household including the cook should still be asleep. So from three o'clock sharp, I will be waiting in my car, just down the lane from the estate's back gates. Bring an electric torch, which you might steal from one of the gardeners or whoever maintains the cars. Bring one change of clothes and some food for the boy so that I might placate him when he wakes.

Once I have departed for the hideaway with William, you must leave the ransom note (enclosed) beneath his pillow. The police will be called, but do not draw attention to yourself, my dear. Appear as confused, puzzled and horrified as the other members of the household will be. I will leave instructions for paying the ransom beneath the turf on Ermintrude's grave, which you must then secrete into the house and leave for Sir Richard to find. Make sure you are not seen. Good luck!

Once we have safe receipt of the funds, we will leave the boy as a foundling on the steps of a nearby church — not Holcombe, since the police and locals will be on the lookout for untoward behaviour. We will decide en route to our new life, my dear.

I cannot wait to see you and the boy on Christmas morning. What a fine gift the lad will turn out to be!

Yours, with love,
Miles

'Got you!' Florrie said.

Her heart racing, she gathered up the letters. Here was comprehensive proof of Talbot and Brooke's guilt. All she had to do now was decide whether to hand the letters over to Conway, or whether she should give them to Sir Richard first. There was also the question of Brooke's letters to Dame Elizabeth. Was it time to reveal that Brooke had been blackmailing and extorting the family for decades?

28

'Sir Richard, can I have a word, please?' Florrie asked, poking her head around the door to her employer's study.

She found Sir Richard and Sir Hugh sitting in easy chairs by the French window – Sir Richard sipping from a coffee cup, Sir Hugh nursing a pre-lunch cocktail. Both men wore serious expressions. Florrie realized she'd happened upon a rare meeting between the brothers to discuss family matters. Now she had two pairs of enquiring eyes fixed on her.

'Sorry. I didn't realize . . . I didn't mean to disturb.' She backed away and started to shut the door.

'Nonsense, Florrie. Do come in,' Sir Richard called.

Gripping the bundle of correspondence tightly, she stepped into the study, forcing a smile. How on earth could she ask to speak to Sir Richard alone without Sir Hugh getting wind of some subterfuge? He was the last person she wanted to be privy to Miles T. Brooke's dastardly secret. Right now, Sir Hugh was idly lighting a cigarette, but Sir Richard's searching gaze moved immediately to the sheaf in her hands.

'Honestly, I really didn't mean to intrude. Only I need to talk to you, Sir Richard.' She hid the letters behind her as Sir Hugh looked up, exhaling a plume of blue smoke through his nostrils like a dragon. 'When you've got a minute, like . . . I can come back.'

Sir Hugh grinned. 'I think our Florrie has something to confess. Ha ha. Out with it, Florrie. Tell us your most sordid secrets.'

Sir Richard shot a disapproving glance at his brother. 'Steady on, Hugh. I don't think our esteemed housekeeper needs to be harangued like that.' He turned to Florrie, studying her face. 'You look concerned.'

'It's a serious staffing matter, sir. But I don't want to bore Sir Hugh with the details.' She willed her employer to intuit the need for confidentiality.

Sir Richard leaned over and patted his brother on his shoulder. 'I think we'd just about finished our conversation, hadn't we?'

Mid-sip, Sir Hugh frowned and lowered his drink. 'Pushing your brother aside to satisfy the demands of the paid help? Mama will be spinning in her grave!' Then he smiled and winked at Florrie. 'Only joking, my dear. You two need to get down to brass tacks about feather dusters and laundry. Far be it from me to cramp your style.'

Clutching his drink, he picked up his cigarette, wedged it into the corner of his mouth and pushed past her. 'Adieu!'

Sir Richard pointed to the vacant easy chair. 'Do sit. Please.'

Sir Hugh's footsteps tapped along the parquet floor towards the drawing room. When Florrie was certain he was out of earshot, she turned back to Sir Richard and produced the sheaf of letters.

'I know who's taken your son,' she said. 'Everything you need is here, but I wanted you to see it before Conway lays eyes on it, because it's . . . Well, see for yourself.'

Sir Richard blanched. With shaking hands, he opened

the envelope on top, addressed to Talbot from Brooke. As he read in silence, his eyes grew wider. His face flushed with anger. 'Bastards!' He slapped the letter down on to the side table and got to his feet. 'Isn't Brooke an old college chum of my father? The duplicitous snake! I'm going to find Talbot and place that old witch under citizen's arrest myself.'

Florrie sprang out of her chair and grabbed him by his forearm. 'No, no, no! Wait! Don't. You mustn't rush in where angels fear to tread. You'll jeopardize Sir William's safety. Let the police deal with it. But first, you really need to know the context behind it.'

She handed him the correspondence from Brooke, written on the light blue paper and addressed to Dame Elizabeth.

'My mother?' he asked. 'What has she to do with all of this ghastly kidnapping business?'

'You'll see.' Florrie laced her fingers together in front of her. 'I'm so sorry. I should have told you earlier, but the police had different lines of enquiry.'

She watched Sir Richard's eyes move from side to side as he worked his way through the first letter. For expediency, Florrie had placed only the most revealing letters on top of the pile. The rest, demonstrating the build-up over time of coercive pressure from Brooke, were towards the bottom.

Sir Richard's features seemed to tighten, the more he read.

The tense silence was broken by a knock at the door, and without pause, Lady Charlotte entered.

Sir Richard gasped, sat back down and stuffed the letters hastily down the side of the chair. 'Yes? What is it?'

Lady Charlotte was now dressed in golfing attire. Her

platinum blonde hair was held in place by a broad headband. 'We're off out for a round of golf to take our mind off things. Are you coming?' She stared blankly at Florrie and then turned her attention back to her husband.

'No, thank you,' he said, placing his hands on his knees. The sinews in the backs of his hands were as taut as violin strings.

'But Dickie, you can't just hide away in here with the staff, feeling sorry for yourself.'

'I said, no *thank you*, Charlotte.' Getting to his feet, careful to conceal the letters with a cushion, he then strode to the door and held it open for his wife. 'I'm in an important meeting with our housekeeper and I *must not* be disturbed. But by all means, my darling, if you feel you need to take your mind off our son's abduction, then you absolutely should.' His sweet words were sour with derision. 'But I am happy to stay inside, keeping all the plates spinning.' He escorted Lady Charlotte out of the study, closed the door firmly behind her and locked it.

Under other circumstances, his locking the door might have made Florrie feel awkward, but right now, with so much at stake, she was relieved. Privacy was exactly what they needed.

Sir Richard leaned against the door, his eyes closed, and sighed. After a few moments, he walked back to the chair, took up the letters in trembling hands and resumed reading. As he read, he shook his head slowly.

Florrie could sense the desolation emanating from his every pore, and sympathy and love surged within her. 'Shall I pour you a whisky, sir?' she asked.

Letting the letters settle on the table, Sir Richard met her gaze. 'Florrie, why on earth didn't you tell me my mother was being blackmailed?'

'How could I?' she asked. 'Your mother swore me to secrecy.'

'How long have you known?'

She revealed how she'd eavesdropped in the library, when Brooke had made a clandestine visit to Dame Elizabeth.

'So, all this time – a good eighteen months – you knew that Brooke was claiming to be my real father?' Tears welled in Sir Richard's eyes. 'And how long have you had his letters to Talbot?'

'Only just found them, sir. I suspected something was going on with Talbot and I've been searching for evidence this past week. This morning, I finally hit the jackpot. You know I would never hold back important information like that, not when your son's life is at stake.'

He brandished the letters to his mother. 'These terrible, scandalous lies! Saying I'm not a Harding-Bourne at all, but some bastard child of my father's former best friend, born on the other side of the blanket! And my mother had conducted some sordid affair with this . . . this . . . *rake*, under this very roof – my father's family home?'

Florrie pressed her lips together. 'Dame Elizabeth said . . .' Should she tell him that the old lady had confessed to her indiscretion, confirming that Brooke had indeed fathered her second son? She could already see the bitter disappointment in Sir Richard's eyes. His world was crumbling around him, and she couldn't bear to break his heart any more than it was already broken. 'Look, this Brooke is nowt but a dead-leg conman, an opportunist and a criminal. He's out for what he can get, clearly, and he's got absolutely no proof that he's your real father at all.' She shook her head vehemently. There was nothing to gain and everything to lose from Sir Richard knowing the truth. 'Lord Harding-Bourne was your father. You're a dead ringer for him! This . . .' She pointed to the damning pile of blue paper. 'The rubbish in all those letters . . . it's all bluster and blackmail. Your mother was intimidated by a bad man who was trying to take liberties with a lonely, ageing woman, that's all. She swore me to secrecy, because she didn't want such whopping lies being peddled to the press as gospel. She didn't want you believing for a minute that your dad was some grubby little liar – a nobody. But now that grubby lying nobody has conspired with your nanny to kidnap your son, and we've got hard evidence.'

Sir Richard stood still and seemed to scrutinize her, as though the future were somehow etched into her face like tea leaves in a spent cup. He nodded resolutely. 'I'll stop Talbot from leaving the house. Right now. Perhaps I can force her to confess where my son is being held.'

Shaking her head, Florrie was desperate to reason with him. 'No. Don't you see? She's dangerous and as much of a fraudster as Brooke. They're in cahoots, and they didn't balk at kidnapping a defenceless baby. We're not enough to take her on.'

'So what do we do?'

'You telephone Conway straight away, but be discreet. We can't have anyone tipping her the wink. I'll find some ruse to occupy her with, to keep her out of her bedroom so she doesn't know the letters are missing, and so she doesn't get wind of the police steaming down the drive en masse. I'll hoodwink her into coming with me to the library. Keep her in the stacks.'

He nodded slowly. 'All right.' He gathered up the letters. 'First, these are going straight in the safe. They're evidence.' He marched over to a rosewood cabinet, crouched down and opened the door to reveal a cumbersome old safe. Swiftly and deftly, he twisted the dial until it clicked and the heavy steel door swung open. He shoved the letters inside. 'Is this everything?'

'Yes, sir.' On the shelves in the safe, she glimpsed velvet jewellery cases from Asprey, Van Cleef & Arpels and Tiffany & Co. – presumably filled with the diamonds that Dame Elizabeth had worn to state functions and which Lady Charlotte regularly wore to society balls. Had he taken her bee brooch from that collection? There were ten or more neat, thick wads of paper currency. Was that the ransom in cash, waiting to be paid? A pile of scrolls was stacked up tightly – bonds and contracts and Lord knew what else multimillionaires kept in the sort of safe one might normally see only in a bank. Florrie felt like Alice through the looking glass, gaining a glimpse of a life that was utterly foreign to her.

Sir Richard slammed the safe door shut, locked it with one smooth movement and got to his feet. 'Let's hop to it. We've got a kidnapper to snare and my abducted son to find, before harm comes to him.' He marched over to Florrie and squeezed her shoulder. 'I want you to know how grateful I am to have you on my side.'

She reached up and fleetingly placed her hand on his. *I'd walk through fire for you*, she thought. 'Of course, sir. Let's get Sir William back.'

29

'Miss Talbot, there you are!' Florrie shouted to the nanny as she approached the house, marching up the long gravel drive. 'I've been looking for you everywhere.'

Miss Talbot raised an eyebrow. 'I only nipped down to the post office, Miss Bickerstaff. Surely my movements are no concern of yours, especially given my charge is missing.'

Florrie wondered how she could cultivate a friendly enough rapport with the nanny to get her to do anything at all. She had to think on her feet. 'Sir Richard has asked that you give me a hand. He wants me to go to the library and seek out some books about psychology and crime, and . . .' *Flattery. Will she respond to being flattered?* 'Apparently, there are quite a few. You're the only person under the roof learned enough to help with that sort of thing. All the others . . . they're not bookish.'

By now, Miss Talbot had covered the remaining ground between them. 'And what makes you think I'm bookish, Miss Bickerstaff?'

'Er, you read the bible, for a start. That makes you a woman of letters, doesn't it?'

The nanny came to a halt inches away from Florrie. She scowled, seeming to scrutinize every pore in Florrie's skin. 'Why would his lordship want books on crime and psychology? His son's being held to ransom by dangerous kidnappers. Surely he has better things to worry about?'

Florrie shrugged. She was well aware that her excuse for occupying Talbot was weak, but she was desperate to get her into the depths of the library stacks, where she wouldn't see the police approaching. 'He wants to understand the mind of the kidnapper,' she said. 'Thinks it might shed some light on his son's whereabouts. Look, we're both getting paid to do as we're told, and as you said yourself, you've got nothing better to do. So, follow me and let's get stuck in.'

'What? *Now?*'

'No time like the present, Miss Talbot.'

Talbot started to climb the steps. 'No.'

This woman was the limit! Florrie had to find a way to make her do as she was told. Flattery didn't work, so . . . Florrie gathered her long skirt and marched up the stairs after the nanny. 'As housekeeper, I'm always looking for staffing areas where I can recommend savings. Right now, Miss Talbot, I'm trying very hard to justify you staying at the house, given you've no child to look after. Helping me find the books Sir Richard has asked for will save you from any cost-cutting cull . . . for now, at least.'

The nanny's gimlet eyes narrowed. Did she smell a rat?

'Very well. Let me just put my bag in my room.'

'Bring it to the library with you. Sir Richard said finding these books is an urgent project.'

Miss Talbot frowned and took a step to the side, away from Florrie. She clutched her cumbersome handbag in front of her like a shield. 'This is the most ludicrous thing I've ever heard. What are you about, Florence Bickerstaff? You're behaving very oddly.'

'If my instructions seem queer, it's because they come

from a man under severe mental strain. But that man happens to pay our wages, and ours is not to question why.' Florrie jerked her thumb towards the library. 'So let's crack on, shall we?'

Finally, Miss Talbot relented, and Florrie ushered her into the stacks in the darkest and coolest reaches of the library.

'This is a fool's errand,' Miss Talbot said, pulling a blue fabric-covered book from the top shelf of one of the deepest stacks. She read the title on the ornate cover. '*Hellas: A History of the Ancient Greeks* by Wilhelm Wagner.' She flicked through the first few yellowed pages. 'This was published in 1882! What on earth do they hoard nonsense like this for? Whoever bought this is long dead!'

Florrie took the book from her and set it back on the shelf. 'Rich people like to hang on to things. I think having books knocking around makes them feel clever. Maybe it gives them a connection to the past. I wouldn't know, because the only book I own is a Brontë novel that my sister gave me for my birthday one year. I must have read it a hundred times. Anything else I read has to come from the library. But never mind that. You should be looking for a title called *Crime, Abnormal Minds and the Law* by Ernest Hoag and Edward Williams. I'm looking for *Criminal Psychology* by Hans Gross. Keep your eye out for them.'

Miss Talbot ran her bony finger along the spines of the books on the shelf. She started to read a title aloud when the door to the library at the far end was slammed open. There was frenzied barking and growling. Multiple footsteps thundered along the length of the library towards the stacks.

The police!

Florrie's gut tightened. 'What's all this hullabaloo?' she asked, loud enough to make their position within the stacks clear.

'Police!' Conway's voice rang out in the library.

Wearing a stricken expression, Miss Talbot dropped the book she'd been holding on to the floor. Her hand slid into the pocket of her skirt.

'Miss Fannetta Talbot, come out with your hands up!'

Florrie instinctively turned away from Talbot towards the direction of Conway's voice.

When she felt a bony arm encircle her waist, she realized she'd made a huge error of judgement in ushering Talbot into the stacks. She was trapped, and now the nanny pressed something sharp against her neck. What was it, a letter opener? The nib of a fountain pen?

'You conniving hussy,' Talbot said. 'You called the police on me? Used this library nonsense to trap me like a cat in a bag?' She pushed Florrie forward towards the light that came from the library's many tall windows. 'Well, if I'm not getting out of here, then neither are you.'

Florrie felt her heart flip behind her ribs. Was she about to meet a violent end at the hands of a kidnapper? At that moment, she prayed for Thom to swoop in and save her, but when she emerged from the stacks, there was no Thom. She saw only the fangs and fur of two agitated Alsatian police dogs and a row of policemen in uniform. At the back, she caught sight of Sir Richard, who pushed the police constables aside to reach the front of the phalanx.

'Let Miss Bickerstaff go, you beastly woman!' Sir Richard shouted. 'Let her go this instant, I tell you!' He looked over to the door where Arkwright had just appeared. 'Fetch the hunting rifle, Arkwright! Quickly!'

'Get back, all of you, or I'll puncture her pretty little neck,' Talbot said, shoving her head so close to Florrie's that Florrie could smell the nanny's stale breath.

Conway stepped to the fore. 'Give yourself up, Fanny Talbot — assuming that's your real name — and tell us the whereabouts of Sir William and this Miles T. Brooke. We know he's behind the kidnapping. If you help us, and we find the child safe and sound, perhaps *you* won't hang.'

Miss Talbot started to edge along the stacks towards the door. 'I want a fast motor car ready for me at the entrance. The Bugatti. I'm taking Bickerstaff here with me, but if I get the slightest inkling I'm being followed, I'll cut her throat with this letter opener, and you'll never see William again.'

'Wait! I have the ransom in my safe,' Sir Richard said. 'Raising it quickly has been fiendishly difficult over Christmas, but friends have been generous . . . I've got it all. What if I just give you the money? Let Florrie go, tell Conway here where my son is, and you can have your blasted money. I just want my son back and my housekeeper unmolested.'

Beyond the roar of the blood rushing in her ears and the snarling of the dogs, Florrie heard a window open upstairs, on the mezzanine. She hadn't seen any police officers go up there. Had somebody climbed in? Would Talbot have noticed? 'There's no need to make this more complicated than it is, Fanny,' she said, trying to root herself to the spot so she couldn't be edged closer to the door. 'You heard him. Take the money. Help the police, and this can all be over. Do yourself a favour. Why should you face the gallows for this Brooke cad? Just tell the police where the baby is. Please. You're a God-fearing woman, aren't you?'

Talbot dug the letter opener further into Florrie's neck. 'Am I? You don't know the first thing about me. None of you do. You all think you're so clever, but you've been played for fools for a long, long time. And it's nothing less than this family deserves . . . a bunch of layabouts with silver spoons in their gobs.'

Florrie heard the creak of footfalls on the mezzanine above and watched Sir Richard, the police constables and Conway for a reaction. *Someone's about to do something daring to get this woman off me,* she thought. *Aren't they? I darn well hope so. Please,* please *let it work, and I hope to high heaven that the coppers don't give the game away too early. Talbot's lost her marbles.* Her desperate gaze alighted on Sir Richard, and she noticed his attention flick up to the mezzanine and back down to Talbot.

Closing her eyes, Florrie prayed that whatever was coming wouldn't result in her own death. One, two, three seconds passed and she dared to open her eyes. Talbot was still trying to shove her along to the door, shouting obscenities to the police. She heard a whistle through the air, followed by an almighty thwack. All at once, her captor loosened her grip on Florrie and slumped to the floor, screaming.

Florrie was plucked from the fray by Sir Richard, and she stumbled with him back to safety, behind the phalanx of police officers and dogs. It was then that she understood what had happened: Thom had crept in through the upper library window and on to the mezzanine. He had stealthily straddled the banister that turned the mezzanine into a galleried landing and was now half-hanging off it, spade in hand. On the floor, Miss Talbot writhed and kicked out, clutching her shoulder. Thom had whacked her with his spade in a bid to free Florrie.

'I don't believe it,' Florrie wept. 'I don't . . . I—'

'You've dislocated my shoulder, you giant lumbering gibbon!' Talbot shouted up at Thom. Her eyes flashed with menace but she was unable to lash out, pinned down as she was by a hefty constable.

'Fannetta Talbot, I arrest you in the name of the law.' Conway stood over her while three burly uniformed officers rolled her on to her stomach to put her in cuffs. The nanny screamed angrily when her shoulder was wrenched back.

Sir Richard put his arm around Florrie. 'There, there. You're safe now. They've got her.' He turned to give Thom the thumbs up.

Thom saluted him and then clambered back over the banister. Within moments, he'd descended the staircase and headed for where Florrie and Sir Richard stood.

Sir Richard let his arm drop from Florrie's shoulder. He laced his hands together behind his back. 'Very good show, Thom. Darned valiant, rescuing our damsel in distress like that. And you even managed not to knock Talbot out cold. I pray we'll get the truth from her quickly.'

Enfolding Florrie in an embrace, Thom kissed the top of her head. 'Oh, my love. I couldn't believe it when I saw all them police cars racing up the drive. And then Arkwright came to fetch me. I thought I'd lost you!'

Florrie buried her face in his chest, relieved to breathe in the comforting smell of his warm skin beneath his rough shirt and the earthy undertones of the garden. 'Thank you. Thank you, love. I thought I was a goner there.' *Pull yourself together, Florrie,* her inner voice insisted. *There are more important matters at hand.* She eased herself out of Thom's embrace and turned back to her employer. 'We'll get Sir William back safe and sound, sir. I'm sure of it.'

'I hope you're right Florrie,' Sir Richard said softly.

Flanked by her fiancé on one side and Sir Richard on the other, Florrie observed Conway forcefully demanding that Talbot reveal the whereabouts of Miles T. Brooke.

'I'm not telling you a dickybird!' the nanny yelled as she was dragged to her feet. She shrieked and glared at the officer holding her on the side Thom had whacked with the spade. 'Mind my shoulder, you oaf. I'll not be brutalized by a bunch of overgrown schoolyard bully-boys!'

'You have one last opportunity to tell us where your co-conspirator has the boy before we throw you into the Black Maria,' Conway said, his face mere inches from Talbot's. 'You have the chance to redeem yourself, woman. I advise you to take it.'

She spat at him. 'Don't moralize to me, you big bald lump. You're in the pay of these industrialist parasites. You're nowt but a toady and a moron.'

Conway's eyebrows sank low above his brooding amber eyes. 'You'll hang for this. Let's see how cocky you are when we give you a glimpse of the gallows and throw you in a holding cell.'

With Miss Talbot marched off the premises by the police, accompanied by the barking dogs, Florrie was only too happy to hasten down to the kitchen for a cup of sweet tea and a slice of cake.

'And she did *what*?' Cook asked, both elbows on the table, leaning forward, red in the face.

Florrie recounted how she'd been held with a blade to her throat by a crazed criminal, intent on escaping in the Bugatti with her as collateral. She touched the place where the sharp tip of the letter opener had dug into the soft skin of her neck. 'I just hope they get that baby back.'

Sitting by her side, Thom held her free hand, stroking her knuckles absently. 'I reckon you can get a full week off for this!' he chuckled.

Florrie wrenched her hand free and playfully batted her fiancé in the chest. 'Honestly, Thom. You're so heartless!'

'Saved your life though, didn't I?'

'That you did.' Florrie momentarily put her head on his shoulder by way of appreciation. 'But I didn't get involved in all this – going hunting for damning evidence, like – I didn't do all that for the sake of squeezing some extra holiday out of that poor beggar upstairs.' She'd told the others about the letters she'd found in Miss Talbot's room, but she'd kept the blackmailing correspondence between Miles T. Brooke and Dame Elizabeth to herself. It had been turned over to Conway in the strictest of confidence. 'I just knew something about that horrible old baggage weren't right. I didn't like the way she treated that little boy. She didn't have any caring or motherly instincts at all, and . . . well, I just smelled a rat and I was proved right.'

'You've got a copper's nose, our Florrie,' Cook said, slicing a large slab of sponge cake on to a side plate and pushing it towards her. 'I just thought she were one of them miserable "thou shalt not" types. Never would have thought for a minute she was involved in such terrible goings-on.' She bit heartily into her own slice and spoke with her mouth full. 'I hope they find the little mite in one piece. Bad enough having Lady Godiva for a mother . . .' She looked up at the ceiling pointedly. 'Let alone being snatched from your cot at Christmas and cooped up with some strange feller.'

'Aye, well, if I were Lady Charlotte, I'd be saying my prayers right now that that crow of a woman comes clean about his whereabouts and doesn't take the secret to the grave with her,' Florrie said. 'Talbot's the type to do it out of spite, I reckon.'

She was just about to get to her feet and resume her housekeeper's duties when Sir Richard came down the stairs and entered the kitchen. Uncharacteristically nervous, toying with the buttons on the coat that he held over one arm, he hadn't yet regained any colour to his cheeks. In fact, he looked even more harassed than before.

Everyone sat a little straighter at the table. Thom took his arm off the back of Florrie's chair. Arkwright, who had been reading *The Times* at the far corner of the kitchen table, slapped the newspaper down and got to his feet.

'Sir,' he said. 'Is there anything we can do for you?'

Sir Richard smiled weakly. 'As you were, everyone. Please.'

'Slice of cake, Sir Richard? Cup of tea with us lot below stairs?' Cook took a clean cup and saucer from the sideboard behind her and nodded towards the giant steel teapot she'd brewed up in. 'We'll look after you, your lordship.'

Placing his hand on his chest, Sir Richard smiled as if he hadn't the weight of the world on his shoulders. 'That's very kind of you, Cook, but actually, I need to speak with our housekeeper as a matter of urgency.' He turned to Florrie. 'If you wouldn't mind meeting me by the front entrance, Florrie?'

Florrie sprang to her feet and bobbed a curtsey. 'Of course. I can walk up with you now, if you'd like.'

He nodded. 'I'll brief you en route.'

En route to what? Florrie wondered. She climbed the stairs behind him, trying to second-guess the urgent matter. Was there yet another dreadful twist to this terrible tale?

When they reached the domed marble entrance hall, Sir Richard came to a stop by the portrait of his father and donned his coat. He turned to face her.

'Faced with the gallows, it seems Talbot has weakened,' he said.

'She's given up an address?' Florrie asked.

'Yes. In Huddersfield, of all places. Brooke's holed up in some rented gentleman's residence, apparently.' Sir Richard cast a glance towards the front door, which was ajar. 'Conway's waiting in his car downstairs. I'm to go with him and his task force.'

'Of course.' She crossed her fingers. 'I'm not much of a praying woman, but please God, Sir William's found safe and sound. You can celebrate the New Year by putting all this nasty stuff behind you. I'll keep an eye on things here, sir. Don't worry about that.'

'Well, actually, Florrie, I need you to come with me. If you will.' He bit the side of his lip.

Florrie couldn't disguise her surprise. '*Me?* Why me? Surely Lady Charlotte will go with you.' In truth, she wasn't entirely sure she wanted to witness a second dangerous showdown in the same day.

Sir Richard shook his head and lowered his voice. 'She's had rather too much to drink. Refuses to come out of the music room, where she's playing the piano very badly with Daphne. The pair of them are drunk as lords. They're a liability. My brother and his German guest aren't any better.' He took her gently by the forearm. 'And you've seen Brooke before at close quarters. I can't honestly remember what he looks like – Mama's funeral was a blur of faces. But *you* can identify him to the police. I trust your judgement, and if . . . *when* we find my son, he knows you. He'll be reassured if he sees you.' He released her arm, looking contrite. 'Please. I know you've already endured terrible upset today, but . . . I need you, Florrie. We need you.'

Florrie rubbed her face. What if Brooke was armed? Wasn't it likely he would defend himself if cornered? This drama had the propensity to end badly – of that she was certain. Yet a baby's life was in the balance, and a man she cared deeply for needed her. How could she refuse him? She nodded. 'Sir William will need nappies and milk and rusk. Something comforting and familiar like his teddy bear or favourite book.'

'I've already assembled everything in a bag. Will you do this for me, Florrie? Will you put yourself in harm's way yet again for the sake of my son? Help me identify this scoundrel and get him behind bars?'

'Course I will! We're going to get him back, sir. We're going to bring your baby home.'

Without saying goodbye to her colleagues and her fiancé, who were huddled together in the safety and warmth of the kitchen, without even donning her coat, Florrie followed Sir Richard out to the waiting police car. He took off his coat and put it around her shoulders. Shivering in his jumper, he opened the rear door.

'After you, Miss Bickerstaff.'

30

'Is this it?' Sir Richard asked Conway.

Though it was only four in the afternoon, it was dark outside. The journey to Huddersfield had been conducted at breakneck speed, their vehicle leading a convoy of three police cars and one Black Maria along the winding country roads that criss-crossed the Pennines. It had been a perilous, bone-rattling journey which had left Florrie feeling quite sick. Now, however, she knew she had to quickly shake off any nausea or anxiety, because they had arrived at the address the duplicitous nanny had given to Conway.

The gentleman's residence being rented by Brooke was a sprawling, York stone semi-detached house, three storeys tall and built in the late 1800s, judging by the architectural style. Florrie could imagine that the exterior had once been a warm, sandy hue, but with decades of polluting smoke coming from the local textile mills, its façade was now blackened and foreboding, lit only by the sulphurous glow of the streetlight. No light shone inside.

She shivered. 'Do we stay in the car?'

Conway looked around. 'Yes. Me and my lads are going in. It could turn nasty. You wait here, and we'll bring the baby out to you.'

'I'm coming with you,' Sir Richard said, tensing, as though he was poised to leap out of the vehicle. 'My son's in there.'

Conway shook his head. 'No, sir. It's best for you to stay here. Don't worry though. My men will do everything they can to keep your boy safe.' In the gloom, the rim of his hat cast his features into complete blackness, giving him a menacing air. He opened the car door and left them alone.

Watching one cohort of officers gather silently by the front door, while the others sneaked around to the back, Florrie's breath came short and quick.

'I pray he hasn't got a gun,' Sir Richard said, his breath steaming in the freezing air inside the car. He inhaled sharply. 'Or a knife.' He turned to Florrie. 'What if he puts up a fight and William gets caught up in a scuffle and—'

Unthinkingly, Florrie laid her hand on his wrist. 'Don't trouble yourself with thoughts of *what if*. Just picture getting Sir William back, safe and sound. With a bit of luck, he'll be delivered to you in minutes, safe as houses.'

Sir Richard took her hand and squeezed it. 'Dear Florrie, I pray you're right.' He was shaking with either cold or trepidation or both. Even in the murk, she could see his face was drawn with apprehension.

Rubbing his freezing fingers to bring some warmth to them, Florrie realized Sir Richard was utterly beleaguered and alone, potentially on the cusp of losing his entire world if the baby was hurt or killed during a botched arrest. He would be devastated. She said a silent prayer for the child's safety.

Her thoughts were interrupted by a crash that rent the icy air – the sound of the door being smashed off its hinges. The police were in. Through the house's windows, misty with condensation, they could see torchlight flashing inside.

'Why's there not a light on?' Florrie asked. 'He must be in, surely! I can't imagine him walking the streets with a stolen baby, when the whole country's looking for him!' She knew she was talking rapidly. The nervous energy coursing through her veins was making her jittery.

'Please be there,' Sir Richard said beneath his breath. 'Please be alive and well.'

Suddenly, there was a loud crack and the living room window shattered.

Sir Richard clasped his hands to his head. 'No! William!' He was yelling. 'No, no, no! This can't be happening.' He flung open the car door and ran towards the house.

Two burly policemen standing guard at the garden gate dragged him back, and Florrie watched in horror as a scuffle ensued. She got out of the car to get a clearer view of what was going on, clasping Sir Richard's coat close against the freezing cold. Had a gun been fired? Sir Richard had broken free of the policemen and was sprinting up the steeply terraced front garden path. *Please don't let this end badly,* Florrie thought. Her employer burst his way into the house and another gunshot cracked through the darkness. Had somebody been shot?

Suddenly, the icy air was filled with the desperate shrieking of a baby. Florrie felt tears prick the backs of her eyes. 'Please be all right, William. Please don't be hurt.'

Moments later, Sir Richard emerged from the house, carrying a bundle. Even in the dim streetlight, Florrie could see he was weeping openly.

'Dear God,' she whispered. 'What on earth . . . ?' She

watched in horror as her employer stumbled into the garden and dropped to his knees, sobbing over the bundle.

Fearing the worst was more than she could bear. Florrie climbed the steep path, slipping and sliding on the icy flagstones until she reached Sir Richard. It was only once she was standing directly above him that she realized that there was a wriggling, struggling tiny boy in among the blankets. With wide eyes glassy with tears, Sir William looked up at his father and then Florrie. Hiccoughing from crying so heartily, he was still clearly shocked and confused by whatever dastardly drama had unfolded inside the house. When he started to wail anew, Florrie realized that he was healthy and whole. She clasped the little boy's chubby hand inside hers and kissed it.

'Thank God,' she said.

Sir Richard smiled at her. 'He's safe. We found him, Florrie. Thanks to you, we found him.'

At that moment, shouting came from the hallway of the house and Miles T. Brooke was marched out of the house and down the garden path. Though his hands were cuffed, he was kicking out at his captors and turning the cold air blue with his foul language. As the police constables dragged him past Sir Richard, Florrie and the baby, Brooke twisted his head, clearly recognizing his victim.

'This changes nothing, you know,' he shouted. 'I'm still your father, you spoiled little bastard, and I'll make sure the world knows it.'

Florrie shook her head. Sir Richard tensed.

'*You're* the bastard, you hideous ghoul!' He got to his feet, pushing the baby into Florrie's arms. 'How *dare* you snatch my son? How *dare* you jeopardize his life and extort me and my family? I'll make sure they lock you up and throw away the key.'

He took several steps towards Brooke. Would there be a fight?

'Leave him, sir!' Florrie said forcefully. 'He's insane. No good will come of starting a set-to with the likes of Brooke. Leave it to Conway and his fellers.'

'Come on, if you think you can take me on!' Brooke taunted Sir Richard. 'An older man in handcuffs. That will look pretty on the front page of the *Telegraph*. "Touchy toff tackles real father in shock adultery case." Or how about, "True heir diddled out of inheritance by—"'

'Hey! Pack it in!' One of the policemen shoved Brooke hard in the back. 'I don't want to hear another word out of that foul mouth of yours, or it won't go well for you once we get you in the cells.'

Brooke was hastily bundled into the police van. Conway strode purposefully out of the house, carrying a pistol on the end of a pencil, wedged through its trigger guard. He came to a standstill by Sir Richard, Florrie and the baby.

'Have you searched the house? What did you find in there?' Sir Richard asked. He'd taken the baby from Florrie and was now holding him close.

'Don't worry about all that, sir. We'll search it properly in the morning when the light's better. You recognize him, right? You can identify him in a line-up?' he asked them both.

Florrie nodded. 'Yes. I'd recognize him a mile off. He's Miles T. Brooke.'

Sir Richard peered at his son. 'Absolutely. No doubt. Miles T. Brooke. I wasn't sure I'd recognize him, at first, but I remember him visiting the house when my father was still alive. He was Papa's old college chum. And now I remember him from my mother's funeral.' He sighed and looked up at the night sky, heavy with snow clouds.

'Well, for now, rest assured we've got all the proof we need that Brooke is guilty as hell,' Conway assured him. 'He'll swing for this.'

Sir Richard looked over at the van, whose engine had now started up. Florrie wondered if he had mixed feelings at the prospect of a man who might possibly be his real father going to the gallows. It occurred to her again that her employer was in a wholly unenviable position. There was no way the rumours that he was not the true heir to Holcombe Hall and the Harding-Bourne fortune wouldn't find their way into the newspapers, either. Spreading scandalous gossip was human nature.

In the car, on the considerably less frenetic journey back to Holcombe, the three of them were squashed together on the back seat. Sir Richard calmed Sir William by reading to him from his favourite book, and the little boy was delighted to be reunited with his favourite teddy bear. Florrie somehow cobbled together a bowl full of rusk and milk and fed him in transit.

While he was eating, Sir Richard stroked his hair. 'He doesn't seem to have been maltreated, does he?'

Florrie shook her head. 'I gave him a good look over before we set off, when I changed his nappy on the back seat. He seems absolutely fine.'

'Do you think he knows who I am?' Sir Richard's brow furrowed.

'Of course! I know it's felt like a lifetime, but it's only

been just under a week. He recognizes his dadda, all right. He calmed down very quickly after that hullabaloo, and that's because he knew he was back safe with his loving father.'

'It must have been so traumatic for him.' Sir Richard wiped his glassy eyes with the heel of his hand.

Florrie cast her mind back to the death and burial of her sister, Irene. George had been little more than a toddler. Nelly and Alice had been babes-in-arms, and yet they had all weathered their loss so well. 'Children are *very* resilient. Try not to think about what happened in the last week. Brooke's a scoundrel, but I can't see him mistreating a baby, for all he's a lowlife. Especially not when the safe return of the baby was worth fifty thousand pounds to him.' She kept to herself the thought that Brooke would quite possibly not neglect a baby that was his grandson. As far as Sir Richard knew, Brooke's paternity claims were the ravings of a lunatic or else the cynical lies of a blackmailer intent on manipulating a wealthy man who was at a low ebb.

The miles passed by in semi-darkness, punctuated only by glimpses of the moon, as it emerged from snow clouds to shine on the bare spikes of the hedgerows, the dry stone walls and the glittering reservoirs of the Pennines . . .

When the car crunched to a halt on the gravel drive, Florrie woke from a fitful sleep she hadn't realized she'd drifted into. Finally, they arrived back at the Holcombe estate. Night had fallen in earnest. Sir Richard was snoring, slumped against the window. Little Sir William was asleep on his father's chest, and she had been sleeping with her head on her employer's lap. Florrie jerked awake in earnest and sat up. Glancing through the foggy car windows, she realized a group of staff was gathered around the car. Most were smiling. A few appeared bemused or were they just curious to see that the baby was alive and well? Thom, however, was peering straight into the car, and his expression was not that of a happy man.

1932

31

'Happy New Year, Florrie!' Sir Richard said on entering the dining room for breakfast, carrying his son in his arms. He beamed down at Sir William. 'Say, "Happy New Year" to Florrie, Willy.' Taking the boy's hand, he waved to Florrie.

The baby jabbered to himself blithely and then wriggled to be free. Sir Richard set him down, allowing him to cruise the chairs and stumble unaided from the table to the sideboard.

'What a happy little chap he is,' Florrie said, smiling. She took out her notepad. 'I thought I'd give my maids a lie-in, so I'll take your eggs order this morning.' Remembering herself, she looked up. 'Oh, and a *very* Happy New Year to you! 1932 has begun better than well, eh? Sir William's back, safe and sound, and his kidnappers are behind bars, awaiting trial. I bet you're the happiest man alive.'

Following the baby around the furniture, Sir Richard nodded. 'I'm counting my every blessing, Florrie. I don't feel I can ever let this little bundle of mischief out of my sight again. Heaven knows how I shall run a business empire.' The smile slid from his face. 'I say, have the papers been delivered yet?'

Florrie glanced over to the table by the stained-glass oriel window where Arkwright normally left the papers mounted on reading sticks. There was no sign of them.

'Perhaps they're just late because it's New Year's Day. I'll check when I hand your egg order to Cook.'

'Marvellous. Thank you. And I'll have some scrambled eggs this morning, please.'

She poured him a cup of coffee and left a rack of toast on the table. 'Shall I bring the high-chair from the nursery?' she asked.

Sir Richard nodded and carried a wilful, twisting, wriggling Sir William back to the table. 'Yes, you better had. This little urchin has escape on his mind.' He took a piece of toast and handed it to the boy. 'Any sign of my brother?'

'Not yet, sir.' Florrie pictured Arkwright sitting in his office in a foul mood because he'd been forced to stay up all night serving drinks to Sir Hugh, Daphne, Lady Charlotte and the German cuckoo in the nest, von Grunwald. 'I gather the others were toasting Sir William's safe return and the New Year until the small hours. I'm sure they'll be along later.'

Repairing to the kitchen, Florrie thought about all that had come to pass since they'd arrived back at Holcombe Hall, following Sir William's rescue. Thom had been distinctly frosty with her, having witnessed the physical over-familiarity between her and Sir Richard in the back seat of the car. Her explanation that she'd had no control over her own body once she'd nodded off and slumped on to Sir Richard hadn't stopped him from sulking. He'd expressed relief that she'd made it back from Huddersfield in one piece, at least, and that the baby was alive and well. Despite them having arranged to bring in the New Year with Mam, however, he'd stayed in the big house, complaining of a cold coming on. Even if she had wanted to unpick her feelings over Thom's obvious petulance, she hadn't had the opportunity. The press had apparently spent the daylight hours of New Year's Eve clamouring at the estate gates for an exclusive scoop on the rescue, setting everyone – staff and family alike – on edge. The telephone had rung constantly and late into the night with well wishes from friends and queries from journalists, meaning Florrie hadn't even made it over to the gamekeeper's cottage on her own to see Mam. She'd slept through the stroke of midnight, having fallen into bed at half past eleven, alone and utterly exhausted.

Now she descended the stairs to the kitchen.

'Well?' Cook asked, in the middle of glazing a ham for the family lunch later on.

'Scrambled eggs, and you can see he's dreading the papers. Baby needs someone to look after him, though, because Lady Charlotte's still too busy drinking the cellar dry.' Florrie looked over at Sally, who was chopping onions badly with her index finger bound in a tight bandage. Her eyes were watering freely and she was sniffing dolefully. 'I know *someone* who might make a better nanny stand-in than a chopper of onions.'

Sally looked up and glanced from Cook to Florrie. 'What? Did someone say my name?'

Cook roared with laughter. 'By heck, our Sally. You're going to have done every single job in the house by the time you're twenty-five – none of them well, I might add.'

Sally looked crestfallen and absently sliced into her middle finger. She winced. 'Ow. That's right mean, that is! I thought you said I was the best assistant cook you ever had.'

Cook's ample chest rose and fell with mirth. She slapped the ham with glee. 'Happen I said you were the *only* assistant I ever had. Not the best.' Wheezing with laughter, she pointed to Sally's freshly bleeding finger with her glazing brush. 'But if your chopping is owt to go by, I don't reckon I fancy your chances of potty training little feller-me-lad much either! He'll be like a dog marking his territory on every rug in the house.'

Florrie stifled a grin. 'Take no notice, Sal. You're kind and caring and responsible. I think you'll make a good interim nanny, until Sir Richard's interviewed for someone new.' She turned back to Cook. 'Has Arkwright mentioned the papers?'

Cook nodded. 'And his lordship's going to throw a hissy fit when he sees the write-up, apparently.'

Florrie's heart sank. 'That's all we need. As if he hasn't suffered enough.'

She made her way through the warren of narrow subterranean corridors to Arkwright's office and found the door to the butler's office open. Arkwright was sitting behind his desk with his head lolling forward, eyes shut and mouth hanging open. 'Mr Arkwright?'

He snorted himself awake and blinked repeatedly, looking up at Florrie and frowning, and then seemed to remember himself. 'Blast! What time is it?' He retrieved his silver fob watch from the pocket of his waistcoat. 'Damn. It's not like me to fall asleep on the job. I must be getting old.'

'What time did that lot finally throw in the towel?' she asked.

Holding a fist to his mouth, Arkwright yawned. 'Four

o'clock. Just after. I appreciate there was much to celebrate, but why on earth they needed me to keep their glasses charged, I'll never know. I fear Lady Charlotte was trying to impress that Prussian halfwit.' He took up the newspapers, which were already ironed and on their sticks. 'Brace yourself, Miss Bickerstaff. We are in for a torrid time.'

Florrie grimaced. 'That bad? Shall I take them up? I can hardly do any wrong at the moment, so if Sir Richard takes the headlines badly . . .'

Arkwright shook his head. 'I've put you in the firing line once too often, I admit. But you've gone above and beyond duty in this kidnapping malarkey, and I'm now happy to face whatever ire is misdirected at me. It's the impact it will have on Sir Hugh I think we really have to watch out for.'

Florrie nodded. 'As you wish. Well, I'll be on hand in the dining room to help out if the sparks start to fly.'

She was about to leave Arkwright's office when the butler held his hand up.

'A moment, before you head back to the kitchen, Florrie,' he said. 'Close the door.'

'Oh? What's wrong?' Anticipation caused the hairs to rise on her arms. She pushed the door shut softly.

Arkwright took a deep breath and held it momentarily. He chewed the inside of his cheek. 'Forgive me for seeming to pry, but is everything quite all right between you and Thomas? Only I sense there's been some tension between you, and I also sense there's a . . .' He smoothed his pencil moustache with a manicured index finger. 'A closeness between you and Sir Richard that's been developing for a long while now, but which has become more pronounced of late.'

Florrie blinked. She felt her cheeks flush hot and started to scratch at her neck. 'Er . . . whatever gave you that idea?'

Arkwright leaned on his desk. 'Look, I've been butler here for decades. I watch people, Florence. It's part of my job: to observe, to act only where necessary, to maintain a happy equilibrium under this roof. And . . . all I'm saying is that you must remember – for *your own* sake – remember the line between employer and employee. However much that lot upstairs present that line as blurred when it suits them, it is still very much there. If you cross it, it can come back to bite you very hard. We staff are *always* the ones to bear the consequences of crossing that boundary. So, think on.'

'I don't know what you're talking about, Mr Arkwright. I never—'

'You're an adult, Florence. And I'm a grown man, too. You know what you're doing, and I know what I see with my two eyes. I can't tell you what to do with your affections, but be careful. What Sir Richard might feel, and what he does – what *he's able* to do – are two very different things. I don't want to see you hurt. And as for Thomas . . .'

Florrie bit her lip and looked down at her fingernails. She felt tears welling but steeled herself not to shed them in front of the butler. 'That big soppy bugger? What about him?' She looked up, feigning levity.

Arkwright lowered his voice. 'Thom is an old-fashioned sort of man. You, Florence, are an independent, intelligent and very *modern* kind of woman. Ask yourself, are you engaged to Thomas because you're a good match, or is he just the first man that asked?'

'Oh.' Open-mouthed and aghast, Florrie stared at the butler, processing what he'd said. She had no answer.

'Are you even the marrying kind?' Arkwright cocked his head to the side and fixed her with searching eyes.

'My mother thinks Thom's a terrific catch,' she said.

'That's not what I asked.'

'I think Thom's just annoyed I'd gone off with Sir Richard without telling him, and then came back with my head in his lap. Honestly, we'd all just conked out with exhaustion on the journey back!'

'I told you, I can see closeness between you and Sir Richard, and I've told you what I think about that. But I don't think for a minute that you two were canoodling on the back seat of a police car, with a baby between you and detectives in the front. That's preposterous, and Thomas is jumping to unfair conclusions ... because he sees Sir Richard as a threat. And is it right he should demand that you tell him your whereabouts at any given moment? You're the housekeeper, and this was a high-profile, high stakes kidnapping, in which you'd inadvertently become embroiled as a witness of sorts.'

Florrie shook her head. 'I don't see what you're trying to say.'

'Is Thom your keeper? Is it right he should be giving you the cold shoulder for a turn of events that was beyond your control?'

'Er ... well, he was worried sick.'

'And is it right he should be treating you as though you've been conducting some clandestine love affair behind his back, simply because you fell asleep in the back of a police car?' Arkwright tucked the papers under his arm. 'An obvious close rapport with your employer is one thing, but... If Thom's possessive of you now, what is he going to be like after five years of marriage? After ten? More?' He raised an eyebrow. 'Think on it. I don't say these things to make you doubt your own feelings. I just want you to make big decisions like marriage for *you*. Not for Thom, or your mother, or anyone else, for that matter. Just you.'

Nodding, Florrie whispered her thanks and followed him out towards the kitchen, silently wiping a tear from her eye. She picked up the domed plate of scrambled eggs from the ever-perceptive Cook, insisting that she had merely poked herself in the eye by accident, and returned with Arkwright to the dining room.

Sir Richard was sitting at the table, bouncing his son on his knee, while the boy chomped on a sausage clutched in his hand. Florrie was surprised to see Sir Hugh had appeared while she'd been gone. He was seated at the far end, scratching his scalp. Still in his pyjamas and dressing gown, he had the sickly grey pallor and puffy eyes of a man who had spent the night drinking heavily and smoking. She could smell the excess on him from where Sir Richard was seated, several place settings along.

'Your eggs, sir.' She removed the dome, which the baby instantly tried to grab. 'No, Sir William. Hot! Ouch!' Setting the dome out of reach, she ruffled the baby's silken hair, took a napkin and wiped his greasy mouth. 'There! That's better.'

'Where would you like your papers, sir?' Arkwright asked.

'Just spread them out on the table, there's a good chap. Let's see what the world has to say about my son's ordeal and his kidnappers.' He exchanged a knowing glance with Florrie.

Would the papers have reported on Brooke's scandalous claims?

Putting on his spectacles, Sir Richard pulled the *Manchester Guardian* towards him first. There was a photograph of Brooke, taken at Dame Elizabeth's funeral service, accompanied by a headline.

KIDNAPPER CLAIMS TO BE MOGUL'S TRUE FATHER

'Good Lord, no,' he whispered.

'What is it, Dickie?' Sir Hugh set down his coffee cup. He took a drag of his smouldering cigarette and tried to pull the paper towards him.

'You don't need to read it. It's stuff and nonsense.' Sir Richard tried to pull the paper back.

'I'll be the judge of that.' Sir Hugh's bloodshot eyes narrowed. 'What are you trying to hide?' He snatched *The Times* from under the *Guardian* and held the paper up, reading aloud: '"High-society kidnapping paternity claim – is the Harding-Bourne nightmare just beginning?"'

He shook his head and squeezed his eyes shut, then re-read the headline just beneath his breath. 'Paternity *what*? Sorry. I'm rather hungover, but what on earth is being proposed here?'

'Oh, it's just rot,' Sir Richard said. 'Take no notice. That Brooke fellow tried to insinuate that he'd had an affair with

Mama. Ludicrous.' He waved his hand dismissively. 'He was just being provocative, and it seems one of the constables has leaked it to the press. Probably got paid handsomely for it. But it'll blow over. I mean, it's absolutely preposterous. Mama, having an affair! Imagine! If he wasn't already in the dock for murder, I'd be inclined to sue Brooke for slander or defamation of character or something.'

Sir Hugh seemed to study his older brother. He dragged on his cigarette and blew a plume of smoke into the air. 'So, Brooke's claiming to be your father?'

'Yes. He's insane, obviously.'

'Wasn't he a college chum of Papa's? Came to the house a lot when we were small?'

Sir Richard forked some eggs into his mouth. 'I can't say I remember any visits.' He didn't meet his brother's gaze, Florrie noted.

'Papa was away a lot on business, wasn't he? So, if Mama *did* have an affair with Brooke, it's possible he *is* your father? I mean, you and I look nothing alike. And you only resembled James because he took after Mama.'

'You're looking for scandal that isn't there, Hugh, and I resent what you're implying about our mother, may she rest in peace. She was an unimpeachable, honourable woman, who doted on *our* father. This Brooke ... he's a kidnapper, for God's sake! He's a dangerous criminal. Tried to shoot me dead when I entered the house in Huddersfield. Are those the actions of a sane man? Does a sane man shoot at his own son?'

'Being a criminal who's motivated by money, and being the type of man to bed another's wife and impregnate her, seem to be attributes that make comfortable bed fellows, if you ask me.'

Sir Richard finally locked eyes with his younger brother. 'Why are you so keen to believe Papa was not my father?'

'Because, dear boy . . .' Sir Hugh leaned in. 'If you're *not* the second son of the late Lord Harding-Bourne, then that makes *me* the heir to the family fortune, including this house.' He slapped the paper down triumphantly and poked himself in the chest. 'Me!'

32

'Morning, Mam,' Florrie called out, as she pushed open the front door to the gamekeeper's cottage. She was carrying a basket of Cook's freshly baked bread, covered with a cloth. It was only the 2nd of January, but since it was Saturday morning and she'd seen hardly anything of Mam and the children over Christmas, Florrie had decided to share an early breakfast with her family. 'Only me!'

'Auntie Florrie!' George shouted from somewhere upstairs. Thunderous footsteps preceded his appearance on the staircase. 'Auntie Florrie! At last!' He ran to greet her, grabbing her in a tight hug. When he broke away, he spied the basket. 'Ooh, what's in there? Has Cook sent something yummy over?'

With her free hand, Florrie cupped George's chin, then leaned down and kissed him noisily on the cheek. 'Yes, chuck. Lovely bread and some fancy cheese left over from New Year's Eve. Where's Nana and the girls?'

'They're in the bathroom. Nan's washing their hair because Alice peed the bed and it got everywhere. Where's Thom? Isn't he coming too? Did I tell you what Father Christmas left us under our tree? It was a day late, but Nan said one of Father Christmas's reindeers might have been poorly and made him late. Guess what it was!'

Florrie chuckled. 'Ooh, slow down, our Georgie boy. You're making me dizzy with so many questions.'

She walked into the scullery and started to lay the table for breakfast.

'I got a bike, Auntie Florrie! I got a lovely *brand-new* push bike. It's right big and it's red and all. I love red. It's my favourite colour. I must have been a right good lad last year, because Father Christmas left us that. Can you believe it?'

Midway through slicing the loaf, Florrie paused to consider what her nephew had just told her. A children's bike was beyond her mother's pocket, and she had clubbed together with Thom to buy each of the children new winter coats and boots. So, who had bought the cycle? It seemed unlikely, given he'd been preoccupied with the abduction of his son, but surely it could only be Sir Richard. She smiled. 'You're a grand young man, our George. I'm very proud of you. And getting a big boy's bike means Nelly can have your old one.'

'Will Thom teach me how to fix punctures?' he asked.

Florrie thought about her fiancé, whom she had seen only briefly at the staff's New Year's Day meal. He had deliberately (or so it had seemed to her) chosen to sit with the other gardening staff on the far side of the table, even though she'd saved him a seat next to her, and he had stayed in the kitchen only to eat a main course, still grumbling about nursing a cold. How she wished Thom wasn't prone to sulking. 'Aye. I'm sure he will.' She could picture Arkwright's sceptical expression in her mind's eye, asking her searching questions about the suitability of their match. She swallowed down an unexpected lump of woe.

When the table was set and George had told her all

about his more practical presents of a new coat and boots, which Father Christmas had apparently delivered late and which he seemed less enthused by, her mother and the girls entered the kitchen.

Mam opened her arms wide. 'Here's my *big* girl! Happy New Year, chuck. I've heard you're quite the heroine up at the big house. I want you to tell me all about your sleuthing adventures.'

Florrie revelled in her mother's embrace, drinking in the smell of Derbac soap, which she'd used on her nieces' hair to ward off headlice. 'It's just a tale of all's well that ends well, Mam. I didn't really do owt, apart from follow my instincts. The main thing is that baby's back where he belongs, and the kidnappers are under lock and key awaiting trial.'

Mam put some water on to boil for tea, and they sat at the table to enjoy the early breakfast.

'Last night, Mr Arkwright brought me over yesterday's papers,' she said, scraping butter on to the bread. 'Is it true? Is Sir Richard this Brooke's son?'

Florrie shook her head. 'I wouldn't believe a word you read. Brooke's a madman and a crook. I think he's just trying to make Sir Richard's life as difficult as possible because his dreadful ransom plot came to nowt. The man clearly has no morals, and neither did Talbot.'

'Shocking. Right under our noses, too.' Mam reached out and stroked Alice's damp hair. The little girl was happily gnawing on a chunk of cheese. 'I'm glad she never got her hooks into *our* babies.'

At that moment, there was a knock at the back door. Who could be visiting at such an early hour?

Florrie looked up and saw Thom peering in at the kitchen window. She felt her pulse quicken. 'Look who it is!'

'Uncle Thom!' the children cried.

Glancing at the clock on the kitchen wall, Florrie wondered if she should make her excuses and go back to the big house. She wasn't sure she could bear another awkward exchange with her disgruntled fiancé.

'Come on in, love,' Mam shouted through the window.

The back door opened and Thom entered, carrying a paper bag. 'Happy New Year Matilda! Kids!' He shot an apprehensive glance at Florrie. 'Florrie.' He pecked her perfunctorily on the cheek and set the bag on the table. 'I picked you some tangerines from the orangery. Them lot won't notice a few going missing.' He handed the jewel-coloured fruit out, to the delight of the children. 'Couple of fresh lemons from the tree for baking.' He proffered those to Mam. 'And what's this?' He frowned quizzically, a smile playing on his chapped lips. 'Could it be something for George?'

He set a small object wrapped in brown paper in front of the boy.

George opened the package, wide-eyed and grinning. 'A bell! Is this a bell for my new bike?' He held it up for the others to see and started to ring it.

'Ooh, hey! Pack it in, young man. That's quite enough of that!' Mam said, covering her ears in jest. 'They'll hear you coming from Batley to Blackpool.'

'A little birdie told me Father Christmas had brought you a new bike.'

'It's a belter, Uncle Thom,' George said. 'Nearly *man*-sized!'

'That right? Well, happen now you've got a bell, you

can cycle to school,' Thom said. 'Maybe on the pavement, mind, if Lady Charlotte or Daphne are out in the car. Ha ha.'

Yet again, Florrie considered how thoughtful Thom was. Was it possible *he* had saved up to buy George the bicycle? Perhaps she had judged him too harshly. Had she got so embroiled in the affairs of her employer that she'd forgotten where her true loyalties lay? She reached out and took Thom's hand. 'Got over your cold, then?'

'Seems so.' Thom still seemed aloof. He didn't even look her in the eye.

She held on to his hand a while longer and squeezed it. 'You going to give us a New Year's kiss then?'

'I just did, didn't I?' No. He still wasn't looking at her, and his demeanour was stiff.

Florrie let her hand sink to her lap.

'Cup of tea and some bread and cheese do you?' Mam asked, looking from Thom to Florrie and back. Did her mother sense the tension in the air?

'Aye. That'd be lovely. Ta.'

'Do you want to see it, Uncle Thom? My bike, I mean. You can put the bell on for me.' George spoke excitedly, with his mouth full of bread. 'It's fire-engine red. A Raleigh!'

'Sounds like a cracker, son. I'll put your bell on it after I've eaten.' Finally, he turned to Florrie. 'Father Christmas has been *very* generous this year.' He raised an eyebrow. 'A flashy new bike for your nephew? Makes a new coat and boots look a bit ordinary. Seems *Father Christmas* wanted to make a grand gesture.'

Ah, so that was it. Thom's ego had been bruised. He

hadn't bought George the bike after all – as she'd initially thought, it was most likely from Sir Richard. Florrie tried to see everything that had gone on over Christmas from Thom's perspective: Florrie had been inattentive towards him, preoccupied as she had been with the kidnapping; she'd hared off to Huddersfield without saying goodbye and had returned wearing Sir Richard's coat, asleep on his lap; George had received an expensive gift from another man. Yes, she supposed she could see why Thom might be jealous. It was just as well she hadn't shown him the bee brooch.

'Is that the only posh present someone in this family's got this Christmas?' Thom asked.

Mam collected Thom's empty plate, eyeing the two of them all the while. 'Father Christmas only gives lavish gifts to the children, because that's his job, Thomas.' Her voice had a no-nonsense tone to it. She turned to George. 'Go and show Uncle Thom your bike. Me and your Auntie Florrie can nit-comb the girls.'

Thom's smile didn't quite reach his eyes. He visibly swallowed hard. 'Oh. Right. Aye. Come on, lad. Let's leave the ladies to their own devices.'

Once Thom was out of earshot, Mam took out the nit combs and handed one to Florrie. 'You do Nelly. I'll do Alice.' She divided the toddler's hair into sections and started to comb through, wiping the comb on to a clean cloth each time. 'What's going on with you two? Out with it.'

Florrie shrugged. 'He's jealous. I think he thinks Sir Richard's . . . trying it on with me or summat. Which is ridiculous. The man's just been to hell and back. The fact he bought George a bike . . .'

'Didn't Father Christmas buy George the bike?' Nelly asked.

Mam looked aghast at Florrie. 'Of course Father Christmas did!' She silently mouthed the following words: 'Arkwright bought the bike. *Arkwright.*'

Florrie mouthed a surprised, 'Oh!' and started to laugh at the unexpected revelation. 'Good old Father Christmas.'

'Listen, Florrie,' Mam said, busily examining the contents deposited on the cloth, while the girls sang a nursery rhyme at the tops of their squeaky little voices. 'I can see there's bad feeling between you and Thom.'

Was she about to be admonished yet again for getting too close to the Harding-Bournes?

'And I think you need to put him in his place before he starts making a habit of calling everything into question. What you did – the way you found them letters to track down that baby ... That was the act of a heroine. You saved the day, love. You saved that baby's life and Sir Richard and his useless missus from heartbreak. I love Thom to bits, but he's out of line on this.'

Florrie surprised herself by starting to cry. She spoke haltingly through a veil of tears, still trying to comb a wriggling, protesting Nelly's hair, even though she couldn't see a thing. Her pent-up frustrations from the last few months – since the proposal – spilled out unchecked. 'Oh, Mam. I don't know what to do. He's so jealous all the time, and moody. If I do something he doesn't like – like, when I made him wait for an answer after the proposal – he'll just not talk to me for days. I don't like sulking. And he's always quick to tell me what I should do, how I should think – as if he's my dad, not my fiancé. It's only now we're engaged I can see he wants to change the way I am, the person I am. But I'm the housekeeper of the biggest stately home in the northwest. That means something to me. I'm like Arkwright. You'd never ask Arkwright to just drop everything and become . . . this *mouse*, would you?'

'Course not.'

'And then, when I was in Huddersfield, Sir Richard went into the house and there was a gunshot and I thought . . . I thought . . .' Her sobbing wracked her entire body and she was forced to step away from Nelly, who was so busy yelling a rendition of 'Baa Baa Black Sheep' that she hadn't noticed her aunt was overcome. 'I mean, I know he's my boss and I know where the line is, and I know not to overstep it. But . . . I still *care*. It's all right to care, isn't it?'

Mam prised the comb from Florrie's hand and clasped her in a tight hug. She patted Florrie's back. 'There, there, chuck. You let it all out. Oh, my poor girl. If I'd known this was making you so sad, I wouldn't have pushed you to make such a big commitment. It's a brave new world, I suppose, and women don't have to live their lives the same as they did in my day, when I were a girl.' She chuckled. 'It's not fifteen years since women got the vote. I mean, it's only four years since they passed the Equal thingy Act.'

'Franchise. Equal Franchise Act.'

'Aye. Things are changing, but Thom doesn't seem to have worked that one out.'

'You sound like you've been talking to Arkwright,' Florrie said, wiping her eyes on the unused half of the nit-comb cloth. She chuckled.

'Mr Arkwright's not the only one realizing the world

doesn't stand still.' Mam rubbed Florrie's hand. 'Do you want me to have a word with Thom? Set him straight?'

Florrie shook her head. 'I will when I'm ready.' She peered through the window to where Thom was tinkering with George's new bike bell. 'I do love him, you know. I just . . . I suppose I'm just tired.' She sniffed. 'I'm being daft. Forget any of this happened. I've got to get back to the house for them reporters coming. No doubt I'll have to referee a fight between Sir Richard and Sir Hugh. They're at each other's throats at the moment over this Brooke feller and who's the rightful heir.'

'You'd better pray there's nothing in this rumour,' Mam said. 'Because if Sir Hugh takes over Holcombe Hall and the Harding-Bourne businesses, we'll be out of collar and out on our ears, fast enough to give you a nosebleed. If you gave that berk a shilling, he'd spend a thousand pounds . . . on drink, most likely. He's a walking disaster, that man. Mark my words. As long as this rumour circulates, and those brothers don't present a united front with Sir Richard still at the helm, we're all facing ruin.'

33

'The point is, Hugh . . . *Hugh!*' Sir Richard clicked his fingers impatiently. 'Are you even listening to me?' He leaned forward to catch his brother's eye. 'This is important.'

As Florrie bent to light the brazier that would heat the orangery ready for the reporters' arrival in just under an hour's time, she felt Sir Hugh watching her. She glanced over her shoulder and found him gazing absently at her. He shifted his attention listlessly to the gardens outside, where tiny snowflakes had begun to whip around in eddies on the freezing wind. Obviously, Florrie couldn't demand that Sir Hugh listen to what his older brother had to say, but she silently willed him to take the scandal and the impact it was already having on the family seriously.

Sir Richard put the collar of his coat up and rubbed his hands together. When he spoke, puffs of steam escaped his lips. 'You've seen this morning's share price. A third of our stock's value has been wiped out overnight. *A third!*'

Finally, Sir Hugh turned to his older brother, looking exasperated. 'The share price will bounce back.'

Thumping the glass-and-rattan table, making the contents of the tea tray rattle, Sir Richard raised his voice. 'For heaven's sake, Hugh! Don't you realize what it's taken to save our companies and this household from financial ruin? I've had to lay off over a *thousand* employees to cut costs, not to mention travelling from America to India to drum up new custom. I've had to shutter half our mills; ordinary people are starving because of the Depression and what it's forced industrialists like me to do to keep us afloat.' His eyes were flashing with anger. 'I've been working in our family's businesses since I graduated, learning from Father. *Our* father! And when I took over the reins after his death and after we lost James in the trenches, I knew what I was doing because I already had more than fifteen years' experience under my belt, from shop floor to boardroom. Whereas you . . .'

'What about me?' Sir Hugh's tone dripped with insolence.

'All you've ever known is hedonism. You've never had a day's responsibility in your life. You don't know one end of a ship from the other, let alone one end of a shipbuilding contract from another or the wholesale price of coking coal for steelworks furnaces. You have no business acumen. You have no love for industry.'

'That's simply not true.'

'It bloody well is, Hugh, and you know it. Your instincts are shockingly bad. Even your attempt to become a kingmaker in politics failed because you backed the wrong horse. Thousands of pounds wasted on Mosley and that idiot, Walter!'

'Mosley's the future. You'll see. And then you'll owe me an apology.' Sir Hugh lit a cigarette and blew the smoke towards Florrie, indicating with a flick of his fingers that she should turn her back to them and face the garden.

Florrie stifled an urge to tip the dustpan full of ashes on him. She continued to eavesdrop, watching the men's reflections in the orangery's gleaming windows.

'You've *always* loved spending the proceeds of everyone

else's toil, without ever contributing one iota,' Sir Richard said. 'But now you want to jeopardize the equilibrium I've restored to our family's fortune and future over a kidnapper's baseless ruse to sow discord between us?'

'I'm the heir. I always was. *I* should be running HB Enterprises.'

Sir Richard got to his feet and grabbed his younger brother by the collar, hoisting him out of his chair. 'We will lose everything. *Everything*. Over nothing but your ego and idle rumours. No more Holcombe Hall. No more living the high life and moving in the right social circles. You will be a nobody, and so shall I. A pair of bankrupts, living alone in some dosshouse in Bury, perhaps, because our wives will leave us for better men, and the house will be sold to pay our debts.'

'Let me go this instant!' Sir Hugh pushed Sir Richard hard enough to send him and the table skittering over.

At that point, Florrie stood tall, cursing Brooke for having blurted his paternity claim in front of those policemen on the night of his arrest. She calmly helped her employer up and turned to Sir Hugh, unable to contain her irritation.

'Sir Hugh, if I may . . . I've known poverty all my life, and I certainly can't recommend it. Believe me if I say that risking the markets turning on Harding-Bourne's businesses because it's your highly experienced and trusted brother they want at the helm . . . it's simply not worth it.'

At her side, Sir Richard dusted himself off. 'I say, Florrie. Thank you, but it's quite all right. Nothing you can say will bring my arrogant brother to his senses.'

Sir Hugh stubbed his spent cigarette out in the uranium

glass ashtray and lit another. 'I'm rather sick of your insubordination, Florrie. You're sacked. And I say that as the head of this household and true Harding-Bourne heir.'

Sir Richard rushed at his brother again. 'She is nothing of the sort, and neither are you.'

The two engaged in another scuffle. Helpless, Florrie watched them, not knowing how to break up the argument before it came to earnest blows.

'Stop it! Please! The reporters will be here any minute.' Neither man was listening to her. 'Don't let Brooke tear your family apart. It's exactly what he's after.'

It was no use. Florrie dropped the ornate brass lid on the brazier and ran to find Arkwright. When they returned together several minutes later, they entered the orangery to find Sir Hugh lobbing a vase at Sir Richard's head. The vase missed by only an inch and smashed on the tiled floor.

'Er . . . gentlemen!' Arkwright called out, clapping his hands. 'Gentlemen! One cannot entertain the country's pre-eminent reporters when one is brawling like—'

'It's damn lies, I tell you!' Sir Richard yelled, seemingly oblivious to Arkwright's presence. He was holding his hands up defensively while Sir Hugh took a swing at him. 'Would you sacrifice your lifestyle on the basis of a madman's lies?'

'If it's lies, why did Mama enter into correspondence with him without involving the police?' Sir Hugh poked himself in the chest. 'You've spent years enjoying *my* birthright. Yes, Sir Richard, this. No, Sir Richard, that. Where's the deference I'm overdue?'

'Sirs! I must ask you to stop!' Arkwright shouted, trying to come between them.

Sir Hugh shoved the butler aside and advanced another step towards Sir Richard.

Florrie exchanged a concerned look with Arkwright. The reporters could arrive at any moment, and the only story they would have to share with the world would be one of discord and mistrust. If Arkwright couldn't break up the fight, she would have to take matters into her own hands.

'Grab Sir Hugh from behind,' she said. 'On the count of three.'

Arkwright nodded.

'One, two, three.' Florrie darted between the two brothers, placing herself in the path of Sir Hugh's flailing fist. Catching a glancing blow to her temple, she stumbled back into Sir Richard.

Mercifully, he caught her. 'Hugh! You utter bastard!' he yelled, righting her. 'Florrie, my dear. Are you all right?' Grimacing, he lifted her hair to check for damage.

'I'm fine, sir.'

Sir Hugh had finally fallen silent. Now he was staring in horror at Florrie. He clasped his hand to his mouth. 'Florrie, I didn't mean . . . It was an accident.'

'Was it?' Sir Richard asked sourly. 'You're lucky you didn't knock our housekeeper unconscious, you ungentlemanly oaf.'

'I'm dreadfully sorry, Florrie,' Sir Hugh said.

'I'll fetch ice,' Arkwright said, haring back towards the hall.

Florrie finally had her opportunity to end the quarrel. 'Look, what's done is done. *The Times* has their top journalists arriving any minute – a reporter and a photographer – so let's present a united front and keep the family's reputation beyond reproach.' Though her temple smarted, she steeled herself to look Sir Hugh in the eye. 'Now as far as I know, those letters from Brooke to your mother were simple extortion, same as the kidnapping of Sir William. Brooke and Talbot are arch-criminals, and there's not a shred of evidence says Dame Elizabeth was anything but true to your late father. Sir Richard's a dead ringer for him, for a start, in looks and temperament. He's even got his ears!'

'Thank you, Florrie,' Sir Richard said softly.

Sir Hugh took out his pack of cigarettes and removed one, tapping it on the pack. He shoved it into the corner of his mouth with something bordering on defiance. 'I'm owed my share of this house. And the business.'

'Didn't you hear a word Florrie said?' Sir Richard said, exasperation audible in his voice. 'Brooke's a fraud, and you're just jumping on the bandwagon because you feel my being head of the family somehow puts your nose out of joint. But think about it, Hugh! Could you really cope with the sort of responsibility I shoulder, year in, year out? No fun. No parties. Greying hair. Sleepless nights. Board meetings. Business meetings. Serious and dreadful tasks, like expressing condolences when miners die in bloody cave-ins? Facing the press? Shouldering the burden when shareholders are disgruntled? Aren't you better spending your extremely generous inheritance on your hedonism and political ambitions?'

Sir Hugh scowled and regarded his brother with undisguised contempt. He lit his cigarette and blew smoke up to the glazed lantern roof of the orangery. 'I want an extra allowance. I'll discuss the sums with you privately, but I want my loss of prestige and my lesser share of the businesses compensated for in cash, Dickie. If I'm to make a difference politically, I need money. Give me what I ask for, and I'll refute Brooke's claims in front of these journalists. Present a united front and all that.'

Pressing his lips together, with exhaustion etched deep into the lines at the corners of his eyes, Sir Richard nodded. 'A good leader puts his people before himself.'

Florrie exhaled heavily with relief. 'I'll clear this smashed vase up and get that brazier sorted, shall I?' She picked up the dustpan and brush.

'No need,' Sir Richard said, taking the dustpan and brush from her. 'Leave it to me. I'll clear this mess up and get the brazier going. You go and get some ice on your head.'

She bobbed a curtsey, trying desperately to hide her wooziness. 'I'll show the reporters through when they arrive, shall I?'

'Please do. And Florrie . . . I'm *dreadfully* sorry you had to take a punch from my idiot brother before we saw sense.'

The following day, the exclusive interview appeared in *The Sunday Times*. Brooke's claims were wholly denied by both brothers, Florrie noted, and the exposé of Sir William's abduction by his ruthless, heartless nanny and the gutless, money-grubbing family friend was so sympathetic, she was certain it would repair the damage to the family's reputation and help to restore the share price. Sure enough, by Tuesday the following week, the share price was back to normal, and the news had moved on.

That afternoon, Florrie took a light lunch of a ham sandwich and an apple into Sir Richard's office.

'Where would you like me to set down the tray, sir?' she asked.

Sir Richard put down the letter he was reading and removed his spectacles. 'On the table by the window will be fine, thank you, Florrie.' He got to his feet and emerged from behind his desk. For the first time in a while, he was smartly dressed in a tweed suit, and though, almost overnight, his hair had begun to turn grey at the temples, he looked back to his handsome, well-groomed self.

Florrie smiled when she saw the copy of the newspaper that was on the board table. 'I told you all's well that ends well, didn't I?'

Unexpectedly, Sir Richard approached her and took her hands in his. 'Florrie, how ever can I thank you? You've saved my son's life, my family, my business . . . you saved me.'

Suddenly, Florrie found she was losing herself in his grey eyes – no longer full of woe, but today, lit up with a lively spark. 'Oh, not at all! It was my pleasure.'

'Dear, darling Florrie.' He gently pushed her hair aside to look at the spot where Sir Hugh had inadvertently punched her. His eyebrows bunched in obvious sympathy. 'Does it hurt?' He stroked her cheek.

Florrie shook her head. Her mouth was dry. The words wouldn't come out.

He held both her hands in his, now. His face moved ever closer to hers. She didn't want to blink, lest the current of spellbinding electricity that flowed between them be broken. The tip of his nose touched hers. She felt the warmth of his skin, and then, when she closed her eyes, the touch of his lips. At that moment, Florrie wanted to kiss Sir Richard more than anything in the world, and she could feel his yearning crackle hot on the cold January air. But the thought of Thom came flooding into her mind, as did the enormous social gulf between them, and she opened her eyes and broke away.

'Enjoy your lunch, sir.' Her voice was breathy. Her heart thumped like a rabbit's hind leg. Could Sir Richard hear it?

His cheeks were flushed pink. He swallowed hard. 'Y-yes. Thank you, Florrie.'

'Will that be all?'

He grinned quizzically, but his smile quickly melted away and he looked crestfallen. 'I suppose it must be.'

34

May 1932

'I can't believe that we *still* haven't managed to find a suitable nanny,' Sir Richard said, as he wrestled with the heavy jug of water that Florrie had brought to his study. He was clad casually in a short-sleeved cream silk shirt with an open collar that was suitable for the first truly summery day of the year. He refilled his glass then leaned over the board table and filled a fresh glass for the next interviewee. 'The ones we want suddenly find reasons why they're not available any more. I just don't understand it. The ones who *do* want the position are never quite up to scratch. The last woman at least seemed reasonably intelligent and friendly, but Willy wouldn't sit on her lap happily.' He looked over to where his son was kneeling on the floor, playing with some brightly coloured wooden bricks, chattering to himself enthusiastically. 'Charlotte?'

As Florrie set the spent glasses on a tray, she contemplated Lady Charlotte's listless behaviour. Was she drunk at eleven in the morning? It was possible, even though she'd announced some days earlier that she'd decided to forgo her mid-morning gin and tonic, preferring to start drinking only at lunchtime, because she'd read that her favourite aviators practised self-discipline where drinking was concerned.

Lady Charlotte waved her hand dismissively. 'I'm sure if she says yes, she'll be fine. Willy seems happy enough with the maid, though. Or Florrie.'

'Yes, darling. But Florrie's our housekeeper, not the nanny.' He looked up at Florrie. 'I say, thanks for sitting in on these interviews. It does help tremendously to have an extra opinion. Such an important decision.'

Florrie curtseyed. 'Of course, sir.'

He turned back to his wife. 'Anyway, Sally, enthusiastic and caring though she may be . . .' He looked back up at Florrie, clearly making his excuses to her, since she was in charge of her friend. 'She isn't qualified to teach Willy until he's old enough for a governess.' He looked at his wristwatch. 'When's the next one due, Florrie?'

Florrie lifted the tray, uncomfortably hot in her long-sleeved, long-skirted uniform. 'Quarter to, sir. She might have already arrived. I'll send her through if she's waiting in the entrance hall, shall I?'

'Please do.' He got to his feet and walked over to the French doors. 'And let's get some air in here. It's incredibly hot already. I swear, if today's anything to go by, May holds great promise.'

Making her way along the hall, Florrie thought how swiftly spring had come around. Hans von Grunwald had finally returned to Germany in early January, at the insistence of Sir Richard and much to the consternation of both Sir Hugh and Lady Charlotte. Few other visitors had been to the house on social calls since the scandal of the kidnapping, leaving the staff of Holcombe Hall to re-establish domestic harmony, as far as was possible. Florrie noted that Sir Richard and Sir Hugh now barely spoke to one another, but they had not engaged in further fisticuffs, and she had not heard Brooke's paternity claim brought up again, even when the subject of his and Talbot's trials came up – set for July. At least Sir William had settled back happily into his routine at home, with Sally acting as his interim nanny.

As for Florrie, she had made renewed romantic efforts with Thom in a bid to salvage their engagement, though notably, Thom hadn't recently pressed her to name a date for their wedding, and she only wore his ring when they ventured out on a rare date. She and Sir Richard hadn't spoken about their almost-kiss since it had taken place, though she occasionally caught him observing her with a wistful look on his handsome face. She kept the fact that she found herself daydreaming about him rather too frequently, and against her better judgement, to herself, and the bee brooch remained a secret, hidden in her shoe. Florrie couldn't help but feel that Thom deserved a different woman. Sir Richard was a silly, unattainable dream, and perhaps she would be better off alone.

Spotting the next interviewee sitting on a chair beneath the portrait of the late Lord Harding-Bourne snapped Florrie out of her reverie.

'Are you Miss Gladstone?' she asked the young woman.

Surely no older than twenty-two or twenty-three, she was neatly dressed and plain, but with a kind openness to her face. Her shoes appeared to be new, as if she'd made a special effort for the occasion. She didn't have the stuffiness or arrogant air of some of the older nannies.

Miss Gladstone nodded. 'That's me. Are they ready for me? Ooh, blimey. Fingers crossed, eh?' She seemed flustered, perhaps awed by the strangeness and size of the house.

Florrie remembered how daunted she had felt when she had first come to Holcombe Hall as a girl of fifteen. 'Follow me, please. And try not to be too nervous. Sir Richard and Lady Charlotte are perfectly friendly.'

'Oh, that's good. I read all about the terrible to-do at Christmas. Those poor people must have been in pieces.'

Florrie had been advised not to discuss details of the kidnapping with anyone outside the household – even job interviewees – lest a member of the tabloid press try to infiltrate their ranks in the search for slanderous headlines. 'Are you in post currently?' she asked, changing the subject.

'Yes, miss. I'm the nanny to an American diplomat's twins, but the family's moving back to Washington at the end of the month. I've had a couple of job offers already, but I want to find the family and the house that's a good fit for me, as much as the other way round. Happy nanny, happy baby.'

Raising an eyebrow, Florrie reassessed the applicant. Here was a young woman who was both sought-after and confident in her own abilities. 'And there was me, thinking you were nervous!'

'Oh, make no mistake, I am!' She clasped her well-polished handbag over her stomach, glancing up at the portraits that hung above the great staircase. 'But a few nerves are healthy. I do hope Sir William takes to me. Is he a good-natured boy?'

'I think he's a little sweetheart, but you'll see for yourself.'

'And Lady Charlotte? Is she a loving mother?'

How could Florrie possibly answer that question honestly? Had Miss Gladstone read the ruinous press coverage of Lady Charlotte? 'Well . . . she likes to juggle her role with her passion for aviation. Amelia Earhart will have to watch her back. Ha ha.' At last, they'd reached the study. 'Here we are.'

Florrie ushered Miss Gladstone in and introduced her to Sir Richard and Lady Charlotte. The nanny curtseyed, so at least she had an understanding of etiquette. Instead of making small talk about her journey to Holcombe, however, she made straight for Sir William.

'Ooh, I like those bricks, Sir William. What colour is this one?' She held up a red brick, on which the letter 'A' was painted in yellow. 'This is red.'

Sir William giggled and lunged for the brick. 'Bick. Bick. Red bick!'

So far, so good. This nanny had established a rapport with the baby instantly. How well would she get on with the Harding-Bournes, though? When the interview began in earnest, the nanny sat with Sir William happily on her lap, tugging at her red hair. She answered Sir Richard's questions fully, detailing her training at a leading nanny academy and the experience she'd gained, from raising her own siblings to adulthood, following the untimely death of her mother, to working for a cabinet member's wife and then the American diplomat. When asked by Sir Richard if she had any questions, she asked about Sir William's nap times, eating habits, exercise routines, play and health. Each time, Sir Richard answered wearing a proud smile.

'Ah, well he adores cheese,' he said. 'If everything was

smothered in cheese, he'd be the happiest boy alive. And he sleeps ...' He frowned. 'Well, after the incident, he slept fitfully for about a month, but he's much improved now. I must say, I've taken to reading to him every night, and I hold his hand until he's nodded off.' With a dry chuckle, he glanced at Lady Charlotte. 'Letting go can be quite a trial, and I know I'm making a rod for my own back, but ...'

'Sounds like he's still feeling insecure, though it's easy for bad sleep habits to creep in.' The nanny looked directly at Lady Charlotte. 'What's *your* routine with him, milady?'

Lady Charlotte was examining her nails.

'Milady?'

She looked up. 'Sorry?'

'What's *your* routine with your son?'

Clasping her hand to her pearl necklace, Lady Charlotte looked nonplussed. 'I see him most days for half an hour or so. He's brought to me in the drawing room. You know?'

'His favourite toy?'

Lady Charlotte shook her head and waved the question away. 'I don't get involved in any of that. When he's old enough, I'll take him flying and teach him how to dance. My husband is the more involved parent, though I do think he's setting our son up for a rude awakening when we pack him off to Eton.' She laughed conspiratorially. 'Only five years to go!'

Florrie noticed that at no point did Lady Charlotte even look at her own son. Had she always been so disengaged, or had she become more detached since the kidnapping?

When the interview came to an end, Sir Richard tapped

his collar three times – a tell they had agreed on if he was keen on a candidate. Florrie had been tasked with sounding the favourite out on her walk back down the hall to the front door.

As they made their way along the hallway, Florrie quizzed Miss Gladstone about her post-interview impressions.

'Well? How do you think it went?'

The young nanny smiled and nodded. 'Sir William was adorable. And I liked his father very much. He's a fine and honourable father figure, full of love for the boy. I could tell.'

'Oh, you're absolutely right. He dotes on Sir William. So, if you were offered the job, do you think you could settle into Holcombe Hall?'

They came to a halt beneath Lord Harding-Bourne's portrait. The nanny pressed her lips together and looked up at the painting. 'Oh, I don't think this post is for me.'

Florrie blinked hard. 'Eh? How come? Is it because we're up north and out in the sticks a bit?'

Miss Gladstone shook her head. 'It's not that. It's Lady Charlotte. I'm afraid I don't want to work for a woman who's quite so uninterested in her own child. I know rich people are busy, and that's why they have nannies, but babies and toddlers don't do well when they rely on a nanny as a mother figure. Lady Charlotte . . . there's no love there. And she was drunk. If you ask me, I think she's a very unhappy woman.' She looked down at her shoes. 'Sorry. You seem lovely and all, and I liked Sir Richard very much. I don't even mind the remote location. But Lady Charlotte . . . This job's not for me, I'm afraid.'

*

When the interviews had finished for the morning, Florrie took Sir William back to the nursery, intending to return him to Sally's care. When she entered the room, she found Sally sitting in the rocking chair, clutching her face and whimpering.

'Whatever's the matter, Sal?' Florrie set Sir William on his little wooden rocking horse.

'I've got *rotten* toothache. It's my back molar. Think it's abscessed. It's been giving me gyp all week, but this morning . . .' She growled. 'Christ almighty. I reckon I'm going to expire with the pain if I can't get this tooth yanked. I went to help Cook, but I were getting on her nerves so much, she sent me back up here. I'm like a dog in a manger, Florrie.'

Florrie heard the door to Lady Charlotte's room slam across the landing. She had an idea. 'Tell you what, get yourself into the village before the dentist shuts, and see if he'll sort you out.'

Sally wore a look of confusion. 'Where am I going to get the money for the dentist? Graham normally yanks teeth if you ask him nicely. He does them with a pair of pliers.'

'Don't be daft. You can't be having a molar yanked by the chauffeur-cum-mechanic. Go to Arkwright and tell him I said you could have money for the dentist. All this extra work you've been doing, nannying Sir William . . .' She turned to the boy, rocking merrily on his horse and singing a tuneless song at the top of his voice. 'That's extra responsibility, that is, so you're owed a bonus. Tell Arkwright I'll get it back from Sir Richard.'

Sally held her jaw. When she spoke, her words were muffled. 'Who will look after the baby?'

'Leave him to me.'

With her friend out of the way, Florrie crouched down by Sir William. 'Do you want to come with me to visit your mama? We can play on her big bed.'

The tot looked at her blankly, so Florrie picked up his favourite teddy bear. 'Let's take Mr Dribble for a walk, shall we?' Coaxing the boy off his rocking horse, she led him out of the nursery and across the landing to his mother's room. She knocked on the door.

'Who is it?'

'It's Florrie, milady.'

From inside, there was a clatter. 'Oh, just the gal. Come in! Come in!'

Florrie pushed the door open and led Sir William inside.

Lady Charlotte was peering at her own reflection in the cheval mirror, wrinkling her nose and frowning as she struggled to pull up the zip on an elegant red dress. 'I'm trying on some things for my visit to Burrough Court at the end of the month. Viscountess Furness is throwing a bash – the first I've been invited to in *aeons*. It's dreadfully exciting. The Prince of Wales wants me to meet this Wallace Simpson woman, so one must look one's best. Here! Help me with this zip, would you?'

Finally, she turned around and saw that Florrie was with her son. Her expression slackened. 'Oh. Why have you brought William in here?'

Florrie picked up the boy and set him on his mother's bed, where he started to spring up and down on his strong little legs, giggling with delight. 'I thought he could have a bounce on your bed, milady. Perhaps we could play with him together. Sally has an abscessed tooth, you see, so I packed her off to the dentist as an emergency.' She smiled at Sir William. 'And I thought, after a morning of sitting on the laps of strangers, perhaps this little man would enjoy some fun with his mama.'

Lady Charlotte turned back to the mirror. 'But I'm busy planning my wardrobe for my trip to Melton Mowbray. I should think looking one's best for His Royal Highness is rather more important than unplanned playtime with my son.' She turned towards Sir William but didn't look at him. 'Like I said in the interviews, I'm not interested in playing with a toddler. I find children far more interesting when they're older. Much older.' She picked up a diamond-studded hair clip from her dressing table and pinned it into her flaxen waves, examining the effect in the mirror, though the dress still hung open at the back. 'I rather like red and diamonds. What do you think? Red and diamonds or red and rubies? Or jet, perhaps?'

The room brightened suddenly with lightning. Outside, there was the rumble of distant thunder. The pleasant weather was turning fast, just as Lady Charlotte's mood was cooling in the bedroom. Florrie felt certain that if she could only interest Lady Charlotte in her own child, the best quality, most sought-after applicants for the role of nanny would warm to the family and look favourably on the vacancy. 'Isn't he adorable? I swear, he has Sir Richard's nose and your eyes. Whose hair do you think he has?'

Without warning, Lady Charlotte yanked the clip from her hair and flung it on to the dressing table. She turned to Florrie with angry tears in her eyes. 'Stop it! Just stop it, Florrie! I know what you're doing. Has Richard sent you up here to stoke up my maternal instincts or some such bunkum?'

Dare Florrie tell Lady Charlotte the truth? 'Oh, not at all! Like I said, Sally has gone—'

'Yes. You already said. The dentist.' Tears rolled down her cheeks and she wiped them away roughly with the back of her perfectly manicured hand. 'But I'm sick of this nanny business and everybody treating William like he's made of porcelain. And for some reason, I'm expected to spend more time with him, as though mothering is the most natural instinct in the world.'

'Isn't it?'

Sir William must have recognized the sharp change in the women's tone, because he stopped bouncing and stretched his arms out to Florrie to be held. She picked him up.

'No, it isn't,' Lady Charlotte snapped. 'And I don't see why I should have to demonstrate my affection to these idiot nannies, just because the newspaper printed lies about me.'

There was another flash of lightning and thunder rumbled closer. Rain started to pelt the window. The boy started to whimper.

'Oh, dear. Sir William's upset. You're upset.' Florrie lifted the boy towards his mother. 'Will you take him? A cuddle might be just what you both need.'

'Are you deaf? Or simply insensitive?' Lady Charlotte backed away from them towards the wardrobe. 'I don't want to hold him.' She started to sob. 'You don't understand, do you? It's all right for you. You're working class. You earn your own money. You're engaged to someone you chose. You can't possibly know what it's like to be married off to a much older man, simply because you have the social standing and he has the money. "A good match", my parents declared it. I was hardly over twenty – a girl – when I had to leave my old life behind to come and live in this backwater, with a man I have nothing in common with. Imagine! And then I was expected to breed immediately, to provide an heir in haste, with my fertility under the watchful, judgemental gaze of my mother-in-law, who never liked me!'

Florrie held the startled Sir William close. She could feel his body tremble as the pitch of Lady Charlotte's voice rose higher and higher. 'But . . .' What could she say to calm Lady Charlotte down? 'But he's such a lovely child, and you almost lost him!'

With tears falling on to her rouged cheeks, Lady Charlotte wrenched the red dress over her shoulders and stepped out of it. Standing in her underwear, she bundled the dress into a ball and threw it on to the bed in temper. 'I'm well aware I almost lost him, and because of that, I also lost my reputation. I'm the laughing stock in high society! Do you know how many invitations to parties I've had since the kidnapping? Three! Three measly invitations, two of which were from people lower down the pecking order.'

'Parties don't matter though, do they? And you're off to visit the Prince of Wales at the end of the month.' This spoiled society wife clearly had no perspective on her own good fortune. 'What matters is you've brought a beautiful child into the world, and he's safe. Look at him! He just wants you to love him!'

The fight seems to drain suddenly from Lady Charlotte. She sank on to her dressing table stool. 'Florrie, when I look at my son, all I see is my husband – a stultifying, unattractive man, who doesn't love me, and whom I don't love.'

Unattractive? Florrie wondered. *Stultifying? Are we talking about the same feller?* 'I'm sure Sir Richard adores you, milady.'

Lady Charlotte scoffed. 'Richard loves his work. He loves his role as head of the family and business. He dotes on William, of course, because William is a faithful copy of him. Richard loves . . . why, my husband probably loves *you* more than me, because this house and the staff in it mean a darn sight more to him than I ever could. If he wasn't so utterly lacking in passion, I'd suspect he had a mistress or, at least, designs on another woman.' The bitterness in her voice seemed to acidify the air in the bedroom. 'Maybe he does. I don't know, and I no longer care. What is clear, is that my husband's affections lie everywhere but with me. And my son, the spitting image of his father, is a constant reminder of that. So take William to bounce on someone else's bed, please.' Her tears had stopped now, leaving streaks of make-up down her cheeks. 'And tell my husband to stop using you as a go-between, in some misplaced bid to bring me to heel and domesticate me, as if I'm a wayward pet.'

'He didn't—'

'Just do your job!' She glared at Florrie. 'You're a housekeeper. Nothing more. Get out, both of you! Have Arkwright bring me a Tom Collins.'

Feeling that she had failed in her attempt to encourage a bond between mother and child, despite her best efforts,

Florrie carried a quietly weeping Sir William with her down to the kitchen, where she knew Cook would be able to cheer him up with some ice-cream. She realized that she had over-reached in her role as housekeeper, going far beyond the boundaries of the house and its upkeep into the lives of the Harding-Bournes. Perhaps Thom had been right all along. And if she had foolishly enmeshed herself in the complexities of the family, how could she extract herself without jeopardizing her position?

35

Still fatigued from a night of patchy sleep, having shared her single bed with a restless Thom, until she'd finally sent him packing to his own room at four o'clock in the morning, Florrie found herself yawning surreptitiously at breakfast. It was the last Friday in May, and as if a metaphorical cloud was still hanging over the household, the rain had fallen almost incessantly since Florrie's confrontation with Lady Charlotte over motherhood. The search for a suitable nanny continued unfruitfully, with Sally providing most interim care, and Sir Richard and Florrie sharing the rest of the load. Florrie's limbs were heavy. The view of the heavy rain and the sodden grounds through the tall windows didn't lift her spirits either. She felt like butter spread too thinly.

Sir Richard, however, seemed unaffected by the malaise that afflicted Florrie. He sat at the large dining table, with Sir William to his right, strapped in his wooden highchair. Both father and son seemed wholly content in each other's company.

'Open wide, Willy,' Sir Richard said. 'The choo-choo train is coming through the tunnel. Choo-chooooo!'

The baby opened his mouth wide expectantly, and his father spooned in some cheesy scrambled egg.

The sight lifted Florrie's spirits, as she stacked that morning's papers on the table by the stained-glass oriel window, ready for Sir Hugh, who didn't usually put in an appearance until mid-morning. 'He looks like a baby bird in its nest, waiting to be fed worms.'

'His appetite is insatiable at the moment.' Sir Richard glanced over his shoulder to smile at her. 'I swear, he's the size of a five-year-old. He's already eaten at least two sausages this morning.'

As if in agreement, Sir William bashed the little wooden table attached to his high-chair with a greasy fist full of half-eaten sausage. He opened his mouth for more egg and kicked his legs in anticipation.

'He's going to be tall, I reckon. And he's the absolute image of his daddy, aren't you, Sir William? Yes, you are!' she cooed at the boy. 'Oh, you're going to grow up to be a *very* handsome young man. The girls will be falling at your feet.' Florrie blushed when she realized what she'd said.

Sir Richard smiled at her coyly. 'I'll take that as a compliment, Florrie. You've just made my morning. Thank you.'

Before the flirtation could develop further, the dining room door swung open. Lady Charlotte and Daphne entered, already fully dressed in their aviatrix's garb of jodhpurs, shirt and high boots.

'Good Lord, ladies!' Sir Richard said brightly. 'To what do we owe the pleasure of your company at such a bright and early hour?' He cast an eye over their attire.

'We're excited to see more coverage of Amelia Earhart's triumph,' Lady Charlotte said. 'Daphne and I decided last night we're going to fly down to Burrough Court a day early, instead of taking the train or having Graham drive us. In Earhart's honour!' She made a beeline for the table with the newspapers and snatched up a reading stick. She lifted the front page of one of the broadsheets aloft for Daphne to see. 'They've reported on it, but no photograph! Look! "Mrs Putnam completes transatlantic hop to Irish coast in fourteen hours, fifty-four minutes." That's it. How tedious.'

Daphne took a seat at the table and placed a napkin on her lap. 'The first woman to fly solo across the Atlantic, battling fire and fuel leaks and storms, and they won't print a photograph? How very mean-spirited of them.'

Scraping up the eggy remnants from the dish, Sir Richard frowned. 'Do you think it's wise to fly in this weather?' He peered outside at the torrential downpour and then caught Florrie's eye. '"Coming down in stair rods" – isn't that how the villagers refer to it?'

'Aye, sir. It's set in for the day and all.' Florrie poured coffee into Daphne's cup. She could smell alcohol on her. 'Where will you be sitting, milady?' she asked Lady Charlotte. 'I'll pour you a coffee.'

Crossing the dining room to join Daphne on the far side of the table to her husband, Lady Charlotte rubbed her hands together. 'Actually, I'll have a coffee and a Bloody Mary, I think. Something to warm my cockles, ready for the flight.'

Sir Richard set down the baby's bowl and spoon. He looked at his wife over his spectacles and laced his fingers together. 'Didn't you have a little soirée with my brother and Walter Knight-Downey last night?'

Lady Charlotte took a piece of toast from the toast rack and started to spread marmalade on it. 'What of it? Hugh and Walter are driving up to Scotland for a boys' golfing weekend tomorrow. Why shouldn't we visit Edward and his new American divorcée a day early?'

'That's not what I meant. I meant, you had an awful lot to drink last night, and now you're asking Florrie for a Bloody Mary at breakfast.'

'So?'

'And you want to fly in a storm? Is that entirely wise, Charlotte?'

Florrie watched, intrigued, as Lady Charlotte started to spread the marmalade with something bordering on aggression. A shadow seemed to pass over her thin face, and the breezy demeanour she'd walked in with was replaced by something colder and darker. 'I'm mistress of my own destiny, Richard. If Earhart can weather the storms of the Atlantic, I can certainly hop down to Melton Mowbray in a May shower. I telephoned Viscountess Furness last night, and she's already found me a field to land in. We're going. Today.'

'It'll be *such* a wheeze!' Daphne said, beaming, clearly oblivious to the silent conflict between her brother-in-law and sister-in-law. 'I can't wait to meet Wallace.'

'Your luggage will be soaked.'

'Don't feign concern, Richard,' Lady Charlotte said. 'The invitation was also extended to you, but you opted to stay at home.'

'I have contracts to read. But contracts notwithstanding, this weather is—'

'You be a stick-in-the-mud all you like.' She closed her eyes emphatically. 'But don't moan when we gals go off and have fun on our own.' When she opened them, her stare was hard and unyielding.

'Well, at least telephone me when you get there, so I know you both landed safely.'

'Yes, yes. If I remember, I'll call.'

Feeling as if a tight fist held her innards in a vice-like grip, Florrie soaked a cloth in a bowl of soapy water she'd set aside for Sir William and proceeded to clean up his face and hands. She wondered if the tension in the household would ever ease.

An hour later, when she was supervising a plumber who had come to instal a radiator in the living room, Florrie heard the put-put-put-whirr of the biplane as it took to the air. She glanced out at the dismal weather, shaking her head as the aircraft skimmed the treetops. It then started to climb steeply. She could just about make out Lady Charlotte and Daphne in the cockpit and passenger seats, wearing their leather helmets and goggles. They made her feel drab and unadventurous.

After lunch had been served above stairs, Florrie joined her colleagues below stairs to eat.

'By heck, this weather's making my joints ache something rotten,' Cook said, glancing up at the high window, which was still being battered by sideways rain. 'I've never known a May like it. A handful of decent days we've had. That's it. The rest has been a wash-out.'

'Aye,' Thom said, taking a bite from his enormous ham sandwich. He spoke with his mouth full. 'The gardens are all getting waterlogged. I've already got blackspot on the roses, and the peonies are rotting on the stem. We're going to have a right moss problem later in the season, if it doesn't dry up.' He turned to Florrie. 'Me and you were meant to go to Blackpool for the weekend, weren't we? It's set to do nowt but piss heavens hard. It's freezing and all.'

Cook leaned towards them. 'I'm sure you two'll find ways to warm yourselves up in some cosy little bed and breakfast.' She winked and then guffawed. 'Sea air makes men more virile, I heard. Better not come back with a bun in the oven, our Florrie.'

Florrie tutted and shot embarrassed looks at the junior maids and valets, who were all giggling and nudging one another. 'That's quite enough of that kind of talk in front of the youngsters, Cook.'

The frivolity in the air was punctured and deflated quickly with the sight of Sir Richard descending the stairs. Clad in a grey V-neck cashmere sweater and charcoal gabardine slacks that he normally wore in winter, he strode into the kitchen. He waved, though his serious expression said this was anything but one of his impromptu social calls. 'Hello, hello! Sorry to disturb your lunch.' He sought out Arkwright, who was puzzling over the *Daily Telegraph*'s crossword at the far end of the table. 'I say, Arkwright, have you taken a phone call from my wife?'

Arkwright set down the paper and sat bolt upright. 'No, sir. Is anything the matter?'

Sir Richard pursed his lips. 'Well, she should have landed in Melton Mowbray by now. Normally, I wouldn't give a second thought to not having heard from her, but in this weather . . .' He now looked to Florrie for corroboration. 'She did say she'd call, didn't she?'

Florrie swallowed her mouthful and dabbed at the corners of her mouth with her napkin. '"If I remember" – I think those were her words. I shouldn't worry too much.' She checked the time on Cook's large wall clock. 'Perhaps she landed around lunchtime, and she's too busy having fun. I should imagine lunch will be a lavish affair if His Royal Highness is there.'

Sir Richard nodded and turned back to Arkwright. 'Do come and find me in my study as soon as she makes contact, won't you?'

At that moment, the sound of the telephone ringing upstairs in the hallway drifted down to the kitchen.

Arkwright got to his feet. 'Perhaps that's Lady Charlotte now.'

Marching smartly past Sir Richard, Arkwright climbed the stairs to answer the call. Sir Richard followed him up. Once he was out of earshot, chatter resumed among the domestic staff at the table, and Florrie took up her sandwich again. She had just taken another bite and was nodding at some observation Thom had made about the tide at Blackpool being five miles out, when a disturbance from above caused them all to fall silent.

'Wait. Was that Sir Richard shouting?' Florrie asked.

'Aye. I think it were,' Cook said. 'Sounded in pain.'

Florrie flung down her napkin and hastened upstairs. She ran towards the entrance hall, where the telephone table was situated, and balked at the sight of Sir Richard, ashen-faced and staring horrified at the telephone transmitter and earpiece in his hands, as if it were made from radioactive material.

Arkwright was wide-eyed, his mouth hanging open.

'Whatever is the matter?' Florrie asked. She placed her hand on Sir Richard's arm. 'Sir?' He was trembling.

'They – they've crashed.' The telephone fell from Sir Richard's shaking hands on to the marble floor. 'Why didn't I stop her?' he whispered. 'Why did I let her go?'

Seeing that Arkwright was rooted to the spot with shock and hearing a tinny voice coming through the earphone, Florrie took up the telephone apparatus. She held the earphone to her ear and spoke into the mouthpiece. 'Hello? Hello? This is the housekeeper of Holcombe Hall.'

The Derbyshire police were still on the other end. After a brief exchange, Florrie learned the grave news, just as Sir Hugh ambled along the hallway.

'What ho, chaps! What's all this hullaballoo then? I could hear Dickie from the music room.' He seemed to finally notice Florrie's serious expression. 'Why are you that funny shade of puce, Dickie? You look like you're about to vomit. Did Cook poison you?'

Two fat tears rolled down Sir Richard's cheeks. He wiped them away abruptly with the back of his hand, shaking his head.

Florrie exchanged a glance with Arkwright. The butler also had a haunted look about him. She cleared her throat. If anyone were to tell Sir Hugh, it was going to have to be her.

'Sir Hugh, I'm afraid it's the worst news.' She took a deep breath, watching the bemused smile slide from his face. She exhaled slowly and steeled herself to go on. 'Lady Charlotte and Daphne flew to Melton Mowbray this morning. The plane went down in heavy rain over the Derbyshire peaks. That was the local constabulary on the telephone. I'm sorry to say . . . I'm so sorry.'

'What? What is it, woman? Spit it out!'

'Your wife . . . Daphne's gone, sir. She was pronounced dead at the scene. And Lady Charlotte is gravely injured. She's been taken to the infirmary with a fractured spine.'

36

'Right, first things first,' Florrie said, wringing her hands as she tried to marshal her thoughts. She locked eyes with Arkwright, who was still in a stunned stupor. 'Sir Richard needs to go to his wife's bedside. So let's get Graham to bring the Rolls-Royce round. Yes?'

At last, Arkwright seemed to register what was being said. He nodded. 'Yes. I'll get to it right away.'

Sir Hugh regarded her through a veil of tears. 'What about me? What about Daphne?'

'The police said you need to identify her since you're her next of kin, so you'll need to go too.' She addressed Sir Richard. 'I'll pack overnight cases for both of you and book you into a local hotel. Yes?'

Sir Richard nodded. It was clear he was barely containing his shock at the devastating news. 'Thank you, Florrie. You're so level-headed in a crisis.' He faced his younger brother, with whom relations had been more than frosty for months since Brooke's assertion that Sir Richard was a cuckoo in the Harding-Bourne nest. 'Hugh. I don't know what to say. I'm so, so sorry.' Abruptly, he wrapped his arms around him, but Sir Hugh remained stiff and inconsolable.

'She should never have been in that biplane,' Sir Hugh said. He shook himself loose. 'My Daphne . . . Charlotte had no right taking that plane up in such foul weather conditions. She's your wife. You should have stopped her!'

'S-steady on, Hugh,' Sir Richard said, shaking as if he had a fever. 'N-neither of us has . . . had any real dominion over our wives. They're headstrong g-gals. And it's not as if Charlotte's walked away unscathed. She has a bro-broken back. She may never walk again.'

Through gritted teeth, Sir Hugh said, 'My wife is *dead*.'

At that moment, Walter Knight-Downey ambled along the hallway to meet them. 'I say, chaps, what's this powwow in the hall that I'm being left out of? Why are you both looking so earnest? You're not going to start brawling again, are you? Ha ha. I thought we'd got over all that.' He winked and grinned, hands in his trouser pockets like a man with not a care in the world, and a conscience unbothered by the fact that he'd been conducting an affair with Daphne for years behind Sir Hugh's back – of that, Florrie and the rest of the domestic staff were certain.

Sir Hugh turned to his friend. 'The gals' plane went down,' he said, his voice wavering. 'Daphne's been killed.' He sobbed loudly.

'Good Lord, no! No, no, no!' Walter clasped his hands to his head. 'No. Not Daphne. No. It can't be. I don't believe you.'

'I'm afraid it's true,' Florrie said.

The colour drained from Walter's face and his eyes seemed to lose focus. He started to slump.

'Hey up. He's going,' Florrie told Arkwright. 'Grab him under the arms.'

Together, they manoeuvred Walter safely on to the floor.

'I'll fetch some smelling salts from my office,' Arkwright said.

Sir Hugh looked down at his friend, tears splashing on to the floor. 'This family's cursed. Since Mama passed away, it's been cursed, I tell you.'

Sir Richard reached out to put his hand on his brother's shoulder. 'It's not a curse. It's just a damned tragedy.'

Sir Hugh stiffened at his brother's touch again and glared at him, but when Sir Richard didn't let go, he gradually curled into his older brother's embrace, as though they were boys, suffering some great misfortune together. The sight of them moved Florrie, but she steeled herself to remain calm and dispassionate. Right now, they needed her to lead.

'Once we've got Mr Knight-Downey back on his feet, I suggest you get yourselves into the drawing room. I'll have Cook send up some sweet tea for the shock, and I'll come and get you when Graham's ready to depart.' She looked down at Walter, whose eyelashes were fluttering as he came round. 'I'll ask Thom to drive Mr Knight-Downey to the station. Family only at a time like this, eh?'

'Quite so, Florrie.' Sir Richard nodded, stroking his brother's hair. 'You're a rock. Thank you.'

'And I'll call ahead to the mortuary in Derbyshire to ask about . . . transport back.' It wasn't so long ago that Florrie had helped to organize the funeral of Dame Elizabeth, and here she was, having to sort out an untimely send-off for the young, vibrant starlet who had most recently joined the family. Perhaps Sir Hugh was right about a curse.

Sir Hugh returned several days before Sir Richard and all but shut himself away in the drawing room, smoking one cigarette after another and drinking until he was incoherent. He refused to eat anything beyond the odd snack that Cook browbeat him into accepting. He didn't rise until gone three in the afternoon, preferring to languish in bed (according to Arkwright, who checked on him daily) with the curtains closed.

Below stairs, most staff members went about their business in sober fashion, though there was understandable speculation as to the root cause of the crash.

With Sir Richard away, everyone was seated around the kitchen table on the night before Lady Charlotte's return, some three weeks after the crash. Even Mam had brought the children over to the big house for dinner, and Sally had set up a corner of the kitchen where Sir William, Alice and Nelly could safely play together with spare pastry dough at a low table, while George sat up with the adults.

Cook folded her arms emphatically. 'Well, my money's on the weather. I mean, it were grim that day, weren't it? And I seen her doing loop-de-loops over the estate for the last year without crashing. By crikey, she's a daft ha'porth, that one, but she seemed to know what she was doing in that cockpit.'

The other women nodded.

'A right Amelia Earhart,' Sally said. 'Except for that time she nearly took the roof off.'

'Well, I reckon she were drunk,' Thom said, putting his cutlery together on his empty plate. He turned to Florrie. 'Didn't you say she already stunk of booze at breakfast, the morning of the crash? But then she had a couple of Bloody Marys – hair of the dog, like?'

Florrie shook her head. 'Look, it's no use us trying to guess what happened, and I'm not getting into a conversation about that lot's drinking habits. Let's just see what the police say. Her ladyship's coming back in a wheelchair, and we've got Daphne's funeral in a week's time at the chapel.' She grimaced. 'Closed coffin.'

A chorus of 'oof' rippled around the table.

'So, just be sympathetic to the family's feelings, please. No tittle-tattle. They're grieving, and it's going to take a while for things to get back to some kind of normality.' She cast her mind back to the newspaper coverage of the kidnapping, where Lady Charlotte had been singled out for a public drubbing. 'And absolutely *no* talking to reporters.'

'They'll be all over this like flies on horseshit,' Thom said.

'Said like a true gentleman, Thomas!' Cook said.

Florrie shot Thom a disapproving look. 'We're in the middle of a depression, and we can't risk another scandal that could jeopardize the value of either the businesses or the family's reputation. Just remember we're reliant on them for our wages. Anyone found talking to the papers gets sacked. Right?'

'Right. Line up on the steps, you lot,' said Arkwright. 'They're due back any minute.' The staff had all gathered in the entrance hall to welcome Lady Charlotte home. The butler tucked his fob watch into his waistcoat pocket and opened the front door. Though June was now well underway, the weather was still drizzly and miserable, as if God was matching the Holcombe weather to the family's dreadful fortunes. 'No let-up with the rain, I'm afraid, but I want respectful, sympathetic smiles on your faces when she turns up.'

Despite his orders, the staff remained sombre.

Florrie chivvied her maids and the kitchen staff into lining up on the steps. 'You heard Mr Arkwright. Concerned smiles when the car comes up the drive.' From the bottom of the grand stone staircase, she looked back at the house and noticed Sir Hugh looking out from his bedroom window. It was the first time she'd seen him up and about before three o'clock since his return from identifying Daphne's remains, and she silently feared he'd cause a scene as soon as Lady Charlotte emerged from the car.

'Do you think she's scarred for life?' Cook asked.

'I have no idea. All I know is she's broken her back. But if she looks rough, just act like nothing's the matter.'

Within five minutes – just long enough for them all to become thoroughly damp – the Rolls-Royce appeared at the end of the drive, followed by an ambulance. Out of the corner of her eye, Florrie could see Cook nudging Sally, who held a disgruntled, damp Sir William in her arms. She cleared her throat pointedly and turned back to the ambulance.

Graham emerged from the driver's seat and opened the passenger door for Sir Richard, who clambered out alone. He waved at the staff, grim-faced. The drivers opened the back of the ambulance, and two nurses emerged. From the boot of the car, a wheelchair-cum-bed type apparatus was retrieved and set up on the gravel. The drivers stretchered a supine Lady Charlotte from the back of the ambulance, and while Graham held the wheelchair steady, the two nurses helped to move Lady Charlotte from the stretcher to the lie-flat wheelchair.

'Ow! You're hurting me!' she cried. 'For heaven's sake, *I* can do it!'

'Don't be ridiculous, darling,' Sir Richard said. 'You need to lie flat and let the fracture heal.'

'Let us help you, milady,' the older of the nurses said. 'Remember what the doctor said.'

'I know what the doctor said. He's an ass, and I hate this damned contraption. I feel like an overgrown baby.'

Though Lady Charlotte's head was bandaged and her entire torso was in plaster, she was still wearing make-up like a Hollywood silver screen star. *How draining it must be,* Florrie thought, *to feel you have to keep up appearances even when your best friend has just died and you've lost the use of your legs in a plane crash.* At that moment, she felt she was the luckiest woman alive not to be Lady Charlotte.

Once she was ensconced in the wheelchair, Sir Richard left his wife's side to retrieve his son from Sally. 'There's my little champ. Oh, how Papa has missed you, Willy!' He thanked Sally and carried the boy over to Lady Charlotte. 'Say hello to Mama.'

Sir William wore a puzzled expression when he looked down at his mother. It quickly gave way to a sorry, crumpled little face. He started to cry.

'Even my own son thinks I look like a monster,' Lady Charlotte said. 'Take him away!' She looked at the staff and then locked eyes with Florrie. 'It's not a freak show. Stop staring and get back inside, for heaven's sake!'

For another couple of days, the staff of Holcombe Hall tiptoed around, not wishing to intrude on the family's grief. Another two nurses arrived from the local infirmary to take over care for Lady Charlotte from those who had travelled from Derbyshire, but the yelling from behind the bedroom door spoke of a reluctant patient. When finally the day of the funeral arrived, the entire staff were granted permission to attend the service in the Hall's private chapel, so that they could bid farewell to Daphne.

Several members of the press had been waiting at the estate gates for days, desperate to get a glimpse of the star-studded list of mourners who were travelling to Holcombe for the send-off. No reporters or photographers were allowed entry to the estate, though Thom and the gamekeeper chased several trespassers off the premises.

Florrie led the female domestic staff who weren't on cloakroom duty into the chapel.

'Ooh, look!' Clary said. 'Isn't that Gary Cooper in the second row?'

'Give over, will you,' Cook said. 'That's Doctor Haslam from the village. Daphne were a starlet, but she weren't in the same league as Gary bloody Cooper, you daft beggar. Do you think the likes of him would show up to a funeral wearing a corduroy jacket?'

Florrie shushed them both. 'No chattering through the service.'

When the coffin arrived, festooned with white calla lilies and borne by Sir Hugh, Sir Richard, Daphne's father and two younger brothers and Walter Knight-Downey, tears flowed freely among the glamorous female mourners in the chapel. They dabbed at their eyes beneath elegant black net veils. The men all stood stiffly, pale-faced and red-eyed, determined not to show any grief. Daphne hadn't been particularly popular with the staff, Florrie mused, but she couldn't deny it was heart-rending to see such a young and vibrant woman laid to rest. At that moment, Florrie was glad her mother had stayed in the gamekeeper's cottage with the children. Unlike her sister, Irene, at least Daphne was being bidden farewell with all the trappings of a rich woman, and at least she left no children behind.

The Anglican priest conducted a formal service that Florrie was certain Daphne would have hated. The Harding-Bournes occupied the front row to the right, with Lady Charlotte laid flat in her wheelchair-cum-bed, attended by her two nurses. Daphne's family were to the left, her father's arm wrapped around her mother's quaking shoulders.

After a succession of readings and hymns, Sir Hugh was invited to give a eulogy. Clutching a piece of paper, he stood at the lectern, looking unhealthily thin in the black double-breasted suit that had fitted him perfectly at his mother's funeral. *He's a shadow of himself*, Florrie thought, *aged by years in a matter of days. Poor soul.*

Sir Hugh unfolded his speech and started to read. 'My wife was a true English rose.' He paused, inhaled raggedly and looked up at the vaulted ceiling of the chapel. Exhaling hard, he glanced over at the coffin and continued. 'I loved her from the moment we met. She brought real warmth and sunlight into a drab bachelor's life that I'd tried and failed to colour with lavish parties and champagne. I have spent my entire life standing in the cold, long shadows cast by giants of the industrial world. My father. My brothers . . . Daphne made me feel like I mattered. She was everything. Talented, beautiful, magnetic. She was the flame, and I happily danced around her like an enchanted moth. I thought she would shine and we would dance for a long and happy lifetime. But here we are. And now she's gone.'

He turned to the front row with a venomous look in his

eyes. The skin on Florrie's arms turned to gooseflesh. She felt certain a confrontation was about to happen.

'And that's all because of you, Charlotte Harding-Bourne.'

A sharp intake of breath and shocked gasps rippled around the chapel. Guests started to look askance at one another.

'Hugh!' Sir Richard said, with a warning tone to his voice.

'Thank you, Sir Hugh, for those heartfelt words,' the priest said, returning to the pulpit.

Sir Hugh, however, held his hand out, staying the priest's progress. 'I've not finished. That bitch, my sister-in-law, killed my wife.'

'Hugh! That's not true!' Charlotte shouted.

Sir Hugh nodded. 'Oh, it's the truth all right. The police told me that when they got you to hospital, they had you breathe into that new invention from America that they're trialling. The "drunk-o-meter".'

'Lies!' she shrieked. 'We were caught in a storm over the peaks. I lost control of the aircraft.'

'Rubbish! You were drunk as a skunk from the night before – we all were, so don't deny it – and you were drinking again at breakfast, before the flight. *That's* why the plane went down. *That's* why my Daphne's dead. You have blood on your hands, Charlotte. I hope you never walk again. I never want to speak to you again. I hate you.'

The sound of Lady Charlotte's wailing came from the front row. 'How could you say such cruel things, Hugh? Daphne was my bosom pal.'

By now, Sir Richard had stepped up to the lectern and

was attempting to pull his brother back to his pew. 'That's quite enough, Hugh! You're making a fool of yourself.' He turned to the gathered mourners. 'It's grief,' he said. 'Just grief. Please take no notice. My brother's understandably not himself. It's all very tragic.' He looked towards the staff at the back. 'A little help, please?'

Watching the drama unfold, Florrie realized she was blushing on Sir Richard's behalf. She sought Arkwright out in the congregation and mouthed, 'What shall we do?'

Arkwright pushed his way past his stableboys and valets into the aisle and clapped his hands. 'My lords, ladies and gentlemen, refreshments will now be served in the banqueting hall. Please make your way over to the house and allow the family to compose themselves at this dreadful and difficult time.'

None of the Harding-Bournes attended the funeral reception, retiring instead to different parts of the house, where they could indulge their grief away from prying eyes. Florrie served Sir Hugh and Walter in the drawing room, where they listened, glum-faced, to Daphne's favourite jazz records on the gramophone and toasted her memory with a bottle of champagne; Lady Charlotte in her bedroom, accompanied only by a bottle of vodka, fed to her through a straw by one nurse, while the other helped her to peruse a scrapbook containing clippings of her and Daphne, cut from society magazines; Sir Richard in his study with a pot of strong coffee and a stack of medical bills. Florrie then oversaw the serving staff in the banqueting hall, ensuring the guests were all served refreshments. To the untrained ear, the conversation between the guests was respectful, but as she moved surreptitiously between groups, when she listened carefully, Florrie heard them lower their voices to speculate over the accusations that Sir Hugh had levelled at Lady Charlotte in the chapel, and whether or not Lady Charlotte would ever walk again.

When the guests were gone, Daphne was laid to rest in the family's burial plot, her graveside attended not only by her parents and siblings, but also by her husband, her lover, her brother-in-law and, if Sir Hugh was to be believed, her killer. Florrie watched from the window in her third-floor room, wondering if Lady Charlotte would recover from her fractured spine, and if Holcombe Hall and the Harding-Bournes would ever recover from their fractured relationships.

1933

37

Two pages away from finishing the chapter of the library book she was reading, Florrie heard a knock on her bedroom door. She set the novel on her lap and pulled the covers up over her thick nightdress. Before she'd had a chance to respond, the door opened, and Thom walked in.

'Only me,' he said, rubbing his hands together against the cold of an early March. Orange light from the dying embers of the fire picked out the rugged contours of his face, accentuating the redness of his cheeks, wind-burnt from working outdoors in all weathers. When he smiled, the lines at the corners of his eyes crinkled deeply. 'You tucked up already? It's early.' He walked to the window, stooping to avoid hitting his head on the gabled ceiling, and pulled the thin curtains closer together.

Florrie frowned at the sight of his work boots. 'Get them muddy boots off in here, will you? And I told you I wanted an early night tonight. We've got von Grunwald arriving from Germany tomorrow and there's a special dinner in his honour, so I'll have to be up at half four to get everything ready.'

Thom started to undress, flinging his heavy cable-knit sweater on to the old wicker armchair by the fire. He hopped around, pulling off his boots, dropping them and his trousers willy-nilly on the floor. Finally, he stood before her – a giant in his long-johns and woollen socks. 'Hutch up, then, love.'

Reluctantly, Florrie lifted the covers to let him into her bed and shuffled up against the freezing cold wall. 'You're such a scruffy ha'porth, you are! I thought I had my bed to myself tonight.'

'Too cold for that.' He put his arms around her. He smelled of dried sweat and the mildew of the shed. 'You need me to keep you nice and warm.'

Florrie wrinkled her nose. 'But you stink and you're freezing cold. Get them socks off in my bed, please!' She sighed with exasperation, imagining what life would be like when they married.

Thom's hands wandered over her body. He started to kiss the back of her neck, making his passionate intentions clear.

'I've got to get up early, I told you,' she said. 'And you smell of shed. Put the light out and pack it in, will you?'

'Aw, you're no fun, you.' Thom turned out the light and wrapped her tightly in his embrace. 'I've got manly needs.'

'Listen! Either shut up and go to sleep, or you can take your "needs" and all your mess back to your own room. See if it's more fun there. Oh, and I want you up and out as soon as my alarm goes off.'

'They all know we're engaged.'

'Aye, but we're not married yet, Thom. I have to set a good example for the other girls, which means keeping up respectable appearances. I'm the housekeeper, after all.'

'Not for long. You'll be my missus soon.'

Florrie sighed in the darkness, wishing for sleep to take her quickly.

'Which room shall I prepare for Prince Hans?' Agnes asked the following morning.

Florrie was standing on the first-floor landing with the young maid, holding fresh bed linen over her arm. She looked from the door to the master bedroom, where Lady Charlotte slept, to the door to the Chinoiserie-themed guest bedroom, where Sir Richard now slept. Was it feasible that there were still extramarital goings-on between Lady Charlotte and the Prussian, even following the crash? Was Sir Richard so preoccupied that he had still not worked out that his wife had betrayed him under his own roof? She shook her head to free herself from the complex tangle of family drama. 'Best to put him at the far end of the guest wing, so he won't be disturbed if Sir William wakes in the night.'

'Is that you, Florrie?' Lady Charlotte's voice came from her bedroom. 'Can you come and give me a hand, please?'

Passing the bed linen to Agnes, Florrie went to her aid.

In the master bedroom, two lots of wardrobe doors stood open. Several outfits lay strewn on the bed. Florrie found her mistress trying and failing to don a navy blue jumpsuit, reminiscent of a sailor's uniform.

'I just can't balance,' Lady Charlotte said. 'It's frustrating in the extreme. I simply can't hold the dratted walking stick *and* pull the thing on, and I do so want to wear it.'

'Will this be warm enough in this weather?' Florrie asked, offering her shoulder for Lady Charlotte to grab on to. She stifled a gasp when those long red nails dug into her flesh.

'Oh, it will be fine. What's important is that I don't let my standards slip. I can hardly greet our esteemed guest looking like one of the domestic staff in some frumpy old sack of a dress, out of vogue by a good decade.'

Florrie caught a glimpse of her own old-fashioned uniform, darned in places where the fabric had worn gossamer thin over time and with repeated washing. She turned away, but was faced instead with the contents of the wardrobe on show, rack upon rack boasting the latest Paris fashions. 'Here you go, milady. We just need to undo the zip a little more. Put one leg in. That's right. I've got you.'

After some fussing, Lady Charlotte was dressed. The recovery from her fractured spine, years of heavy drinking and the loss of her best friend had aged her. Now she looked some years older than Florrie, though their birthdates were separated by only one day, and despite Lady Charlotte having every beauty treatment and the finest couturiers at her disposal. Her once soft features had hardened, yet she still had good bone structure. And though the muscles in her legs had wasted somewhat from diminished use, she still had the long limbs of well-fed nobility.

'You look a treat,' Florrie said.

Lady Charlotte smiled and then pouted in the mirror. The smile slid. 'It's a long time since the *Tatler* asked to photograph me.'

Florrie glanced at the contents of the wardrobe and thought about the hand-me-down trousers and fine-knit, plus the two Sunday best dresses (fashioned by Mam from offcuts of curtain fabric) that hung in her own wardrobe in her modestly furnished attic room. 'You're as glamorous as ever. You worked so hard at rehabilitation and got yourself walking again—'

'And stopped drinking.'

'That sort of thing requires real grit and determination. Qualities worth a darn sight more than fame.'

'Ha. Infamy, in my case.'

'And now you've got the silver-topped cane, you've got the air of a mysterious lady adventurer or summat.'

The smile was restored to Lady Charlotte's lips. 'Oh, Florrie. You are a gem. *Ta, chuck!*'

She gave thanks in her ridiculous approximation of the local accent, but Florrie knew that in this instance, it was heartfelt. 'Not at all. Will you be joining Sir Richard and Sir William for lunch in the dining room?'

Lady Charlotte shook her head. 'I have no appetite for sitting with my family. No, I'll come down when Hans arrives.' She looked wistfully at her wall of wardrobes and then at a large trunk that she'd asked to be brought to her room. 'Have one of the maids bring me a salad for lunch. I might as well attend to this clear-out I've been planning. Out with the old, in with the new. It's terribly good for one's mood when one finishes an exercise like this.' Leaning on her stick for support, she reached up and pulled out a mink coat.

'You're not getting rid of your furs, are you?' Florrie asked, thinking that a discarded mink from a fine furrier would look exquisite on Mam. 'They're perfect for this weather. There's snow in the air, Cook reckons.'

Lady Charlotte pulled out a silver fox coat. 'That'll be all, Florrie. Thank you.'

'Herr Hitler is already proving himself to be an exemplary chancellor,' von Grunwald said at dinner.

Sir Richard, looking elegant in black tie, sat in the middle of the dining table, flanked by his widower brother. Lady Charlotte had changed into a glittering red evening dress and was seated to the Prussian prince's right. It was a tiny gathering, compared to the dinners of old, but Florrie knew Lady Charlotte had pestered her husband into putting on a lavish formal dinner for their guest. Florrie and Arkwright had also been tasked with being the only staff members to serve, since Lady Charlotte had confessed she had a surprise announcement to make at the end of the dinner, and she'd insisted on having only the most trustworthy servants in attendance.

Now, Hans von Grunwald held his crystal goblet of red wine up to the light contemplatively and twisted the stem around. Taking a sip, he nodded to Sir Hugh. 'Your man Mosley should follow his example.'

'Hitler's been in power how long?' Sir Richard asked, slicing into his lamb. 'A month? Just over a month.' His tone was disparaging. 'How can he have achieved anything worth any salt in that time?'

Von Grunwald raised a pale eyebrow. 'Two days after Herr Hitler took office, he took the bold decision to rearm.'

'*Rearm?* What about the Treaty of Versailles?' Sir Richard asked. 'Germany made a commitment to disarm after the Great War. Does that now count for nothing?'

'Adolf Hitler is the Chancellor of Deutschland, Richard. He can do as he wishes – what's best for the Fatherland.'

Sir Richard glowered at the Prussian prince. 'Sounds to me like he's planning another war.'

Florrie stood in silence at her serving station, eavesdropping on the conversation. Arkwright, who was standing like a silent sentry by the fireplace, caught her eye. She knew he loathed von Grunwald and his love of fascism.

'Well, the Chancellor has announced his policy of *Lebensraum*, giving Germans the right to move east,' Von Grunwald said. 'But that's not war.'

'It's expansionism!'

'Nein, Richard. That's the reunification of territories that always belonged – culturally, ethnically and historically – with the Fatherland. Aryan peoples.'

Sir Hugh sipped from his wine. 'Sounds eminently sensible to me. It's too easy to lose one's national identity and history when great empires become fragmented and infiltrated by immigrants with their foreign ways. Think what would happen to Britain if she lost dominion over her colonies or all the colonials suddenly flooded into Britain to live! And take Communism . . .'

The Prussian pointed to him triumphantly. 'Ah. You make exactly the correct point. Here in England, the status quo is constantly under threat from Communism, ja? Well, already Herr Hitler has removed that threat. He's had Göring ban all Communist meetings and demonstrations, and he's clamped down on press freedoms, because you know, that lot spread lies and un-German ideas. He's planning a boycott of Jewish businesses for the start of April also.' He looked to Lady Charlotte, clearly seeking her approval. He leaned in closer, as if sharing some great secret. 'And because I'm privy to the plans of Herr Hitler's inner circle, I know that Jews are soon to be banned from public office and the legal profession.' He bristled with obvious pride.

Sir Richard shook his head, frowning. 'That's ridiculous. There are some of the finest minds in the world among Germany's Jews. Scientists, entrepreneurs, writers, artists, thinkers . . . What will they do for a living if they're being outlawed from key professions?'

Von Grunwald sliced a bloody piece of rare lamb from his fillet and forked it into his mouth. There was menace in his cold blue eyes. 'The party will find other ways to put them to work. *Arbeit macht frei.*'

'What does that even mean? *Work makes free?*' Sir Richard spat the words out with undisguised derision.

'It's a slogan for some new labour camps that are in the pipeline. One has just opened in Dachau.'

'Sloganeering! It's poppycock. You're excusing the shocking persecution of one of the most loyal and economically productive groups in your country.' Sir Richard drained his glass and slammed it back on the table. 'You should be ashamed. And much as this family has been on the receiving end of some rather unfair coverage in the news over the years, a healthy democracy needs a free press. Governments must be held to account!' Florrie could see he was incensed. The flames of the open fire reflected in his grey eyes like sparks of ire.

Lady Charlotte blithely patted von Grunwald's hand.

'Well, I think Herr Hitler is setting a splendid example for the rest of Europe. He's a strong leader. Germany's starting to sound like the promised land.'

'Forty-three percent of the vote can't be wrong,' von Grunwald said. 'If anyone can take Germany out of this depression, Hitler and our National Socialist Party can.'

'Hear, hear!' Sir Hugh said, raising his glass. 'I propose a toast: to fascism heralding the end of the Great Slump. I only wish my Daphne had lived to hear this promising news.'

Lady Charlotte raised her glass of water. 'To fascism!'

Florrie rolled her eyes at Arkwright. The butler merely closed his in response and ever so slightly shook his head.

Just as the three friends were clinking glasses, Sir Richard threw down his napkin and got to his feet. 'Yet again, Hans, you dine at my table and put me off my own dinner. I don't know why my wife invites you. You're a guest in my house, and you know I deplore fascism. Must you sit here, boasting about the hellish depths of depravity Germany's quite clearly sinking into?' He turned to his brother and his wife. 'And need you two jolly him along?'

Sir Hugh waved his concerns away. 'You're out of step, old chap. Germany's not the enemy any more. Mosley reckons that even if Hitler does have expansionist plans, Chamberlain's all for appeasement. Nobody wants war. Our government doesn't want war. We must see Germany as a friend and ally.'

At her serving station, Florrie swallowed hard. She'd seen the clips on Pathé News of Hitler and his brownshirts when she and Thom had visited the cinema. They looked like bully-boys, in her opinion – no different from

Mussolini's fascists, no different from Mosley's New Party militia, the Biff Boys. Thinking of all the antisemitic chatter her predecessor, Bertha Douglas, had had to endure while serving dinner, keeping her Jewishness secret for decades until the day she died, Florrie felt nauseous. Like Sir Richard, she wanted von Grunwald to stop enthusing about the rise of Hitler and his Nazi party. Sir Hugh and Lady Charlotte should demonstrate better judgement than to pander to the Prussian's ego.

She gestured to Arkwright that she needed to get some air. The butler tapped his fob watch pointedly.

As she unobtrusively slipped out of the dining room and into the hall, Sir Richard followed her.

'Florrie, are you quite all right?' he whispered, laying his hand protectively on her shoulder.

She came to a halt and turned to him, pressing her hand to her chest. 'I can't bear it. Sorry. I know everyone's entitled to their own opinion, it's just . . .'

'I completely agree. He's foul. His boastfulness . . . and those disgusting Nazi policies . . .' He peered apologetically up at a portrait rendered in oils of his ancestor – the first Harding-Bourne to find success as an industrialist, who had also built the house. 'I feel ashamed having him under this roof. I may be little more than a nouveau riche who has hung on to the family fortune and married well, but I come from a long line of men who have always worked for the betterment of people. Not *this* . . .'

Florrie grabbed his arm. 'Then do something about it! It's *your* house. Turf him out!' She looked down at his tuxedo-clad arm, clutched in her workworn hand. She let go. 'Sorry.'

'No, Florrie, you're absolutely right. Come back in with me?'

She nodded, her pulse quickening in anticipation.

Sir Richard returned to the dining room. Florrie slipped in behind him, resuming her place at the serving station, looking straight ahead.

'Get out,' he told von Grunwald. 'I want you to pack your things immediately and get out of my house. And take your despicable politics with you.'

'Richard! How could you be so rude to our guest?' Lady Charlotte cried.

'Steady on, Dickie!' Sir Hugh said, toying with his bow tie. 'Charlotte and I live here too, and Hans is our friend.'

'He's no friend of mine. He's a pompous oaf, and I'll tolerate him no longer.'

Oddly, Florrie noted, Hans von Grunwald stayed in his seat, grinning slyly to himself. He took Lady Charlotte's hand and squeezed it.

Lady Charlotte got to her feet. 'Well, actually, Dickie, I was saving this announcement until coffee and petits fours, but I may as well tell you now, since you're being such a nincompoop.'

38

Lady Charlotte smiled down at von Grunwald before turning back to her husband, who had suddenly paled. She took a deep breath, then nodded to herself. 'I want a divorce. There. I said it. I don't love you. I never did. I love Hans. And I'm leaving for Germany tomorrow to be with him.'

'*What?*' Sir Richard yelled. 'But we have a son. We're a family.'

Lady Charlotte scoffed. 'I'm not mother material. I never was. Willy loves *you*, not me. I'm just ... I was a brood mare for your mother, there to carry on the great Harding-Bourne line and to add a little minor royal cachet to the family.'

'Charlotte, that's a cynical lie.'

'It's not, though, is it? And let's face it, Dickie, you don't love me either. I don't know where your true affections lie, beyond our son and this house and the blasted business. You're an enigma. Actually, no. You're not that intriguing. In fact, you're the most buttoned-up stick-in-the mud I've ever met. So I'm letting you go.'

Sir Richard blanched. He seemed to have run out of words.

Lady Charlotte turned her attention to her brother-in-law. 'I didn't survive a plane crash that almost saw me joining dear, *dear* Daphne in the family burial plot so that I could fritter away the rest of my prime years ...' – she turned back to Sir Richard, eyebrow raised like an insolent youth, arms folded – '... in an unhappy marriage to a bore like you.'

Finally, von Grunwald drained his glass, wiped his mouth with his napkin and got to his feet. He held his elbow out for Lady Charlotte. 'I think it's time we retired to bed, darling. We'll leave after breakfast.'

The clandestine couple exited the dining room, leaving both Sir Hugh and Sir Richard open-mouthed.

'Will you just stand there and let him take her?' Sir Hugh asked. 'She's one of my best friends. I don't want her to leave Holcombe!'

Sir Richard met his gaze. The dark fury in his eyes from earlier seemed to have melted away, leaving a look of relief on his handsome face. 'As long as she doesn't take my son, I won't stand in her way. It's for the best, old chap. She's right. It's over.'

As soon as the family had dispersed to different parts of the house, Florrie and Arkwright almost sprinted down to the kitchen, where Cook, Thom and Graham were drinking strong tea around the kitchen table and discussing football.

Florrie was the first to speak. 'You'll *never* guess what just happened.' She felt herself grinning.

'Miss Bickerstaff, shouldn't we be a little discreet?' Arkwright asked, taking a seat at the table.

'You legged it down here, same as me!' Florrie said.

'Go on! Go on!' Cook said, her cheeks flushing and her eyes glittering as they always did when gossip was in the offing.

Florrie related all that had been said at the table, and how she'd encouraged Sir Richard to confront von Grunwald. Arkwright related the second part to the tale, with the revelation that Lady Charlotte wanted a divorce and was running away to Germany with the Prussian.

'So that's why she was flinging all her furs into a trunk earlier today,' Florrie said. 'She was packing to leave.'

'Blimey!' Cook said. She rummaged in the cabinet beneath the Welsh dresser and brought out a bottle of brandy and five glasses. 'That's the *best* gossip I've *ever* heard, our Florrie. This calls for a little tipple to calm the nerves.'

Sitting with their brandies, Thom frowned. 'I don't think you should have got involved, Florrie. If Sir Richard wakes up tomorrow and reckons he's made a mistake, he'll blame you for starting it all off.'

'Give over, Thom!' Florrie said. 'Lady Charlotte said she had an announcement for the end of the dinner. That was clearly it. Nothing I said would have changed anyone's mind. It just meant Sir Richard kept some dignity.'

'You're always putting your two penn'orth in and getting involved, you are,' Thom said clearly irritated. He swilled his brandy ruefully. 'What have I told you? "Remember your place!" It's not your business what gets said in that dining room. You're not being paid for your opinions. Keep 'em to yourself.'

Florrie felt the other three scrutinizing her. There was a sharp intake of breath from Cook; her lips formed a scandalized O. How should she react to Thom's effort to dictate how she conducted herself in her job? Should she let his comments go and turn the other cheek, just as Sir Richard had spent years turning the other cheek when Hans von Grunwald had been taking liberties with his wife?

She chose her words carefully, looking at her outstretched fingers. 'Last time I looked, Thomas, you weren't the boss of me.'

'Aye, but we're getting wed, aren't we? I'll be head of household, so . . . As your husband-to-be, I'm *telling* you, Florrie: keep your neb out of their business.' He tapped his nose. 'The sooner you leave your job, the better. You've got too involved.'

Florrie could barely believe what she was hearing. In giving her a dressing-down in front of the others, Thom had nullified her hard-earned position of respect and authority. She balled her fists and closed her eyes tightly, grappling with the urge to give him a piece of her mind. *If in doubt, do nothing*, said a small voice inside her that sounded rather like Mam. *Remember he's a good catch*.

'Are you going to let him talk to you like that, love?' Cook's voice cut through the maelstrom in her head.

'Hey! Don't *you* be getting between a man and his wife!' Thom snapped. 'What is it with women these days, eh?'

'Watch your mouth in my kitchen, Thomas! She's not your wife yet, and you're not too big that I can't put you over my knee. I'll have that brandy back if you can't take a drink without getting a mouth on you.'

Florrie got to her feet. 'I'm going to bed,' she announced. '*On my own*.'

The next day, after a sleepless night of replaying the previous day's events over and over in her head, like a news reel on a loop, Florrie rose, washed and dressed as normal. She found Sir Richard in his study by six, when he rang for coffee.

'Good morning, sir.' She bobbed a curtsey. 'I won't ask you if you slept. I certainly didn't. I'm *very* sorry about last night.'

He smiled uncertainly at her, removing his tortoiseshell spectacles and absently examining the arm. 'I'm not, actually. I just want them gone.'

This morning, he was back in his thick cashmere jumper, to which Mam had recently attached leather elbow patches. His hair was immaculately Brylcreemed, and he looked fresh-faced, resembling a handsome young academic (Florrie imagined) rather than a captain of industry.

'I'm not going to fight her,' he said simply. 'We need to remain amicable for Willy, you see.'

Florrie nodded. 'Very dignified, given the circumstances. Lady Charlotte's very lucky you're such a gentleman.'

Sir Richard chuckled. 'Dear Florrie. How kind you are. But it takes two to end a relationship, and I am not without blame.' He laced his hands together and pursed his lips. 'Have a couple of the lads bring her trunks and things down while she's having breakfast. I'll stay in here. I have no desire to wave the two of them off.'

'Of course, sir.' Should she apologize for having egged him on? Had Thom been right?

Sir Richard studied her face. 'What is it, Florrie? I can see you've something on your mind.'

Florrie bit her lip. 'I'm sorry if I played any part in this . . . parting of ways.'

Her employer's cheeks flushed pink. He smiled shyly. 'Oh, well, you and I . . .'

'I mean encouraging you to chuck von Grunwald out.'

'Oh. Right. I see.'

Now it was her turn to blush. 'Perhaps I stuck my oar in, and it wasn't my place.'

He shook his head. 'No! Nonsense. You were absolutely right to advise me. It's only because of you that I saved any face at all. I'm thankful for your intervention, Florrie. There's a fine line between being gentlemanly and being a sop, and I needed reminding where that line was. Don't spare it another thought.'

It was sleeting when Lady Charlotte and von Grunwald's taxi came to take them to the aerodrome. By now the gossip had spread throughout the household, and the entire staff gathered in the drawing room, jostling for space so they could peer out at the departing couple through the tall French doors and windows. Only Sir Hugh stood at the bottom of the grand stone staircase, hands stuffed in his trouser pockets.

'He looks like he doesn't know what to do with himself,' Graham said. 'Drunken buffoon.'

'Let's keep insults for the brothers to ourselves, please,' Arkwright said. 'Let he who is without sin cast the first stone and all that . . .'

'She must be mental, giving all this up for a German,' Cook said. 'That lovely Sir Richard, with all his money and nice manners. And she chooses a big Günther in *lederhosen* over him?'

'Hans!' one of the valets said. 'And he's Prussian.'

'Günther, Hans . . . same difference. He's still a kraut.'

'Maybe he's got a massive schloss!' Ginny said, giggling.

'That's enough,' Florrie said. 'Let's behave with a bit of decorum, please.'

When the taxi was loaded, von Grunwald climbed in without a backward glance, but Lady Charlotte turned to look at the house. Leaning on her cane, she looked fragile, as if Holcombe Hall had taken something from her, leaving her an impoverished shadow of the girl who had arrived as the new high-society bride to the heir to the Harding-Bourne empire.

Florrie felt an unexpected pang of sadness at seeing her go, though Lady Charlotte had often been her tormentor, always seeing her as the easy butt of a cheap joke, and never appreciating that she was married to a king among men – the man Florrie had loved from the moment she'd been introduced to him by Mrs Douglas, on her very first day of domestic service. She sighed.

'Well, that's that then,' Thom said, watching the taxi begin its journey down the long driveway. 'End of an era, I suppose.'

'Think of it more as the start of a *new* era for Holcombe Hall,' Arkwright said. 'We're all still here. The brothers and Sir William are still here. All that's changed is the future. I'm sure it won't take long for another lady of the house to turn up on the horizon. That lot never waste time getting wed again.'

Florrie swallowed hard at the prospect of a new woman in Sir Richard's life – a fresh source of suffering that the future held in store for her. But there was one painful conversation she could put off no longer. She took Thom by the hand and pulled him to one side.

'Have you got a minute?' she asked.

He smiled at her, as if he hadn't reduced her to nothing with his harsh words the previous evening. 'Aye. Only a minute though. I've got to go out and sow some seeds in the veg garden.'

Dear, dear Thom. The man who grew things from seed, nurtured food for the table and who made toys for her nieces and nephew by hand. A man of principle. An old-fashioned provider. Florrie couldn't abide the thought of what would come next, but she knew it was unavoidable.

'You all right, love?' he asked, frowning.

Florrie put her hands in the pockets of her skirt, digging her nails into her thighs, chivvying herself to get on with it. 'Let's go for a walk to the library, shall we? Somewhere with a bit of privacy.'

'Oh, aye? Not sure I like the sound of this.' He let go of her hand. 'What's going on?'

'I need a word . . . about us.'

Acknowledgements

It takes a good many people to turn my early draft manuscript into a book that readers can purchase and enjoy, and *A New Era for Holcombe Hall* is no exception. As a result, I'd like to thank the following people for their hard work in helping me turn a story set in 1931 – one that I'm sure you'll agree resonates with us in the here and now of 2025/2026 – into a book that will hopefully entertain you, warm your heart and thrill you as well as provoking interesting conversations.

Thanks first go to my family for putting up with my insane work schedule (I also write crime as Marnie Riches, and two books per year plus teaching means seven-day working weeks!) and frequent whingeing that I can't get into the garden to take the dahlias up/plant the dahlias out. They really are stoic and loving, and boy, do they need to be!

Next, I'd like to thank my incredibly loyal and supportive agent, Caspian Dennis, who has been my most trusted ally and firm friend for some twelve years and counting. He's a gem of a man. Thanks also to Sandy, Rebecca, Jasmine, Ray, Tom and the rest of the team at my excellent literary agency, Abner Stein, for all their contractual, accounting and cold, hard, cash-money ministrations throughout the year(s).

Obviously, you wouldn't be reading this series at all without the magnificently good reading taste and editorial nous of my lovely editor, Hannah Smith at Penguin Michael

Joseph. She is the equivalent of a top-class obstetrician in facilitating the birth of my book babies, except she runs marathons too! What a Wonder Woman! Her editorial notes are never less than spot-on, and she has a keen understanding of the market – i.e. how to reach you readers. I thank her for that and for championing the delightful, heart-warming genre of historical romance/saga.

Thanks to all the PMJ team for their part in putting Florrie's story into the hands of readers – Katya Browne, Sarah Bance, Beatrix McIntyre, plus everyone in marketing, sales and PR. Thanks too to Claire Storey, who narrates the *Housekeeper* audiobooks so well, bringing Florrie and the large, varied cast of Holcombe Hall to life.

I feel very blessed to be writing this series, set at such an important juncture in modern history, doing my part to document (through fiction) the conditions that led to World War Two. I feel even more blessed that so many of you are enjoying the books. If you happen to read *A New Era for Holcombe Hall* first – and you absolutely can read the stories out of sequence if you wish – please do pick up *The Housekeeper of Holcombe Hall* to see where Florrie's adventures begin. And if you enjoy my writing, please do look up my Nurse Kitty series of three books, set in Manchester at the end of World War Two and the start of the 1950s. And if you like cosy crime, please do try my contemporary-set series (also published by Penguin), which starts with *The Gardeners' Club*. I think you'll enjoy it! In the meantime, stay tuned for book three of Florrie's epic story . . .

Discover where Florrie's story began . . .

Out now

NURTURING WRITERS SINCE 1935

SIGN UP TO OUR SAGA NEWSLETTER

Penny Street

The home of heart-warming reads

Welcome to **Penny Street**, your number **one stop for emotional and heartfelt historical reads**. Meet casts of characters you'll never forget, memories you'll treasure as your own, and places that will forever stay with you long after the last page.

Join our online **community** bringing you the latest book deals, competitions and new saga series releases.

You can also find extra content, talk to your favourite authors and share your discoveries with other saga fans on Facebook.

Join today by visiting
www.penguin.co.uk/pennystreet

Follow us on Facebook
www.facebook.com/welcometopennystreet

On a station platform, with nothing to read,
and a four-hour train journey stretching ahead of him...

That's where the story began for Penguin founder Allen Lane.
With only 'shabby reprints of shoddy novels' on offer,
he resolved to make better books for readers everywhere.

By the time his train pulled into London, the idea was formed.
He would bring the best writing, in stylish and affordable
formats, to everyone. His books would be sold in bookstores,
stationers and tobacconists, for no more than the price
of a ten-pack of cigarettes.

And on every book would be a Penguin, a bird with a certain
'dignified flippancy', and a friendly invitation to anyone who
wished to spend their time reading.

In 1935, the first ten Penguin paperbacks were published.
Just a year later, three million Penguins had made their
way onto our shelves.

Reading was changed forever.

—

A lot has changed since 1935, including Penguin, but in the
most important ways we're still the same. We still believe that
books and reading are for everyone. And we still believe that
whether you're seeking an afternoon's escape, a vigorous debate
or a soothing bedtime story, all possibilities open with a book.

Whoever you are, whatever you're looking for,
you can find it with Penguin.